SO-AKL-139

The Excitements

The Excitements

· · · · · · · · · · · · ·

A NOVEL

CJ Wray

WILLIAM MORROW

An Imprint of HarperCollins*Publishers*

This is a work of fiction. Names, characters, places, and incidents are products of the author's imagination or are used fictitiously and are not to be construed as real. Any resemblance to actual events, locales, organizations, or persons, living or dead, is entirely coincidental.

THE EXCITEMENTS. Copyright © 2024 by CJ Wray. All rights reserved. Printed in the United States of America. No part of this book may be used or reproduced in any manner whatsoever without written permission except in the case of brief quotations embodied in critical articles and reviews. For information, address HarperCollins Publishers, 195 Broadway, New York, NY 10007.

HarperCollins books may be purchased for educational, business, or sales promotional use. For information, please email the Special Markets Department at SPsales@harpercollins.com.

Originally Published in Great Britain by the Orion Publishing Group Ltd. in 2023.

FIRST U.S. EDITION

Library of Congress Cataloging-in-Publication Data has been applied for.

ISBN 978-0-06-333748-0

23 24 25 26 27 LBC 5 4 3 2 1

To Mum,

With all my love.

One

• • • • •

London, Spring 2022

John Betjeman was right. Nothing bad could ever happen at Peter Jones. Thus thought Archie Williamson as he sipped his cappuccino and looked out over London's rooftops from the Sloane Square department store's sixth floor café. The café was Archie's happy place. Even on a grey day the atmosphere was sunny as people took turns at the window tables, understanding that one did not linger for hours over a single latte in front of this fabulous view. Archie nodded with satisfaction as a young woman with a laptop ceded her place to a frazzled mother with two small children, saving him from having to do the same.

With his own lunch companions still *en route*, Archie shook out the copy of the previous evening's *Standard* left behind by his table's last occupant and turned to the puzzle pages. Codeword was his favourite. He was getting faster each time, though it would be a while before he was able to crack the puzzle as quickly as his great-aunt Penny could.

As he pondered whether the number twenty-four represented an "a" or an "o," Archie's phone buzzed with a message. It was Arlene, Penny's housekeeper, letting him know that she'd put Penny and her older sister Josephine into a taxi which should reach Sloane Square at any moment. Archie thanked Arlene for letting him know. She really was a treasure. But after forty minutes more there was still no sign of Archie's beloved great-aunts. Then, just as he was about to call Arlene and ask her to check the taxi's progress on her app, a managerial-type with a Peter Jones partner's badge came flying up the escalator, calling out as she went, "Mr. Archie Williamson? Is there a Mr. Archie Williamson in the café?"

"Right here," said Archie, standing up and giving her a wave. Two customers seated on the first inner row of tables stood up at the same time, ready to take Archie's place by the window the very second it was vacated. They eyed each other like Olympic athletes at the start of the hundred metres and would move just as quickly the moment Archie stepped out of the way.

"Thank goodness," said the woman, whose name, according to her badge, was Erica. "It's your great-aunts. The Misses Williamson? I need you to come with me."

Archie was immediately worried. "Are they OK? Are they hurt?"

There had been an incident the previous month when Josephine slipped on a discarded burger outside McDonald's on the King's Road and took Penny down with her as she fell. They'd both had to spend the night in the Chelsea and Westminster Hospital with suspected concussion.

"No, no," said Erica. "They're both fine. At least physically they are." She dropped her voice. "It's something else. Something . . . Mr. Williamson, I think it might be easier to discuss this somewhere private. Would you mind?"

Archie followed Erica back down the escalator. When they reached the ground floor, Erica led Archie through the shelves of neatly-stacked towels and bed linens to a door he hadn't previously noticed. She pushed the door open so that Archie could go ahead of her.

"Your great-aunts are in here," she said.

Archie found it difficult, letting Erica hold the door for him when manners dictated it should have been the other way round, but he nodded and stepped inside all the same. He still didn't know what to expect.

In a plain room decorated with tasteful pastel prints (available for sale on floor four), Archie's great-aunts sat side by side on two chairs opposite a very tidy desk. Though it was a balmy spring day outside, they were both well-muffled in coats and scarves. Josephine was wearing a blue fisherman's cap; Penny, her favourite mohair beret. Archie was always surprised by how small his aunts looked when he saw them out of the context of their South Kensington home but this time they looked tinier than ever. Perhaps it was the contrast with the two enormous men flanking them like sentries. Plain-clothed security officers, Archie realised with growing concern.

"Oh, Archie. Thank goodness you're here," said Josephine. "There's been a terrible misunderstanding."

"What's going on?" he asked.

Auntie Penny looked down at her size three-and-a-half feet in their neat Velcro-fastened shoes. When she looked up again, her face wore the expression Archie recognised from every photograph of his younger great-aunt taken between 1924 and the beginning of World War Two. She'd been up to something. What on earth was this "misunderstanding" about?

"Archie, dearest, I'm so sorry to embarrass you like this," Penny began. "I only picked it up to have a look but I must have let myself get distracted and before I knew what I was doing I had put it in my handbag and closed the zip quite without thinking."

The "it" in question was a small Swarovski-style crystal elephant, now standing on its hind legs in the middle of Erica's desk.

"Are we calling the police?" asked one of the security guards.

Lovely Erica chewed her lip. She looked from the guard to the sisters to Archie and then back to the guard again. Her discomfort was palpable.

"I don't think calling the police will be necessary," Archie interjected quickly. "As you can see, my auntie Penny is . . ."

How to not say "ancient" in front of her?

"Well, I'm sure she won't mind me saying that there are occasions when she becomes a little forgetful, but she does not have a dishonest bone in her body and she would *never* have sought to deprive Peter Jones of its property by stealth. She's as honest as the day is long. It's just . . . it's just, she has . . . you know . . . she's got . . ."

No. He couldn't say the "d" word either, even if it might help keep Penny out of jail.

"It's just that she's recently turned ninety-seven."

Penny nodded wretchedly, suddenly looking every one of her years.

"I was in *The War*," she said.

"So was I," said Josephine.

"In fact," Archie continued. "I came here today to meet my great-aunts in the café to discuss their taking part in the VE Day celebrations at the

Royal Albert Hall. VE Day? To mark the anniversary of the end of World War Two?"

"In Europe," Penny qualified. "The War didn't end in the Far East until much later the same year."

"That's absolutely right, Auntie Penny." Archie turned back to Erica. "They're going to be meeting Prince Charles in their capacity as representatives of the women's services."

The security officer who wanted to call the police seemed unmoved but Archie could see that the younger man and Erica at least were impressed to hear they were in the presence of real live World War Two veterans.

"I was in the Wrens," said Josephine.

"Women's Royal Naval Service," said Archie.

"And I was a FANY," said Penny.

"First Aid Nursing Yeomanry," Archie quickly explained.

"Thank you for your service," said the younger guard.

It was a platitude that Archie knew both his aunts hated but that day they had the grace (or the sense) to simply thank the young man for his kindness.

"I'd be very happy to pay for the elephant," said Archie, in an attempt to bring the situation to a conclusion. "Perhaps then we can put all this behind us and let you get on with your day."

"Store policy . . ." the older officer began.

"Is that every incident like this has to be processed in the official way," Erica jumped in. "I know, John, I know. But perhaps in this case since, technically, *Mizz* Williamson hadn't exited the store . . ."

Archie smiled gratefully and handed over a credit card. "For the elephant."

"You don't have to," said Erica.

"But I'd like to," said Archie.

He reasoned that Penny must have wanted it.

"Well, if you really want to. We'll have to take it to one of the tills."

"Are we not calling the police then?" asked John.

"We're not calling the police," Erica confirmed. "Not today. Ladies?" She opened the door to let Penny and Josephine back out onto the shop floor.

Archie parked Penny and Josephine in the cushion aisle while he paid for the hideous crystal knick-knack. It was astonishingly expensive. Excruciatingly so for something so very, very ugly. Who on earth bought these things out of choice? Who would ever bother to steal one?

"I think we'll have lunch at Colbert today," Archie told the sisters when he rejoined them. He felt the need to be outside and well away from the scene of the crime. The two security officers had headed in the direction of the main doors which opened straight onto Sloane Square, so Archie ushered his great-aunts out via the scented candle department onto Symons Street instead, making it clear by his body language that this was no time to stop and sniff the Cire Trudon Abd El Kader candle that reminded Penny of her time in Algiers.

Two

• • • • •

Archie Williamson's earliest memory of his great-aunts was of an afternoon in the Highlands in the summer of 1987 when he was six and a half years old. Archie's parents had taken him to Scotland to see Grey Towers, the Williamson family's ancestral home (now in the care of the National Trust for Scotland), and Josephine and Penny were staying nearby in all that remained of the once vast family estate: a small bothy without running water or electricity. The sisters were on a fly-fishing holiday. They'd arrived at the self-catering cottage where Archie and his parents were staying, laden with freshly-caught trout and bickering over who had hooked the biggest.

"These are your grandfather's sisters," said Archie's father Charles.

Archie was immediately fascinated by the two women, who were far older than anyone he had ever met before, though they could only have been in their sixties at the time. Still, sixty is ancient when you're not even seven. They were from another era—might as well have been from another planet—yet somehow by the end of the afternoon, Archie felt a kinship with Penny and Josephine despite the many decades between them. Perhaps it was the way they spoke to him. From the very beginning they treated him like a small adult, expressing great interest in his preferences and opinions. When they offered to teach him how to fish, he was delighted.

The following day, the sisters took Archie to the loch for their first big adventure as a trio. Though Archie's parents worried that their sweet and bookish only child might not enjoy a day's fishing with two sexagenarians, Archie loved it. He only grew more captivated by his newly-met relations;

these exotic creatures who rowed like sailors and swore like builders, yet could keep their hairdos perfect all day long. By the time they brought him back to his parents, Archie had a good grounding in fly-fishing and a greatly expanded vocabulary of swear words. He couldn't wait to see the sisters again.

WHENEVER THERE WAS an opportunity, Archie went to stay with his great-aunts and they were thrilled to have him. On further Scottish holidays in the bone-chillingly cold bothy—which his father had accurately described as, "like camping, only worse"—the sisters gave Archie an alternative education. They taught him how to identify the local flora and fauna. They taught him how to catch his supper. They taught him how to lay a fire. It was all so much more exciting than the late twentieth-century childhood he was enduring back in Cheltenham. At home, he wasn't allowed to touch the matches. With Penny and Josephine, he was allowed to throw cap-gun pellets onto a raging bonfire.

"They're a terrible influence," Archie's mother complained, when he came home from that trip with singed eyebrows.

Certainly the sisters always gave him the most age-inappropriate gifts. Among Archie's favourites was a set of books he received for his tenth birthday. While his godmother worried that she might have overstepped the mark when she sent him something from the *Goosebumps* series, Archie much preferred the antique copies of Major W.E. Fairbairn's *All-In Fighting* and *Get Tough!*—manuals on lethal unarmed combat—that Auntie Penny sent from her personal library. He spent that whole summer learning the tricks of Defendu, Major Fairbairn's trademark "ungentlemanly" martial art, unfortunately managing to break his own wrist in the process. Nevertheless, when he got back to school, the rumour that Archie Williamson had broken his wrist single-handedly defending his household from a burglar, *à la* Kevin in *Home Alone*, briefly made him rather popular.

Penny and Josephine introduced him to more refined activities too. At the big white house the sisters shared in South Kensington, Archie learned how to cook *cordon bleu* and dance the foxtrot. He accompanied the sisters to London's museums and theatres and listened in awe as they talked in French, German, Italian, and Hausa to the eclectic guests who thronged the house on Saturday evenings to eat, drink, and play cards, while a teenage Archie mixed martinis.

"A little heavier on the vermouth, dear."

The sisters were mad for vermouth. And gin. They liked their martinis stronger than Molotov cocktails.

As Archie got older, the sisters took him with them on trips abroad; first to Europe, then further afield.

"Always pack a party dress!" was their sage advice for travelling.

Thanks to their careers and family connections—Josephine was an academic whose diplomat husband's job had taken them all over the world, while Penny had been in overseas aid—it seemed that the sisters could turn up in any city in any country and be guaranteed to know someone interesting who would invite them to tea: writers, artists, disgraced ex–government ministers . . .

When Archie moved to London to take up a job in a gallery, one of the things that excited him most about living in the capital was that he would be able to see much more of his great-aunts. He lived with them, in the spare room stuffed with knick-knacks from their travels, until such time as he was able to afford the deposit on a flat of his own.

Truth be told, had it not been that he felt a little bit shy about bringing dates home, Archie would happily have stayed in the sisters' spare room forever. Joining them for a sherry or something stronger—"This needs *much* more vermouth, dear"—when he got home from work was the highlight of his day.

"How on earth can you enjoy living with two old biddies?" someone once asked him.

"They're much more fun than people our age," was Archie's honest reply. People of the sisters' generation were vastly more interesting than Archie's contemporaries; so much more cultured. He would far rather listen to their stories than hear one of his peers yakking on about another lost weekend in Ibiza.

Modern music left Archie cold. Likewise modern literature and film. Thanks to the sisters, by the age of fifteen, Archie had read every important forties book and watched every forties movie anyone cared to name. Perhaps it was inevitable that Archie became a specialist in 1940s paintings.

Archie thought that the sisters had lived through the best of times, even if those times had included the Second World War.

Most importantly, the sisters taught Archie how to live life by their philosophy, which they in turn had borrowed from a fictional alley cat called Mehitabel. The *Archy and Mehitabel* books by Don Marquis that the sisters had enjoyed in their childhood became some of their great-nephew's favourites too.

"One must be *toujours gai*, Archie, *toujours gai*."

"*Toujours gai*" was Mehitabel's motto and now it was theirs. It meant remembering there was no room in life for gloom or self-pity. Every opportunity for fun must be seized with both paws.

When Archie decided that he was actually *toujours gay*, the sisters were perfectly pleased about it and helped him navigate the delicate task of informing his parents, whom he rightly suspected would be less relaxed. He felt the sisters had saved him from years of parental estrangement with their careful intervention. For that alone he would always love Penny and Josephine dearly. He vowed to be there for them just as they had been there for him.

Three

. . . . .

That late April day in Sloane Square, post–Peter Jones debacle, Archie knew that what he had planned as a quick lunch was unlikely to be over before five. It was impossible to have a quick lunch at Colbert. After the sisters had both ordered steak frites with extra frites—they may have looked birdlike but their appetites were anything but, unless you were thinking "herring gull"—Archie excused himself from the table to call his assistant. Archie had his own gallery now and was considered an authority on the official war artists of World War Two. Once he'd given instructions to divert any calls for the rest of the day, he returned to the table and settled down for a lazy afternoon.

It was Josephine who asked the question this time.

"So, Archie, what *excitements* do you have for us today?"

It was the question the sisters always asked. *Excitements* was their term for any sort of social engagement and since Archie had somehow become their *de facto* manager, it was up to him to provide them. Sometimes it filled Archie with dread, hearing those words, when he didn't have anything to offer or when he suspected that the excitements he did have planned wouldn't cut the mustard. As two of a fast-dwindling number of Second World War veterans, the sisters were always in demand for speaking engagements but Archie knew they were both bored stiff of talking to university students and pedantic history buffs.

"Always the same bloody questions," Penny would sigh. Sometimes within earshot of the unhappy questioner.

Penny in particular was dangerous when uninterested. Just the previous week, when a boy of eleven asked the sisters, as often happened at a school talk, "Did you ever kill anyone?" Penny had responded, "I could tell you but then I'd have to kill you too," with such a cold look in her eyes that for a moment she even had Archie believing she could be a stone-hearted assassin.

Thank goodness that, today, Archie was sure he had an excitement worth getting excited about.

"Well, as I was saying to the nice young lady in Peter Jones . . ." Young lady? She was almost certainly a decade older than he was. "You've both been invited to take part in the VE Day service at the Royal Albert Hall. Prince Charles and the Duchess of Cornwall will be in attendance."

"Those two again?" Penny scoffed. "Given how few of us there are left these days, you'd think they would roll out Her Maj."

"She is getting on a bit," said Josephine, who was older than The Queen by two years.

"That's true," Penny agreed. "All the same. It could be our last time."

"No, Auntie Penny!" Archie protested. "You mustn't say that. You're both going to live to be at least 117, like that French nun who survived the coronavirus. Didn't even know she had it."

"A nun?" said Penny. "What's the saying? If you don't drink, smoke, or have sex you won't live forever . . ."

"But it will certainly feel like it," Josephine chimed in.

They both cackled.

"Tell us about the service," said Josephine. "Will we be expected to say anything?"

"I don't think so. You've been invited in the capacity of honoured guests. You'll be sitting in a row in front of the orchestra with other veterans."

"Who's left these days?"

"Not that old Dambuster . . ." said Penny. "*Handsy,*" she mouthed at her sister.

"That was an accident," said Archie, remembering 2017's Remembrance Day affair. "He stumbled on his way up the dais and . . ."

"Fell straight into my bosom?" Penny crossed her arms.

"I'll ask that you're seated well away from him."

"I don't mind," said Josephine. "If you can get me between him and that lovely army man we met last year. So charming . . ."

"Then you're both happy to take part?" Archie asked.

"What else are we going to do?" Penny responded. "Nothing much happens when one gets to our age. So few *excitements*. It can be *vraiment* hard to stay *toujours gai* when there's so little left to look forward to."

Archie didn't remind his aunts that just a fortnight earlier he'd arranged for them to be interviewed by Dan Snow for his World War Two podcast. Most people their age would have been over the moon at the prospect of being interviewed by that delightful young man. So good-looking. Josephine instead had fixated on the fact that Snow had been wearing odd socks when he turned up at their house for the recording.

"Well, I understand you can't actually see anybody on a podcast," said Josephine. "But he might have made an effort all the same."

Archie thought Josephine might really have taken against Snow not because of his socks but because, as his team was setting up to record the sisters' segment, he let slip that he had come straight from interviewing Davina Mackenzie. Davina Mackenzie, at 101 years old and still completely *compos mentis*, was the actual oldest Wren in town.

"And granddaughter of an admiral, in case she didn't mention it," as Josephine would always add whenever her name came up. Needless to say, Davina Mackenzie never failed to mention her late grandfather's illustrious rank.

Josephine asked now, regarding the VE Day celebration and in a tone Archie knew was meant to be throwaway, "And Davina Mackenzie? Will she be there too? As the granddaughter of an admiral . . ."

Archie knew he had to tread carefully when he answered.

"The BBC producer said I was the first person she'd spoken to regarding guest appearances. She's terribly keen to have you both on board. There are very few places and you two have first refusal."

Josephine was happy enough with that.

A waiter placed three mini-baguettes in the middle of the table and the sisters dived upon them.

As he buttered a delicate bite of his own bread, Archie asked, "Why were you ladies so late to meet me anyway? You're usually on naval time." Which was to say, five minutes early.

"We popped into Tiffany," said Josephine. "We needed a christening present for the Browns' new great-grandson."

The New York jeweller's second London store was on the corner of Sloane Square and Symons Street.

"Did you find anything?" Archie asked.

"Nothing worth buying," said Penny.

Moments later, a waiter arrived with a bottle of champagne that the sisters must have ordered while Archie was telephoning his assistant. He tried not to look shocked when he saw that it was Ruinart and not the house fizz.

"This one is on me," Penny reassured him with a pat on the arm.

"But what are we celebrating?" Archie asked.

"Getting away with it," said Penny, presumably referring to the Peter Jones incident, which Archie hardly considered "gotten away with." But as she rifled through her handbag for a tissue, the glitter of a diamond solitaire caught Penny's eye.

Four

• • • • •

By the time lunch ended, the sisters were ready for supper but Archie had an exhibition launch to attend and could not be persuaded to miss it. Neither could he be persuaded to take them along with him as he sometimes did. The sisters and champagne were a dangerous mix and, to put it bluntly, they'd already had a skinful. Instead Archie loaded his great-aunts into a taxi at the Sloane Square rank, stuffed two twenty-pound notes into the driver's hand, and instructed him to make sure he took both ladies right to the front door of their house.

The driver, who was a member of the Poppy Cab service that ferried veterans to the cenotaph every Remembrance Sunday, promised that the sisters would be safe in his hands. Thus reassured, Archie leaned into the back of the cab to ensure that both Penny and Josephine were buckled up.

"Try to stay out of trouble until I see you next," he said.

Penny and Josephine assured him that they would.

"Good. Because I can't keep buying crystal elephants."

THE SISTERS HAD shared Penny's South Kensington house since 1983, the year Josephine was widowed. Penny had lost her husband many years before, back in the 1960s. Though, by their own admission, as children they had fought like cat and dog, the sisters found they enjoyed living together as adults, and what they had thought would be a temporary arrangement— just while Josephine was in the deepest depths of grief for her beloved Gerald—soon became permanent. They would be together in that house until the very end. In their mid-eighties, they made a pact that if either one of them ever needed to go into an old people's home, they would both buy a one-way ticket to Switzerland.

The day after Archie first heard this macabre plan, he locked his great-aunts' passports away in his office, with strict instructions that the sisters were not to be allowed to have them without his say-so. And he would never give his say-so if Zurich was on the itinerary.

A decade on from the announcement of that gruesome pact, Archie was delighted that his great-aunts were still so independent but he was also very glad they had Arlene, their live-in housekeeper. The sisters told themselves, and anyone who asked, that Arlene's duties were limited to cooking, cleaning, and making cocktails—"Though she always skimps on the gin!"—but Arlene Blomerus was trained in first aid and just knowing that she was on hand helped Archie sleep more soundly at night.

THAT DAY, WHEN Penny and Josephine returned from Sloane Square, Arlene was ready to welcome them with tea and cheese toasties. Arlene made a mean cheese toastie. She thanked the cab driver profusely for his assistance in getting the sisters all the way to the front door. It had turned out to be a bigger favour than the cabbie had bargained for, with Penny making all sorts of inappropriate suggestions as he helped her up the steps.

"Old ladies are the worst," he would later tell his mates at the rank.

Arlene asked the sisters about their day and they told her that it had been *vraiment gai* and left it at that. Though Arlene already knew about the Peter Jones debacle—Archie had called her with the lowdown while the sisters were on their way home—she didn't push to hear more about it. She didn't want to embarrass Penny over this latest memory lapse. It was almost certainly a symptom of dementia and Arlene believed that the elderly deserved nothing but compassion in their decline. "After all," as she often said to her own sister Peta, "We're all going to get there in the end."

After supper, Arlene gently suggested to her charges that an early night was in order.

"I know you're both high on your lovely day out but if you don't get to bed in a timely fashion, you'll pay for it tomorrow."

With much grumbling and a tot of whisky apiece, the sisters took Arlene's advice and bid each other goodnight on the landing.

"Watch the bugs don't bite," they told one another, just as they had when they were small.

JOSEPHINE WAS ASLEEP minutes later but Penny wasn't ready for bed. She had some research to do. Firing up the tablet Archie had given her for her ninetieth birthday (preloaded with a sudoku app to help stave off mental decline), she went straight to her favourite diamond dealer's website to check the value of the ring that had spent the afternoon nestled next to a packet of cough sweets at the bottom of her handbag. Had the shop assistant told her it was two carats or three? Having decided it was only two (still not bad for fifteen minutes' work), Penny made a note to put in a call to an old friend the following day. After that, a quick google of upcoming jewellery sales revealed an interesting auction taking place at Brice-Petitjean in Paris: "Notable jewellery from the early twentieth century." The June sale was advertised with a photograph of a ring set with an enormous emerald in a dazzling halo of tiny baguette-cut diamonds. A ballerina setting, as it was called.

"There's a story behind every piece . . ." the accompanying text assured the interested reader.

Penny enlarged the image on her tablet screen as far as it would go, then picked up the magnifying glass she kept on her bedside table for such occasions, to get an even better look. Her mouth dropped open in disbelief as she studied the picture more closely. Was it? No. It couldn't be. And yet . . . Oh yes, it was. There was definitely a story behind this piece.

Chapter Five

. . . . .

Despite Archie's concerns, the VE Day celebration at the Albert Hall went well. The sisters were seated together in the middle of a row of six veterans. Penny had the dashing army officer to her right. Josephine had the handsy Dambuster to her left. Former Third Officer Davina Mackenzie was not in the line-up (Archie did not tell Josephine this was because Davina was recording a special segment for the ITV news), though there was another ancient Wren in attendance: Sister Eugenia Lambert, a nun with The Sisters of the Sacred Heart, whom Archie's great-aunts referred to as The *Prinz Eugen* on account of her having the demeanour of a battleship. Funnily enough, Sister Eugenia had been in the Y Service—the wartime intelligence service that listened to enemy radio traffic at sea—and claimed to have intercepted signals from that infamous German ship amongst others, including the notorious *Bismarck*.

"Anyone who was ever in the Y Service intercepted signals from the *Bismarck*," Josephine would sometimes scoff. "Even if they joined up after it was sunk."

The sisters proudly wore their medals: Josephine had two, Penny had three. Archie had polished them up. He'd also had Penny's sewn onto a set of new ribbons, the originals having been chewed by Penny's most recent dachshund, Flaubert the Third. The sisters both had the War Medal, of course, with its red, white, and blue ribbon. In addition to that, Josephine had the Defence Medal and Penny the 1939–1945 Star and the Italy Star for the periods she'd spent in Algiers and Puglia.

Every time he helped the sisters pin those medals on, Archie thought back to the very first time he saw the gongs, one Christmas in South Kensington. While the adults talked about things that didn't interest him, he'd been allowed to play with the medals as if they were toys, pinning them onto a large and love-worn teddy bear that had once belonged to his great-grandfather Sir Christopher Williamson. Neither sister worried that Archie might lose or damage them as he played. They wore their wartime adventures so lightly.

"Everybody's got *those* medals," said Penny at the time. "You only had to turn up and put on a uniform."

And lately Josephine had told him, "We weren't heroic, Archie. We had very easy wars. We get invited to these ceremonies purely by virtue of having lasted longer than anybody else."

Possibly that was true, but Archie was proud of his great-aunts all the same, and when the cameras panned round to rest on Josephine and Penny's faces as the veterans present at the VE Day ceremony were named, he felt tears spring to his eyes, as they did every time. No matter how the sisters tried to minimise it, their contribution *had* been important and now they were doing the vital work of keeping the memory of the greatest generation alive.

WHEN THE CEREMONY was over—Charles and Camilla did not stay long—Archie caught up with the sisters in the green room beneath the Albert Hall's vast stage for tea and sandwiches.

"You'd think they'd have laid on some proper drink," Penny complained. "Who knows how many more of these ceremonies we've got in us."

"*Toujours gai*, Auntie Penny," Archie reminded her.

"I'd be much more *gai* if I had some alcohol."

"What excitements do you have for us next?" Josephine asked then.

Blimey, Archie thought. They'd barely finished one excitement and they needed another. It was like finding worms to feed chicks.

"I'm working on something," he assured them.

"An interview with Andrew Graham-Dixon perhaps?"

"But he's an art historian."

"So tell him we're both works of art," was Penny's answer.

Archie was relieved when two twenty-something television researchers came over to pay homage. The young people, called Pongo and Tiger (at least that's what it sounded like through their tongue piercings), spoke to his great-aunts as though the nonagenarians were half-witted, as seemed to be the habit of so many when addressing the elderly. On the surface, the sisters seemed fine with that, but after one of the youngsters—possibly Pongo—said "ah, bless" in response to Josephine telling them about her plotting room role in the Battle of the Atlantic, Archie noticed Penny begin tapping her right forefinger on the ceremony programme in her lap. To an ignorant outsider, it might have looked like a tic but Archie recognised the Morse code for "moron." She'd often tapped it out on his forehead.

Archie surreptitiously checked his phone. There was a voicemail from a number he didn't recognise. He was about to listen to the message when the charming BBC newsreader Huw Edwards wandered over for a chat and Josephine, Penny, and Archie all went into full flirt mode. For the moment, the voicemail was forgotten.

LATER ARCHIE ACCOMPANIED his aunts back home.

As the taxi drew up outside their house, Archie looked up at the façade with a critical eye. The house had beautiful bones but it was definitely looking shabby. He would have to arrange for the stucco to be painted again though he felt sure only six months had passed since the last time. The maintenance was never-ending but he knew his great-aunts would never countenance moving to somewhere a little easier to keep from falling down. They were "settled," as they put it, surrounded by two lifetimes' worth of treasures and with all their friends nearby.

"I bet you can't wait to inherit this place," an old boyfriend had said to Archie when he first saw number 63 Pelham Road. He couldn't believe it when Archie told him that he wasn't going to inherit a thing from his great-aunts, least of all this prime piece of real estate.

Though he was their closest relation, after his own father—"And our very favourite," as they often said—Archie had always known that his great-aunts' house would never be his. The sisters had been quite clear about it since he was old enough to understand what inheritance meant. The house was to be sold and the proceeds given to the charitable foundation Penny had set up in memory of her late husband, the horse trainer Connor O'Connell, who'd died suddenly in the South of France in 1966 (on their honeymoon, as it happened). Since then the O'Connell Foundation, supported by Auntie Penny's exceedingly clever investments, had cared for hundreds of orphans in dozens of war-torn countries, providing them with a home, healthcare, and education. Archie had met many of those children when he accompanied Penny on trips to the Foundation's projects and he did not begrudge them a thing. He knew he'd had a lucky start in life.

"It's what your great-uncle would have wanted," Penny said.

Archie wished he'd met his great-uncle Connor. In the one photograph he'd seen of him—a group shot from a 1960s party which was pinned to the back of the downstairs loo door—Connor looked as though he had a good sense of humour. He'd probably needed it, Archie thought from time to time.

ARLENE WAS MAKING lunch when her charges returned. Archie leaned against the kitchen counter while she put the finishing touches to a salad that was made up of all the colours of the rainbow. He was very glad to see she was making enough for four. The Albert Hall sandwiches had been disappointing.

"Anything to report?" Archie asked.

Arlene rinsed her hands and dried them on the tea-towel. When she turned back to Archie, he could tell there was something she wanted to say and he wasn't sure he was going to be happy about it.

"There have been lots of phone calls," she said.

"Go on."

"There's a new telephone scam, where they pretend to be from the HMRC, so when Penny got a third call from a particular gentleman in as many days, I asked him exactly who he was and why he was phoning. He hung up and I blocked his number. Suspicious, eh?"

"Hmmm," said Archie.

"Don't worry, Archie. I'm keeping an eye on things. No one is going to get near the ladies without me knowing what their business is. These people who target the old and the vulnerable with their scams are disgusting.

I don't know how those thieves can live with themselves. No matter how lowly one's position in life, there's no excuse for dishonesty."

Archie nodded. "Well, hopefully it's nothing sinister."

Archie's own phone rang then. It was the number he hadn't recognised from earlier that day. In the excitement of meeting Huw Edwards, he had quite forgotten to listen to the voicemail. He excused himself to the garden to take the call and when he came back in he was all a-flutter.

"Good news?" Arlene asked.

"Oh yes! Very good news indeed."

Here was the excitement to end all excitements.

"Auntie Josephine! Auntie Penny!"

The sisters, who were upstairs changing, poked their heads over the banister to see what was going on.

"I've just had a call from the office of the French ambassador to London. You've been nominated for the *Légion d'honneur!*"

"The what?" Penny asked.

"The *Légion d'honneur*. The highest French order of merit. For your services to France in the war."

"Both of us?" asked Josephine.

"*Tous les deux*," Archie confirmed.

"Then *je suis ravis d'accepter*," said Penny.

"*Moi aussi*," said Josephine. "Oh, this is *vraiment gui*."

The sisters came downstairs and Archie danced them both down the hall. Arlene joined the impromptu polka when they reached the kitchen.

"The *Légion d'honneur!*" Archie sang. "Aunties, we're going to Paris."

Six

. . . . .

7TH JULY 1939

I HATE PARIS!!!

I'm so bored I could scream. I was so looking forward to this visit but it's been nothing but ennui *from the very first day. I might as well not be here. Nobody pays me any attention. Uncle Godfrey is too busy in his wine cellar. Aunt Claudine is too busy with her painting lessons—though we all know that Monsieur Lebre isn't really an art teacher—and now even Josephine has abandoned me.*

She's spent the past week drifting round like a mooncalf. Since August Samuel started making eyes at her, she's entirely forgotten I'm here. Yet I was the one who spoke to him first. Josephine just blushed and hid behind The Code of the Woosters *whenever August came into the courtyard. I was the one who dared to say "bonjour" and I was the one who found out all about him. He was supposed to be our* joint *friend.*

Without me, Josephine would never have come to know August at all—her French is vraiment épouvantable—*but she says she has no use for me as translator now she's decided that August is her* l'amour vrai *and he, apparently, feels the same way about her. While I was inside getting lemonade for us all, he kissed her! Now they are officially in love and I am chopped liver. I've half a mind not to give her the bracelet I stole from Galeries Lafayette.*

I should say that I didn't mean to steal the bracelet. I fully intended to buy Josephine's birthday present. I asked the sales assistant to show me the five I liked best but as I was trying them on and imagining how they would look on Josephine's fat wrist instead of my own far more slender one, a woman in a fancy hat came up to the counter and, as far as the assistant was concerned, I might as well have disappeared in a puff of smoke.

Why does everyone seem to think I'm so easily dismissed? The sales assistant straight away tidied up the bracelets, which I was still looking at, and sent me off with a flick of her hand. She clearly thought I wasn't worth bothering with now that Madame Moneybags had arrived so I felt much less guilty than I might have done when I realised, as I got to the Métro station, that one of the bracelets was still on my arm.

I had walked out of the store quite without knowing I was shoplifting! I even said "bonne journée" to the doorman as I stepped into the street. I couldn't believe it, though I have to admit it was quite a thrill to think I'd got away with an actual crime, even if it was by accident. Perhaps the fact that nobody takes any notice of me could be an advantage, if only I had the gumption to do it again. I'm not sure that had I taken the bracelet on purpose, I could have left the store quite so calmly. I'd have gibbered out a confession and been locked up in La Bastille.

The bracelet probably isn't to Josephine's taste but it's the thought that counts. She's only interested in what she might get from August anyway. I'll bet she thinks he is going to give her some real jewellery. His father was a gem-dealer in Vienna before they fled the Nazis.

By the way, if you have read this far without my say-so, I hope you are thoroughly ashamed of yourself. This is, as it says quite clearly on the cover, my TOP SECRET diary and anyone who reads these pages without my express permission is cursed. Especially you, Josephine Cecily Williamson!

17TH JULY 1939

Today was Josephine's seventeenth birthday. I gave her the bracelet over breakfast. She pronounced it "divine" and declared me her favourite sister (in a field of one and obviously not so dear to her that she wanted to spend the day with me).

As soon as Uncle Godfrey and Aunt Claudine departed the apartment—Godfrey to his cellar and Claudine to an outdoor "painting lesson" in the Bois De Boulogne—Josephine went straight down to the courtyard to wait for August Samuel. She left in a cloud of Aunt Claudine's Eau De Divine. It was absolutely choking. I'm not sure it's ladylike for your scent to announce your arrival quite so far in advance.

Josephine told me that under no circumstances must I follow her down to the garden, neither must I spy on her from the lavatory window, which is the only one that overlooks. She and August had important things to discuss which were not for my "tender ears." I asked how she would know what August was discussing with her if I wasn't there to translate. She said, and I quote, "When you get to my age, Penelope, you will understand that there are some things in life which need no translation."

Naturally, I watched from the lavatory window. Josephine perched on the bench below, pretending to read Aunt Claudine's copy of The Constant Nymph *but really only thinking about how she would look when August came downstairs. She pinched her cheeks and tried various different poses. All of them made her look like a second-rate show-girl at the Moulin Rouge.*

Finally, August arrived, sending Josephine into paroxysms of excitement, and they disappeared through the gate onto the street. I put my foot in the toilet bowl as I was stepping down. Tant pis.

Considering she is relying on me not to tell our godparents what she's been up to, Josephine could really be a good deal kinder, instead of telling me I'm too young to understand the "mysteries of love." I'm only eighteen months younger after all and I've read all of the same books.

Besides, Josephine isn't the only one men find alluring. After she and August left this morning, I went down into the courtyard. I was writing my diary when Gilbert, the son of Madame Declerc, the concierge, sat down on the bench beside me. As usual, he was carrying his gas mask.

He said, "You are the prettiest sister."

I told him it's actually prettier, when there are only two sisters to compare.

I was going to ask him why he thought I was the prettier, since no one has ever said that before and I should like to know what particular aspect of my face is nicer than my sister's, but his mother came back from the market. She only had to scowl in his direction and he went running to help her carry the groceries inside without saying au revoir. Madame Declerc is a vieille vache terrible. She seems to resent everyone who lives in the building, even though they pay her wages. Uncle Godfrey says that being unpleasant is an important part of the concierge's role.

Josephine and August came back around lunchtime. August told me I had good taste in jewellery, regarding Josephine's bracelet.

"Though you know the stones are only glass," he said.

Of course I knew that.

Then he added, "I can show you something real."

He invited us both then—Josephine and me—into his family's apartment. His parents were out, as was Lily, his little sister. I was glad she wasn't there today. August has taken to foisting his sister onto me so that he can go smooching with mine. It really is very annoying.

"My father would kill me if he knew what I'm about to do," August told us.

It turns out that the Samuel family have a safe hidden beneath the floorboards in their bathroom, full of jewels smuggled out of Austria.

Josephine went completely gaga when she saw what was inside, especially when August pulled out a ring he said once belonged to a Russian Grand Duchess who had to sell it to escape to Vienna during the Bolshevik Revolution. There were plenty of big diamonds in the safe as well but this ring was far more lovely. It was an emerald the size of a Fox's Glacier Mint.

Josephine asked if she could try it on and held out her hand as though graciously accepting a proposal. It was absolutely sick-making. It was all I could do not to snort with laughter when the ring got stuck on her knuckle. Then I tried it on too and on me it looked quite beautiful. It turns out I have the hands of a refined Russian aristocrat.

The sight of the emerald fitting me so perfectly made Josephine even more spiteful than usual and after lunch she sent me away again so she and August could talk about more untranslatable things. It was raining so I sat in the stairwell with Gilbert. He says he is as fed-up as I am with August and Josephine both mooning about like they invented love. Before Josephine came along, August was his best friend. They did everything together. Now August has no time for him at all.

Gilbert let me try on his gas mask, which his mother makes him carry at all times. Madame Declerc is convinced that the Germans are going to attack at any moment. Gilbert's father was gassed in the Battle of Verdun and never really recovered. He died when Gilbert was four. That's when he and his mother had to move from their little farmhouse in Brittany to Paris and the concierge flat.

Gilbert wants to be a lawyer when he leaves school though he doesn't know how he will be able to afford the training. I told him I want to be a writer like Colette. I've read all her books in the original. Gilbert says that must be why my French is so good for an English girl's. He says I must always write in French as it is the natural language of the poet. He's really not so bad if you don't look too closely at his spots.

18TH JULY 1939

Gilbert kissed me! It's not the first time I've been kissed but it couldn't have been more different from when Eric Bullingham kissed me in the churchyard on Easter Sunday. That was disgusting. Luckily, the French do things differently. When Gilbert took my face in his hands and told me I might be beautiful one day, I thought my knees were going to buckle underneath me. As he looked deep into my eyes, it was as though he was looking straight into my soul!

I didn't let him use his tongue, of course. I'm not a fast girl. He said he understood and didn't press me to change my mind, thank goodness. It was still SOOOO romantic. I don't care if Josephine doesn't want to spend time with me anymore. I am IN LOVE.

20TH JULY 1939

Just my luck! Today we got a telegram from Pa, saying, "War imminent. Send girls home." Aunt Claudine said Pa was being dramatic but Uncle Godfrey isn't so sure. He said the Germans are getting ready to march on Poland and when that happens, France is honour-bound to go to Poland's defence alongside Great Britain. It could be worse than 1914, so he's sending us and Aunt Claudine to Dieppe to catch the boat to Newhaven on Saturday night. Aunt Claudine protested that she has too much to do in Paris to have to leave right now, to which Uncle Godfrey responded, "You mean your painting lessons?" in a way that said everything the rest of us have been thinking all along.

Josephine is simply desperate at the news, as am I. Gilbert was going to take me for a picnic at a secret grotto in the Jardin du Luxembourg on Sunday afternoon. I'm sure he was planning to tell me he loves me. I told Josephine as much and she told me I had nothing to be upset about. She said my passion for Gilbert is a passing fancy and I'll have forgotten all about him by the time we get home. Not so for her and August, of course. They are "as real as Romeo and Juliet."

I met Gilbert in the stairwell and told him we're leaving at the weekend. Gilbert asked if we could kiss with tongues, seeing as we didn't know how long we might have to be apart. I didn't let him. Now I'm wondering if I should have. Probably for the best that I didn't. Ma and Pa would go berserk if I came back from France with a baby.

22ND JULY 1939

Still another three hours to Newhaven. Aunt Claudine and Josephine are both moping about the cabin sighing at having to leave their loved ones behind—and Uncle Godfrey, though he says he's going to follow in two weeks. Nobody seems to worry about how I'm feeling. Gilbert wished me farewell this morning and gave me his copy of Baudelaire's Fleurs du Mal, *which I will have to hide from Ma and Pa as he's underlined the rude bits. He has promised to write. He is sure that the war, if it happens, will be short.*

Before we left, August took me to one side and made me promise that whatever happens I will always look after my sister. "Always," he insisted, quite dramatically. He's told Josephine that as soon as they are old enough, they will elope and be married. The Russian duchess's emerald will be her engagement ring. He'll have to get the band enlarged.

13TH AUGUST 1939

Arrived for the annual two weeks with the olds at Grey Towers this afternoon. While I was still unpacking my suitcase, Josephine went straight to find Connie and they ran off to our secret hiding place in the gardens without me. When I caught up with them, they immediately went silent so I knew they'd been talking about something they didn't want me to hear. Probably the same sort of "grown-up things" that Josephine wouldn't tell me in Paris. She's still miserable about having to leave August Samuel behind.

I told Connie that her mother wanted her back in the kitchen to peel potatoes for our supper. It wasn't true, and when she'd gone Josephine pinched me and told me it was unkind of me to be so haughty with Connie and remind her that she's staff now when she's always been our friend.

At supper, Connie deliberately spilled cock-a-leekie soup on my best plaid skirt but Grandmama told me off for being clumsy and said, "If you can't manage to sit still and eat like an adult, Penelope Williamson, you'll have to have your meals in the nursery."

I can hear Connie and Josephine through the wall between Josephine's bedroom and mine now. They're sniggering about me, I know. Ugh. I hate Scotland almost as much as I hate Paris. I can't wait to go back to school.

3RD SEPTEMBER 1939

WAR DECLARED!!!

Prime Minister Chamberlain made the dreaded announcement this morning. The Bullinghams came round to listen to our wireless as theirs is broken. The vicar joined us too and we all crowded into Pa's study for the broadcast.

Chamberlain sounded terribly serious when he imparted the bad news to the nation. Josephine, Ma, and Mrs. Bullingham were soon in tears. Cook started wailing. Eric Bullingham looked like he might be sick. He kept asking if he's old enough to fight. Pa and the other men were grave but, I think, relieved to know what's what at last. George was delighted. He and the younger Bullingham boys raced straight outside to check for German bombers.

Given the circumstances, I thought we might get out of going to church. Alas the vicar told us he would simply move the Eucharist an hour later saying, "People need the word of God more than ever today." This was the worst-case scenario since it meant an extra hour until lunch. Cook was not pleased. She said the beef would be ruined. Pa muttered he'd always thought "ruined beef" was Cook's speciality.

The rest of the day was taken up with the news. Pa will go wherever the army needs him, of course. He'll contact his old regiment first thing. George was most disappointed that he's too young to fight. When I could get away from having to help Cook make endless cups of tea for all the visitors who wanted to know what Pa thinks about it all—since he fought in the Great War, he's considered quite the expert on the Boche—I wrote at once to Gilbert. He's fifteen so he won't have to fight yet. I'm not sure about August. He is sixteen already. France has declared war on Germany too. Josephine is distraught. She says she is terrified by the thought of all the men she loves being sent to the front line.

"Oh, lamentous day!" she cried at one point.

I'm not sure lamentous is a word.

I can still hear her crying on the other side of my bedroom wall now. Really, she can be unbearably wet. I know I should be scared too but I can't help feeling thrilled. <u>WE ARE AT WAR. At last!</u> It's all terribly exciting!

Seven

• • • • •

1939

To begin with, the war wasn't actually very exciting at all. At least not for the Williamson sisters.

The day after the declaration, Josephine and Penny's father Christopher went straight to rejoin his old regiment. He continued to live at home while the regiment trained in the evenings and at weekends and waited for their weapons to arrive. Guns were suddenly very hard to come by. There was still the family business, a cardboard box factory, to run in the meantime. The machines were quickly retooled to produce boxes for military supplies.

The sisters' mother, Cecily, joined the Women's Voluntary Services as an ARP warden—Air Raid Precautions. Her job was to cycle around the lanes as dusk fell every evening, making sure all the villagers were obeying the strict new blackout rules. Compliance was high and most evenings the only people she had to tick off were her own children and Mrs. Glover, the cook, who claimed the blackout blinds in the kitchen were giving her "claustrapedia."

The sisters' little brother George was only eleven—much too young to worry about signing up, thank goodness—so he contented himself with building hideouts from where he could fire his catapult at any German spies who might dare parachute into the garden. There was a rumour that they would come disguised as nuns, which made life rather uncomfortable for the sisters at the nearby Convent of The Holy Infant Jesus. They were interrogated for several hours by the local bobby, PC Pilkington, who was zealous about rooting out the enemy within.

"Evil walks among us," he told Christopher Williamson.

"I think the Reverend Mother's evil days are long since over," Christopher remarked after PC Pilkington accused the convent's ninety-one-year-old Mother Superior of taunting him with her German sympathies by offering him a slice of bundt cake.

George wore his gas mask whenever he had an excuse. He also tried to train the family dog, Sheppy, a six-year-old Labrador who was notoriously relaxed about visitors, to spot and attack German agents. Alas, George only succeeded in making Sheppy so jumpy that for the first time ever she tried to bite the vicar when he arrived for tea on Sunday afternoon. She still rolled onto her back for the postman and passing burglars.

A week after the declaration, Josephine and Penny had to go back to school. They were boarders at an old-fashioned establishment called St. Mary's School for Girls near Leamington Spa, where much importance was placed on deportment and very little on anything that might actually be useful in real life, particularly in a country newly at war. School was much the same as ever. In their spare time, the girls were made to knit sweaters for soldiers. Penny could never quite get the hang of knitting and made, unmade, and remade the same single green sleeve for the first six weeks of term.

Josephine still wrote to August and he to her. They had come up with a ruse to get their letters past the school matron, who would have burned them all had she known that Josephine was writing to a boy. Josephine had August sign his letters "Augustine" and pretended he was a Parisian girl she'd met during the summer holidays. Penny backed up Josephine's innocent penfriend story, in exchange for a permanent loan of Josephine's treasured copy of Elizabeth Bowen's *The Death of the Heart*, and Matron was convinced. In fact Matron was so touched by "Augustine's" charming letters (of course she still read them) that she even suggested Augustine's parents might be persuaded to send the young French girl to St. Mary's to keep her safe from the Nazi menace raging across the Continent.

• • •

THE FAMILY'S FIRST wartime Christmas was a little different from usual though there was still a tree cut from the coppice on the estate and carol-singing around the village, and on Christmas Day Mrs. Glover did her best to prepare a sumptuous feast within the constraints of the shortages that everyone was sure would have to lead to rationing in the new year.

"Tell her we'd be perfectly happy with corned beef straight from the tin," Christopher Williamson told his wife when he heard how their cook was planning to re-create her traditional roast with various substitutions that threatened to make the whole even less palatable than usual.

There were still parties to go to even if the talk at every gathering was of military strategy. Penny found it interesting to listen to the local armchair generals. She read her father's copy of the *Times* each morning and longed for someone to ask her opinion on developments at home and abroad. Of course they never did.

"You needn't worry your pretty little head about it," said Rear Admiral Anthony Featherstonehaugh (RN retired) when Penny asked him to clarify Chamberlain's plans for defending Britain's merchant shipping in the North Atlantic. She suspected he didn't want to have to worry his pretty little head about it either.

AT THE BULLINGHAM's traditional Boxing Day sherry party, Mrs. Bullingham told the assembled ladies about her niece Margaret, who was intending to join the WAAF, the Women's Auxiliary Air Force. Mrs. Bullingham did not know what her brother was thinking, allowing his only daughter to indulge such a fanciful notion.

"The Air Force! She'll be surrounded by the very worst types. It's all most untoward."

The more Mrs. Bullingham expounded on the horror of allowing "decent young girls" like her niece to serve alongside "predatory airmen," the more Penny thought the WAAF sounded like great fun. *Untoward?* How exciting!

Meanwhile Josephine moped and sulked and moped. On the day after

Boxing Day, she completely refused to get up, saying she had never felt so ill in her life. Suspecting gastric flu, Cecily let her eldest daughter stay in bed. Mrs. Glover sent Penny up to Josephine's bedroom with all the usual sick-room treats but even two days later Josephine couldn't be tempted into eating (not that anyone was ever really tempted by Mrs. Glover's creations). She could hardly keep a sip of water down.

JOSEPHINE'S MALAISE PERSISTED and in January, Penny went back to school alone. At the time of her departure, she hugged her father especially tight, since on New Year's Eve he'd told the family that his regiment was off to train on Salisbury Plain ahead of being sent to the front line.

On the train to Leamington Spa, Penny sat opposite a young soldier heading home to Coventry on "a forty-eight" (two days' leave), who amused her with stories and swearwords she didn't yet know. The soldier seemed to appreciate Penny's rapt attention and as she prepared to get off at her stop, he gave her a gift of a whole pack of cigarettes. Twenty Craven A!

"Think of me facing the Boche when you smoke them," he said.

A WEEK INTO the new term, Penny received a letter from her mother, confirming that her father's regiment would indeed be leaving for Salisbury in a matter of days. Cecily also wrote that Josephine would not be returning to school that term. The doctor recommended that the best remedy for what ailed Penny's sister would be a spell in the fresh air. To that end, it had been decided Josephine would be going up to Scotland, to Grey Towers, to stay with their paternal grandparents until such time as she was well again.

Cecily concluded, "The doctor has asked that you do not write to Josephine, nor she to you, since she is to avoid any unnecessary excitation."

Penny wasn't unduly upset. She'd always felt overshadowed at school by her big sister, who was a senior prefect and captain of the lacrosse team—The Jolly Girls, as that clique was called. The sentimental soldier's gift of cigarettes had made Penny very popular among her peers in the boarding house and suddenly she was never short of company outside the classroom. Gathering her new friends together in the sports equipment shed to share a smoke and a cough during lunch break, Penny told and retold the story of her encounter with the young private until it took on the air of a grand but doomed romance. Even the head girl, Judy Farmer-Jones, squeezed into the shed to hear the lurid details of Penny Williamson's tragic love story, which had come to incorporate a stolen kiss in the train corridor as the soldier helped Penny with her baggage.

"Penny Williamson, you are terrible," Judy breathed in admiration.

No, Penny did not miss Josephine at all.

JOSEPHINE HAD RECOVERED from her illness by Easter time but still did not return to school. When the sisters were briefly reunited at home during the holidays, Penny noticed that Josephine seemed somehow changed but put that down to the general atmosphere around the house.

Their mother was extremely distracted. They knew now that their father had been sent to France, but since he'd arrived there, news had been frustratingly infrequent. Many of the families in the village had a father, son or brother in the same regiment. Anyone who received a letter would rush from house to house reassuring the others all was well. At least, all had been well when the letter was written and posted.

In the evenings, Penny joined her mother to listen to the news on the wireless in Pa's study. Josephine said she couldn't bear it. She spent a lot of time crying. Suddenly anything could make Josephine cry. She even cried when one of the farm dogs had puppies.

Penny was bewildered. "They're puppies, Josephine. *Toujours gai!*"

In the end, Penny was glad to go back at school. She didn't realise as she tossed a careless "goodbye" through Josephine's bedroom door that it would be the last time they saw each other until the Christmas of 1945.

IN JULY 1940, DURING the week of her eighteenth birthday, Josephine applied to join the Women's Royal Naval Service. Mrs. Bullingham approved. She told Cecily Williamson that Josephine was making the right choice in choosing to work alongside the "Senior Service," as the Royal Navy was known. As Mrs. Bullingham had feared, her beloved niece was absolutely changed for the worse since joining the WAAF. She was wearing trousers when she came home on leave.

"She even asked for a scotch before dinner! Scotch! I ask you. She's ruined. You must be so relieved," Mrs. Bullingham said. "That Josephine is such a sweet, sensible girl."

Cecily and Josephine shared a small, sad smile at that.

Eight

• • • • •

HMS Pembroke I,
London

30TH JULY, 1940

My Perfect Penny,

Well, I did it. I joined the Wrens and here I am on HMS Pembroke for my basic training. Don't worry. I haven't gone to sea. Pembroke is what they call a "stone frigate"—naval parlance for a building. It's terribly funny. Though we're very much on dry land, we have to talk as though we're on the ocean wave, so our dormitories are cabins and the kitchen is a galley, that sort of thing.

I am sorry we didn't have a chance to say goodbye. I so hoped we'd have a last weekend together while you were home on exeat, especially with all the excitement of Pa's regiment getting out of Dunkirk, but in the WRNS one turns up when one is asked and I had to be here in London earlier than I expected.

I know I was being an awful drip when we saw each other at Easter but it was just the effects of my convalescence. I promise I feel very much better now I'm here on the good ship Pembroke, getting plenty of exercise in the brisk sea air. Well, of course it's not real sea air but you know what I mean!

Write soon and tell me how you've been getting on in the tennis team.

> *Toujours gai, little sis.*
> *Your Josie-Jo*
> *xxx*

One of the first things Josephine did when she left home for WRNS basic training was write a letter to August in Paris, telling him where he could find her. She received no reply. Paris, of course, was occupied now. German soldiers sat outside the cafés on the Champs-Élysées. She'd read that the occupation had been relatively calm but knew also that more than two hundred Parisians had died in the process. Was August one of that unhappy number? She felt sure he would have put up a fight.

Josephine thought about the summer of 1939 all the time. Was it just the fact that August was her first sweetheart that had made those few weeks so very special? Would Josephine have fallen anywhere so deeply in love had it not been for the thought that at any moment war might tear them apart?

Before it actually came about, Josephine had been excited at the prospect of war. She'd grown up on the Great War stories of her elders. Her father had been in the army. Her mother had joined the Red Cross and learned to drive a truck. Josephine had always loved the thought of her mother as a brave young woman on the front line (though in reality, Cecily drove dignitaries around the Home Counties) and often wished she too could have such a life-enhancing adventure. It was all so glamorous. Of course, she understood now that her parents had spared her the worst of their experiences. Her father had never talked about the horror of the trenches. Her mother never talked about the soldiers who came home minus legs, arms, eyes, and minds.

In the summer of 1939, August had been altogether more worried that at any moment France might declare war on Germany and open itself up to invasion. Josephine remembered one of their last conversations, as they sat beneath a horse chestnut tree in the Tuileries.

"Hitler means to eradicate us."

"The French? He'll seek some sort of non-aggression pact, surely,"

Josephine parroted the words she'd heard her godfather and his friends throw about.

"I'm talking about the Jewish people, Josephine."

August reminded her that he'd already fled his homeland. In Vienna, people the Samuel family had long considered friends turned their backs on them when it became clear that the Anschluss was going to happen.

"But that wouldn't happen in France," Josephine said. "The French will stand up to Hitler, you'll see, and they certainly won't turn against you. And if they do, you can come to England. My father will find you a position in our cardboard factory."

"Do you think he'll be happy to hear you've made a Jewish friend while you were supposed to be improving your French language skills?"

"Pa couldn't care less where people come from so long as they are good and kind," Josephine said with certainty. "Anyway, you could try harder to teach me the language of love."

"*Je t'aime*," August told her then. That didn't need translating.

HER BASIC TRAINING finished, Josephine was appointed to a secretarial position at WRNS HQ off Trafalgar Square. She was billeted in a "wrennery" in Hampstead, where she shared a room with three other girls, one of whom had the most awful laugh. Other than that, they were perfectly fine, if not the kind of girls that Josephine could ever imagine becoming great pals. They were very different from the lacrosse crowd at St. Mary's (though Josephine didn't have much in common with those "jolly girls" anymore either).

Josephine's new roommates were making the most of being in London. She admired their persistence in trying to have a social life when, given they had to be back by ten o'clock each night, sometimes it was hardly worth getting ready to go out.

Every night that autumn of 1940, the Luftwaffe swept in across the Channel and the air raid sirens wailed. It was a hellish sound that some of the girls nevertheless secretly welcomed if they heard it while out and about. Jane, one of Josephine's roommates, had had to spend a whole night sheltering in the basement of a theatre with her airman beau, after the warning sounded while they were watching a comedy revue. She said it was one of the best nights of her life. She acted as though the war was one great big game. Not so Josephine.

Even on a quiet night with no raid directly overhead, while the other girls in her room slept and snored, Josephine would find herself awake and staring at the ceiling, reliving those last days with August over and over. Had he received her letter from London? Or the one before, from Scotland? Was he angry with her? Did he *hate* her? Was he even alive? Without him, was there any point in living through the Blitz?

ONE TUESDAY IN November, Josephine received a letter. Whenever mail arrived, Josephine would race to fetch it, only to be disappointed when she saw that the only envelopes addressed to her were in her sister's or her mother's hand. They were never from France. Neither was there anything from France on this particular day, but there was a letter in a familiar scrawl from someone she'd not expected to hear from again. Why now? Unexpected news was always bad news in wartime. That was what Josephine was learning. She tore the envelope open.

> *Dear Josie-Jo,*
>
> *It took me ages to find out where you're living. I didn't want to send this letter via your ma and pa. I'm in London now. I'm driving an ambulance in Battersea. I'm sorry I didn't say goodbye after you know what. I couldn't come back to the house. They wouldn't let me. I need to see you. There are things I have to tell you that I can't put in writing. Write to me at my station and tell me when we can meet.*
>
> *Yours faithfully and sincerely,*
> *Connie Shearer*

Connie—the youngest housemaid at Grey Towers, her grandparents' house near Arisaig—had been a friend and playmate to Josephine since they were small children. They'd been as close as any sisters but there was nothing about Grey Towers that Josephine wanted to be reminded of now.

Especially given that Connie had run away and left Josephine all alone there after everything they'd been through. Josephine folded the letter up again. She didn't think she could bear to write back. What could she say?

JOSEPHINE WENT OUT that evening with one of the other Wrens. After an early supper at the Lyon's Corner House, she and Iris caught a bus to a cinema on Baker Street. They saw *Let George Do It*. The cinema was full of laughter at George Formby's antics as a ukulele player mistaken for a British intelligence agent. Josephine had never found Formby particularly funny but she told Iris she'd enjoyed the film all the same.

"Keeping our sense of humour is our national duty," said a man who'd been sitting on the row in front of them as they filed out afterwards.

"Too right," said Iris.

The man, seeing that Iris and Josephine were both in uniform, gave them a salute. "You make us proud, girls," he said.

Iris and Josephine saluted him back.

They had only just got home to the wrennery when the air raid sirens began to sound. Josephine was in the bathroom as the horrible wail went up. She could hear the other girls shouting to one another in the bedrooms.

"We need to get downstairs! Who's in? Is Evie back from the theatre?"

"I bet she's trying to get herself stuck there all night like Jane did!"

"Lucky so-and-so," said Jane. "Tonight I get to be in the stinking cellar with you lot."

Josephine spat her toothpaste into the basin but remained standing there, staring at her face in the murky mirror as though it belonged to a stranger.

"Where's Josephine?" someone shouted.

She didn't respond.

"Tell her to get downstairs quick. It's going to be a bad one. I can feel it in my bones."

"Not in your waters?" someone else joked.

"I'm definitely going to wet myself if this raid is anything like last night's."

Josephine could hear the unmistakable desynchronised sound of German engines drawing close now, but still she didn't move to find safety.

Jane swore as a plane roared overhead.

"There's no need to swear," said Maureen, a new arrival at the Hampstead house. She was planning to join a convent after the war.

"There's every need to swear!" Jane responded. She followed up with a few more carefully chosen curses.

"Where is Josephine?" Maureen asked this time. "We all need to be downstairs."

Still Josephine didn't move. She was so very unhappy. Perhaps it wouldn't be so bad if the Luftwaffe did their worst and she didn't make it to the shelter.

There was a banging right on the bathroom door now. It was Iris.

"Josephine, come on."

The whistling noise they had all come to dread was followed by an awful crump—close, very close by—that made the whole building shake.

Iris hammered on the door again.

"They're flying right over us. Come on, you goose. I don't want to die."

I do, thought Josephine. *And I deserve to.*

"Josephine," Iris shouted through the door. "It isn't fair to make us worry. Come now."

"I'll be right down," Josephine promised.

She heard Iris thundering down the stairs. Somewhere nearby, another stick of incendiary bombs made contact. Maureen shrieked. Jane cursed all the saints.

"I've had enough," Josephine looked at her reflection in the mirror as she spoke to her own god. "I don't want to live anymore. Put me out of my misery. I know I can never be happy again so I'll be grateful to be dead. Just make it quick and don't hurt the others. They're good girls. Not like me."

Someone seemed to be listening. A moment later Josephine heard a German plane right above the house. She closed her eyes and waited for the inevitable.

Down in the cellar, the young Wrens said their prayers and crossed their fingers, pleading for salvation like the children they'd been not so very long ago.

THE ALL CLEAR did not sound for what felt like an eternity. When it did, with barely a word to one another, the Wrens climbed up from the cellar and filed out through the front door of their house to see the devastation on the street. *Their* street. The Germans had never got so close before.

The smell of cordite, which had filled the basement, was just as strong outdoors. The air was thick with smoke and choking dust. Opposite, where a big house that exactly mirrored the one in which they were living had stood, was now a smoking ruin. Only one wall of the once grand villa remained intact, revealing fireplaces, wallpaper, and treasured family photographs and paintings still hanging. There was a strange intimacy to the sight of a charred dressing gown on the back of a door that led to nowhere. It was as though a monstrous child had taken a hammer to a dolls' house.

The fire brigade and the air raid wardens were already there, attempting to move a large beam.

"Is someone under there?" Iris asked one of the firemen who was taking a breather on the wrennery steps.

"No one alive," he said.

On the street lay five bodies, carefully shrouded with blankets, awaiting the undertaker.

"It's a wonder there aren't more," the fireman observed.

The Luftwaffe had taken out every other house on the side of the street opposite the wrennery. There was an awful precision to the way the bombs had fallen.

Maureen muttered a prayer. Iris and Jane clung to one another. Only Josephine was dry-eyed. Iris folded her into a hug.

"You goose," Iris said. "We were so, so worried when you stayed upstairs."

The warmth of her friend's arms made Josephine remember how long it had been since she'd last been held. When she'd waved her off to London, Josephine's mother had hardly seemed able to look at her, let alone share one last embrace.

VERA LAUGHTON MATHEWS, the venerable director of the WRNS, was apprised of the near miss and appeared at the wrennery at breakfast time to make sure her girls were as well as could be expected after such a frightening night. Her stalwart presence was reassuring.

After that, the young Wrens returned to their various roles about the

city as on any other Wednesday morning. Josephine and Iris caught the
bus into central London. The journey took far longer than usual. The Luftwaffe had been busy all over the city and had rendered many roads all but
impassable. Iris didn't chatter away as she normally did but as they turned
into Baker Street she grabbed Josephine's arm, leaning across her to get a
better look at one bombsite in particular.

"It's the cinema," she breathed. "We were in there just last night."

The cinema, like the house across the road from the wrennery, had been
obliterated. The burgundy velvet seats were scattered throughout the ruins
like the seeds of a pomegranate crushed beneath a cart wheel.

Iris crossed herself.

"God was looking out for us," she breathed.

Perhaps he was.

As she looked at the wreckage, Josephine felt the inexplicable sensation
of something like the beat of a second heart keeping time with her own.
Something like hope.

During her lunch hour, Josephine wrote to Connie Shearer at her Bat-
tersea ambulance station, suggesting they meet at the Lyons' Corner House
on Coventry Street on Saturday afternoon. Her mind was suddenly busy
with the reasons why Connie might want to meet. She must have news
from August—she'd been their go-between after all.

Returning to the wrennery that night, Josephine picked up a tiny piece
of shrapnel from the road outside. It was only the size of a cinema ticket,
yet she knew that at high speed it might have caused significant damage to
the fragile body of a human being. She wrapped that shrapnel in her handkerchief and put it in her pocket. Holding it tightly, like a talisman, Josephine resolved to get through this war and to find August when it was over.

ON SATURDAY, JOSEPHINE got to the Corner House ten minutes early.
Fifteen minutes after the appointed time, Connie Shearer was still nowhere
to be seen; instead a young man who said he'd been Connie's colleague
arrived in her place to buy Josephine a cup of tea and offer his condolences.
He'd wrung his cloth cap between his hands as he told her, "Connie died
in the raid on Tuesday night. The house she'd been called to took a direct
hit. She didn't stand a chance."

The news Connie had been so keen to impart had died with her.

"Will you be alright, miss?" the young man asked nervously as he waited for his message to take effect.

"Of course." Josephine nodded briskly. She was well used by now to holding back her emotions. She thanked the young man for the tea and left the Corner House with her mascara still intact. But on her way back to the wrennery Josephine had to duck into an alleyway as the tears finally broke through.

She pounded a cold brick wall with her fists.

"Not Connie. You were supposed to take me, God, not Connie. Not Connie too . . ."

MORE THAN EIGHTY years later, Josephine pressed her thumb to the edges of her "lucky" piece of shrapnel, safe inside its little cotton pouch, and smiled and nodded and smiled as Archie outlined the excitements ahead. Archie seemed so very pleased about the trip to Paris that Josephine decided she would just have to play along with his enthusiasm and make her excuses later.

"Wonderful, Archie!" she said. "Oh, it will be ever so *gai*."

But she didn't want to go to Paris. If she'd never been to Paris, things might have turned out very differently indeed.

Nine

• • • • •

Present Day

Paris in June. The timing could not have been better for Archie. As it happened, a trip to the City of Light was already pencilled into his diary for the week of his great-aunts' inauguration as *Chevaliers de la Légion d'honneur*. He was due to be in France for a series of antiques and art fairs. The fairs were one of the highlights of Archie's year. He relished the opportunity to see what was "new" in the world of old paintings and catch up with friends in the business.

Thus when the date for the inauguration came in, Archie was very pleased indeed to see that it perfectly matched his tentative plans. However, almost as soon as he'd told the sisters about the excitements ahead, he started to worry.

It had seemed such a grand idea, taking his great-aunts to France on a jolly, but perhaps he should have asked the French Embassy if they might receive their gongs in London instead. The sisters were in their late nineties, after all.

As it was, Josephine had expressed some reluctance to take the trip but was quickly overruled by Penny, who pointed out that this might be their last hurrah. For his own selfish reasons, Archie had backed Penny up, promising that he would make sure it was all very easy and a smashing adventure, to boot.

"What's happened to the daring great-aunt I once knew?" he'd asked when Josephine demurred. He'd jollied her into letting him book her ticket. But perhaps Archie should have accepted her concerns. Were the sisters really fit enough to travel overseas for the ceremony? How would Archie make sure they stayed out of trouble if they did?

In the week following the news of their election to the *Légion d'honneur*, Penny had twice walked out of Waitrose on the King's Road without paying. On the second occasion, she had secreted a tin of sardines in chilli oil in the pocket of the fishing jacket she wore for most casual outings. She didn't even like sardines! The security staff had been lovely about it, thank goodness. They accepted that Penny's memory was perhaps not what it should be and made her a cup of tea while she waited for Arlene to come and find her. But Penny's accidental shoplifting—and of course it *was* accidental—was becoming a worrying habit. Where had it come from? Archie googled "shoplifting and dementia" and was horrified to discover that it was not at all uncommon for people with dementia to unwittingly commit petty crime. The ubiquity of the phenomenon did not make it any less concerning. What if Penny did the same in Paris and fell foul of a gendarme who didn't have the empathy of the lovely team at Waitrose? Would Archie be able to talk their way out of that? He realised with a sinking heart that he wouldn't be able to keep an eye on both sisters and do all the things he had hoped to do. Like seeing his old friend Stéphane.

STÉPHANE BERNARD HAD been Archie's school French exchange partner. When they first met, Stéphane was a sixteen-year-old history geek obsessed with the Renaissance. He now headed up Brice-Petitjean, one of the biggest auction houses in Paris. Twenty-five years had passed since Archie and Stéphane shared their first illicit kiss in the garden of Stéphane's parents' house in Annecy but the memory of that day was still special to Archie. He suspected it remained special to Stéphane too. They'd stayed in touch ever since, meeting whenever they found themselves in the same city. On their occasional meet-ups, Archie thought he still sensed a frisson between them but fate decreed they had never been simultaneously single and thus able to act upon it.

By very happy coincidence, Stéphane was hosting a fancy reception the week of the antiques fair to celebrate Brice-Petitjean's upcoming "important twentieth-century jewellery" sale, which included headline items from the estate of one of France's most popular actresses of the 1950s. Archie was over the moon to receive an invitation. Though he didn't know Stéphane's current relationship status, the fact that Stéphane responded to Archie's instant RSVP with matching alacrity gave him great hope that this could be the moment he'd been waiting for.

"It will be <u>wonderful</u> to see you," Stéphane wrote.

Archie knew he simply had to be at that party. But it might mean having to leave the sisters alone in Paris for an evening and in the light of recent events that was just too big a risk. What he needed was a reliable auntie-sitter, so he was extremely relieved when Arlene said that she would love to accompany her charges to France. Worth every penny, Archie thought, as he booked her Eurostar ticket.

With Arlene on board, Archie felt reassured enough to put the rest of the plan in place. He booked four rooms at the Hotel Maritime just off the Rue du Faubourg Saint-Honoré. It was expensive but he knew the sisters would love its old-school style. Soon the trip was coming together nicely and Archie dared to start believing he might be in line for some excitements of his own.

OVER SUNDAY LUNCH in South Kensington, the day before they were due to travel, Archie outlined their Parisian itinerary to his great-aunts and Arlene. Josephine and Penny approved whole-heartedly of the booking at The Maritime and the news that Archie had upgraded their Eurostar tickets to Standard Premier class with his *carte blanche* points.

"We will arrive in time for tea tomorrow afternoon," Archie told them. "Tuesday is the big day. We need to be at the ceremony venue by nine-thirty in the morning. A French veterans association will be hosting lunch in a nearby restaurant. In the afternoon, you have an interview with the BBC's Paris correspondent. That might take an hour or so. After that, I expect you'll both be happy with room service and an early night. Meanwhile, I . . ."

The sisters looked at him expectantly.

"Well, I've been invited to a reception at Brice-Petitjean, Stéphane's auction house . . ."

"Stéphane!" Josephine and Penny echoed his name.

Archie's great-aunts knew all about Stéphane. He'd visited them in London a number of times over the years. They both adored the charming young French man almost as much as they adored Archie.

"It's to launch a jewellery sale. Terribly boring," Archie continued. "I won't drag you ladies along."

"Oh no," said Penny. "A reception at Brice-Petitjean sounds right up my street. It seems a shame to be in Paris and not make the most of every moment. I would love to see Stéphane again."

"Me too," said Josephine. "Such a lovely young man. Is he single?"

"I'm not sure."

"Well, you can rely on us to ask the right questions."

The very idea made Archie blanch.

"So you both want to come to the auction house reception?" he asked them, heart sinking.

Penny nodded. "Yes. Absolutely. That would be terribly *gai*."

Archie could only hope the sisters would have forgotten all about it by the time they boarded the Eurostar.

Ten

• • • • •

That same afternoon, Penny packed her suitcase for the trip. Arlene had offered to do it for her but Penny wanted to be sure she had everything she needed and it wasn't a task she could delegate.

She could hardly believe she was going to Paris the following morning. Thank goodness Josephine had allowed herself to be persuaded. Had Josephine refused to travel, the whole trip would have been off and that would have been a disaster. Penny felt only a little guilty for having turned on the waterworks when Josephine first expressed her reservations.

"It's only the thought of excitements like this that keep me going," Penny had lied.

Alone in her bedroom, Penny shook out the jacket she'd bought at Marks and Spencer the previous Friday. Archie had insisted the sisters go shopping for something new to wear for the inauguration, though both Penny and Josephine would have been perfectly happy to wear the same suits they wore for every public occasion. Josephine always wore a navy-blue trouser suit. Penny had a preference for brown. Funny how more than three quarters of a century since they'd left the women's services, they both still resorted to uniform dressing for important occasions. But Archie wasn't having it. Not this time.

"One isn't awarded the *Légion d'honneur* every day," he'd reminded them. "You've got to be wearing something fresh and modern when you step up to receive those medals. We're going to Paris after all. It's the fashion centre of the universe."

"I think we're beyond fashion," Josephine told him.

But the sisters had eventually agreed to some new outfits and Arlene, who was very interested in fashion, had done the honours, escorting them to the Marks and Spencer flagship store at Marble Arch and acting as their personal stylist. At least, she had tried to act as their personal stylist.

Josephine may have somewhat submitted to Arlene's suggestions but Penny had ignored the younger woman's exhortations that she should go for a "pop of colour" and settled instead for a trouser suit in a dark mahogany shade, which was as close as Arlene would let her get to brown. Entirely plain and polyester, it was the sort of suit one could wear for all occasions—sober or festive. Penny's first thought, when she spotted it, was that it would make good funeral wear for those tiresome modern occasions when people insisted "no black."

As Penny emerged from the M&S changing room, Arlene was talking to a sales assistant, explaining why the sisters needed new outfits.

"Ah, bless!" said the assistant, when she saw Penny in the jacket and trousers.

If there was one thing Penny really couldn't stand, it was people who said "Ah, bless." Such a patronising phrase and a reliable signifier that the person who uttered it was a half-wit.

"You've won a medal, haven't you?" the assistant added in the tone she probably used for three-year-olds and puppies, compounding her mistake.

"Yes, I know I have, dear," said Penny. "I may be old but I am not yet entirely gaga so please take your inane 'ah bless-ing' somewhere else."

The assistant pursed her lips and scuttled away to rearrange a pile of cotton sweaters.

"Penny," Arlene scolded. "That lady was helping us and now you've upset her."

"She needed upsetting."

The moment gave Penny a small frisson of satisfaction. She hated to be underestimated, even though she knew that was *exactly* what she would be hoping for in Paris.

• • •

"ONE SHOULD ALWAYS pack a party dress," Penny said to herself now as she folded the suit into her suitcase. "And some sparklers to go with it."

She tossed her old medals in their velvet pouch into her handbag. Then, having taken a quick look out of her bedroom door to reassure herself that Josephine, Arlene and Archie were still downstairs watching—for the hundredth time—a DVD of *In Which We Serve*, she set to work.

Penny's knees and hips let out a sharp protest as she knelt to roll up the rug on her bedroom floor. It was a beautiful rug. She'd bought it on a trip to India with Jinx, back in the 1950s. Every time she thought about it she was transported to the dingy shop in a back street in Agra, which had looked so unpromising yet was stuffed full of treasures. She remembered the scent of the small glasses of tea they'd been offered and the beautiful young boys who demonstrated how the fine silk threads looked different depending on which end of the rug you were standing. They'd unfurled those rugs with such indifferent aplomb; it was almost like watching a ballet. What a fabulous adventure that had been. The Taj Mahal by moonlight was a sight Penny would never forget. It had been a successful business trip too.

With the rug carefully rolled back, Penny took out her old Swiss army knife and knelt down again to work loose the screws that were holding the floorboard in place. One, two, three, four. The board took some prising up but she managed it without too much swearing or making any other noise that might attract Arlene's attention. That woman had the ears of a bat. Finally, Penny sat back with a section of the board in her hand. And there was her safe.

Of course, any professional burglar worth his salt would know that beneath the floorboards was the place to keep something *really* valuable but Penny was happy that this safe would at least escape the notice of a casual thief. There wasn't much left inside it now anyway. The pieces of jewellery that Archie would recognise as his great-aunt's favourites were always on her body or in the pottery bowl on her bedside table (it was a very ugly bowl but Archie had made it when he was nine and for that reason alone it was infinitely precious). What remained in the safe were things Penny didn't ever wear but couldn't sell, and the thick wad of notes she'd received in exchange for the diamond solitaire she'd lifted on the way to meet Archie at Peter Jones back in April. Not entirely a fair exchange, she suspected, but she was a little out of the loop when it came to finding reliable fences and it was very difficult to conduct such delicate business when Arlene was always first to the phone. Ah well, it was still enough to fund the Foundation's school in the Democratic Republic of the Congo for half a year.

The cash was not what Penny was after that day, though she would need to deal with it soon. She didn't want to leave it to Archie. He wouldn't have a clue how to get it into the Foundation's bank account without having to answer too many questions. Archie, dear Archie, could not tell a lie, to the extent that sometimes it was hard to believe he was her blood relation. Penny was looking instead for a particular piece of jewellery, something she had not worn in a very long time. Something she had never worn in public.

"Ah! There you are!"

From the corner of the safe, Penny pulled a little newspaper package. She unfolded it and slipped the ring that had been hidden inside onto her finger, surprised to find it so easy. Her knuckles were gnarled and swollen with arthritis, but with just a little effort, she could still get the ring on. She held her hand to catch the light from the window and turned it this way and that so the green stone in the centre sent coloured shards across the white walls. Everything grows old, thought Penny, except for the stones. The Stones! She had a little chuckle at her own joke. She'd met Mick Jagger at one of her husband Connor's parties, before the band became famous. He'd flirted with her, Penny remembered, suggesting she might like to go upstairs for a quickie. She wondered if he would ask her now. She wondered if it would be worth the bother of saying yes if he did. What was that line? "Come upstairs and make love? These days it's one or the other."

The ring had aged considerably better than Penny *or* Mick Jagger. Its ballerina setting was as pristine as the central stone. The design was timeless. Simple. Not that the simplicity meant it had been easy to create. It had taken a special jeweller to make a setting so fine. It took a trained eye to appreciate the skill. Penny had that eye.

She put on her glasses and brought the ring closer to her face. It was as good as she remembered. Briefly, her mind flashed back to the first time she'd seen it, on a velvet tray in a jeweller's workshop. She could see the jeweller's face as he waited for her to tell him what he already knew. It was perfect.

"An excellent idea," he'd told her. "To have a replica made of such a fine piece."

If only she had the original.

With the ring on her finger, Penny flattened out the newspaper cutting in which it had been wrapped. The scrap of paper dated from June 1966. It held a story that had been tucked away on page eight of *The Times*.

"French police are searching for a mysterious benefactor who left an emerald ring in a church in Antibes on the Côte D'Azur. The woman visited the church's confessional at around three o'clock in the afternoon before depositing the priceless gem in the offertory box on her way out. She is described by a witness as well-dressed, of medium height, wearing a scarf over her light brown hair. She spoke perfect French with a slight English accent . . ."

Just then Penny heard Arlene in the hallway downstairs. The film must have finished.

"I'll get us all some tea," Arlene said in the loud voice that suggested Josephine's hearing aid was on the blink. "I've got a special treat as well. I'll ask Penny if she'd like to join us."

Penny wrenched the ring from her finger and quickly tucked it into the breast pocket of her shirt. She just about managed to stand up and kick the rug back into place before Arlene got to the top of the stairs. She'd have to nail the floorboard down again later. Arlene knocked lightly on Penny's door. She was good like that at least. She would never just barge in.

"Tea and lemon drizzle?" Arlene asked when she popped her head around the door.

"Oh, yes please," said Penny. Arlene made excellent cakes.

"And you asked me to remind you about the five-thirty at Haydock Park. I put that money on Carningli like you asked."

"Thank you. Let's hope the old nag isn't having an off day."

Penny still had the *Racing Post* delivered. Connor's lessons in how to read form had proved invaluable over the years. She remembered how he'd called her a "natural" when it came to picking horses. Penny could read things in a horse's body language that other people missed. She always thought she could read things in human body language that other people missed too. Until she met Connor.

Arlene was hovering and Penny was sure she was looking at the rug. Had she put it back the wrong way round?

"I'll be downstairs momentarily," she said.

Thankfully Arlene understood she was being dismissed. With Arlene gone, Penny fished out the ring and gave it one last appraising look before she secreted it more securely in the inside pocket of her handbag next to her lucky silver matchbox. She wasn't going to Paris without that.

THE LEMON CAKE was excellent and Carningli romped home two lengths ahead of his nearest rival.

"Wonderful." Penny clapped her hands. "I shall spend all my winnings at Galeries Lafayette. Oh, I am so looking forward to Paris."

"What are you most looking forward to?" asked Arlene.

"Catching up with an old friend," Penny said.

"Who's that?" asked Archie, jumping on the suggestion. "You haven't mentioned any old friends in Paris to me. Who are you planning to catch up with?"

When Penny didn't answer but merely continued to smile a distant smile as the racing results scrolled down the screen, Archie and Arlene both assumed she hadn't heard the question.

"Give me your hearing aids now," Arlene told the sisters, holding out a palm. "You both need new batteries before we go to France."

Penny happily handed hers over. From time to time, she quite liked being without her hearing aids. She could go inside her head and tune into her thoughts far more easily without them whistling in her ear. Now, momentarily almost completely deaf, she buried her nose in the catalogue for Stéphane's auction which Archie had brought along to show them. Archie had thought, rightly, that the sisters would be interested in Stéphane's new corporate mug-shot but that wasn't the only thing Penny wanted to see. The emerald ring she had spotted online warranted a full catalogue page to itself. A single line on the ring's provenance confirmed Penny's suspicions.

Then the racing was finished and, on the television, a film was about to begin. It was the 1945 version of *Blithe Spirit*.

"It's your favourite, Auntie Penny," Archie observed, extra loud.

Eleven

Purgatory
Otherwise known as St. Mary's School for Girls.

19TH NOVEMBER 1940

Dear Josie-Jo,
How is my favourite Wren? Thank you so much for the photograph of you in your uniform. I am awfully proud to have a sister in the navy, though I see what you mean about the floppy-looking hat. Hopefully it won't be too long before you're made Petty Officer and you can have that natty tricorn.

I am dying of boredom here at St. Mary's, though there was some excitement last week. I was on fire watch on the school roof when the dreaded Luftwaffe flew over on their way to bomb Coventry. Trudy Sargeant, who can't tell a Spitfire from a seagull, thought they were our boys and actually waved them on their way! You can imagine how much stick she's been getting this weekend.

Anyway St. Mary's was spared—as usual. Doesn't seem to matter how hard I pray for a bomb on the biology lab—but the girls at Wroxall Abbey woke up to find an unexploded parachute mine in the middle of their lacrosse court. Bad news for The Jolly Girls, whose away match against them was cancelled. Bad news for us too, since old Miss Bull has decreed that we must now have a fire drill before breakfast every morning. She said that while it's unlikely that Herr

Hitler would ever command a direct attack on St. Mary's School for Girls, the incident at Wroxall Abbey was a timely reminder that a Luftwaffe pilot might offload unused ordnance anywhere on his way back to Germany.

I'm in the upper dorm now so of course my fire escape is down a rope into the courtyard—you must remember that. It's quite exciting actually. I've got my technique down pat. Not that Old Bull is impressed. This morning she said to me, in front of the whole school, "There's no need to look quite so pleased with yourself, Penelope Williamson. You're not in training to be a commando."

Oh, how I wish I were! How envious I am of the young men who are off to be trained for the new Special Service Brigade. I read about it in The Times. *Did you? I can't believe I have to pretend to be interested in the womanly arts for another two terms before I can bid goodbye to this old dump. The minute I am old enough, I'm going to follow you into the services, though it probably won't be the Wrens. Judy Farmer-Jones went to enlist last week and was told they're only recruiting catering staff right now. I do not want to spend my war serving pink gins to old admirals!*

Enough about me. You've got awfully important war work to be getting on with, no doubt. Oh, how I envy you, my favourite girl in blue.

Toujours gai!
With kisses from your Perfect P.

P.S. 21/11/40 Your letter arrived this morning, before I had time to send mine. I can hardly believe the news about Connie. I am so sorry, Josie-Jo. I know she was your very best friend. A little sister hardly makes up for it, I'm sure, but I will always be here for you. PP

A whole fourteen months later, in January 1942, the moment of Penny's liberation arrived.

She was sitting at the breakfast table with her mother and George when she opened her invitation to an interview for the FANY—the First Aid

Nursing Yeomanry. When her face was suddenly bright with joy, George and Ma thought she must be reading news of her father, whose regiment was again overseas.

"It's the best news in the world!"

"No," said Cecily, when she read the short letter herself. "Absolutely not. I will not have both my daughters in uniform. I simply cannot allow it. Penelope, you are needed here at home."

"No, she isn't," said George. "You said the other day she's more of a hindrance than a help around the house."

Cecily did not bother to contradict her son but was still adamant that Penny would not be going to London to join the FANY and thence find herself sent goodness only knew where.

"Why on earth do you want to go to war?" Cecily asked.

"I won't be going to war. In all likelihood, I'll be stuck in an office like Josephine. But I do want to do my bit. You did your bit, Ma, in the Great War. If you hadn't signed up to drive an ambulance, you might never have met Pa. And then what would have happened?"

"I might have met a sensible man and had two sensible daughters who I could rely upon in my old age. Why can't you be happy in the Voluntary Service with me?"

"Because I can't spend a worldwide war making cups of tea! You know if Pa were here he'd say I should join the FANY."

"He probably would," George agreed.

"Well, he isn't here. Oh!" Cecily exclaimed. "What have I done to deserve this?"

In the end, rather than put up with Penny's pleading and pouting, Cecily said she would think about it. That evening, she gave Penny her grudging permission to attend the interview.

"I'm going to join the FANY," Penny told Sheppy the dog. "It's so exciting."

Sheppy greeted the news with an extravagant, tongue-curling yawn.

UNLIKE HER SISTER, who had practically sleep-walked into the Wrens, Penny prepared well for her FANY interview, determined to wow the recruitment board into giving her a position of responsibility from the start.

She'd heard that the FANY were keen to recruit a "certain kind of girl": the serious kind; practical and efficient. To that end, Penny made sure she looked suitably serious, practical, and efficient for her first meeting at FANY headquarters. She wore no make-up—she *had* no make-up—and made sure her nails were short and scrubbed. They were always short. They weren't always scrubbed.

On the train down to London, Penny read the book she had bought with her birthday money. It was martial arts expert Major W.E. Fairbairn's newly-published *Self-Defence for Women and Girls*. Mr. Clark, who ran the bookshop, was most surprised when Penny put in her order.

"But I've been saving you this new Agatha Christie," he said. "What do you want to read about self-defence for?"

"Mr. Clark," said Penny. "We are at war. All over Europe, women are finding themselves face-to-face with the enemy in the most terrifying of circumstances. Every woman should know how to defend her own honour."

Mr. Clark nodded thoughtfully and made a note to order three further copies for the shop and one for his daughter.

When her W.E. Fairbairn arrived, Penny took the book straight up to her bedroom and pored over the photographs, in which a middle-aged man in a suit and an immaculately groomed young woman in a puff-sleeved tea-dress demonstrated a variety of strangleholds. The book warned against trying out the defensive moves described therein on one's friends but George—now thirteen—was only too happy to play the evil attacker so Penny could practise escaping various methods of restraint. He pointed out when she demurred that he definitely wasn't her friend.

"Though I suppose you're alright for a sister," he admitted when she got him in a headlock.

It was all good fun until Penny gave George a black eye—a proper shiner—while practising her umbrella drill. "The umbrella," wrote Major Fairbairn. "Is an ideal weapon for the purpose of defence . . ."

So it is, thought Penny as George rolled on the floor.

Luckily, George was not too badly wounded and he was prepared to forgive Penny everything in exchange for a whole month's sweetie rations.

"Or I tell Ma I *didn't* fall out of a tree."

Harry and Larry, the ten-year-old twin evacuees from Coventry that

Cecily had taken in (much to Mrs. Glover's chagrin), were watching as George and Penelope negotiated.

"You'd better save some of next month's ration to buy their silence too," George warned her.

ONCE IN LONDON, Penny alighted the train and marched across the platform with purpose; head up and shoulders back. It was very important to look as though one knew where one was going in a city this size, where all sorts of terrible people might be waiting to take advantage of a young woman travelling alone. Penny managed to brush off the attentions of several people who wanted to help with her case—"Or steal it, more likely!"— but her veneer of invincibility was somewhat punctured when she realised she had left the station via the wrong exit and was heading north instead of south, adding half an hour to her journey.

Thus she arrived at FANY headquarters, in a requisitioned vicarage just south of Hyde Park, feeling a little flustered. In the waiting room, she surreptitiously eyed the other girls. They'd all got the memo about looking sensible. Too sensible. They didn't look as if they would be any fun at all.

As she waited to be summoned, Penny brushed up on her W.E. Fairbairn. She looked closely at the photographs of the gutsy young woman in puffed sleeves dealing with a seated assault in which her besuited attacker placed an unwanted hand on her knee. It was described as "A defence against wandering hands."

"Catch hold of the hand with your right hand . . . Although it is essential that the initial hold of the offending hand should be as near as possible to that shown, you should not have any difficulty in obtaining it, as the person concerned will most likely be under the impression that you are simply returning his caress . . ."

Unconsciously, Penny mimed the steps, which earned her a few funny looks from the other candidates. In response, Penny waved the book.

"Vital information for the modern girl."

FINALLY, PENNY WAS called to the interview room, where two magnificent middle-aged women, resplendent in the FANY's khaki uniform, awaited her. They took it in turns to ask the questions Penny had expected. Which subjects had she liked best at school? Did she play any sports? Did she know the history of the First Aid Nursing Yeomanry?

"It is the oldest and most venerable of the women's services," Penny said. "First conceived in 1907 as a cavalry of nurses to support front line troops. Original recruits were expected to be accomplished horsewomen. As am I," she added. If always coming bottom of the league table at Pony Club counted.

Both her interviewers nodded with satisfaction.

"Can you drive?" they asked.

"I learned in my father's Bugatti."

"Can you lay a fire?"

"Had to brush up on my skills after our housemaid ran off with the gardener's boy. Took ages to find a replacement."

"Do you ever do the *Times* cryptic crossword?" the younger interviewer asked.

"Well, yes," said Penny.

"And do you usually manage to complete it?"

"Always."

"Wonderful." The more senior FANY slapped her hands on her knees and stood up. "You're exactly the sort of girl we're looking for."

SUCH JUBILATION WHEN confirmation of Penny's acceptance into the FANY arrived a few days later! She had just a week at home with Ma, George, Mrs. Glover, and the evacuees, before she was expected back at FANY HQ to embark upon basic training. The night before she left, Mrs. Glover made a special cake, using everybody's sugar rations. They all agreed it was the best thing that had ever come out of the kitchen on Mrs. Glover's watch, though perhaps that was because, two and a half years into the war, everyone's standards were very much lower.

After supper, George and the evacuees invited Penny to try her self-defence skills on them one more time. As she fended the boys off with sofa cushions, she warned them that by the time she had completed her FANY training, she would be able to take down a Messerschmidt with a catapult and finish the pilot off with her bare hands. The boys were delighted. They made solemn vows to protect the home front while Penny was off fighting the Nazis.

THE NEXT DAY, Penny returned to London and was thence transported to a large country house in the Home Counties to be put through her paces. She was so excited but alas, basic training turned out to be awfully dull. There were endless, pointless drills and lots and lots of housework. Every day started with the clearing of numerous fireplaces.

"I feel like Cinderella," Penny complained to another trainee, who simpered and said she hoped their princes would turn up soon. Most of Penny's fellow new FANYs were sensible but wet. There were definitely no opportunities for Penny to try out her W.E. Fairbairn on a willing and worthy adversary.

At the end of the fortnight of grate-scraping and square-bashing, Penny returned to FANY HQ in London to await further instructions. She was billeted in a requisitioned house near to FANY headquarters, where she shared a room with three other girls. Every surface was always festooned with drying stockings, that were inevitably still slightly damp when you put them on again, and the air was thick with scent.

One of the girls, Pamela, was a little older than the rest at twenty-two. She had joined the FANY in a rush of blood to the head after a broken engagement, though she told the girls they should not feel sorry for her for having lost her man at a time when they were in short supply. She'd been the one to break it off.

"I couldn't have spent the rest of my life with him. You've got to be sexually compatible with the man you marry," she said. She underlined the importance of her pronouncement by taking another drag from Penny's cigarette and exhaling a long plume of smoke out through the window. She didn't give the cigarette back but Penny didn't mind. She hung on Pamela's every word.

"Besides," Pamela continued. "I heard that shortly after I called the engagement off, he was seen in the company of a submariner at The Pink Sink."

Pamela's audience gasped at the mention of the notorious gay club beneath The Ritz Hotel, where it was said the men took it in turns to take the ladies' part on the dance floor.

Penny had quickly developed a huge girl crush on Pamela, who was the big sister she wished she had, instead of boring old Josephine, whose letters lately were only ever about weather and books. Pamela was the very essence of *toujours gai*, so Penny was delighted when she chose her to accompany her on a double date. Pamela's beau Ginger had four tickets to see *Blithe Spirit*. Would Penny like to come along as company for his friend?

"He's really nice," Pamela assured her.

"Have you met him?"

"Well no, but I'm sure he's a perfectly decent sort."

"Then why not?"

Penny didn't tell Pamela that it would be her first proper date, assuming sitting in the stairwell with Gilbert Declerc didn't count.

DRESSED IN THEIR brand-new FANY uniforms—made-to-measure if a little bit dowdy when compared to the Wrens' chic navy blue—Penny and Pamela met Ginger and his friend in the American Bar of The Savoy. Ginger's friend was called Alfred and Penny was relieved that on first impression he seemed like a nice enough chap. He had a friendly round face and thick brown hair. He was tall too, which was good. He was an army man, on a forty-eight from training on Salisbury Plain. Penny was glad to find out more about the place where her father had been sent ahead of his going overseas.

At The Savoy, Alfred and Ginger bought the girls two pink gins apiece, but Penny was careful to make sure she didn't drink all of the second one. The first made her feel sophisticated and warm inside. She suspected the second might unravel those happy feelings, or, worse, turn her into a fast girl. While Alfred wasn't looking, she tipped half of it into a plant pot.

Since the theatre was not far from the hotel, when the time came to leave they decided to walk. Ginger and Pamela had been stepping out for a while, so she let him put his arm around her waist. Alfred lent Penny his arm. She didn't need his support but she took it all the same. It brought her close enough to smell his aftershave. Old Spice. That made her feel much giddier than one and a half pink gins.

Penny sneaked a glance at Alfred's profile. Could she love him? He was no James Stewart but perhaps he'd be her romantic hero yet.

As they walked, it began to drizzle and Ginger and Pamela charged ahead to save Pamela's hair. Meanwhile Penny tried to impress Alfred with her air of *toujours gai*. It seemed to be working. Alfred took off his coat and draped it around Penny's shoulders in a thrillingly gallant gesture. What came next was somewhat less so . . .

"Are you a virgin, Penny?" Alfred asked as they waited to cross the Strand.

Penny was too shocked to tell him it was none of his business. Instead, she meekly said, "Why, yes. Yes, of course I am," then tried to pretend he hadn't asked. Alas he wasn't going to leave it at that.

"So no one ever tried it on with you?" he persisted. "No one ever touched you under that nice khaki skirt?"

"I . . . er . . ."

"I bet you'd be a right little goer once someone got you started . . ."

Penny was exceedingly grateful to see Pamela reappear up ahead, waving programmes.

"Show starts in three minutes," she yelled.

INSIDE THE THEATRE, they sat right in the middle of the stalls. Even before the house lights were dimmed, Penny was extremely aware of Alfred's arm pressing against hers and she wasn't at all certain she liked it.

She'd heard such wonderful things about *Blithe Spirit*, and had been terribly excited to see it, but the presence of Alfred at her side made it very hard to concentrate. Rather than listening to Coward's perfect lines, she found herself going over and over the awful conversation they'd had on the walk from The Savoy. There was nothing witty about it and she wished she had not brushed it off so easily. She should have dropped Alfred's arm and slapped him. She was sure that was what Pamela would have done. Pamela would never have accepted such nonsense.

While the audience all around her laughed their heads off at the action on stage, Penny's expression hardened and her mouth settled into a thin tight line that her siblings would have recognised as a warning sign. All the time, Alfred was edging further and further into her space, quite oblivious to her discomfort. His arm was soon taking up all their shared armrest. It wasn't long before his thigh was pressing against hers too. She tried to evade him, moving as far towards Pamela as she could. Pamela didn't notice. She was too busy necking with Ginger. Still Alfred continued his offensive. Then he let his hand fall into Penny's lap and gripped the top of her thigh so hard she was sure he must be leaving bruises.

As she recovered from the initial shock, Penny found herself feeling a strange mixture of emotions. She was horrified that Alfred had made such an unacceptable advance and yet she was also thrilled. She was thrilled that at last she was going to be able to put into action one of the most interesting moves in Major W.E. Fairbairn's *Self-Defence for Women and Girls*. This was quite literally a textbook situation.

Penny remembered the instructions under "A defence against wandering hands" almost word for word; how her assailant would not have the faintest clue what was going on because he would assume, when she took his hand in hers, wrapping her thumb and fingers tightly around his palm, that she was merely returning his expression of interest.

Poor Alfred. He had no idea what was coming.

Breathing slowly to keep her heart from racing, Penny waited for her moment. She would have just one chance. She had to get it right.

Keep calm, keep calm, she told herself.

When the audience erupted into laughter at a particularly pithy line on stage, she made her strike. With all her might, Penny pulled Alfred's rogue hand across her body with a jerk, causing him to suddenly double forwards and—in a development Penny hadn't planned for—crack his nose on the back of the seat in front of him. Sitting up, stunned and with blood pouring from both his nostrils, Alfred let out a roar of outrage followed by a long stream of expletives that had everyone within a fifty-seat radius shushing.

While Alfred railed, Penny quickly got up and left, stepping on numerous feet as she made her escape. She managed to keep relatively calm until she got to the lobby, then she burst from the theatre onto the blackout dark street and ran all the way back to the FANY boarding house, with her hair flying and her gas mask bumping against her hip.

What had she done? What had she done! She was astonished at how well the move had worked. Good old Major Fairbairn.

As Penny reached the boarding house, an air raid siren rent the air. The other girls in the house, many of whom were already tucked up in bed, quickly made their way down to the shelter, but Penny lingered outside the building, taking her time, waiting until she saw the deathly shadows of the Luftwaffe planes overhead. She felt exhilarated, liberated, strong. Tonight she was an Amazon.

"Come on, Hitler," she shouted at the sky. "Come on, all you Nazi bastards. I'm ready!"

Twelve

. . . . .

London, 2022

Archie stayed overnight in the guest room in South Kensington to be certain that the journey to France would go without a hitch. They were to be taking the 12:24 Eurostar, which, by Archie's reckoning, meant they needed to leave the house at ten at the latest to ensure they had enough time to get through security and passport control. Archie booked a taxi and tried not to panic when, at nine o'clock, the sisters were still eating their breakfast in a frustratingly leisurely way.

He tried to calm his rising fear that the sisters would somehow transpire to miss the train by leaving them to it and absenting himself to the sitting room to go through a box of letters he'd brought down from the attic.

Over the years, Archie had spent many hours in the attic at Penny and Josephine's house, sifting through boxes of letters, telegrams, ration books, and photographs of goodness only knew who—the sisters certainly didn't remember. In one box he'd found a diary dated 1817, belonging to some long-forgotten Williamson ancestor. Unfortunately, the faded handwriting revealed nothing particularly interesting, unless you were fascinated by livestock prices in the early nineteenth century. There were still at least a dozen more boxes to catalogue however and any one of them might contain something really exciting. Something for the history books.

Perhaps it was because Archie was the only child of an only child on his father's side that he felt such a responsibility to record all the memories that might otherwise be lost. Though it wasn't just on the Williamson side that Archie had appointed himself family historian. Recently he'd started to trace his mother's line too.

Archie's mother Miranda came from a very different background to his father. Charles Williamson was an old Etonian who'd grown up cocooned by layers of unimaginable privilege. Archie's mother Miranda was a grammar school girl from Cirencester who'd won a scholarship to Oxford. They met while they were both working in the city. Charles was instantly captivated by Miranda. She was five years his senior and seemed so sophisticated and worldly-wise. In return Miranda loved Charles' confidence and his upper-class polish, which soon began to rub off on her. No one meeting Miranda Williamson for the first time nowadays would guess she hadn't been born to the pony club life.

In fact Miranda's parents Tom and Clara Smith had both worked at a biscuit factory. Archie had fond memories of visiting them in their ugly seventies house where they let him eat his tea from a tray on his lap in front of the television, something that only happened at home if he was off school with tonsillitis.

With fond thoughts of those happy times, Archie had initially applied the same enthusiasm to tracing the Smith family line as he had the Williamson but there was so much less to work with. Even when Archie was old enough to hear about it—warts and all—Tom and Clara had never talked much about the past. Whenever Archie visited, they were much more keen to hear about his plans for the future.

"Any sign of a girlfriend yet?" Clara would ask. "The girl who gets her hooks into you is going to be very lucky."

Tom and Clara had died before Archie felt ready to come out.

The Smiths had left behind boxes of papers but there were no distinguished war records, no deeds to great family estates or handwritten letters from long-dead dukes and princes such as were rotting in his paternal great-aunts' loft. Only gas bills and ten pounds' worth of premium bond certificates and, poignantly, a pile of birthday and Christmas cards handdrawn by Archie as a child. The 1970s house belonged to the council and was quickly passed to a new family. There wasn't even any old furniture that might have a story behind it. Tom and Clara preferred new, not understanding how the late Tory Minister Alan Clark's snide comment regarding his colleague Michael Heseltine's having bought his own furniture could possibly be seen as an insult. Why wouldn't you buy new if you could afford to?

Yes, the Smith family history was all very boring. Until Archie's mother dropped a bombshell.

Over Easter lunch Miranda had told Archie that, on her death bed, his grandmother Clara had muttered something about Miranda's parentage being "not exactly as described." What could it mean other than that the identity of her father was in doubt?

"I think he might have been a GI," Miranda confided. "There were thousands of American servicemen down the road on the airbase at Fairford. Your grandma used to go to dances there."

The more Archie thought about it, the more it seemed a distinct possibility that his mother was not Tom Smith's child. Miranda didn't look like any of her siblings. She was different in personality and in her interests too. She was the odd one out long before she married well and "got above herself." But how could she find out for sure?

Archie already subscribed to a genealogy website on which people raved about DNA testing. They'd found cousins, half-brothers, and even full sisters that way. Some of them had discovered they were not in fact related to their own fathers, which must have been hard. Archie had no fear of that. His "difficult" feet were one hundred per cent inherited from Charles Williamson.

Confident that there would be no nasty shocks regarding his own parentage, Archie ordered one of those DNA kits and—putting aside his absolute horror of spitting—filled a test-tube with saliva which he duly sent away to be analysed. He couldn't wait to get the results.

Thirteen

• • • • •

The journey to Paris went quite smoothly. Far more smoothly than Archie had dared to hope. Both his great-aunts were in a good mood and on good form, determined to be *toujours gai* for the occasion. Despite the slow start, Arlene had them both ready by ten o'clock, as promised. The taxi to Kings Cross St. Pancras was on time and the staff at the Eurostar terminal were top notch, ensuring that the sisters were whisked through security and border control on account of their advanced years. It never failed to amuse Archie that while for the most part his great-aunts were insistent on not being treated like "little old ladies," when it came to cutting a queue, they were only too happy to jump into a wheelchair and have some nice young person whizz them past the hoi polloi.

At the other end of the trip through the Chunnel, there was a brief moment of panic when the disembarking Eurostar passengers were rushed by one of the beggar gangs that frequented the area around the Gare du Nord. Archie squawked with alarm when one of them targeted Penny and he thought he might have to intervene—he really didn't want to have to get hands on—but Penny assured him that she had not parted with a centime when the young woman tried to sell her a "diamond ring" she claimed to have found on the station floor. It was a classic scam and thankfully Penny was wise to it.

"But you let her shake your hand!" said Archie. "That's how they make off with their victim's watches."

Penny assured him that she still had her watch, which had been stuck at half past three since 1989.

After that excitement the Williamson party quickly found a taxi though the traffic was against them. The taxi driver blamed Madame Hidalgo's "improvement works." Thus the going was slow, but they did make it almost all the way to the Hotel Maritime before Penny started saying she needed to stop for a wee. They were on the Place Vendôme at the time. Archie tried to persuade Penny she could hang on for another five minutes but she was insistent. So they stopped the car and Penny spent a penny at The Ritz and then took twenty minutes to find her way back to the hotel lobby where Archie was just about to ask a Ritz employee to check that his great-aunt hadn't come to some terrible harm in the ladies'. Then when they got back to the taxi, it was to discover that Arlene and Josephine were missing. While Archie went to find them—Josephine had also decided she needed to answer a call of nature—Penny disappeared again.

After a search lasting another half an hour Archie eventually found Penny in the Blanchet jewellery boutique on the other side of the *grande place*, chatting to a sales assistant in perfect French while trying on some baubles. There were dozens of glittering jewels laid out on the velvet tray on the counter. Archie appreciated the young assistant's efforts to humour an old lady in a knitted beret but where on earth did she think Penny was planning to wear a diamond parure complete with tiara?

"Well," Penny said, when they were outside and Archie admonished her for going AWOL. "I thought Josephine might be ages. She's been complaining about her bowels since Ebbsfleet."

"No she hasn't," said Archie, before Penny tapped out the SOS in Morse on his arm. "Ah, I see . . ."

Josephine was apologetic when she and Arlene finally returned to the car.

"Never get old, Archie," she said. "There's nothing quite so frustrating as being unable to trust one's own inner workings. Arlene and I were just saying there should be one of those app things. How many minutes to the next public convenience . . ."

"Yes," said Penny enthusiastically. "With star ratings. Archie, we could make a fortune."

"It would certainly be useful," Archie grumbled. "Now is everybody momentarily in control of their bodily functions *and* their faculties?"

The sisters and Arlene nodded.

"Then *allons-y*."

THEY EVENTUALLY ARRIVED at the Hotel Maritime in time for an early supper, over which Archie gave the sisters and Arlene their instructions once again.

"Ladies, tomorrow morning you will need to be downstairs for breakfast at 0800 hours local time. That's London time plus one. I know that's earlier than you would ordinarily prefer but we need to be at the *Mairie* by quarter past nine in order to go through security. Because of the level of dignitaries attending, there will be enhanced checks. For that reason, you should lay out the outfits you intend to wear to the inauguration tonight so that after breakfast you can change into them *tout de suite*."

"I'll be in charge of that," said Arlene.

"Excellent. Aunties, I also think it would be a good idea for you both to hand over your medals to me right now so we know exactly where they are when we need them for the ceremony tomorrow."

"We've kept those medals for seventy-five years, we're not going to lose them tonight," Penny grumbled.

"It would give me peace of mind," Archie said, not mentioning the fact that in the thirty-five years he had known her, Penny had mislaid her medals on many dozens of occasions. Most recently they'd lain at the bottom of Flaubert the dachshund's bed for at least three months, only coming to light when the old dog crossed the rainbow bridge and Penny was persuaded to throw away his tatty blanket. "I will sleep far better knowing exactly where they are," Archie persisted.

Ordinarily, the sisters would have protested such infantilising measures, but they could both see that Archie was about to go into headless chicken mode so, after a quick shared glance, they did as he asked, dipped into their handbags and handed the medals over.

Archie looked at the medals with a critical eye. "I'll give them a bit of a polish. This Italy Star hasn't been the same since Flaubert got hold of it, Auntie Penny. That dog . . ."

"Flaubert?" Arlene had joined the household after the dachshund's demise. "I've always meant to ask . . . That's a very fancy name for a dog. Are you a big fan of French literature, Penny?"

"Something like that," said Penny.

The two dogs before Flaubert had been called Browning and Walther, as had all her dogs before them in rotation since she bought her first dachshund puppy in 1966 (just after Connor died. It was easier than bothering to find another husband for company). She was still waiting for someone to make the connection and it was nothing to do with books.

PENNY WAS THE first to retire to her bedroom but she had no intention of going straight to bed. Archie had told her to "get some beauty sleep" but short of being put into cryogenic suspension, there was nothing Penny could do now to hold back the ravages of time. Besides Penny had things to do, plans to finesse. Tucked into one of the many pockets in her capacious handbag was the page torn from the Brice-Petitjean catalogue and an old but detailed floor-plan of the auction house building itself, which she'd printed from the internet during a visit to the library on the King's Road.

For two-thirds of her very long life, Penny had promised herself that one day she would have vengeance. The only question in her mind was "when." At last the universe had sent her an answer. Penny's "when" was suddenly "tomorrow night."

Fourteen

· · · · ·

Alone at last in her own hotel room, Josephine fell into a reflective mood. It had been truly exhausting, staying *toujours gai* all day long for the sake of Penny, Arlene, and dear, dear Archie. All the same she knew that if she got into bed now she would not be able to fall asleep. Instead, she settled herself in a chair by the window. Archie had done very well with the hotel reservation and her room had a spectacular view over the rooftops of Paris. How unchanged those rooftops seemed even after so many years. Still so beautiful.

But looking at that beautiful view made Josephine's eyes prickle with tears, and she berated herself again for not having been braver, for not having insisted that she would really rather stay at home, in the face of Archie's enthusiasm and Penny's pouting. Apart from anything else, she wasn't sure she entirely deserved to be invited to France to receive another medal. For quite a while now, Josephine had been far from certain that this seemingly endless appetite for celebrating World War Two was a good thing.

So many had lost so much, and the hope that revisiting their sacrifices again and again would convince their descendants that history must not be allowed to repeat itself didn't seem to be working. Just as the Great War—H.G. Wells's "war to end all wars"—had led inexorably to World War Two, the horrors of World War Two had far from ended the cycle of human violence. Instead, Britain's part in the conflict had been reduced to a triumphant football chant—"Two world wars and one world cup"— combative and provocative; missing the point altogether. No matter how hard Josephine tried to emphasise the futility of war when she addressed school groups and history clubs, most people only seemed to take away the fact that this little old lady and her sister both knew how to strip a Sten gun. "How cool is that?"

Why hadn't she made a stand and told Archie she'd had enough and asked him to say "thank you, but no thank you" to the kind *Légion d'honneur* committee?

It was because of Penny, Josephine told herself. Because all these excitements did seem to keep Penny going. Penny needed to be kept distracted. Always had. And it was for Archie too. After he had gone to such an effort to find something else for the sisters to look forward to, it would have been churlish to complain. He was so very good to them.

Josephine worried about Archie. What would he do when the sisters weren't around anymore? She wished he could meet a nice young man who filled his days with love and happiness, so that he no longer felt the need or had the time to entertain two old haggises like his great-aunts. She offered up a little prayer to the god who hadn't listened for a very long time. "Let Stéphane be single." She was glad, at least, that the *Légion d'honneur* ceremony had given Archie a rock-solid excuse to be in Paris for that party at Stéphane's auction house.

Thank goodness it was at least somewhat easier to be openly gay these days than it had been when Josephine and Penny were young. Life in the forties, the fifties, even the so-called "swinging sixties" had been so strictly bound by moral certitudes that birthed so many toxic secrets and ultimately caused nothing but damage. Looking out over Paris, Josephine thought of the toxic secrets she herself had kept over the course of her lifetime—was still keeping in some cases—her own secrets, her husband Gerald's secrets, her sister Penny's secrets. Even those of Penny's secrets that Penny had no idea Josephine knew. Josephine understood that she and Penny couldn't have much longer to go on now. Was it time to let some of those secrets out into the light?

As she asked herself that, Josephine considered that perhaps subconsciously she *had* wanted to come to Paris all along; to share her own darkest secret in the place where it all began.

Pressing her thumb against the edge of her lucky shrapnel for comfort, Josephine thought back to the last time she'd been in the city. July 1947. She'd been to France a few times since, most notably to the south the summer Penny's husband, Connor, died—oh, what a terrible business that was—but not Paris. She had thought she would never be in this city again.

Fifteen

. . . . .

Paris, 1947

At Christmas 1945, when Penny finally returned from her FANY posting in Italy, the sisters were reunited for the first time since 1940. Josephine had not moved back to the family home after being demobbed, preferring instead to stay in London, where she was working as a secretary for a firm of accountants. She waited until Penny arrived from overseas to make the trip to the countryside and the big stone house that had been their childhood home. Both sisters looked forward to seeing George, who was over the moon to have his big sisters with him again. Sheppy, now an old dog, was likewise thrilled to see them.

However, there was tension between the sisters and their parents. Their father in particular didn't seem able to appreciate that the war had turned his girls into women, with their own ideas and opinions about what to do next. Penny's time with the FANY in Algiers and then in southern Italy had given her a passion for travel. Much as Ma and Pa would have preferred it, there was no way she would ever settle for a husband and the Home Counties now she'd seen what the rest of the world had to offer. On Christmas Day, she told them that she'd accepted a job in Germany, in the British sector in Hamburg, with an organisation that helped to rehome people displaced by the war. Needless to say, there was plenty of work to be done on that front.

As for Josephine, she simply couldn't pretend that things would ever again be as they had once been, much as she wished she could and even though she believed Pa didn't actually know what had happened in the spring of 1940, while he was stuck in France. Ma had at least promised her that. Josephine had come home for Penny and for George. That was all.

She was glad to go back to London after a couple of days. Waiting for her at the house where she rented a room was a letter from the University of Cambridge, offering her a place to read English on an ex-service grant.

There was another letter too. This one was from her dear friend Gerald Naiswell, containing a marriage proposal that broke her heart, even though she knew for sure she hadn't encouraged it.

She'd met Gerald while she was working in the plotting rooms in Plymouth, when his submarine, HMS *Uriel*, docked for repairs and Josephine's Wren colleagues dragged her along to a party on board. While the party roared in the narrow, stuffy mess, she and Gerald sat and shared a quiet cigarette on the conning tower. They'd become firm friends since then but they'd never been lovers. But here he was, proposing marriage.

> *My darling Josephine, I might not be the husband you hoped for but I feel sure I could be the husband you need and you, in return, could be my ideal wife. Please say you agree. I know this is not the most romantic proposal and I'm sure you must have hoped for better, but I also think that we could make each other very happy indeed. I promise I will always be your safe haven if you only say you'll be mine. Just say the word.*

Josephine sent her "no" by return. She wrote that she hoped she and Gerald would be able to stay friends but her heart still belonged to one man and one man only. He knew that. Just as she knew why Gerald's heart could never really be hers.

EIGHTEEN MONTHS AFTER that uncomfortable first post-war Christmas, Penny was still in Germany and did not have time to come back to England for a visit, so she proposed that Josephine meet her in Paris for the second week in July.

"*I'm not sure it's a good idea,*" Josephine wrote. "*It won't be the same as it was in 1939.*" She stopped short of giving her real reasons. Penny still had no idea what had happened in Scotland.

Penny wrote back at once. "*Don't be such a rotten spoilsport, Josie-Jo. Aunt Claudine says they'd be so pleased to have us and I would be really pleased to see you. Work has been terribly difficult lately and I need to have some proper fun. Come to Paris. If it's awful, we'll jump on a train to Biarritz. I'm paying for everything and I promise it will be totalement gai.*"

After a flurry of letters, Josephine had given in and agreed to the plan. Looking back in later years, she would understand that there must have been a part of her that *did* want to go to Paris, that wanted to know for sure. But for a month before her rendezvous with Penny, she would wake in the middle of the night, every night, and wonder what she might find in the city she had tried to forget. The creeping dread she felt in the small hours started to seep into the day. She was constantly distracted. She couldn't concentrate on her studies. Her heart told her with every beat that it was a bad idea to go to France. A *very* bad idea indeed.

Josephine had not heard from August Samuel since February 1940. After her mother found out that Augustine was in fact a boy—there was incontrovertible evidence of that—she was forced to write a letter telling him she no longer wished to be in contact. Then Cecily sent Josephine to Scotland to "think about her future." Whenever she could—and it wasn't easy under the constant vigilance of her Victorian grandmother—Josephine sneaked letters to August. Connie Shearer had acted as go-between.

Josephine had sent one last letter in March 1940 but there had been no response. Seven years had passed since then. The reasons why August might not have written in that time were many but none of them were good. Either he'd decided that he no longer loved her—and in the light of her last letter from Scotland that would hardly be surprising—or something far worse had happened. She hoped it was the former. Even after all the awful things that had befallen her because she had fallen in love with him, she still wished him happy and well.

The night before she was due to leave for France on the ferry train from Victoria, Josephine pulled her old suitcase from under the bed and found the secret hiding place in the case's silken lining. She hadn't looked at August's letters since the summer of 1940, when she realised he wasn't going to turn up and save her like a knight in shining armour on a stupid white horse, and to see his curly handwriting suddenly became more of a torture than a comfort. Before then, she had read those letters so many times that she knew them by heart and their creases were so worn that the light shone through.

She tried to read the letters now but found she still couldn't bear it. Instead she tucked them back into their hiding place and started to pack the things she would need for her trip. Her clothes, her notebooks, and her courage. She had to go to Paris whether she wanted to or not. It was too late to let dear Penny down. She suspected from the tone of her little sister's most recent aerogram that Penny really *needed* her to be there. That was Josephine's excuse.

UNLIKE POOR OLD London with its bombed-out terraces that looked like broken teeth in a tired and dirty face, Paris had at least escaped the worst attentions of the Luftwaffe. Though the city was decidedly grubbier than Josephine remembered, it was still very much recognisable as its beautiful self. Life had come back to the grand boulevards. The cafés were buzzing. People were ready to enjoy themselves again.

"I've been so looking forward to seeing you," Penny said, as they whizzed up the Champs-Élysées in a taxi. Uncle Godfrey and Aunt Claudine had moved back into their old apartment and that was where the sisters would be staying, sharing a room again for the first time since the summer of '39. Penny was excited but Josephine was not at all sure how she would feel when she walked into the courtyard of 38 Rue du Mont Olympe.

As the sisters got out of the car, Penny looped her arm through Josephine's and brought her close. Though Penny had not mentioned August's name once as they made their plans for the trip, and had continued to steadfastly avoid the subject on their taxi ride, Josephine took that gesture to mean her sister did perhaps understand how hard this was going to be.

An unfamiliar concierge let them through the gate that day. Walking into the communal garden where so much had happened, Josephine couldn't help but turn to look at the names on the letterboxes. Her eyes automatically flickered to the top row. Where once had been written "Famille Samuel," now there was a different name. Though not a stranger's name exactly.

"Declerc." Josephine said the word out loud.

"Oh. That's a coincidence," said Penny.

Josephine felt her heart ache as she looked at that nameplate and tears pricked at her eyes. Penny noticed and clasped Josephine's arm a little tighter.

"*Toujours gai.*"

AUNT CLAUDINE WELCOMED them with kisses. Though she was as beautiful as ever, the war years had left their mark on her, overlaying her much celebrated beauty with an ethereal veil of sadness. Two of Claudine's brothers—Ernest and Roland—had died in The Battle of Normandy. Josephine and Penny remembered the young men well. At Godfrey and Claudine's summer wedding back in 1932, Claudine's brothers had each scooped up a little Williamson girl for a riotous piggyback race around the garden. Now they were forever frozen in time, forever in their twenties, smiling out from portrait photographs in their smart army uniforms, in a sitting room that was much smaller and darker than Josephine remembered.

"How wonderful to see you both," Claudine said.

"Good to have you here, girls," agreed Uncle Godfrey. "Bringing some life to the place."

Godfrey was not the man he had once been. He was much slimmer and had lost a lot of hair since they'd last been together in this room. When he kissed Josephine on the cheek, she smelled alcohol on his breath, though it was still only ten in the morning. Indeed, while Claudine brought coffee to her visitors, Godfrey remained in the kitchen, adding another slug of brandy to his elegant porcelain cup, then knocking back another one direct from the bottle. When he came to join his wife and their guests again, he bounced off the door frame on his way into the room.

"Who put that there?" he joked, but Josephine could tell he was embarrassed.

They exchanged news of Penny and Josephine's parents and of George, who was finally in the army but finding it a lot less exciting than he'd imagined back when he was eleven years old pretending to shoot German paratroopers out of the sky over the kitchen garden. His regiment had been posted to Malaya and his letters home were full of complaints about the heat, the food, and the leeches.

Then they spoke about their war. Godfrey told the sisters how proud he was they had both gone into the women's forces. "Not that I'm in the least bit surprised. You were always both fine young women with a proper sense of duty."

Penny took Josephine's hand and squeezed.

Claudine seemed much more tender with her husband than Josephine remembered. There was no mention of her painting—the hobby that had obsessed her in the summer of 1939. The sisters knew better than to ask after Monsieur Lebre, though privately Josephine wondered what had become of him. In 1939, he must have been in his twenties. Had he joined up the moment France entered the war? Had he taken part in the Battle of France? Or had he been shipped off to Germany to join the groups of young French men forced to labour for the Axis powers? Had that been the fate of their old friends August and Gilbert too?

"You've got a new concierge," Penny observed. "What happened to Madame Declerc?"

"Ah yes," said Uncle Godfrey. "The Declercs have rather gone up in the world since you saw them last. Well, they've definitely gone up in the building. They came into an inheritance—an obscure uncle from Bordeaux who died in '43 or thereabouts. It was the best sort of inheritance, since apparently they didn't know the uncle well enough to miss him—and after the war they used the money to buy apartment four."

So it was them.

"From the Samuels?" Josephine asked. It was the first time she had said that name out loud in years.

"I don't think the Samuels ever owned it," said Uncle Godfrey, unaware of what that utterance had cost her.

"Have you heard anything about them?" Penny wanted to know too. "The Samuels? Anything at all? Did they get out of Paris before the occupation?"

Godfrey and Claudine shared a glance.

"Perhaps you should talk to the Declercs," said Claudine. "We've invited Madame Declerc and Gilbert for supper. We know how friendly you girls were with Gilbert when you came to stay here before the war and his mother remembers you both very fondly."

"She used to chase me with a broom," said Penny.

"You'll find she's quite different these days."

MADAME DECLERC, THE former concierge, was indeed very different from the brusque country woman the sisters remembered. Though she had only to walk across the courtyard and up the stairs to Claudine and Godfrey's apartment, she put on a purple velvet opera cape for the trip. Gone was the filthy apron she used to have wrapped around her waist at all times. Now she was dressed in the very finest garb the best department stores of Paris had to offer. When Godfrey went to take her cloak, she let it drop from her shoulders in a manner that reminded Josephine of a film star arriving at a Hollywood premiere.

Madame Declerc's voice had changed too. The gravelly snarl that spoke of too many cigarettes and not enough kindness had been replaced by an accent that would not have sounded out of place in the dining room of any of the city's grandest hotels. There was no trace of the Breton farmer's widow at all.

Gilbert arrived half an hour later. He was studying to be a lawyer now, just as he'd always hoped.

There is, of course, an enormous difference between a boy of fifteen and a man of twenty-two. Gilbert had grown into the big hands and feet Josephine remembered as being so enormous that he sometimes looked as though he'd trip over himself. His face also seemed to have caught up with his nose, which must have been a relief. His jaw was more square. His eyebrows were heavier. Somehow they made his brown eyes seem more intense. He greeted the sisters with "bises" and Josephine thought she saw Penny bat her eyelashes at him.

Over an aperitif, the sisters and Gilbert and Claudine and Godfrey listened politely as Madame Declerc talked about her busy day. She'd been to lunch on the Left Bank with her friend Madame Richard. Had they met Madame Richard? Her husband was a doctor. They'd both eaten *sole meunière*. It wasn't the best since, thanks to the war, many Parisian establishments were still short of a well-trained chef or two but . . .

It seemed like a very long time before Josephine was able to ask the question she was burning to ask.

"Where are the Samuel family now? What happened to August? And Lily?"

At the mention of their names, it was as though a needle had scratched across a gramophone record. There was no pretending that everything was "*toujours gai*" now. Madame Declerc closed her eyes and her heavily bejewelled right hand fluttered to rest over her heart.

"Of course you want to know about your friends," she said. "But I cannot be the one to tell it!"

When she clutched Gilbert's forearm and entreated him to tell the story instead, Josephine already knew this was not going to be a tale with a happy ending. It couldn't be. Gilbert looked stricken.

"Please go ahead, Gilbert," Godfrey encouraged him.

With his eyes on the tablecloth, Gilbert began.

Sixteen

. . . . .

"As soon as the Germans crossed the Maginot Line, we knew we needed to be ready for them to take Paris. August and his father already understood what it was like to live under the Nazis and they wasted no time in preparing for the worst. August and I were too young to join the army but when Paris was occupied August did not have to persuade me that I should join him and his father in small acts of resistance, though I know Maman was not keen . . ."

"Not keen to see my son executed on a street corner, you understand. The Germans were ruthless. I supported what August and his father were doing with all my heart."

"Of course, Maman. Of course," Gilbert said.

Madame Declerc clucked like a hen.

"To begin with, August and I were tasked with delivering anti-German leaflets across the city. It was easy for me to get by the German soldiers with those leaflets in my school bag."

"I was so scared," Madame Declerc interrupted. "If he had been caught. Claudine, can you imagine?"

"I didn't have the looks to draw much attention. Well, you girls know that."

Penny protested politely.

"Only once, a soldier asked to search my bag. Having checked my papers, he noticed I had a gramophone record. He confiscated it of course but I didn't care. He was so pleased with his new treasure that he entirely overlooked the notes I was carrying, which outlined details of a meeting that very night.

"August had it harder. It was obvious from his accent that he wasn't native French and he got stopped all the time. I warned him the attention he drew made him a danger to himself and the rest of us, but he was so angry at the occupation and so determined to draw Nazi blood . . . It was very hard to reason with him and convince him of the need for discretion; that it wasn't only his safety at stake, but that of his whole family and the rest of us too."

Madame Declerc nodded along.

"In the winter of 1941, we were plotting to blow up a police station. We were in contact with the British and we had explosives and grenades and rifles hidden in various places all over the city. As well as the weapons, we had false papers and identity cards, cash, and other valuables that might be needed in the event we had to leave in a hurry. Everything was going to plan.

"But on the day of the attack, I woke up hardly able to move with a fever. I could only lay in bed raging while August and Monsieur Samuel went to the cell's appointed meeting place. I wanted to be there so much. We had planned the biggest attack the city had ever seen. It was going to be spectacular. But when the cell members got to the rendezvous, it was to discover that the police had already been tipped off. They were arrested and taken away."

"And?" Josephine clung to the hope of a plot twist.

Madame Declerc looked at Josephine as though she thought she was simple-minded. "Why, they were executed, of course."

AS THE WORDS landed, all Josephine could hear was her own blood in her head. The voices in the room seemed underwater.

"I just thank my lucky stars Gilbert was unwell that day and wasn't there when the Carlingue arrived," Madame Declerc kept talking.

"I've never forgiven myself for not being with them," Gilbert said.

"You were saved by God," his mother told him.

"God was not on duty that day. Or on any other day that year."

Madame Declerc picked up the story. "Madame Samuel was insane with grief. For six months, I looked after her as though she were my child. She could not leave the apartment. She could barely get out of bed. She could not feed and care for herself or for Lily. I did everything I could. With her husband gone, Madame Samuel had no money so I shared what we had—me and Gilbert. The only good thing was that Monsieur Samuel and August had not been carrying their real identification papers so the police did not come to the apartment, because surely the Carlingue would have executed Madame Samuel too, to make her an example."

"We should have moved them out of Paris right away," said Gilbert.

"How could we? You were ill. Madame Samuel was sick and half-mad with sadness. And Lily was so young. We could not have done it without attracting attention. The safest place for them to stay was here."

"Until it wasn't."

"There were so many collaborators," Madame Declerc suddenly burst out. "You never knew who you could trust. People were denouncing their neighbours for a loaf of bread. Desperation turned decent citizens into animals. You know that, Claudine."

She turned to the sisters' godmother for corroboration.

"After her husband and August were taken, I told Madame Samuel to change her name and tell anyone who asked she was a Catholic. I even took her with me to church, so that she would know what to say if anyone asked if she went to mass. Madame Samuel was a beautiful woman. She was educated but not at all snobbish. She treated even me, a lowly concierge, as her equal. But there were people who were envious of her elegance and class; people who wanted to take her down a peg a two. People who would have turned her in . . . I tried to help her." Madame Declerc gasped for breath.

"What happened?" Josephine cried. "What happened to Madame Samuel and Lily?"

She listened in horror as Gilbert told them about the night of the 16th July 1942, when Madame Samuel and Lily were dragged from the building, rounded up and corralled with more than 13,000 other Parisian Jews, including 4,000 children, at the city's Vélodrome D'Hiver—the "Vél D'Hiv." They were held there, without food or proper shelter and not even a single lavatory between them, until such time as they could be transferred to the internment camps at Drancy, Pithiviers, and Beaune-la-Rolande. Thence to Auschwitz . . .

Seventeen

• • • • •

After that, dinner was abandoned. Josephine wanted to go back to England as soon as she possibly could but the following day she could hardly stand. The shock had taken the legs out from under her. Claudine insisted Josephine stay in bed then called a doctor, who prescribed at least a week of rest before she even thought about taking the boat-train home.

"You can't travel in this state," Penny agreed. "You'll be better off here, surrounded by people who love you. Let us look after you while you come to terms with the news."

Penny wasn't being entirely selfless. Josephine's intuition from Penny's letters that her little sister needed her company in France wasn't wrong. Penny wanted Josephine with her because she really had to spend some time pretending that the war had never happened and everything was fine and dandy again, like it had felt back in the summer of '39 when they were still young and naive. She was desperate for a break from all too much reality.

The months before she and Josephine met up in France had been challenging. In January, Penny had found herself sitting in the gallery at a war trial in Hamburg, hearing one of the displaced people she hoped to help—Marguerite, a Jewish woman not so very much older than she was—give evidence against a concentration camp guard.

Penny had promised she would be there so that Marguerite could look up from the witness stand and see a friendly face whenever she needed to, but it was a harrowing experience. Penny was no stranger to stories of terrible violence, thanks to her own wartime experiences, but Marguerite's testimony somehow got straight to her heart. She could not even begin to imagine what it must have taken for Marguerite to describe the casual cruelty with which the guard in the dock—a woman who looked like any suburban housewife you might have passed on any German street in 1939—meted out the beatings that had left Marguerite blind in her left eye. The same woman had beaten Marguerite's sister to death and laughed as she did it. And yet Marguerite delivered her testimony with such grace and such dignity, her voice steady and clear. Penny was left in awe of her bravery.

As the former guard heard her sentence with blank incomprehension—"But I was only following orders!"—Penny at least hoped that when she got back to work she would be able to make sure that Marguerite and her children, who had miraculously escaped the camps thanks to the kindness of a neighbour who passed the children off as her own pure German brood, might at last have a home of their own where they could start to feel safe again. Now they were staying in a boarding house where they shared a bathroom that had no lock on the door with twenty other displaced people. An old man had exposed himself to Marguerite's seven-year-old daughter while she was cleaning her teeth.

Returning to the office, Penny was determined to do something to help but her boss told her flatly that there was no money to find Marguerite a new home. The boarding house Marguerite hated so much was a good deal better than many other billets in the city. Penny mentioned the flashing incident, in the hope that it would underline the urgency with which Marguerite needed to be moved somewhere better.

"They'll just have to go to the bathroom as a family," was the solution. "And put something heavy against the door when they're in there."

It wasn't good enough but Penny could do nothing more about it, though she tried on a regular basis. She understood that her boss's hands were tied. There were many hundreds of similar cases in Hamburg alone. But Penny was exhausted from the constant disappointment. She'd been avoiding Marguerite for a couple of weeks now and resolved not to think about her and her children while she was in Paris.

•••

OF COURSE, JOSEPHINE was not going to be the companion Penny so needed for the rest of the trip—Penny was surprised at how badly Josephine was taking the news about the Samuel family. They'd known them for just a few weeks after all. Instead, she found herself asking Gilbert if he would accompany her to a museum or to the pictures. He was only too happy to oblige.

Gilbert was nicer than Penny remembered; less pretentious and more fun. He laughed at the earnestness of the young man who had given her that book of poems by Baudelaire, carefully annotated to impress. Now that he was studying to be a lawyer—thanks to his inheritance from the mysterious uncle in Bordeaux—he seemed a good deal less chippy to boot.

Penny found she enjoyed spending time with Gilbert. He made her laugh at a time when she needed to laugh very badly. It seemed, after that awful first night over dinner, that they had both made the decision not to talk about their war years. Though Penny would have liked to have heard more about Gilbert's adventures in the Resistance, she understood more than he could ever know why he wanted to close the door on the last few years and live entirely in the present. She felt exactly the same way. They could do nothing about the past; its humiliations and pain, or about those times when they had fallen short of what the long fight required of them while others went on to make the ultimate sacrifice. Right then the weather in Paris was beautiful and there was fun to be had.

It was inevitable, she supposed, that they picked up where they had left off when they were love-struck teens. She didn't stop him from using his tongue when he kissed her now. They went to bed together while Madame Declerc was on her shopping excursions. That happened most days.

One afternoon, while Gilbert slept off his exertions, Penny tiptoed to the bathroom of the Declercs' apartment—the apartment that used to belong to the Samuel family—and found herself rolling back the fancy new rug that covered the bare wooden floor. She couldn't resist. It was here, wasn't it, the secret hiding place? But while Penny was on her hands and knees, trying to find the loose board, she heard a key in the front door of the apartment and had to abandon her mission and sprint back to the bedroom to wake Gilbert before his mother caught them in flagrante.

ON THE MORNING of the sisters' departure from Paris, Penny told Josephine she wanted to take one last spin around the shops, to find gifts for the girls in her office back in Germany, where luxury was still in very short supply. Josephine declined to join her, so Penny found herself alone in Galeries Lafayette, which seemed remarkably unchanged since the last time she'd been there, shopping for Josephine's seventeenth birthday present with her pocket money; accidentally stealing the bracelet with the green glass stones that Josephine still occasionally wore. In fact, Penny thought the woman on the counter might even have been the exact same one who served her all those years ago.

The woman's mean little eyes lit up as Penny approached and asked, in impeccable French that was greatly improved for having spent time with Gilbert, if she might see a couple of items.

"Bien sûr."

Penny talked all the while she tried the pieces on. It was easy to make small talk. Penny was good at that. Soon they were talking about the sales assistant's son, who had been in the Resistance (of course he had), and how she was hoping to move out to the countryside and live with her sister on a farm. She was tired of having to work so hard, only to go home to a tiny apartment that was all but falling down.

"After such a terrible few years, you deserve a little happiness," Penny agreed. The sales assistant's eyes glistened with gratitude.

"What an understanding young woman you are," she said.

Had there not been a counter between them, Penny was sure the sales assistant would have tried to hug her. Instead, she reached across and squeezed Penny's hand. She described her sister's farm in more detail as Penny pulled her short white gloves back on. Penny nodded along. She knew how to look interested in talk about sheep and cows.

"I am sorry we couldn't find something you liked today," the sales assistant said as she and Penny concluded their encounter.

"That's alright," said Penny brightly. "I'm sure I'll be back. Good luck on that farm!"

Penny wished the doorman a *"très bonne journée"* as he waved her out into the street.

Walking back towards the Métro, Penny felt shaky but ecstatic. She had pulled it off. She had actually pulled it off! It wouldn't be until closing that the sales assistant noticed she was a ring short, by which time she would have served several customers. She would never suspect that the kind and beautiful young woman who had shown such interest in her hopes and dreams could possibly have been a thief.

ON THE TRAIN back to Hamburg later that day, Penny examined her haul. The ring she'd stolen was set with a very small stone, barely a chip and definitely not a real diamond. It was not worth much, but it was worth enough to enable Marguerite and her children to move out of the boarding house into a place of their own for a while. Arriving in Germany, Penny went straight from the station to a pawnbroker. By the time she had finished telling the owner of the shop about her broken engagement—a most convincing cover story—he had raised the amount he first offered her by twenty-five per cent.

"Such a fool, your fiancé," he said, holding her hand a little too tightly.

Marguerite cried when Penny handed her the money the following day. "But where is this from?" she asked.

"It's an emergency grant," Penny lied. "I have authority to give it to you but you must not mention it to anyone else because I might not be able to help them in the same way. It's a one-off. It will not happen again."

That's right, Penny promised herself. It would not happen again.

FROM GERMANY THAT autumn, Penny sent Gilbert Declerc several jaunty letters. At first, Gilbert matched every one but it wasn't very long before their correspondence fizzled out, ending on a last pompous letter from Gilbert that made Penny furious with herself for having ever gone to bed with him. She thought she'd been doing him a favour!

Ma chère Penny,

How slowly time passes when you are not here. I miss you very much. At the end of the day, however, I cannot make a promise to you in the way you deserve. I must ask you to move on from me and look for a man who can bring you the life you have always wanted: marriage, a home, and children. You will always have a special place in my heart.

Your ever affectionate,
Gilbert

Eighteen

●　●　●　●　●

Paris, 2022

Breakfast on the morning of the sisters' inauguration to the *Légion d'honneur* was a fraught affair. Though the hotel restaurant had laid on the buffet of dreams, Archie could not enjoy it. While he waited for his great-aunts and Arlene to come downstairs, he chucked back a double espresso and ate a perfect buttery croissant in two bites, not tasting a thing. The moment they walked into the dining room, he hurried his great-aunts straight to the buffet and set about preparing plates for both.

"What kind of eggs do you want, Auntie Penny? Eggs? Penny? Eggs? What kind?"

"My hearing aid *is* working this morning," Penny said. "But I will need more than two seconds to decide whether I want scrambled or fried."

"Someone should invent an app for that," said Josephine. "To tell you exactly what you fancy to eat. Wouldn't that be *gai?*"

"Oh very," Penny agreed. "What do I want for breakfast today, Thingy?" she pretended to speak into a phone.

"It's *Siri*," said Archie, through gritted teeth.

When they were finally at the table, Archie watched the sisters impatiently, constantly checking his watch. At 8:15, he suggested, while Josephine still had most of a *pain au chocolat* left on her plate, that it might be time for the ladies to go upstairs and change.

When they came back downstairs half an hour later, he inspected them both as though he were a senior naval officer and they his hopeless ratings. He pinned their medals on, then re-pinned them, then realised he had mixed them up and given Josephine Penny's Italy Star while Penny was wearing Josephine's Defence Medal. He made sure each sister was wearing the correct gongs then decided they looked a little wonky and had to start all over again.

"Should we be wearing our medals on the other side today?" Josephine asked, quite innocently. "So our new medals can be pinned on the left?"

That sent Archie into a total panic. "Should medals be worn on the right or the left here in France? I have no idea!"

"It's going to be fine," Arlene assured him. "Someone at the event will let us know."

"Will you just make sure both my aunts have spent a penny before we get into the taxi?" Archie asked her. "Two pennies," he added as an afterthought.

BY THE TIME they arrived at the Mairie in the 7th arrondissement, where the special inauguration was to take place, the people who were to be honoured that morning were already beginning to assemble in the courtyard. Having checked the sisters' medal placements against those of the other decorated ex–service people present, Archie allowed himself to think that from now on everything would be plain sailing. They were all present and correct. There was a good half hour before the ceremony started. Then Archie heard the all too familiar sound of a boatswain's whistle . . .

"A bosun's whistle? Who on earth?" asked Josephine when the sound reached her hearing aids.

"Oh no." Arlene closed her eyes tightly. "No. It can't be."

Arlene did not need to turn around to know exactly who was piping the "stand still" in their direction.

Proceeding across the courtyard in a wheelchair pushed by a very harassed looking young woman in a smart carer's uniform was former Third Officer WRNS Davina Mackenzie. She was dressed in a neat navy-blue skirt suit (which Josephine eyed enviously, having been persuaded by Arlene to buy a floral dress that really wasn't her style) and an extravagant feather-bedecked tricorn hat, in a nod to her wartime career and her proud naval heritage. She wore her own war medals on the left side of her jacket and her late father and grandfather's service medals on the right.

"She looks like a North Korean general," said Penny.

In Davina Mackenzie's wake came another wheeled veteran, pushed by a novice nun in a plain grey habit. It was Sister Eugenia. The *Prinz Eugen*.

"Mrs. Mackenzie! Sister Eugenia!" Archie at least managed to respond to the arrival of Josephine's nemesis and her sidekick with something other than obvious horror. "How lovely to see you both and what a shock . . . I mean, a surprise."

"It certainly is," said Davina. "Sister Eugenia and I are to be added to the illustrious roll of the *Chevaliers de la Légion d'honneur*." She pronounced the words with an extravagant Franglais accent that made several francophones in the vicinity wince.

"Well, isn't that a coincidence," said Archie.

Josephine's smile stretched into a tight straight line. "What lovely news."

"Yes," said Davina. "As the granddaughter of an admiral, I only wish my late grandfather could be here to see it."

"You're here for the same reason, ladies?" asked Sister Eugenia.

"We are," said Josephine. "I drew maps for the D-Day landings in my final posting at Whitehall."

"How exciting," said Sister Eugenia. "I've been nominated for my role in intercepting the signals from the *Bismarck*."

"The *Bismarck*? You were in the Y Service in '41?" Josephine asked. "I didn't think you were *that* old."

"Arlene," Davina Mackenzie interrupted the competitive swapping of war records. "I thought it was you. I recognise that horrible jacket."

Arlene pulled her favourite jacket—a bright orange number that she had thought just perfect for the occasion—a little tighter around her.

"But what are you doing here with these old dears? I thought you emigrated to Jamaica after you left me in the lurch. Do you mean to tell me you're back in England and working as a carer again? Why didn't you let me know? I would have had you back. Despite everything."

At her interview, Archie had warned Arlene that she must never, ever admit to having once worked for Davina Mackenzie. He felt sure Josephine would refuse to have her in the house in case she was a double agent. Arlene had assured him she was so traumatised by the experience, she would only reveal that she'd spent time with Mrs. Mackenzie under torture. And this was torture. Arlene suddenly deeply regretted having spun the "moving to Jamaica" line.

"We don't have *carers*," said Penny, before Arlene could stutter an excuse. "Arlene is here as our guest."

"Your guest?" Davina seemed unconvinced. "I see."

Archie tried to rescue the situation by quickly changing the subject. "And how have you been enjoying Paris, Mrs. Mackenzie?"

"Terrible food," she responded. "The French will insist on serving everything half-cooked and smothered with unnecessary sauces. The beef we had last night was practically mooing."

Archie nodded sympathetically.

"I rather like my meat rare," said Sister Eugenia. "I know it isn't very Christian of me to say so, but there are definitely moments when I wish the sisters in the convent kitchen were a little less concerned with salmonella and a little more concerned with preserving the flavour of God's alimentary gifts."

Archie nodded again. Having spent so much of his young life in the company of Josephine and Penny, Archie was skilled at giving absolutely everyone the impression he agreed with them whole-heartedly even if that meant taking two opposing positions within the space of half a minute.

"Where are you staying, Archie?" Sister Eugenia asked in her amiable way.

"The Maritime."

"How extravagant," Davina snapped.

"But very lovely," said Josephine. "We are so lucky to have a great-nephew like Archie. He organises such wonderful excitements. We're fortunate that he's even interested in our war years, which are in the quite distant past now."

"It's nice to meet a young man who is interested in the history of his country. Arlene barely knew anything about at all about Great Britain when I took her on."

Why would she? everyone else wondered. Arlene was born and raised in South Africa.

On the steps of the Mairie, a young woman with a large clipboard was trying to attract the attention of the crowd. Seeing that she was failing, Davina took out her boatswain's whistle and blew the "Word to be passed," the traditional British naval command for silence. It certainly focussed everyone's attention, if in the wrong direction.

Archie blushed on Davina's behalf. There were times when he was almost grateful that most people assumed someone as old as Davina Mackenzie must have lost her marbles.

THE YOUNG WOMAN with the clipboard ushered that morning's honorees and their guests inside the building. Having made sure that the sisters and Davina and Sister Eugenia were safely settled in the front row of seats in the grand reception room, Archie and Arlene found their places in the audience.

Fortunately there was an aisle between Josephine and Davina. It was such a shame they couldn't talk about their war years without getting competitive. They had a great deal in common, having both spent time in the Western Approaches plotting rooms—Davina in Liverpool and Josephine in Plymouth—translating radar signals into visual representations of shipping movements on vast maps of the Atlantic Ocean. "Like a giant game of battleships," was how Josephine had described it to Archie when he was a child, though of course it was much more complicated than that. Archie would have loved to hear more about Davina's experiences during the Battle of the Atlantic. He didn't dare ask in front of Josephine.

Finally in his own seat, Archie took a moment to regroup. He'd got his great-aunts to the ceremony and so far nobody had come to any harm. He felt his shoulders loosen as he looked around the elegant reception room. A large portrait of the President of the Republique hung over the desk on the stage. There was also a bust of Marianne, symbol of the Republique, in her Smurf-style liberty cap. A small Union Flag was dwarfed by the European flag and a Tricolore as big as a bed sheet, but flowers had been placed in every alcove and the man to Archie's left suggested that the roses were meant to represent England while the lilies represented France.

◉ ◉ ◉

THE CEREMONY WAS supposed to start at ten o'clock but it wasn't until ten past that the functionary who was to oversee proceedings swept into the room wearing a *tricolore* sash and a gigantic medallion to signify his lauded position. Everyone stood for "La Marseillaise." Josephine and Penny sang along. As did Archie. His great-aunts had taught him the words when he was a child. It was one of the ways they passed long car journeys, singing national anthems. Archie knew the words to a great many and "La Marseillaise" was one of his favourites (after Poland's magnificently stirring "Mazurek Dąbrowskiego"—"Poland Is Not Yet Lost"). As the chief functionary stepped up to the lectern, a lesser functionary stepped forward with a sheaf of papers and handed them over. Tightly typed papers. Dozens of them. The chief functionary began to address his audience.

"To the glory of La Republique . . ."

Archie hoped that his great-aunts would make it through the speech without needing to spend another penny.

Nineteen

• • • • •

Forty-five minutes later, the functionary was still talking. Meanwhile, the sun had moved through the sky so that it was now shining directly into the room where the ceremony was being held, raising the temperature until even Archie was tempted to take off his jacket. Not that he ever would. He remained as immaculate as when he'd left The Maritime after breakfast, but he worried for Josephine and Penny, who were sitting in a shaft of bright sunlight. He wasn't sure how they would get on if it started to get very much hotter.

As it was, the sisters were fine, if a little bored. Josephine glanced at Penny, who had her hands on her knees. No one would have thought it unusual for an old woman to be fidgeting from time to time—age brought with it all sorts of embarrassing tics and tremors—but of course Josephine knew that the movements of the fingers on her sister's right hand were anything but random. "Dash dot dot pause dash dash dash . . ."

Josephine tuned in.

"Dot dot dash . . ."

Penny was talking in Morse.

"Do U think speech go on longer? Need spend penny."

Josephine responded, "Dash dot dash dash . . . Shld have gone b4 ceremony started."

As the man on the podium continued to praise the tenacity of the French Resistance, Penny tapped back, "Did. Bladder shot." Then, "Dash dash pause dot dot . . . Might wet self."

To which Josephine replied, "U smell of pee anyway."

"Dot dash dot dot . . . Like Prinz Eugen."

Josephine tried not to snigger. "Unkind," she tapped back. "Ashamed to be sister."

Penny grinned at that. "My work is done," she whispered.

As the dignitary continued his interminable speech, oblivious to the discomfort of his audience, Josephine and Penny tapped out their private jokes, trying not to laugh out loud.

But what Josephine and Penny were forgetting was that they were not the only people in the room with impressive Morse code speeds honed in the theatre of war. Sister Eugenia had been one of the fastest coders in the Y Service and since those days when she tapped out messages all day long and often dreamt in code at night, she had not lost the ability to recognise a Morse pattern when she saw one. Thus she easily intercepted the sisters' messages, just as they were tapping about wee.

At first Sister Eugenia couldn't believe it. Prinz Eugen? Having established that they were not reminiscing about the battleship, Sister Eugenia realised it could only be her that the Williamson sisters were discussing. She felt a blush rush the full length of her body from her head to her toes (which usually felt very little).

"People who eavesdrop never hear good of themselves."

She remembered the words of Sister Elizabeth, the first nun she ever met, back when she was a small girl at convent school in Sussex. Sister Elizabeth was fond of a morality tale and a clip round the ear to underline its message.

This is God's punishment, Sister Eugenia told herself. *I intercepted a signal that wasn't meant for me and found out the Williamsons have nicknamed me after a battleship!*

Perhaps it was a sign of affection, she tried to convince herself. It was just that Eugenia was easily shortened to Eugen, wasn't it? And that she had been in the Y Service and actually taken down signals from that vessel? It wasn't anything else . . . It wasn't anything about her girth? She knew gluttony was a sin, but really, when you were a ninety-eight-year-old nun, there was very little to keep one going through the long, long days. And during lockdown, the younger nuns had had such fun making cakes for the local community. It would have been churlish to refuse to taste their samples.

Sister Eugenia could hardly bear to think about it, yet her eyes were drawn back to Penny and Josephine's hands, tap-tapping away.

Josephine coded, "Dash dash pause dot dash . . . Mac's hat. Monstrous."

Just then Davina Mackenzie fell into a micro-snooze and her head dropped forward, leaving the feathers atop her tricorn all a-quiver.

"Dash dot pause dot . . . Never wear thing telegraph movements," Penny observed.

Sister Eugenia had to agree with that. Davina's hat was rather ridiculous. And it did make it all the more obvious when Davina woke herself with a sudden snore that set her feathers trembling and the people in the row behind tittering.

Then at last—at long last—the honourees were called up to receive their medals. Josephine and Penny gave two short speeches in perfect French. Sister Eugenia shyly muttered, "*Merci à Dieu et à la France.*"

Davina Mackenzie seemed to speak for almost as long as the functionary, beginning her speech, naturally, "*En tant que petite-fille d'un amiral . . .*"

Once all awards had been given out, the assembled crowd stood once again for "The Marseillaise." Archie and the veterans all sang out with gusto.

ON THEIR WAY to the lunch reception afterwards, Archie and the sisters caught up with Sister Eugenia and Mrs. Mackenzie in the courtyard.

"Well, wasn't that a lovely ceremony," said Archie.

"If you ask me, it went on for much too long," said Davina. "That man rather liked the sound of his own voice."

"Oh I thought he gave a wonderful speech," said Penny, just to be contrary. "Of course, I imagine it was much more interesting to those of us who speak fluent French."

"It's true I would have been much better able to grasp the nuances of his discourse had it been in German, Danish, or Norwegian," Davina replied.

"Well, you've got me there. My Norwegian is strictly conversational," said Penny.

"I always get my Norwegian mixed up with my Swedish," Josephine claimed.

"I wish I had your facility for languages, ladies," Sister Eugenia sighed. "Apart from my schoolgirl German, the only other 'language'—if you can call it that—that I've ever mastered is Morse. Still, that was all I needed when the *Prinz Eugen* was communicating in Enigma Code. You know I had a Morse speed of twenty-five words per minute, back in the day. I think I could still follow it at that speed though I'm not sure I could tap back so fast with my poor arthritic fingers."

Penny and Josephine shared a worried look and Sister Eugenia felt an unchristian thrill at the thought that they knew they'd been rumbled.

IT WAS VERY warm in the courtyard that morning. While Penny and Josephine were still digesting Sister Eugenia's Morse speed revelation, and Davina Mackenzie was expounding on the difficulty of procuring a decent cup of tea on "The Continent," Davina's carer suddenly swayed and fell to the floor like a sunflower chopped halfway down the stem.

Archie, Arlene, and Sister Eugenia's young companion, Sister Margaret Ann, immediately went to the young woman's aid. Archie took off his jacket—with a secret degree of relief to have an excuse—and made a pillow of it for her head.

"Too hot," she murmured, as she came round from her faint.

"For goodness' sake," said Davina Mackenzie. "You simply cannot get the staff . . . This is really most inconvenient."

Arlene shot her former employer a poisonous look that would have finished off anyone else but it bounced off Davina Mackenzie like a rubber bullet off a Sherman tank.

It was decided that Hazel, as the unfortunate young woman was called, needed to have a lie down and a proper rest before she could return to her duties. She certainly couldn't push Davina's wheelchair all the way to the veterans' lunch, which was taking place in a restaurant two streets away. Not far, but far enough.

"I'll do it," said Archie.

He gallantly stepped in. But though Archie was used to looking after ancient veterans, he was not used to pushing a wheelchair—it was hard even to persuade his great-aunts to use their sticks when they were out and about—and as he tried to move Davina Mackenzie's chair out of the courtyard, he somehow got the small front wheels stuck in an invisible rut and very nearly deposited his demanding passenger face first in the gravel. Davina was unamused. She gave a blast on her bosun's whistle and shouted, "This simply will not do!"

Flustered, Archie's attempts to move the wheelchair only grew more panicky and less efficient, until Arlene could stand it no longer and said, "Get out of the way, Archie. I'm used to that old thing. I've got the biceps to prove it."

It was true that Arlene had very impressive arms. Back in London, Arlene had seen off all-comers in the impromptu arm-wrestling contest Auntie Penny had arranged at the sisters' last Christmas party. Archie couldn't compete. He didn't even try. His wrist had never truly recovered from when he broke it at ten years old.

"I'll take Mrs. Mackenzie to the lunch and get her back to her hotel afterwards," Arlene said now. "You keep an eye on the others."

Archie gave Arlene a brief salute then they formed a convoy for journey to the restaurant, with former Third Officer Mackenzie (at the front, of course) occasionally blowing the "haul" on her boatswain's whistle as "encouragement."

The third time it happened, Penny blew an impressively loud raspberry in response and blamed it on her sister when Davina Mackenzie demanded, "Who was that?"

Twenty

• • • • •

The restaurant where the veterans were to have lunch had been chosen for its wartime links to the French Resistance. It had actually been a popular haunt with the occupying German troops. They'd had no idea that the friendly proprietor and his winsome young waitresses were eavesdropping on their conversations and passing on the information to a Resistance group that met in the restaurant's wine cellar. The décor of the place had changed very little since the 1940s, one of the French hosts from the veterans' association explained to the British guests, adding in a whisper, "Upstairs in the proprietor's office, you can still see the bloodstains on the floor where a brave Resistance fighter slit the throat of a Gestapo officer she lured up there with the promise of sex."

"Bloodstains." Penny nodded enthusiastically. "We must see those."

LUNCH WAS DELICIOUS, though Davina sent her food back three times before the meat was cooked to her satisfaction.

"Are they trying to kill us all off?" she asked loudly. "What happened to the *Entente Cordiale*?"

You're dismantling it single-handedly, thought Archie.

Though Davina wasn't one of Archie's charges, strictly speaking, he felt an overwhelming need to apologise to the waiting staff on her behalf. She overheard him.

"What on earth are you apologising for, Archie?" she asked, in her foghorn voice. "They've had three opportunities to get my lunch right. Never say sorry for someone else's mistake."

Archie wondered whether the waiter had wiped Davina's steak across the kitchen floor on the third occasion of it being sent back. That was what the chef at the restaurant where he'd worked as a teenager would have done.

Thankfully, Penny and Josephine were being slightly less difficult than usual about the food though Archie began to worry when he noticed that somehow they had ended up with three wine glasses apiece by the time they finished the main course—champagne, white, and red. He should have kept a closer eye on them.

"Don't forget the BBC interview at three!" he reminded them from across the table. Josephine raised a glass of burgundy to him to acknowledge the remark and in doing so spilled half its contents down the front of her dress.

Archie got up and swiftly removed the rest of his great-aunt's wine stash, hissing, "If you get too merry, the BBC will have to interview Davina Mackenzie instead."

"Well, I suppose she is the granddaughter of an admiral . . ."

"What's that about an admiral?" Davina shouted down the table. Her hearing aid batteries never wore out.

AS HE HELPED her blot the wine stain on her skirt, Archie noticed that Josephine's new medal was already half hanging off its smart red ribbon.

"Let me pin that on again properly," Archie suggested.

"It's too heavy for this dress," Josephine complained. "If I were wearing my navy suit, it wouldn't keep drooping like this."

"It is quite big," Archie agreed, admiring the intricate medallion with its white five-pointed Napoleonic star interwoven with bright green enamelled laurel leaves. "The French certainly know how to do bling."

"It's less a medal than a hub-cap," Sister Eugenia commented from the other side of the table as she admired her own new French decoration. "Or a shield. It rather overshadows my Bletchley brooch."

"How did you get a Bletchley brooch?" Davina asked sharply.

"Well, we Y Service girls were the source of a good deal of Bletchley's raw material . . . If we hadn't been listening in to the Kriegsmarine, they would have had nothing to decode."

Meanwhile Penny was deep in conversation with a young man from the *International Herald Tribune* who was intending to cover the veterans' inauguration and lunch for the paper's weekend edition. Archie couldn't help but tune in as the young man asked, "The First Aid Nursing Yeomanry were famously linked with the Special Operations Executive. Were you involved with any of that, Miss Williamson?"

"Well, I did work as a code and cipher officer for a while," Penny confirmed. "But if you're asking if I was an SOE agent . . ."

Of course the journalist was asking that. Everyone always asked that. Archie asked it all the time. Hovering just behind Penny and her interlocutor, Archie wondered what sort of answer the journalist would get.

Twenty-One

● ● ● ● ●

Josephine's retelling of her war years had always been quite straightforward. No matter how many times she recounted it, her story never really changed: basic training in London, a desk job at WRNS HQ, a stint in the Western Approaches plotting rooms in Plymouth, before finally returning to London to draw D-Day maps in a basement office in Whitehall. It was all very different with Penny.

In the course of researching the family history, Archie had already tracked down Josephine's official war records, which confirmed exactly where and when she'd been posted during her four years with the Wrens. There were reports too, from her seniors. "A capable girl, if a little aloof when it comes to her fellow ratings," wrote her commanding officer at WRNS HQ. Later, that aloofness would be to Josephine's advantage in the eyes of the officers who put her forward for promotion from secretarial rating to young petty officer. "Not silly and given to gossip like some of the other girls."

Archie had not been able to find anything like the same sort of information for Auntie Penny. It had taken a while to persuade the FANY archivists to look for the papers he wanted—he had to have Penny's written permission and somehow she was always forgetting to give it—and when they finally did get back to him, the news was bad. They confirmed that Penny had indeed joined the FANY in 1942, shortly after her eighteenth birthday, but there was scant little information regarding Penny's career between her basic training and her being posted first to Algiers in late 1943 and then to Southern Italy.

There was a gap in Penny's records of more than a year and Archie found it maddening. Penny insisted she'd told him everything she could remember about those missing months—"Oh, I just had an admin job at an army training camp"—but he had hoped her official records might contain some tiny detail that would unlock a new and exciting anecdote. Where had those missing months gone?

A newly published book on the FANY, which Archie had downloaded onto his Kindle the very moment it was released, revealed that many of the FANY's service records had been destroyed in a fire not long after the war. Archie had at first accepted that explanation but the more he thought about it, the more oddly convenient it seemed.

As the journalist talking to Penny had pointed out, it *was* now common knowledge that during World War Two the FANY had close links with the SOE—the Special Operations Executive. The covert wartime intelligence agency, commissioned by Churchill himself with the instruction that it should "Set Europe Ablaze," was also known as the Ministry of Ungentlemanly Warfare or the Baker Street Irregulars (its head office was on Baker Street). It was tasked with supporting resistance groups behind enemy lines in occupied Europe—often by sending in specially-trained agents. Its methods were subterfuge and sabotage. Its very existence was controversial.

Many FANY recruits were sent to work at the SOE in administrative and other support roles, but the FANY's unique position as a voluntary organisation—a charity on the army list but not actually part of the army—meant that it was also perfectly placed to offer military status to the civilian women the SOE sent into the field as undercover agents, affording them the official protection due to military personnel under the 1929 Geneva Conventions, should they ever be captured.

A memorial on the wall of St. Paul's Church in Knightsbridge commemorated the many FANY officers who had risked all as SOE agents behind enemy lines; women such as Violette Szabo and Odette Hallowes and the ethereally beautiful Noor Inayat Khan. Their names were immortal. Was it possible that Penny's wartime work had brought her into contact with those wonderful women? Was it possible that she had been one of their number?

• • •

THAT PENNY HAD spent her missing year as an agent behind enemy lines was Archie's greatest fantasy. She would have made a fabulous spy, he thought, remembering the many adventures they'd had together over the years. Like the time she took him to Greece when he was fifteen and they jumped off the side of an enormous ferry as it was leaving the dock in Igoumenitsa. It was a slightly extreme way to avoid having to talk to the "boring old boyfriend" Penny claimed to have seen at the other end of the deck, and their luggage was soaked, but it was very exciting and left him exhilarated. Likewise, young Archie had always loved it when halfway through a trip Penny would tell him that to liven things up, they were going to travel under aliases.

"We're from Belgium," was a typical suggestion. "We have never been to London in our lives . . ."

They'd once kept up aliases for an entire transatlantic crossing, pretending they were Peggy and Arnie Wilhemsen from Seattle. Penny reeled off their backstory with great aplomb for the "criminally dull" people who shared their table in the ship's dining room each night. She told them, in a north-west American accent (she was an excellent mimic), that the Wilhemsens had migrated to the US from Norway after the war. They were descended from the great King Cnut . . .

They almost came unstuck when Archie, whom Penny had claimed was a medical student, was asked to take a look at someone's rash. Quick-thinking Penny immediately put her hand to her forehead and told Archie she thought she was about to have "one of her turns." He gratefully escorted her back to her cabin, suggesting the poor unfortunate with the rash "put some ice on it" as he went. Back in Penny's cabin, they collapsed into fits of giggles.

"Oh that was killingly funny!" Penny cried. "Put some ice on it! Archie, you are a card."

"I feel terrible, Auntie Penny. We shouldn't have lied . . ."

Luckily, the chap with the rash found his way to the cruise liner's sick-bay and didn't ask Archie's opinion again.

That whole trip was one Archie would never forget. They'd disembarked in New York and painted the town red, with Penny paying for everything with thick wads of cash. She didn't trust credit cards. Still didn't. "It's never a good idea to leave a trail," she said.

There was one sticky moment when they found themselves nose-to-nose with a would-be mugger as they walked back to their hotel from a Broadway show but Auntie Penny quickly dispatched the unfortunate chap to the gutter with a move using an umbrella that was straight out of W.E. Fairbairn's *Self-Defence for Women and Girls*.

Archie was both thrilled and appalled at the way things unfolded. He would never have believed his great-aunt, who was then in her seventies, could move so fast if he hadn't seen it with his own eyes. He was sure he couldn't have reacted so quickly.

"I should have been looking after you, Auntie Penny. But it's my wrist . . ."

"I know, dear," Penny told him. "I know. And for that I do hold myself accountable."

You see, once upon a time, Archie had shared Penny's brand of chutzpah. In the summer of 1990, he was ready for all-comers, imagining his pillow as the school bully when he practised the moves in Major Fairbairn's *Scientific Self-Defence*.

One of the hardest Fairbairn manoeuvres to perfect was a backwards roll from lying flat to standing—page forty-three—designed to put our hero back on his feet after being laid out by a blow. Archie remembered how proud he'd been when he finally got it right. When Penny and Josephine visited for a family party, he insisted they come into the living room and watch him execute the perfect flip before they even took their coats off.

That first flip *was* perfect, though Archie did take out a standard lamp in the process.

"Imagine if that had been an enemy," Penny reassured him while Josephine got out her chequebook.

"We feel rather responsible for this sudden mania with martial arts," Josephine told Archie's mother Miranda as she pressed the price of a new lamp into her hands.

At the time, Auntie Penny was less apologetic. "Everyone needs to know how to handle themselves. You can't make a hero without breaking lamps, Miranda dear."

She whispered to Archie, "I knew you'd be good at Defendu. You see, you're a clever boy and cleverness always wins out over brawn in the end."

"Do you think I could have been an agent in World War Two, Auntie Penny?" he asked her.

"Oh yes. They would have snapped you up. You're clever, you're brave, and you can do a perfect back flip to standing."

He'd felt himself grow a little taller at the thought.

Then he tried the back flip again—in the garden to avoid any more breakages—and that was when he broke his wrist. He had to wear a plaster cast for the whole of the school holidays and the first two weeks of term. The sisters wrote on it. Josephine drew an old-fashioned Chad cartoon, with its nose hanging over the wall. "Wot no tennis?" she scribbled underneath. Meanwhile Penny scrawled a line straight from Fairbairn.

"There are no rules. Only kill or be killed."

"Do *not* encourage him," Miranda wailed when she saw what Penny had written.

But Penny had encouraged Archie. She had encouraged him enough that when he went back to boarding school in September, he walked a little taller and the rumours that swirled around the reason for his plaster cast made the bullies a little less quick to pick on him. Then the cast came off and Archie's courage seemed to come off with it.

"It doesn't matter," Penny assured him that night in New York. "I had us covered with my brolly and I know that if I hadn't, you would have stepped in in an instant. You'd have found the strength to defend us both had you needed it. As it was, I rather enjoyed that little episode," she added. "Took me right back."

Right back to what, Archie wondered.

SAILING HOME TO Southampton—thankfully not having to put on accents this time—they heard from other passengers that their outbound voyage had been hit by a string of thefts.

"That's why I'm wearing all my jewellery at once," said the American matron who passed on the news.

"You cannot be too careful," Penny agreed.

Bizarrely, when Archie got home to his parents' house in Cheltenham and was decanting clothes from his suitcase back into the wardrobe, he discovered a single diamond earring in the breast pocket of his dinner jacket. He had no idea how it got there. He took it with him to his next lunch with the sisters.

"Must have happened when that old biddy from Atlanta gave you a hug on the last night of the cruise," Penny suggested.

Archie couldn't remember that having happened.

"I should hand it in," he said.

"After all those thefts onboard? I wouldn't put yourself through it. You'll only put yourself in the frame. No good deed goes unpunished."

"But it's a big diamond, Auntie Penny."

Penny examined it. "Two carats max. She won't miss it. But if you're worried, I'll hand it in for you, dear."

IT WAS FUN to pull the wool over the eyes of nosey fellow travellers, but lately Archie realised that he'd often felt Penny was holding something back from him too. Many times he had asked her a question about that "admin job" during the missing year only for her to start fiddling with her hearing aid. Did hearing aid batteries really run out so frequently?

Suddenly the chairman of the French veterans' association tapped the side of his wine glass with a spoon.

"Mesdames et messieurs . . ."

Another speech. By the time the chairman had finished talking, Penny had probably forgotten what the journalist had asked her in the first place and it was time to introduce the sisters to the nice people from the BBC.

Twenty-Two

. . . . .

Unfortunately, the interview with the BBC Paris correspondent did not go exactly as Archie had planned. The presenter's eyes lit up when she realised that not two but four female World War Two veterans had been given the *Légion d'honneur* that day and she insisted that Davina Mackenzie and Sister Eugenia take part in the recording too. What could Archie say? He could hardly tell her about the rivalry between his great-aunt Josephine and Davina Mackenzie. All he could do was ask Arlene and Sister Margaret Ann to help him gather all four elderly ladies together in front of the screen the cameraman had set up in a back room at the restaurant and hope that Josephine was able to get a word in.

"Archie, why didn't you tell me this interview was happening before," Davina Mackenzie barked at him. "Will there be hair and make-up?"

When Archie told Davina that the BBC had sent only a cameraman and a presenter, he found himself being despatched to a nearby pharmacy to purchase a comb, face powder, and a coral-pink lipstick. These accoutrements were for Sister Eugenia.

"I find that grey rather washes me out on camera," she said, indicating her neatly-pressed habit.

THE INTERVIEW WENT horribly, with all four of Archie's ladies (he seemed to have assumed responsibility for *all* of them now) talking over each other all the time.

"Well, we've certainly got plenty of material to choose from," was the

BBC presenter's tactful summing up when the recording was finally finished.

As Archie trotted out after the presenter to take her a notepad she had left behind in the restaurant, he heard her saying to the cameraman, "We can't use any of that last segment. I guess it just goes to show that not everybody gets better with age."

Archie didn't dare ask the BBC presenter exactly what it was that they couldn't use. He could only hope that it hadn't come from either one of his great-aunts.

After that, Archie decided that it was time for everyone—himself included—to have a little rest. While poor Arlene accompanied Davina Mackenzie and Sister Eugenia back to their hotel, Archie summoned a taxi for The Maritime. En route, Penny asked, "Well, that was a very nice lunch but what excitements do we have for tonight?"

"We're going to a party at Stéphane's auction house," he said.

"Oh yes," said Penny. "I knew that."

But a look of confusion flickered briefly in her eyes, followed by something that looked a lot like frustration.

"Yes. I knew that," she said again.

Archie hated these moments, when he had to remind the sisters of something he'd already told them several times. It wasn't the having to repeat himself, but the implications of it that made his heart sink. He wasn't ready to lose his great-aunts, especially not by increment. Even now they were in their nineties, he wanted them always to be as brilliant and funny as they had been when they first rowed him around the loch and taught him how to swear in pig latin. They'd done pretty bloody well so far. When it came to recognising the creep of dementia, Archie wanted to remain just as deep in denial as Penny was.

ARCHIE SAW BOTH his great-aunts to their rooms, Josephine first. As he pushed open the door to Penny's room, she told him, "Come in for a minute please, Archie. I've got something I've been meaning to give you."

She reached into her handbag and pulled out an old 1930s silver matchbox that Archie hadn't seen in years; not since Penny gave up smoking in her late-eighties.

He gasped at the sight of it. "You've still got that old thing?"

"Of course. But I thought you might like to have it now."

When Archie had first known his great-aunts, Penny was still what you might have called a "chain smoker." She'd given him his first cigarette, when he was nine years old.

"The sooner you learn how vile these things taste, the better," she'd said, before taking a long drag on the filter to get it started.

There was method in her madness. Archie had eagerly helped himself to one of Penny's Camels (the brand she had smoked since Algiers), coughed his lungs up, and never tried again. He certainly never got round to learning to blow magnificent smoke rings as Penny could.

Back in those days, Penny had carried that silver matchbox everywhere. Archie liked to help by filling it with England's Glory when she ran out. He'd been fascinated by it, especially having read in his W.E. Fairbairn books all the ways one could incapacitate a man using a metal matchbox as a makeshift knuckle-duster.

"Never practise these moves on yourself as you will likely knock yourself out," the author warned. Naturally, whenever Archie could get hold of Penny's matchbox, he *did* practise the moves on himself—albeit in slow-motion—in the mirror.

Penny's matchbox was engraved on one side but Penny would never tell him what the engraving referred to or how she had come by such an unusual item. Eventually Archie came to know that the engraving was a stanza from a poem—"Invictus"—but he still didn't know how she'd come to own it.

"I know you don't smoke," she said as she handed it over in her Paris hotel room. "But you always liked this silly box when you were a child."

"Gosh, Auntie Penny." Archie held the box as though it were solid gold. "I've always *loved* it. But why are you giving this to me now?"

"Oh. You know . . . Seems like the right time."

Archie threw his arms around Penny and hugged her to him tightly. "Thank you, my dear, dear auntie. I will look after it. But you can have it back whenever you like."

"I don't think I'll be needing it again."

"You never know. Have you had a lovely day, Auntie Penny?" Archie asked all of a sudden. "I hope you've had a lovely day. We've got so many more excitements before bedtime and lots to come in the future. Auntie Josephine's hundredth birthday next year. And yours right after that. There's so much to look forward to. I'm so glad to have you both in my life. I don't know what I would do without you."

"Are you quite alright, Archie?" Penny asked. "You seem a little agitated."

Archie *was* agitated. Truth was, the unexpected gift of the matchbox had worried him. That matchbox was one of Penny's most treasured possessions but now she'd decided she no longer needed it? He'd heard about this sort of thing; read about it while searching online for dementia resources. If she was giving away something that had once meant so much to her, she must be preparing to go.

Though the sisters had made that horrible pact to avoid the old people's home more than a decade before, Archie had never really believed they would orchestrate their own exits. He'd met many people their age over the years. Some people definitely decided their time was up and simply let themselves fade away. That had been the case with his maternal grandmother. But not Penny and Josephine. They'd always wanted to squeeze life until its pips squeaked. Had something changed? Was Penny worried about the memory lapses that had led to her accidentally shoplift from Waitrose and, most alarmingly, that temple of the high street, Peter Jones? What was she planning? He subconsciously patted the jacket pocket which contained his passport and those of both his great-aunts. No one was going to Switzerland on his watch.

Archie had always been able to turn to his great-aunts when he was worried. His parents had too many expectations for him. They were too closely interested in his progress through life; too invested in his being a certain way—their way. With Penny and Josephine, he had always felt as though he could be his authentic self. Whenever he'd shared his fears with them, he'd always come away feeling reassured and absolutely supported. He wanted to be able to do the same for them.

"Can I use your bathroom?" he asked Penny now.

"Of course."

Running the taps in the basin to cover the sound, he quickly rifled through Penny's wash-bag, taking an inventory of the tablets therein. He knew her medication regime by heart and didn't think any of it might be dangerous in excess, besides which Arlene had carefully packed only tablets enough for the trip and one day extra in the event of a travel delay, but . . . Could one take too many Rennies? He removed half of Penny's supply of the indigestion remedy just in case.

When he came back into the bedroom, he said, "Auntie Penny, you know I am here for you—you and Auntie Josephine—no matter what. No matter what worries you have, you can share them with me. I'm not the little boy you rowed around the loch all those years ago. I'm a grown man and whatever you need, I can make sure you have it." He realised as he spoke that he might be opening himself up to a request he didn't want. "Unless it's, you know, something illegal. Do you remember my grandfather Tom? Of course you do. He couldn't even recognise his own children towards the end but he was always very happy. I don't think he would have shortened his life by a day."

"Archie, dear, I don't think I follow you. Perhaps I'm a little bit tired but . . ."

"I don't . . ." Archie stumbled over the words. "I just don't know what I would do without you. You and Auntie Josephine."

Penny squeezed his hand. "I don't know what we'd do without you either. Look at all the lovely excitements you've arranged for us today. How many old ladies are lucky enough to be having so much fun in their nineties? Now what time are we supposed to be at the wotsit this evening?"

"Seven o'clock."

"I'm looking forward to it. Now you had better go and get yourself ready to see your old flame. *Toujours gai*, Archie." Penny sent him away with a wave.

BACK IN HIS own room, Archie lay diagonally across the enormous bed, staring up at the ceiling as he turned the silver matchbox over and over in his hand. He'd coveted it ever since he first saw it but now he didn't want it one bit. The thought of a future where all he had left of his dear aunts were trinkets such as this made him terribly, terribly sad. He knew that the day would come when they were no longer around—no one lives forever—but he couldn't let them go yet. Picking up his phone, he googled "oldest woman in the world" to cheer himself up. It was still that French nun, Lucile Randon, known as Sister André, now clocking in at 118. 118? Why, Penny might have another twenty years!

While he was looking at other uplifting stories of grand old dames who had made it past 110, while still variously smoking, drinking, and riding horses, his phone pinged. It was a message from Stéphane.

Looking forward to seeing you tonight, mon cher Archie.

Sitting up to respond to Stéphane's sweet text, Archie determined to shake off his worries about Penny for the moment. He replied to Stéphane, then he checked his emails. He was sure that his very capable assistant Tim could hold the fort at the gallery in Mayfair, but he wanted to be certain he hadn't missed any urgent personal messages from his more important clients.

Thankfully, there was nothing happening on the work front that required his immediate attention, but there was something else that definitely warranted action. While he'd been wrangling his great-aunts, Archie had received a message regarding the DNA sample he'd sent away in the hope that it might solve the mystery of his mother's paternity. Now he clicked on the link that led to a breakdown of his DNA profile, excited to know what secrets that little test-tube of spit—ugh, spit—might have revealed.

There were no surprises in Archie's genetic make-up: Scottish, English, and a touch of Scandinavian. That didn't mean he didn't have an American grandfather, of course. There were plenty of people with Scottish, English, and Scandinavian heritage in the US. The surprising part—the delightful part—was that as well as a breakdown of his genes, the report told Archie that an actual genetic match had been found in Canada. That was very nearly the US for the purposes of his GI fantasy. The points of similarity suggested that the match was a close cousin. Would Archie like to be introduced? Too right he would. Archie responded right away.

Oh, it was like Grindr but much more exciting! And with a much higher chance of a long-lasting relationship at the end.

Archie still hoped that his grandfather was a GI, as his mother suspected. Wouldn't it be amazing if he had heroic World War Two veterans on both sides of his lineage? Archie had loved his grandpa Tom but the possibilities for a new thread in the tapestry of his family history were too exciting. As he got ready for the reception at Brice-Petitjean, he allowed himself a daydream in which he met his new cousin and saw a photograph of their grandfather in common—a GI with a face that resembled his own. There weren't many aspects of modern life that Archie approved of, but this DNA sampling business was turning out to be a wonderful thing.

Twenty-Three

• • • • •

1949

After their disastrous Parisian holiday in 1947, the next time the sisters saw each other was in the spring of 1949. By then Josephine was in her final year at Cambridge. Penny was a social worker in Manchester. They'd been summoned to London by their grandmother's sister, who'd arranged for them to be presented to the King and Queen. Great Aunt Helena was very keen on the idea of "society" and thought it a terrible pity that the War had prevented the Williamson sisters from having the debutante season that was their due as young women of a certain social standing.

As children they'd looked forward to being debutantes but the very idea of being presented at court seemed ridiculous to both sisters now. All the same, they did it out of respect for the maternal grandmother they had both dearly loved.

Stepping into that glittering drawing room at Buckingham Palace, for a moment it was as if the War had never happened (though of course even the palace had not escaped the Blitz unscathed). Having served their country with every bit as much courage and intelligence as some young men of their acquaintance, Penny and Josephine suddenly found themselves catapulted back a decade and reduced to white-gloved clothes horses and suitable wives-in-waiting, who had to curtsey—curtsey! for goodness' sake—in front of the Royals. As if that wasn't bad enough, they then had to shuffle back to the receiving line without turning their backs on the monarch. The young woman who went ahead of the sisters caught her heel in the bottom of her skirt as she tried to stick to the protocol.

The Queen looked bored, Penny thought. As well she might. She wondered how many "nice young gels" the Queen had cast her eye over since her husband ascended the throne. Meanwhile George VI looked unwell. His skin was distinctly yellow.

After the assembled loyal subjects of the Empire had been presented, they were ushered through to an anteroom where they were offered tea and dainty little sandwiches with the crusts cut off. An unthinkable waste, not eating the crusts. It wasn't so long ago that bread was on the ration. Still Aunt Helena was delighted to have seen her great-nieces properly launched with royal approval at last and was soon in conversation with another woman, accompanying her daughter, who agreed that "such things are important."

While Helena expounded on the importance of "society," Penny showed her teaspoon to Josephine. It was stamped with the royal crest. "Dare me to pinch this."

"You never would," said Josephine with absolute confidence. "You're much too good. You wouldn't even pinch a sweet from Woollies."

"How much longer do you think we have to be here?" Penny asked. "It's ridiculous, all the curtseying and shuffling about like demented crabs so the King doesn't have to see our bottoms." She launched into a rant that had become familiar to Josephine from her letters. "After everything this country has been through, doesn't it bother you that the old guard are still trying to carry on exactly as before? We should have known this would happen. We should have known no one would make the effort to do things differently and make life better for the average man and woman. All those lives laid down for this nonsense to continue. All that courage and sacrifice so we can carry on tugging the forelock. I could spit."

"Don't though, will you? Not while we're at the Palace."

Penny bit into another sandwich and said, with her mouth full, "I can only imagine what the people I work with would think if they saw me gussied up like this. I'm helping a family who were in Singapore. They spent three years starving in a Japanese camp. Three years! The father died from malnutrition. The mother and children came back here after all that and were given a flipping tin of condensed milk by the local council as a welcome home."

"Nobody here has had much to give," Josephine reminded her.

"Some people have done OK. And here I am eating fancy sandwiches. I should be back in Manchester, helping that family find a decent home where their fourteen-year-old daughter Jinx doesn't have to share a bed with her little brother. Jinx is the bravest child you ever met, Josephine. After VJ Day, when the POWs were left to fend for themselves, she had to pull gold teeth from the mouths of dead Japanese soldiers to get money to buy food for her family."

"Gosh," said Josephine, putting the slice of cake she had been so looking forward to back on her plate, so she could digest the thought.

"She's amazing. Not scared of a thing, even after everything she's been through. I want her to have the opportunities we've had. She's got such grit."

Aunt Helena was looking for them now. "Girls! Girls!"

"Girls?" Penny growled. "We were officers in the women's services, for heaven's sake."

Josephine linked her arm through Penny's. "Come on. It's only one day. You can go back to being a communist tomorrow. Aunt Helena is so pleased we allowed her to arrange this. She thinks she's done us a great favour by ensuring we didn't entirely miss out on our *debut*."

Josephine pronounced the word "*day-boo*" with the intention of making Penny smile.

"Look how happy it's made her to have an excuse to see the King and Queen. And think yourself lucky you didn't have to dress up in white and spend a whole *month* dancing with the chinless sons of the aristocracy. If the war hadn't happened, you'd have been married off to one of them by now. You'd be Lady Chinless Wonder . . ."

"So." Penny nudged Josephine in the ribs. "Is there a chinless wonder on your horizon? You must have met dozens at Cambridge."

A flame of sadness flared in Josephine's eyes so briefly that Penny didn't see it.

"What about that submariner you met in Plymouth?" Penny persisted. "Gerry, wasn't it?"

"Gerald. Never call him Gerry. He doesn't like that. I still hear from him," she admitted.

"He's not married?"

"No."

"But he was so good-looking. You must have done quite the number on him."

"Oh, there you are!" Great Aunt Helena had caught up with them. She frowned at Penny's crumb-covered plate. "I hope you're going to have room for another round of sandwiches. I've invited a couple of lovely young men to join us at The Ritz," she added in a conspiratorial way.

Josephine pressed her lips tightly together and did not look at Penny, knowing that Penny would not be happy about that at all.

AFTER A HURRIED second tea, Penny bid goodbye to the suitable boys, her sister, and Aunt Helena, and carried on alone up Bond Street. She took off her hat as soon as she thought she was out of her aunt's sight. If it hadn't cost so much money, she would have stuffed it straight in a bin, but she thought she'd better hang onto it. She could probably sell it on with an advertisement in the back of *The Lady*. Waste not, want not.

As she drew level with the shining windows of Devrey, however, she put the hat back on and straightened herself up a little. It wasn't often that Penny felt well-dressed enough to visit Devrey, the society jeweller. Dare she step inside now? Smiling pleasantly, she approached the door. An attendant stepped forward to swing it open for her.

Inside, the store was empty but for a single sales assistant. The man, who was in his forties, greeted Penny warmly and asked how he might help.

Without quite knowing why, Penny affected a French accent for her response. "I should like to see some bracelets," she said. "My father is going to buy me a gift for my twenty-first birthday."

"How nice," the sales assistant said. "Let me show you what we have. Do you have an idea what you might be looking for? A bangle style? Or links? Would you like it to be set with a particular stone?"

"Show me everything," said Penny.

It wasn't long before the sales assistant had fifteen bracelets out on the counter. One by one, Penny picked them up and examined them closely.

She had the sales assistant fasten them onto her arm. They looked especially good against the white gloves that were compulsory attire for the Palace.

"They are all so beautiful," said Penny, keeping up her Parisienne. "I don't know which one to choose. Perhaps I could try one on each wrist to compare."

She kept the assistant talking.

"It must have been awful in occupied France," he said.

"Yes. It was frightening but not as frightening as it must have been for you here in London, with all the bombing."

"It wasn't much fun when they started with the V2s," the assistant said with classic English understatement.

During the course of the conversation, the sales assistant revealed he had been among the men evacuated from Dunkirk. Penny's hand fluttered to her throat.

"You must have been so scared."

"Oh, it was too chaotic to be frightening at the time. It wasn't until after we got back that I really thought about it. I'm just glad I didn't have to go back to France. Terrible what happened in Normandy. I lost a cousin there."

"I lost two uncles," said Penny, thinking of Claudine's younger brothers, frozen in time. She did consider them sort of uncles and it was easier to be convincing when your story contained a grain of truth. Of course, had she been telling the whole truth, she could have mentioned that her father was at Dunkirk too. Too risky.

All the time they talked, Penny kept holding out her wrists so the assistant could add and remove bracelets from the stack she was wearing along her arms.

"Not this one," said Penny, turning her right wrist so that the assistant could unclip a bracelet set with rubies and snap one set with sapphires in its place. Backwards and forwards. Forwards and back. Penny's French gamine was finding it terribly difficult to make up her mind. Would the sapphires go with more of her dresses than the emeralds? Perhaps she should stick to diamonds? They go with everything. If she could just try the rubies again?

They continued in this vein until the clocks in the showroom struck five.

"I must go!" Penny said. "I'm supposed to be meeting my father at The Savoy."

"You mustn't be late," the assistant agreed.

"I'll come back with my father tomorrow. I think I've settled on the diamonds," Penny said, giving the diamond bracelet an affectionate stroke with the white-gloved fingers of her right hand. "You will be here tomorrow?" she asked.

"Oh yes," said the assistant. "Just ask for Frederick."

"Frederick," Penny purred. "*À demain!*"

Then Penny walked from the store, bidding the doorman "good evening" as she went. He tipped his hat at her.

As she stepped out onto Bond Street, Penny's heart was hammering so hard, she was sure that everyone within half a mile had to be able to hear it. Knowing she must not draw attention, she walked slowly and steadily as she could to the junction with Burlington Gardens, even forcing herself to pause to look into other shop windows, then as soon as she was out of the direct line of the doorman's sight, she broke into a run, taking off the dratted hat and stuffing it into a dustcart as she went.

Safely on a bus heading east, she finally dared to fold down the cuff of her left glove to see the emerald bracelet nestled against her wrist. She'd done it. She felt half elated and half sick. Poor Fred would be waiting a long time for the French heiress to return with her father's chequebook.

But now what? Penny was overdressed for a visit to the pawn shop but also knew the sooner she got the bracelet off her hands the better. Where should she go to off-load the thing? Jumping off the bus near Hatton Garden, she chose the shop that looked least sleazy, which still didn't mean that it looked like the kind of place where a young woman who had spent the morning at Buckingham Palace would naturally find herself a few hours later.

The old man behind the counter sat up a little straighter as he checked her out.

"I'd like a valuation for this," Penny said in her old friend Marguerite's accent. Her story now, if anyone asked, would be that she was an Austrian refugee. There were lots of them in London and it wouldn't seem so unusual that they had jewellery to sell.

"I'll have a gander," said the old man.

As he studied the bracelet with an eyeglass, Penny hopped from foot to foot. Why was he taking so long? Perhaps it wasn't too late to snatch the bracelet back, return to Devrey and claim she had only discovered the bracelet was still on her wrist when she got to The Savoy. They would believe it was an accident, wouldn't they? No. She had to go through with it. Penny steeled herself by imagining being able to hand a wad of notes to Jinx's mother: enough to rent a decent flat, buy some decent food, get Jinx a proper uniform for the grammar school . . .

Just as the man placed the bracelet back on his velvet desk pad and was about to tell Penny what he'd give her for it, the shop doorbell rang. Penny jumped out of her skin. She turned, half-expecting—more than half-expecting—to see a police officer, come to take her away. She could hardly claim she'd been intending to return the bracelet if she was in the process of getting it pawned. And indeed the man on the threshold was a police officer, in a smart black uniform with a shiny silver badge. But it was much worse than that.

"Bruna?"

It had been a very long time since anyone had called Penny by that name.

Twenty-Four

• • • • •

1942

What Penny didn't know when she used her best Major Fairbairn tactics on Alfred the army man during that long-ago performance of *Blithe Spirit*, was that she had unwittingly passed a test. Alfred of the roaming hands would not bother her for a date again and Pamela was furious, claiming that Penny had all but ruined her prospects with Ginger too, however in the audience at the theatre that night was someone who was extremely impressed by Penny's ability to protect herself. This despite the fact that she'd stamped on his foot during her escape.

Since she'd been wearing her brand-new FANY uniform it was easy for Penny's admirer to quickly find out who she was, not least because by the following morning the incident in the theatre was already the talk of FANY HQ. When Penny's admirer heard, via his contacts, about her language skills, he was even more intrigued.

"Excellent French," Penny's commanding officer confirmed. "Speaks like a local. Spent a lot of time with godparents in Paris before the war, I understand."

Penny was duly invited to a meeting with the "Inter Services Bureau" in an anonymous-looking mansion block near Baker Street.

When she received the invitation, Penny assumed she was to be repri-manded for the *Blithe Spirit* incident. Bashing an army officer's ugly mug against the back of a theatre seat in the middle of a Noël Coward play was surely something one should feel guilty about. Not that Penny did. Not really. Four days on, she was still exhilarated at the memory and enjoying the hushed reverence that now followed her about the FANY dorms. The majority of the girls had sided with Penny over Pamela. No FANY should ever have to put up with the kind of impertinence to which Penny had been subjected! Some of the girls had even asked for a demonstration of the Fairbairn technique.

"We should be taught this kind of thing in basic training," Penny told them to enthusiastic agreement. By the time she had finished, Penny's FANY friends were the most dangerous dates in London.

AT THE MANSION block, Penny was directed by the doorman to a flat on the fifth floor. She understood that the damage wrought by the Blitz meant that many government and military departments were having to work in less conventional surroundings than one might expect, but all the same, she was surprised to be asked to wait in a bathroom. Should she perch on the loo or on the side of the tub? She chose the tub, thinking it was slightly more elegant.

Five minutes passed before she was retrieved by a woman who did not introduce herself. The woman wasn't in uniform, so Penny assumed she must be a secretary. She didn't exactly exude warmth as she invited Penny to follow her to the drawing room. On the way, Penny looked for anything that might give a clue as to why she had been summoned here. There was no FANY regalia and nothing to suggest she'd been called before an army disciplinary hearing either. Everything about the set-up was utterly anonymous. What was this Inter Services Bureau about?

In the drawing room, a man who looked to be about Penny's father's age was waiting by the window. He also declined to introduce himself— "We don't need names here," he said—before he made Penny understand that the conversation they were about to have was not to be repeated in the outside world. "And I hope you won't mind if we speak French," he added.

"French? *Pourquoi pas?*" said Penny. It was an odd request but why not?

"Excellent," said the man. "I understand you're rather good at French. Now, where shall we start?"

Penny blushed as the man revealed that she had squashed his foot as she escaped that fateful performance of *Blithe Spirit*.

"Perhaps I went a bit too far," Penny said.

"*Pas du tout*," he assured her. "You were under attack and you acted swiftly. Let's hope the silly chap learned his lesson."

"But am I in trouble? Is that why I'm here?"

"The incident certainly drew you to our attention. We understand that not only are you fluent in French, Miss Williamson, but you also have basic German and that you've been selected to be trained in code and cipher."

"I don't think I'm supposed to talk about it."

"We know. So tell us a little about what you like to do when you're not at work. Apart from disrupting West End productions . . ."

As the conversation continued—all in French—Penny was reminded of her initial FANY interview. Many of the questions seemed irrelevant but she knew now there was no such thing as an irrelevant question in war time. The crossword question, for example, was intended to get an idea of her suitability for code and cipher work. Now the strangers quizzed Penny about her family, though they already seemed to have all the facts at their fingertips. They knew she had a sister in the WRNS and her father was an army man, currently stationed in North Africa. Did her parents approve of her being in uniform? they wanted to know. Where had she learned her martial arts skills?

"I taught myself," she said. "From Major W.E. Fairbairn's *Self-Defence for Women and Girls*. I haven't had much opportunity to practise."

That seemed to amuse her interviewers.

"We might be able to change that," said the man.

"Am I being sent home?" Penny asked then. She couldn't bear the tension a moment longer. "I don't think I could stand it if I had to go home. You see I've only just escaped."

"You're certainly not being sent home. Penny, we'd like to send you on an assessment course," said the woman, who was obviously not a secretary after all.

"For what?" Penny asked.

"We think we might have an interesting role for you. In France."

THERE FOLLOWED TWO further interviews with the same two nameless people. At the second, Penny was apprised of the "interesting role."

"You'd be living as a civilian behind enemy lines, supporting the local resistance groups by sending and receiving messages to and from London, arranging supply drops, acting as a courier for documents, that sort of thing."

"I'd be a spy?" asked Penny.

"Spying is not our business," said the man.

"We're not after another Mata Hari," the woman told her. "Should you be caught, your status as a FANY officer . . ."

"Officer?" Penny, a mere cadet, was confused.

"Yes. Officer . . . You'd be promoted. It should give you some protection. But, well, the truth is, should you get into trouble, you will be on your own. You'll be prepared for all eventualities but there likely won't be anyone coming to rescue you. Death in service is a strong possibility."

"A very strong possibility," said the man, with a nod. "It's vital work but dangerous."

Penny nodded back.

"Now you must go away and sleep on it."

"I don't need to sleep on it," said Penny. "I'm ready to go."

The dire warning had done nothing to dampen her rising excitement.

"Sleep on it," the woman said kindly. "You can tell us when next we meet."

TWO WEEKS LATER, having signed the Official Secrets Act, Penny was on her way to Surrey to join the mysterious assessment course. As she boarded the train, she felt the same sense of joyful anticipation as someone about to start a jolly holiday. She'd been instructed to travel incognito so she wore civilian clothes and did not talk to anyone, though she was fizzing with excitement. Disembarking, she did her best not to draw any attention to herself. She'd been told that if any locals asked what she was doing in the area, she was to say she was working as a secretary at the country pile that housed the new commando training school.

Ha! She imagined what her old headmistress, Miss Bull, might have to say if she heard that Penny, whose fire drill antics had earned such disapprobation, was going to a commando school. How Penny would have loved to see her face. It was frustrating not even to be able to tell Josephine what was going on. But Penny had been told she was to be incognito even to the other people *on* the course. The less they knew about each other, the safer. Upon arrival, she was informed that from that moment forward, she was to be known only by an alias. She should forget Penny Williamson existed.

"So what is my code name?" she asked the officer who checked her in and handed over her new uniform, which comprised fatigues and ominously heavy-duty boots. "Am I allowed to choose one?"

She was not. She was informed that her code name would be "Bruna."

Twenty-Five

• • • • •

The training course might be being held in a requisitioned mansion house but this was to be no country house party. The morning after her arrival, Penny was shaken into wakefulness at five. Before breakfast, she joined her new colleagues—all but one were men—for a four-mile run around the manor house grounds. It had been a long time since Penny had to do a run, the ground was boggy from all the recent rain, and by the end of the third mile she was ready to go back to bed. Last to the finishing line, she barely had time to retie her bootlaces—they would not seem to stay put—before the recruits were instructed to line up at the start of an obstacle course.

"Here we go," said the other woman, who introduced herself as Francine. "I hope you don't bruise easily."

Penny watched as the first six candidates in their group—all at least a foot taller than she—attacked the course. It was considerably harder than anything she'd ever tackled at St. Mary's or during FANY basic training. And unlike at school, there was no point trying to get out of it by mouthing "monthlies" at the trainer.

"Bruna! Bruna!"

It took a nudge from one of the men to remind her that that was her new name.

"Isn't that you, sweetheart?"

Penny would soon come to learn that in this place, "sweetheart" was never meant as a term of affection.

That first morning was awful. Despite watching her new colleagues closely to see how they handled the course, as Penny approached each obstacle, her mind went completely blank. Even the simple rope swing, which should have been right up Penny's street, was difficult. The rope was wet and slippery and she couldn't get a proper grip. Her hands were soon covered in burns from the rain-sodden sisal. Her legs were still weak from the run, like cooked spaghetti. Why were her boots, which pinched and rubbed, so heavy? Penny seemed to spend a lot of time face down in freezing mud. Why was she even there? Could she ask to be sent back to London now?

"Don't even think that. You've been called to serve your beloved France." Penny was giving herself a pep talk when she was knocked off a six-feet-high wall by a real commando who pretty much landed on top of her. Face down in the freezing mud again.

But Penny could not let any height, depth, length, or weight get her sent back to FANY HQ. Being chosen for this assessment was the most exciting thing that had happened to Penny in her life. Thus she would climb, jump, dive, do whatever it took . . . Though every new obstacle looked as though it would kill her, she reasoned that it had not been designed to do so. She was not on enemy terrain. Not yet. She might get hurt. She might limp away covered in bruises—she was already covered in bruises—but they would fade. Even a broken bone would heal in time. Why would she have been sent to this place, if only to be killed off on the first day?

"*Toujours gai*," she muttered to herself as she threw herself at the rope swing one more time.

THOUGH IT SEEMED on many occasions as though she had reached the limits of her endurance, Penny stayed the course and was not sent back to London afterwards. Instead she was moved straight on to another training course at another country house. This time in Oxfordshire. There was more PT—endless PT—but now there was coding and telegraphy to master too.

Penny had to learn to use radio equipment—and know how to repair it—and get her Morse code up to speed. She'd previously been quite pleased with her coding rate of ten words per minute. Now she had to double that. She and Francine took it in turns to hold the stop-watch and monitor each other's pace and accuracy for hour after hour after hour. The Morse training was so intense that after a couple of days Penny found herself tapping out her thoughts as she tried to get to sleep.

Theoretical training was delivered entirely in French, reminding the candidates that once they were deployed behind enemy lines—as fully-fledged SOE "F Section" agents. The "F" was for France—their cover would depend on their being able to pass as locals. Trainers instructed the candidates in French slang and social etiquette. The students were also brought up to date with the current rules in occupied France. They could not risk being caught out by not knowing, for example, that it was now illegal to order alcohol on a Sunday or that French women were not permitted to have a cigarette ration. There were a great many things to learn.

Over the next few weeks, Penny perfected her French accent—modelled on the voice of her godmother, right down to the little intakes of breath she made at the end of each sentence. She decided she would use elements of Aunt Claudine's family history in her official back story too. It was important for a back story to feel real and thus including fragments of an agent's real story was useful.

Soon Penny's Morse speed was the fastest her telegraphy instructors had ever seen and while she would never be the quickest around the obstacle course, she had learned that taking just a couple of seconds to properly evaluate a situation before she tackled it could make all the difference between successfully jumping a gap between one wobbly platform and the next or landing on her bottom in the mud.

Meanwhile, there were other, more surprising, skills to master. Three times a week, Penny's cohort attended lectures on disguise, forgery, burglary, and house-breaking.

"Nice to have a trade to fall back on when we're done with the war," a fellow trainee quipped.

It was rumoured that some of the house-breaking trainers had actually been criminals before they were asked to lend their skills to the pursuit of victory.

There was weapons training too. Penny had grown up around guns—they were an essential part of country life—but she'd rarely been allowed to shoot. When her father went game-shooting, only her younger brother George was allowed to tag along, unless they were short of beaters. So this was new. She was gratified to discover she was good at it.

Penny was hurriedly trained in the use of several types of gun—both the guns she might be provided with by her handlers (though arming women in the field was still controversial) and the guns she might come across in the hands of the enemy. If she somehow managed to wrestle a Walther P-38 off a German officer, she had better know how to use it. Likewise the Flaubert pistols used by the French police. A whole afternoon was spent learning about the French police, and their more dangerous cousins the Milice, their ranking systems and how to recognise where they stood in it. In the occupied zone, certain of the French were just as much the enemy as the Germans now.

It wasn't long before Penny could strip a Sten gun as fast as anyone and fire four different makes of handgun with deadly accuracy. She easily convinced her trainers that she could handle herself in a gunfight, but what if she was without a weapon?

She was about to find out. Three months after that first strange meeting in the mansion block, Penny was on her way to Arisaig to spend several weeks devoted to guerrilla training, specialising in explosives, evasion, and silent killing.

Twenty-Six

• • • • •

On the first afternoon in Scotland, the instructor who would be leading the F Section candidates through their advanced training in unarmed combat and silent killing introduced himself as "Frank." He didn't look like a Frank, Penny thought. More like a Douglas. He was tall and fair with movie star looks. If a movie star hadn't been able to find the right doctor to reset his nose after a fight.

As Frank outlined the work that lay ahead of them, Penny was thrilled to hear he was going to be teaching them combat techniques based on the methods of Major Fairbairn. Frank claimed he had worked with Fairbairn in the Shanghai Municipal Police.

"My job is to send you all away from here with the skills of a ninja," Frank said. "Unfortunately, I have a matter of days rather than years and, looking at you lot, nothing like the right kind of raw material."

The male candidates shifted and grumbled. They didn't like the suggestion they weren't already the best of the best. Penny too stood a little straighter, determined to prove this Frank chap wrong.

"The first thing I want to impress upon you is how important it is to listen to me carefully," he said. "There is a fine line between practising your combat skills and accidentally committing murder. Not that I think any of you will master the techniques first time round but you never know. I want you to do everything with only half the force you'll use in the field. So, which one of you would like to be first up?"

Penny could have predicted the first volunteer. It was the trainee agent codenamed Jerome, an American. From the moment she met him,

Jerome had teased Penny mercilessly and not in an entirely friendly way. He seemed affronted to have to train alongside women. Now he stepped forward and stood in front of Frank, making himself large. He had a whole head in height on Frank. He was broader too. He was smiling widely and chewing gum, as though getting ready to fight off the advances of an optimistic twelve-year-old.

"I'd take that gum out if I were you," said Frank. "Don't want to choke."

Jerome continued to grin but tucked the gum behind his ear.

"OK, my friend," Frank began. "Come at me from the front and try to get me in a two-handed stranglehold."

"Try?" Jerome turned back towards the other candidates, playing to the audience. "Tell me when you're ready."

"I'm always ready," said Frank.

Jerome rushed at Frank with both hands out in front of him. Before anyone had a chance to draw breath, Jerome was on the floor.

Frank addressed the others. "If someone is coming at you from the front like that, with their hands out, they're telegraphing their intentions and they're already unbalanced. All you have to do is tip them that tiny bit further."

Jerome was still on the floor.

"Nice try," said Frank.

Jerome wasn't grinning anymore.

One by one, the trainees did their worst and Frank planted every single one of them on their backsides in the dirt. There was something about the spectacle of one man fighting off so many others as though they were gnats that made the male trainees eager to take their turn and be the one to reset the balance. It was a while before Penny found her way to the front of the queue.

"I hear you already have some experience in Defendu, Agent Bruna," Frank joked. "Remind me not to ask you to the theatre."

"I don't think being able to defend oneself is a laughing matter," said Penny.

"Of course not. Though perhaps one ought to be more discerning when it comes to telling the difference between a deadly enemy and an amorous army man."

"Is there a difference?" Penny asked. "For a woman?"

Frank had no answer for that.

Penny waited for her instructions.

"OK," said Frank. "I'm going to come at you from behind and I want you to deflect me. Are you ready?"

"Always ready," she said, parroting his own words. She turned her back on him and pretended to be adjusting a pair of imaginary gloves to add a bit of verisimilitude to the scenario.

"Oooof!"

Though Frank had spoken softly, he did not come at her softly at all. He tackled Penny with every bit as much speed and power as he had tackled the boys. Penny was on the floor before she could blink. There wasn't any time for her to adopt a defensive stance. Definitely no time to come up with a counter-attack. This was very different from training with George and the evacuees in the garden back at home.

"Bastard," she muttered.

While Frank was turning to explain her mistakes to the others——"Feet too close together. Not *ladylike* to stand like this, I know, but you've got to . . ."——Penny saw red. Still on the ground, she hooked her right foot through Frank's open legs and around his right ankle, before yanking as hard as she could.

Frank, caught totally by surprise, lurched forward. Penny followed up by using her left foot to kick him in the arse. He landed on his knees. While he was down, Penny quickly scrambled to her feet and adopted a pugilist's stance.

"Always ready," she said. The other trainees cheered.

Standing up again, Frank conceded the point. "And that's the kind of spirit you'll need to demonstrate in the field."

AS THE MORNING went on, all the trainees stayed on their feet for longer. Frank introduced the scenarios, demonstrated on a brave volunteer, then sent them away to practise in pairs. After Francine, the only other female trainee, was paired with one of the men, Penny was left alone. None of the men wanted to be paired with the girl who had brought Frank down, lest she leave them similarly red-faced.

So Penny had to practise with Frank himself. He continued to make no concessions to her relative size. The enemy wouldn't, after all. Every tackle was as hard as the first one, forcing her to put every ounce of her weight behind her punches and her kicks. By lunchtime, she knew that beneath her green overalls, she must be black and blue. *Thank goodness*, she thought, when Frank told the class that "silent killing"—that afternoon's topic—required less brute force and more cunning.

"I think you'll be rather good at it," Frank told her.

AFTER LUNCH, THEY were given a presentation on pressure points and shown exactly where to apply one's fingers to cause someone to black out within seconds. Penny watched intently, marvelling at the fragility of the human body and how easily a life could be snuffed out. How quietly.

Later that same afternoon they were introduced to a new weapon. Designed by W.E. Fairbairn himself, with his colleague Eric Sykes, the double-bladed Fairbairn-Sykes fighting knife was the ultimate commando tool. It was easy to wield, hard to drop unintentionally. It could be used to stab or slice. It could break the skin with only the slightest pressure . . .

"Right, silent killing," Frank continued as most of the trainees tested their new blades on their thumbs and tried not to let on that they'd cut themselves. "So called because the trick is to cut the windpipe so your victim can't draw breath to scream."

"Sounds good," said Jerome.

"It shouldn't sound of anything at all."

Penny paid closer attention to Frank's instructions now than she had ever paid to anything in her life. Her old teachers at St. Mary's would not have recognised her in such an attentive mood. This time, when Frank called for volunteers, they were in short supply. There was something about the glittering blade of the F-S knife that unleashed a primeval anxiety.

"Agent Bruna?" Frank called Penny to the front. "If I may?"

Penny was every bit as nervous as the men who stepped back to let her be first but she would not let them know it. She stood in front of Frank with her feet apart and braced. Taking her by the elbow, he quickly whipped her round, as if in a dance move, so that her back was against his chest and her neck encircled by his elbow. He tipped her head back and brought his sheathed blade to her throat.

"Here." He pointed with the tip to the best place to cut.

He let Penny go. Shaky with shock and relief, she staggered back to the line-up.

"Hang on," said Frank. "It's your turn."

"My turn?"

"To try to kill me."

To the amusement of the other trainees, Frank pulled a lipstick out of his pocket and used it to swipe colour along both sides of the leather sheath of his knife. "So you can see your mark." Then he handed the blade to Penny.

"Do your worst, sweetheart."

"Sweetheart?"

Frank turned his back on Penny and went to walk away. Flooded with anger and adrenaline, Penny went after him. In two steps, she was on his back like an angry cat. She pulled his hair to jerk his head back and used the sheathed knife to draw a line across his neck. When she let him go, he crumpled to the ground in such a way that when Penny rolled him over and saw the slash of red across his bristly throat, for a moment she genuinely believed she had killed him.

"Bloody hell," murmured one of the other candidates. The rest were silent until, at last, Frank sat up, coughing.

"Not bad," he said. "Not bad."

FRANK JOINED THE candidates for dinner that evening. Everyone wanted to be near him. They all wanted to hear his stories of working with the great man Fairbairn. They all wanted to know how often Frank had had to use his silent killing methods in the field.

"I think we all know it's not in good taste to keep a tally," he said, which Penny suspected was calculated to make his awed trainees sure the number must be in the hundreds.

Penny tried not to stare at Frank. She pretended to be interested in the conversation at her end of the table. However, whenever Penny allowed herself to glance in Frank's direction, she always found he was looking back at her. Usually, they both looked away quickly, but once—one glorious time—he sent her a small smile.

"Come on, Frank," said one of the men, after much wine had been drunk. "Tell us how we did today. Tell us which one of us you think is going to make the best agent."

"I have no doubt that every one of you has what it takes," Frank said diplomatically. He was doing his best not to be drawn.

"But some of us are ready to go hand-to-hand with the Nazi bastards, eh?" the candidate persisted. "While some of us should just stick to fiddling about on the radio." That brought a laugh from the men at Frank's end of the table. The other female candidate, Francine, rolled her eyes for Penny's amusement.

"Well, I'll tell you one character trait that's of no use in the field whatsoever," Frank said. "And that's arrogance; a trait some of you have by the bucketload. All of you still have a lot to learn before you come anywhere near the skill of the agents already in France."

There was grumbling at the mild ticking off.

"But Frank," said Jerome. "You must have your ideas. Come on. Just one name. I've got money riding on it."

So the men were running a sweepstake. The women had not been asked to place their bets.

"OK," said Frank. "If you really want to know."

The men hammered on the table. They did.

Frank shook his head, but right afterwards he looked straight at Penny and everybody knew.

ON THE WAY back across the courtyard to the dormitories, two of the male candidates jumped Penny and Francine from behind. Francine shrieked, struggled and was quickly released, but the man who had hold of Penny did not let her go so easily. Instead, he pressed his elbow harder and harder against her throat. It was Jerome. Of course it was.

"Teacher's pet," he hissed in her ear.

Penny stamped down hard on his instep with the heel of her boot. Howling with indignation, Jerome loosened his grip and hopped away swearing.

"Bastards," said Francine. "Who needs the Germans when we've got that lot on our side. Are you hurt?" she asked Penny.

"Not as badly as Jerome's ego must be."

After Francine went to bed, anticipating another day on the assault course, Penny remained outside alone. She needed a cigarette. She found a quiet place well away from the main house, sat down in the shelter of a wall, and gazed out into the darkness until her eyes adapted and the shadowy hulks of the mountains became just visible in the gloom.

Penny blew smoke rings, suddenly remembering that soldier she'd met on the train back when she was still a schoolgirl. He'd blown excellent smoke rings. What happened to him, she wondered? She couldn't remember his name. Had he ever told her?

She thought about Josephine, down in Plymouth working in the Western Approaches plotting room and going to parties on submarines. It sounded like more fun than her former job at WRNS HQ. She thought of their father still overseas. When would he next be home? Would this war be over before George had to sign up and fight? Though she knew her little brother probably relished the prospect as much as she once had, she very much hoped that George would never have to go to the front line.

Hearing the rustle of someone approaching, Penny sank back into the shadows, hoping she wouldn't be noticed. Too late. The glowing tip of her cigarette gave her away. She'd extinguished it slightly too slowly.

"Mind if I join you?"

It was Frank.

Penny scooched along the stone bench. Frank tapped a couple of cigarettes out of his packet of Players and handed one to her.

"I saw what happened with Jerome. I don't think I made you very popular with your classmates."

"I don't think I was very popular to begin with," Penny said. "I don't understand it. We're all fighting for the same cause, aren't we?"

"Let's hope so. Need a light?"

Frank didn't have a lighter. He had an old-fashioned silver matchbox, like the one Penny's grandfather carried. In the glow of the match he struck against it, Penny saw that it was engraved.

"Can I have a look?" she asked.

"Of course." He handed it over. It was inscribed with a verse from a poem.

In the fell clutch of circumstance,
I have not winced nor cried aloud.
Under the bludgeonings of chance
My head is bloody, but unbowed.

"'Invictus,'" Penny said.

"You know it?"

"Learned it by heart for a school poetry competition. I didn't do very well. Too much *passion* in my delivery."

Frank snorted at that.

"But why didn't you have the last few lines?" Penny asked. "Much more uplifting."

"I don't know. I think this is a better verse for our line of work, don't you?"

The fact that he called it "*our* line of work" gave Penny a little frisson of pleasure.

"You have a point," she said. "It does speak of perseverance." She nodded to herself. She hoped she'd proved she could persevere. "You know the FANY motto is 'Arduis Invicta'?"

"In difficulties unconquered," Frank nodded.

"That's right. Kill many people with this?" Penny asked, as she handed the matchbox back. Frank had referenced Fairbairn's "Matchbox Attack" that morning.

Frank just laughed. "Why do you want to do this, Bruna?" he asked then. "You're so young."

"It's better than being stuck in an office at FANY HQ."

"But do you have any idea what you're letting yourself in for? I mean, really? It's not all Mata Hari romance, you know."

"So everyone keeps telling me."

"Well, I'll tell you again. It's not too late to go back to the FANY and have a nice war. Then when it's all over, you could meet a nice fella, get married, have some children . . ."

"Boring."

"So's being dead. Do you know the life expectancy of an F Section agent in the field? Do you know how many young things like you I've waved off to their deaths?"

"I don't. How many?"

Frank didn't tell her. He took another drag on his cigarette.

"It will change you forever, going to France," he said. "If you have to kill someone, you'll never be the same again. You'll lose your innocence."

"Who says I'm innocent?"

"Come on." Frank laughed. "I'm serious. When you end someone's life, you kill a part of yourself too. You stop trusting the world. Every time you look at yourself in the mirror, you're looking into the eyes of a murderer. Do you want that?"

"We're at war. The rules are different."

"I'm not sure the heart knows."

"I will do my best not to kill or be killed. How's that?" Penny said, giving him the Brownie guide salute.

"You are the best I've ever trained." He said it out loud now. "You're bright, you're fast, you're as dangerous as a Jack Russell after a rat . . ."

Penny laughed. "Then if anyone can come back from France alive, it's me. And when I do and this war is over, you can buy me a drink so I can say 'I told you so.'"

He looked at her, saying nothing, for what felt like a very long time. Then he gently put his combat-roughened hand to the side of her face.

"You're something else," he told her.

Was this a seduction? Penny straightened up and inched away from him along the stone bench. The trainees had been warned that under no circumstances should they allow themselves to become too close to the people they worked alongside. Emotional attachments might cloud their judgement at a time when it was vital to be clear-headed. And they could never be sure that their colleagues were one hundred per cent trustworthy. The French Resistance had been infiltrated by German spies in exactly this way.

"Is this a test?" Penny asked, as Frank moved closer and cradled her face in both his hands. "I mean, are you trying to see how easily I give in to temptation?"

Frank shook his head and instead of clarifying anything in words, he brushed his lips against hers.

"You are something else," he said again.

FRANK'S ATTENTIONS WERE not a test. Penny passed her guerrilla training with flying colours ("best in her cohort," Frank wrote on the report she didn't see). She survived a three-night field exercise, hiding out in the mountains with only sheep for company. There was uproar when she made it back to base, having evaded capture by her trainers and the local police, who'd been briefed to bring her in, with a lamb trotting along beside her on a lead fashioned out of her belt. For the rest of the course, she was known as Little Bo Peep, but the majority of her colleagues agreed that managing to evade detection with a sheep in tow boded bloody well for Penny's chances of being able to smuggle herself past the Gestapo.

Her performance in the post-exercise debrief, intended to mimic the kind of questioning and torture she might expect from the Gestapo were she ever captured, was exemplary. She set a course record for endurance during an exercise where her head was repeatedly dunked in a bucket of freezing cold water. No matter what approach the trainers who had been sent to break her tried, she never wavered from the cover story she had worked so hard to learn by heart. Yes, she cried when the torture was over, but so did *all* of the men. When one of them asked how she did it, she told him, "I just kept thinking of that line from 'Invictus.' 'Bloody, but unbowed.'"

Bloodied, bruised, and tempered by fire, Penny was ready at last.

Twenty-Seven

• • • • •

1949

More than six years had passed since Penny said goodbye to Frank in Arisaig. Throughout that time she'd been strangely certain they would meet again, but she had not for one moment expected that their grand reunion would take place in an East End pawn shop.

"Bruna?" Frank blinked theatrically, as though he couldn't believe his eyes. He wasn't the only one.

"Frank," Penny stuttered. There was no point putting on a foreign accent now.

"Well, isn't this a nice surprise. You're the last person I expected to see today. And what a getup!" Frank said, referring to her Buckingham Palace outfit. "I'd never have believed you'd scrub up so well. You look almost presentable."

"Get lost," said Penny.

"Lovely to see you too," Frank rejoined. Penny presented her cheek so he could kiss her hello. When he got close enough, he hissed in her ear, "What on earth are you doing in this place?"

"I've got a bracelet to sell," Penny told him. "It was given to me by an admirer."

Frank glanced at the bracelet glittering on the counter.

"Nice admirer. You should engineer a proposal at once."

"How much will you give me?" Penny addressed the pawn shop owner again.

The man quoted a price. It was enough to rent a flat big enough for a family of three in Manchester for a year. Penny was about to accept it just so she could get out of there when Frank interrupted.

"I think the lady would like a moment or two to think about your offer," he said, picking the bracelet up and dropping it into Penny's palm. "Come on." Frank put his hand on Penny's elbow and guided her back onto the street.

"What do you think you're doing?" Penny protested once they were outside. "I can handle myself, thank you very much."

"Clearly you can't. I can see from half a mile away that you're hawking a serious piece of jewellery there and that old bastard was going to rip you off." Frank prised the bracelet from Penny's fist and looked at it more closely. He whistled through his teeth. "This beau of yours must be smitten."

Penny snatched the bracelet back. "He is. Thank you very much."

"Unlucky guy, since he clearly can't mean that much to you if you're flogging his gifts to one of the city's lowest scumbags. Or have you hit upon hard times? You don't look as though you have."

"I don't have to tell you anything."

"Of course not. Do you think your beau would object if I took you for a coffee?"

"I don't have time."

"Please, Bruna. I've only just found you. I can't let you disappear again."

TRUTH WAS, PENNY didn't want to let Frank disappear again either, not that she would tell him that. The surprise of seeing him in such an incongruous setting—and in a policeman's uniform at that—was giving way to something else. She wanted to throw herself at him, hitting his chest with her fists and screaming out her anger, before sinking into his arms and staying there all night. It took an enormous effort to walk calmly alongside him to the café of his choice as though he meant no more to her than the pawn shop owner did.

The proprietor of the café greeted Frank warmly. She already knew his order. Penny asked for an espresso. When Frank looked surprised, she told him, "Algiers then Southern Italy. Bari. But you probably knew that. And you? The police, obviously . . ."

"It's where I started out."

"Of course. Did you get married?"

"I was married when you met me."

Penny didn't blink. "Children?"

"One of each."

"Well, good for you," she said, like she was talking to one of her aunt Helena's "nice young men."

"And what about you?" Frank asked. "What are you doing now?"

"Social work. Supporting returned POWs."

"And are you enjoying it?"

"I wouldn't say it's enjoyable, seeing what a mess the war made of so many ordinary lives, but I like to feel I'm doing my bit."

Penny wished she'd phrased it differently. Did she sound as pompous to Frank as she did to her own ears?

"You always were a good person," Frank said simply.

This was agony. The coffee arrived. Frank added three sugars to his. He offered Penny the sugar bowl.

"Sweet enough as I am," she said. Then she knocked the coffee back like it was a shot of grappa. She wished she could have a shot of grappa. She felt the need to look tougher than she was feeling in the presence of the man who'd taken her virginity and her heart. He was married . . .

Frank reached for her hand across the table.

"Don't," she said. "You've got a wife. You didn't say."

"You didn't ask."

"*And* you didn't look for me after the war ended."

"You didn't look for *me*."

"I didn't know your real name, did I? You could have found mine out."

"You're crediting me with much more authority than I had. But what is it? Your name?"

"Penny Williamson. And you?"

"I'm really Frank. Frank Smith."

"Sounds made up."

With her coffee gone, Penny made her excuses but Frank would not let her go. As she tried to walk by him, he grabbed her wrist. She could have escaped the hold in a second, using the techniques Frank himself had taught her, but she didn't. As though his touch had taken all the strength from her, she sat back down.

They were still there when the café owner started putting chairs on tables to mark the end of the day. And by the time they parted, they had agreed to meet again. She'd told him the truth about how she came by the bracelet eventually. Penny could never lie to Frank. Never. When he looked at her with the big blue eyes that she remembered so well, it was as though he was shining a torch straight into her mind. If only she could have mustered the mental strength she had on the training course.

"How the hell do you steal a bracelet like that accidentally?" Frank asked. "And why?"

"I wanted to get some cash. Not for me. For a family I know. In Manchester. They were in Singapore. They spent three years in a camp and now they're living in one room. The daughter reminds me of . . ."

"You?"

"Yes. I suppose she does." Penny told Frank about Jinx, the brave teenage girl she'd described to Josephine.

"She deserves more help. It's ridiculous that there is so much money swilling around this country yet there are people who can barely afford to keep a roof over their heads. It isn't right, Frank."

"And you want to set it right. Like Robin Hood."

"Don't laugh at me."

"I would never laugh at you. Not for your dear, kind heart. But if you're going to lead a life of crime, you need to know what you're doing and who you can trust. For a start, if you're going to steal anything that has a name as big as Devrey stamped on the back of it, you need to break it up. Or sell it to someone who can."

"I don't know anybody like that."

"Luckily, I do. I'll sort it out. But it has to be a one-off. You've got to promise me that."

Penny promised.

"In the meantime, I'll give you an advance for your little friend Jinx," Frank said, pulling a roll of cash from his pocket. "Sounds like she deserves a treat."

"I didn't know the police were so well paid," said Penny.

"They're not."

Twenty-Eight

• • • • •

Three days later, Penny arrived at the grotty boarding house where Jinx and her family were sharing a bedroom, laden with shopping bags containing two new school uniforms, a pencil case full of sharp pencils, assorted toiletries, a coat for Jinx's little brother, and a box of Turkish delight that she'd picked up at Fortnum's on a whim.

Jinx's mother Dorothy burst into grateful tears as Penny handed over the bounty and Jinx said all the right words when she tried on her new blazer, but while her mother was busy making tea, Jinx asked Penny, "Where has all this come from?"

"I had some birthday money," Penny lied.

"Blimey. You must have a posh family. Why didn't you get yourself something nice?"

"I wanted to treat you instead."

"Why?"

"Didn't anybody ever tell you not to look a gift horse in the mouth?"

"Someone will always have to pay for a free lunch," said Jinx.

Penny knuckled Jinx in the cheek. "I'll take my reward in heaven, thanks."

Jinx smiled at last. She took the blazer off again and sat with it folded across her lap, occasionally stroking it as though it were a living creature. "I'll look after it," she promised.

Then Dorothy was back with the tea. "Did Jinx tell you about her exam results, Penny? Top of her class in English and in French, she was."

It was worth it, having taken such a big risk at Devrey, to see Jinx in the blazer that would stop her getting picked on at school; to see her little brother Eddy filling his cheeks with Turkish delight like he was a hamster; to see their mother Dorothy so happy she looked like the beautiful young woman she'd been in the family photograph she had kept with her through those awful years in the camps. Penny had had to lie some more to persuade Dorothy to accept the rest of the advance Frank had given her but, "It's a one-off," Penny reminded herself as she caught the bus back to her own flat.

But of course it was not a one-off. After a meeting in a grubby hotel not far from the pawn shop, where Frank handed over the rest of the cash for the bracelet, they began an affair. And it wasn't just to each other that they became addicted.

Penny's work in Manchester had convinced her that a redistribution of wealth was what Britain needed, and she wanted to make that happen in her own small and very direct way. People's lives could be transformed with sums of money that would seem insignificant to the kind of people who shopped for jewellery on Bond Street. Added to that, Penny soon realised that dressing up to rob jewellery stores gave her a kick she hadn't felt since SOE finishing school. She loved to create a new persona for each lift, falling back on the disguise and distraction skills she'd learned with F Section. What an excellent education for this new criminal life that had turned out to be.

Whenever she turned up to their hotel rendezvous with another bracelet or a diamond ring or a pair of sapphire earrings to be turned into cash that she could drip-feed to various charities, Frank would tell her that this really had to be the last time. She had to stop before she got herself caught. But he would always find a way to dispose of the jewellery for her. If there's one thing a policeman has, it's contacts in the criminal world. And soon those contacts were getting curious. Who was Frank's daring jewel thief?

Frank always had money trouble. A policeman's salary wasn't riches and his wife—"In name only but she'll take the kids if I go"—had expensive tastes. Penny's talents offered him a solution. To begin with Penny had just lifted whatever she could, now Frank had her steal to order for his mysterious clients. They started travelling together to Europe's jewellery capitals, and by 1960 they'd expanded their patch to include the United

States. New York. Las Vegas. Penny's chameleon-like ability to blend in with the wealthiest citizens in any of their target cities meant that she could get away with her daring crimes anywhere. Frank provided false papers, using old SOE contacts, who'd returned to forgery for profit now that their skill in faking documents was no longer needed for nobler aims. Penny soon had five passports: British, American, French, German, and Dutch. In her French passport, she was Bruna Declerc, in a nod to her old Parisian friend, Gilbert, and his termagant of a mother.

When they were on a job, Frank would check out the target but it was always Penny who did the steal. Her MO was to strike at lunchtime, which was when the high-end stores they targeted were most likely to be lightly-staffed. Once she was inside, her method had hardly changed since the day she accidentally stole that green glass bracelet from Galeries Lafayette.

Penny relied on the art of distraction, chatting amiably to the assistant she'd chosen as her mark while they laid out their riches before her. She learned that, for insurance purposes, they were not supposed to have more than five items out on the counter at any one time, but Penny could always persuade them to break that rule. The more jewels they laid out the better. Ideally, Penny liked to see at least ten items on the velvet pad. Dazzling. Confusing. Like the three-card tricksters who hung around train stations, Penny knew how to draw a sales assistant's eye away from what was going on right under his or her nose. A favourite ruse was to ask the assistant to step around the counter to examine Penny's eye for an imaginary speck of dust. The time it took for the assistant to get back to their position was usually long enough for Penny to pull an elegant glove over a purloined ring.

Having made the steal, it was straight to the getaway. Frank would have a car waiting to take Penny and her haul straight to the nearest airport or international train station. The important thing was to get over a border and fast. They'd meet up again somewhere safe.

Sometimes Frank had Penny try out her personas in private but he liked it best when she was herself—the upper-class English girl he'd met at the F Section training camp—just as Penny liked it best when she could be herself with him.

• • •

THE DAYS WERE long but the years were short and soon almost fifteen years had passed since Penny re-encountered Frank in the pawn shop. During that time, her sister Josephine had married Gerald Naiswell, the submariner she'd met in Plymouth in '43. He'd become a diplomat and his work had taken them all over the world. Their little brother George had long since grown up. He'd taken over the family cardboard business, married a suitable girl named Serena, and produced an heir, Charles, who was the apple of everyone's eye.

Penny's siblings knew better than to ask about her marital prospects, and perhaps even envied her carefree life (though of course they didn't know the half of it), but sometimes Penny couldn't help but wish she and Frank were on the path to a long and happy old age together. Their passion for one another had not dimmed but after all those years, Frank was still very much married and showed no sign of changing that arrangement. His wife was "vulnerable," he said. He did not know what she would do if he left, though he assured Penny that the marriage was over in all but name.

Frank's heart belonged entirely to Penny. He swore it. His marriage became one of those things they just didn't talk about, like the night in 1943—the disastrous night that had left Penny so ashamed, she had never spoken about it with anyone. They might have carried on like that forever had Penny not broken the silence in the summer of '64.

Twenty-Nine

. . . . .

Paris, 2022

Archie woke from his nap much later than planned. There really wasn't time to read emails before he changed into his dinner jacket for the party at Stéphane's auction house—not if he was going to have to make sure the sisters were ready too—but when he saw he had another message from the DNA testing site in his inbox, he simply knew he had to look.

While he'd been asleep, Archie's newly-discovered cousin had responded to his request for further information. Archie clicked through, eager to find out more. Was this the moment he discovered he was descended from a highly decorated GI on his mother's side? Wouldn't that be a piece of news to take to the party?

Dear Archie. It's great to be in touch with you. So, it seems that you and I are cousins. My name is Madeleine Scott-Learmonth. My friends call me Maddie for short. I decided to get my DNA tested to help find some missing branches on my family tree. On my mother's side, we go all the way back to Champlain. On my father's side, it's a different story. The family tree stops with him. Dad was adopted as an infant in the spring of 1940. His parents—my great-grandparents—weren't ever going to tell him, but after they died there was the usual ugly family inheritance quarrel and that's when his sister, their biological daughter, told him the truth: that he was in fact the illegitimate baby of a housemaid on a big estate in Scotland called Grey Towers. Her name was Connie Shearer.

I'm hoping her name or the name of the estate will mean something to you, since I see you're based in the UK. Are you from Scotland? Is Connie Shearer already in your family tree? Do you have your tree mapped out at all yet? I'd love to work out where we interconnect and share the information I have. Write back soon! Best wishes, Maddie

What? This was not what Archie had expected at all. He read the email again. By Grey Towers, she had to mean the estate in Scotland that had belonged to the Williamson family for generations (until it had to be sold for inheritance tax). Of course he knew it. But Connie Shearer? He'd never heard of her. Or had he?

A faint memory tickled the back of Archie's mind.

He did not want to be late for Stéphane's party, but he was down the rabbit hole now. Just ten minutes, he promised himself.

On Archie's iPhone, he had a folder of photographs of Grey Towers, that he'd taken when he was last there a couple of years previously. He'd been on a fishing trip nearby with the sisters—not that they did much fishing anymore. They preferred to direct from their camping chairs while sipping from flasks filled with the *cocktail du jour*. Josephine had felt unwell the day Archie suggested a visit to the family seat, but Penny had gone with him to the old pile. Inside the walled compound was a private chapel and a graveyard where generations of Williamsons were buried. Around the edge of the graveyard a handful of loyal servants were laid to rest too, alongside the Williamsons' most treasured working dogs.

Opening the file, Archie quickly found the photographs he'd taken that day and, on a hunch, enlarged a picture of one stone in the graveyard in particular. It was the youngest stone in the small, sad collection representing Grey Towers' loyal staff.

"Well, blimey," Archie said to himself. The name on the stone was Connie Shearer. No wonder it rang a bell.

On that last visit to Grey Towers, Archie had asked about the stone and Penny told him that, though she had been sent away from the house "under a cloud, regarding who knows what," in death Connie had been allowed back into the fold, to be interred next to her own grandparents and father, who had all been in service at the big grey house. Her headstone was simple—made from granite to match the surrounding buildings—but it carried her name, her dates and the legend "Ambulance driver. Killed in the Blitz," as per her mother's request.

Now Archie remembered the very first time he'd seen that headstone, when he was at Grey Towers with his parents in 1987 and—though he was a very precocious reader at six and a half years old—he'd had to ask his father, "What does Blitz mean?" It was the dates that had really interested him as a child. Connie was just eighteen years old when she died. At six and a half, Archie didn't understand how someone could have died so young.

Oh dear. It could only mean one thing. None of this new information had anything to do with his mother's side of the family. With a jolt, Archie realised that he had inadvertently uncovered a mystery entirely other than the one he had intended to solve. The only possible explanation for the DNA match between Archie and Maddie Scott-Learmonth was that Connie Shearer, the Grey Towers housemaid, had been made pregnant by one of the Williamson men. But which one? His great-great-grandfather? Surely he'd have been much too old even in 1940. His great-grandfather Christopher, the war hero? No. No way. It was too awful. Archie's great-aunts were devoted to the memory of their father, how could he possibly tell them what he'd discovered? He decided that for the moment he simply wouldn't. Neither would he write back to Maddie with his thoughts. Not yet. He would have to sit on this news and think about it. The last thing he had expected when he took that DNA test was that he would discover a philanderer in the family. Weren't his ancestors supposed to be staunch Presbyterians?

Archie didn't know why the idea of Connie Shearer's illegitimate child upset him so much, except that he had always liked to think of the Williamsons as being a cut above. He wanted to come from a line of upstanding heroes, not common adulterers.

It was 6:20. There was no time to investigate further now. He called Josephine's room to make sure she was up and dressed. Then Penny.

"We're doing what, dear?" she asked.

"We're going to that party at Brice-Petitjean. With Stéphane?"

"Oh yes. Of course we are. You told me. And what time?"

"Now," Archie said. "Get your glad-rags on."

• • •

HALF AN HOUR later, the three were together again in the hotel lobby. Josephine had changed back into her beloved navy-blue trouser suit. Penny was in brown. The dress code for the party was black tie but the sisters had reached an age that exempted them from most conventions, including having to wear silly frocks.

"But you both have to wear your new medals tonight," Archie told them.

"These things are ridiculous," said Penny, as Archie pinned hers in place. "I'm sure we could use them to pick up satellite TV."

"You should wear them with pride," said Archie. "There's going to be lots of incredible jewellery at the auction house tonight, but in my opinion, there are no diamonds on earth as beautiful as a medal for courage and bravery."

"Or for living longer than anyone else who was there," Josephine added.

"Shush," said Archie. "I am very proud of you both."

Archie asked the doorman at The Maritime to summon a taxi, leaving him with just enough time to check that his great-aunts were really ready—"No one needs to spend a penny? Are you sure?"—and that he himself was set for the night ahead. Wallet, phone, Penny's old lucky matchbox; now his. It felt good to have that matchbox in his pocket. It was the perfect accessory for the urbane art dealer. He imagined himself elegantly offering a handsome man a light. If only anyone he knew still smoked. He glanced at himself in the mirrored wall of the lobby and smoothed down his hair. In less than half an hour he'd see Stéphane again.

"Please don't ask any embarrassing questions," he begged his aunts as he bundled them into the car.

Thirty

. . . . .

Arlene was disappointed not to be able to go to the auction house party with Archie and the sisters, but really what could she do? She knew that there was no one else on hand who could handle Davina Mackenzie or her temperamental wheelchair and Arlene was too good a person to leave even an old harridan like Davina in the lurch. Plus, Arlene's boss at the care agency had said she would make sure it was very much worth her while.

But though she was very glad she'd attended the *Légion d'honneur* ceremony, it was the glamorous soiree at Brice-Petitjean that had really captured Arlene's imagination when Archie first proposed the trip. She'd been so looking forward to it. It wasn't often she was invited to something that required the guests to dress in black tie. In fact, she'd never been invited to a black tie event in her life. She only knew what the dress code meant because it was one of the many things Davina Mackenzie had been shocked to discover Arlene didn't know when she started working for her.

"Does it just mean the men have to wear a black neck tie?" she'd asked tentatively.

"For goodness' sake, Arlene. It means the gentlemen have to wear a dinner jacket with a dicky bow or what Americans call a 'tux.' For ladies, formal dresses. How do you not know that?"

"I grew up on a farm in the Karoo," Arlene reminded Davina. "We don't exactly dress for dinner."

"Don't people read there either?" Davina had barked.

It was comments like that which had led Arlene to ask the care agency to find her a placement with another, kinder, softer, altogether nicer old lady: the type of grandma you saw in Hollywood films—apple-cheeked and always smiling. Davina was furious to hear that Arlene was moving on. That's when Arlene had decided that telling Davina she was emigrating to Jamaica was her only hope of making a graceful exit.

"It's not that I want to leave . . ." she'd promised, with her fingers crossed behind her back.

Arlene was glad to get away but over the years that followed, she had to admit she'd found herself in several situations where the arcane knowledge Davina had forced down her neck was almost useful. She was pleased that she didn't have to ask Archie what the dress code for the Brice-Petitjean reception meant. Likewise, she felt quite chuffed she'd been able to tell the various different types of wine glasses apart at the veterans' lunch. She could even read a bit of French, thanks to Davina's—and later the sisters'—insistence on throwing the odd French phrase into their speech. Usually when they were being rude about someone within earshot, Arlene had noted. Though if they were being *really* rude, Archie had explained, the Williamson sisters used Morse.

Arlene tapped out Morse for "cow" on her own knee as she waited for Davina to finish a telephone call to her son, so that she could wheel her down to dinner. It made her feel slightly better about the fact that the long burgundy evening dress she had made for the Brice-Petitjean function would remain unworn.

"Yes, yes," Davina snapped at her youngest child—who had just turned seventy-five, though you wouldn't know it from the way she spoke to him. "Well, it really is most unsatisfactory. Tell the agency that they shouldn't be employing such weaklings."

She was referring to poor Hazel, who was still recovering from her faint in her hotel room. Arlene couldn't blame Hazel for making the most of her doctor-ordered rest.

"Useless child." Davina put the phone down without saying goodbye to her "boy," who had been a high-court judge prior to his retirement.

"Ready," she said to Arlene. "Let's go."

She blew a quick blast on her boatswain's whistle for good measure.

• • •

FORTUNATELY, SISTER EUGENIA was a peach. If Davina seemed to think that having Arlene step in to take over from her carer was her due, Sister Eugenia couldn't stop thanking Arlene for rescuing their long-planned evening out.

"It would have been such a pity for dear Davina to have to stay at the hotel and eat room service," Sister Eugenia said. "Who knows when we'll be back in the City Of Light? Well, probably never, let's face it—I am 98 and she is 101—though the Lord does move in mysterious ways. There's a nun somewhere here in France who has made it to 118, you know. Apparently the secret of her longevity is port and chocolate."

"And prayer?" Sister Margaret Ann suggested.

"Oh yes. I expect that had an effect too."

"Where are we going this evening?" Arlene asked.

Sister Margaret Ann had managed to get a table for four at a pop-up restaurant near the Bourse.

"It's called Chez Mickey and it's the hottest ticket in town," Sister Eugenia said proudly.

"I prayed for a dinner slot," explained Sister Margaret Ann when Arlene congratulated her on the coup. "And they had a cancellation."

"God must think we deserve a treat," said Sister Eugenia.

"Well, let's just hope this 'pop-up' has a proper kitchen where they can cook some proper food," said Davina. "I have had indigestion all afternoon. Lunch was distinctly sub par."

"Oh, I rather liked it. Anyway we looked at the reviews for tonight's place online," said Sister Eugenia. "Five stars all the way."

"In my experience, the sort of people who leave reviews online should not always be allowed access to computers," was Davina's reply.

At the restaurant, Sister Eugenia insisted they all have a cocktail. She had the barman come around the bar and crouch next to her in her wheelchair so she could tell him how to make a perfect French 75, 1930s style: lemon and sugar, mixed in a shaker, with a jigger of gin, topped with brut champagne and a lemon peel twist.

"My father's favourite drink," she explained to the others. "He operated a *soixante-quinze* during the Great War. The *soixante-quinze* was the gun that won the war, you know. Well, that one . . . The first world one. Goodness, there have been so many since."

Davina Mackenzie asked for a "stengah."

The young barman had never heard of one of those.

"Equal parts Scotch and soda, young man. From 'setengah,' the Malay word for 'half' for goodness' sake," Davina put him right.

"We used to drink those when we went to parties on submarines," said Sister Eugenia. "Though the ratio of scotch to soda wasn't always exactly equal. There was also a cocktail called a sinker. I have no idea what was in it but more than one and you were definitely sunk."

"You've been to a party on a submarine?" Arlene asked.

"Lots of them. When I was stationed in Belfast the submariners had the very best parties. They were simply fabulous. I think perhaps it's something to do with spending all that time underwater. The moment they docked, they wanted to live it up. They would send for all the local off-duty Wrens and we'd put on our finest dresses and head down to the dock. The dinners were excellent, because they always had rabbits."

"Rabbits?" Arlene frowned.

"Not fluffy ones, dear. 'Rabbits' was navy slang for illicit goods like alcohol and off-ration meat. They'd pick it up from across the border in the Republic of Ireland. Oh! It was such a treat. And the games were hilarious. On one sub they played 'messroom skittles,' which involved clearing the dining table so that the crew could take it in turns to slide each other down the table to knock over the empty bottles placed at one end. It seemed like an especially dangerous game to play in such close quarters but it was very popular. I remember a rating called Terry who everyone wanted on their team. He was the ideal ball. Round head. Thick skull. I met my fiancé on a submarine," Sister Eugenia finished with a wistful smile.

Arlene couldn't hide her surprise at that.

"Yes, dear, I had a fiancé. He was sunk off the coast of Malta in '44."

"I'm so sorry. And that's why . . ."

"I became a nun? Oh no. I had another two fiancés after that but in the fifties I suddenly realised I was rather bored of men."

"Weren't we all," said Davina, *sotto voce*.

The food arrived. Tiny plates of exquisite beauty that had Davina grumbling the moment they were set down.

"What's this supposed to be? Is this a dolly's tea party?"

Sister Eugenia clapped her hands together. "I'll say grace," she said, offering a vote of thanks so quick that the others barely had time to bow their heads, let alone put their hands together. "Oh, I've been looking forward to this all day. Yum."

"I think they've forgotten to put food beneath this garnish," Davina grumbled.

There was very nearly an old Wren mutiny when dessert appeared.

"A single strawberry?"

"Marinated in a concoction of organic honey from hives on the roof of the Palais Garnier mixed with ancient cognac from the convent of St. Marie, where only novice nuns were allowed to press the grapes," the waiter explained.

"I do hope they washed their feet," said Sister Eugenia.

It was a superlative strawberry, thought Arlene. Though she definitely had room for another one.

"Sometimes it is better to be left wanting," said Sister Eugenia. "I'm sure our Lord must have said something along those lines."

As the evening progressed, Arlene found herself wishing that she had Sister Eugenia's sense of contentment. Was it because Eugenia was a nun, or was it because she had a life well-lived to look back on? As the four women finished their food, Sister Eugenia was full of anecdotes that surprised and delighted the others. Well, Arlene and Sister Margaret Ann at least. But ultimately, the conversation left Arlene a little wistful. When she made it to her nineties—if she made it to her nineties—what would she have to tell a younger audience?

Josephine Williamson had often told Arlene that the war had utterly changed life's direction for many women of her class and generation. With the men away fighting, they'd been pulled into work from which they'd previously been excluded. Joining the women's services had allowed many to rip up the rule book entirely, as they put on uniforms and travelled the world. Josephine and Penny, Davina, and Sister Eugenia had all jumped at the chance to sign up. Would Arlene have done the same?

She hoped she would, but she hadn't had to. Neither had she particularly had to fight for the right *not* to follow in her own mother and grandmother's footsteps. She'd left the Karoo as soon as she could. Couldn't run away fast enough. But had she stopped running too soon? She'd made a comfortable life for herself in London but once upon a time young Arlene had bigger dreams. As a child—in fact, right up until she came to the UK—she'd wanted to be a fashion designer, inspired by the colourful style of the women she'd grown up around. She still loved to dress up (even if Davina had declared her handmade clothes garish). She had even more fun styling other people. When she first arrived in London, she'd thought she might go to fashion school, but life in London was too expensive and it didn't ever happen. And now she was almost fifty. Too late to begin again. Never mind that Davina was explaining to the others how she took her first degree—in art history—at eighty-seven.

"Oooh. That reminds me. Tomorrow, if we have time," Sister Eugenia said, "I would like to go to the Musée d'Orsay and see Manet's *Olympia*. That painting has always been a favourite of mine—ever since an old flame told me there was something of Olympia about my . . . my eyes. I should like to say goodbye to the old girl . . ."

"I'm up for that," said Arlene.

"And I'd like to see how renovations are getting on at Notre-Dame," said Sister Margaret Ann.

"Of course, dear. I'm sure our sisters back at the convent are dying to know. Now a round of cognac, I think," said Sister Eugenia.

"As the granddaughter of an admiral, I should have a rum," said Davina.

Thirty-One

• • • • •

When Archie and the sisters arrived at the Brice-Petitjean auction house for the party, a line of eager guests was already stretching halfway down the street. Clearly the launch of Stéphane's early twentieth-century jewellery sale was a hot ticket, so Archie was especially gratified when one of two young women with clipboards made a beeline for Penny and Josephine. "The Williamson sisters?" she asked. Archie was impressed, though to be fair there weren't many other nonagenarians in the queue. "And your great-nephew Archie? I'm Natalie. I've been asked to look after you. Please follow me."

They were swept past the queue, which contained a number of faces Archie recognised from the French magazines he'd flicked through on the Eurostar. There was a photographer waiting in the lobby to capture the celebrities in front of a huge collage of black and white photographs of the much-loved late actress whose collection formed the bulk of the sale. Natalie tried to arrange Archie and his great-aunts in front of it. Archie put on his best smile but Josephine and Penny kept walking.

"Don't you want a lovely photographic memory of tonight?" Archie asked. "With your spanking new medals?"

"Sometimes it's best to let memories fade," said Penny. "Who even needs to know we were here?"

Well, that was one way of looking at it. Archie posed for a couple of snaps by himself to show willing then skipped to catch the sisters up.

Natalie found Archie and the sisters three seats around a small table and went to fetch them champagne. Spotting Stéphane on the other side of the room, Archie waved excitedly. To his obvious delight, his old flame came right over. There was much "*bise*-ing," which left both Archie and Stéphane bright red with blushes. The sisters shared an indulgent smile. They'd always had high hopes for Stéphane.

"Aunties!" Stéphane had earned the status of honorary great-nephew over the years. "How beautiful you both look this evening. I must have a closer look at your new accessories."

He gently lifted Penny's *Légion d'honneur* away from her lapel.

"Fabulous. Such an elegant design. And you both wear it so well."

"I agree," said Archie.

"Well done, Archie, for finding such a good excuse to bring your wonderful great-aunts to Paris to see me," Stéphane said.

Archie glowed—everybody noticed—but unfortunately his bliss was to be short-lived.

"I'm so glad you're all here tonight because I want to introduce you all to someone special. You know how much your opinion matters to me. Especially yours, Archie."

Stéphane beckoned to a man who was holding court in a circle of admiring young women. The chap's face was familiar. Possibly because they'd seen him glaring intently from every newsstand in Paris. Catching Stéphane's signal, he excused himself and sauntered across to join the Williamson party.

"This is Malcolm," Stéphane said. "My fiancé."

"Oh dear," said Josephine reflexively.

Stéphane was too busy twinkling at Malcolm to have heard, though Penny and Archie both did.

While the rest of the men in the room were dressed in black tie, this Malcolm chap was wearing a somewhat unusual "costume," to use the old-fashioned term. He was dressed in brown trousers, a rough dun-coloured linen shirt without a collar, and a worn leather waistcoat. The toe of one of his decidedly ancient boots was flapping open and out of the side of his mouth poked what appeared to be a piece of straw. Still, despite his getup, Stéphane's fiancé looked Archie up and down in a way that suggested he was making comparisons and deciding that he came off better. Much better.

Archie put on his game face and shook Malcolm's hand. Malcolm was very well-muscled, his big chest stretched that leather waistcoat. When Malcolm released his hand, after pumping it up and down like he was trying to shake Archie's arm off, Archie had to flex his fingers to get some blood back into them. Malcolm's overly-enthusiastic handshake had made the old break in his wrist ache. He cradled it protectively, in a stance that was familiar to Archie's family and friends. He often cradled his wrist when he felt in need of comfort.

"Did I hurt you?" Malcolm asked. His accent was odd. Half-French, half-mid-Atlantic.

"War wound," Archie quipped. "Old martial arts injury, actually."

It wasn't exactly untrue.

"I have heard a lot about you, Archie," Malcolm said. "But I didn't know you were a fan of martial arts. I practise taekwondo and capoeira myself."

Of course he did. "And you?"

"Defendu."

"Is that a real thing?"

"Yes, actually. But I don't have the time these days," said Archie.

"I understand. You have a little gallery in London, am I right?"

That "little" seemed calculated.

"Yes," said Archie. "In Mayfair."

Fifteen all. The sisters watched the exchange as though it was a tennis match, their heads turning back and forth. Malcolm kept the straw in the side of his mouth throughout.

"When I am in London, I spend most of my time in the East End," said Malcolm. "Where the new art galleries are. For the younger energy. Stéphane likes that too."

It had not gone unnoticed that Archie had at least a decade on his rival.

Thirty-fifteen.

"It's hard to keep track of the East End," said Archie. "Half the galleries there have the lifespan of a butterfly."

Thirty-all.

"Better a butterfly than a dusty old moth."

Forty-thirty.

Stéphane, who had been pulled away by a staff matter, was back. He rested one hand on Malcolm's arm and the other on Archie's. Archie flexed his bicep as hard as he could, without making it obvious that he was doing so.

"How have you been getting on?" Stéphane asked. "I'm so glad that two of my favourite people got to meet at last."

"Your favourite *people*?" Malcolm asked, throwing a proprietorial arm around Stéphane's shoulder.

"Well, of course you're my very favourite, dear . . ."

Game Malcolm.

"Did Malcolm tell you he's an actor?" Stéphane asked then, which explained the posters. "I was actually especially looking forward to introducing him to you, Penny, and Josephine, because in his next role Malcolm will be playing a hero of the Resistance. Shooting starts next week. Hence the outfit."

The ladies cocked their heads in polite interest, pretending they hadn't noticed there was anything strange at all about Malcolm's random getup.

"I'm a method actor," Malcolm explained. "Like Daniel Day-Lewis and Marlon Brando. It means that when I'm working, I *live* the part."

"How exciting," the sisters said in unison.

"I believe that to truly inhabit a role, you have to embrace it twenty-four seven."

"And your character chews a straw?" Josephine observed.

"He was never pictured without one. René Tremblay was a country man, even when he was defending this very city."

"Hmmm," said Penny.

"Shooting begins next week," explained Stéphane.

"It has been a long and difficult process to get to this stage," Malcolm continued. "I've had to spend a lot of time looking into the abyss and it's been life-changing. I don't think I'll ever be the same again."

Stéphane put his hand on Malcolm's shoulder and nodded in sympathetic agreement.

"The rehearsals nearly broke me. The risks. The *danger* . . . I've prepared myself for next week like a partisan preparing to die for the love of his country, just as René faced the Gestapo bullets in 1944. The stress has been immense."

"Of course," said Penny. "I can see how one might find it almost as traumatic as actually having been there . . ."

"Thank you." Malcolm gave Penny a little "namaste." "I knew you'd understand. It's been tough but I feel I've grown as a man and an actor and finally I carry the spirit of the Resistance fighter within me." He thumped his fist against his heart, then shot it upwards towards the ceiling. "*Liberté!*"

"Hmmm," said Archie.

There was a quiet moment while Malcolm and the others contemplated the gravity of his career choices, then Stéphane waved at a new arrival.

"Ladies, Archie, you will excuse us. That's Dragomir Georgiev over there. I must say hello. I know he has his eye on several pieces for his, er, goddaughter, I think."

The lizard-like man was accompanied by a young woman several decades his junior. She definitely wasn't his goddaughter. You could tell that just by looking at her dress. Any godfather worth his salt would have worried about her catching a chill and sent her home to change.

Archie recognised the man. Perhaps a month earlier, Georgiev had visited his gallery and bought five paintings for a new holiday home, or was it a yacht? Georgiev had not spoken at all, sending in one of the flunkeys who encircled him and his "goddaughter" now to complete the transaction the following day. Archie had been sad to let the paintings go, sure that Georgiev was buying them for bragging rights rather than anything about the paintings in themselves. But then you didn't have to work in the art world for very long to realise that most of the people who could afford to buy the really good stuff had no idea *why* it was so good. Neither did they care to know. They merely went by the price tag. When guests admired their new paintings, they would be itching to reveal how much they'd paid, not to point out the tiny details that obsessed a real art lover, like Archie.

And now Georgiev was here to splash the cash in Paris. Cash that came from God only knew where. At one point he'd been in politics in some ex-Soviet country, thought Archie, but since then? The kind of money Georgiev had didn't come from after-dinner speeches.

"Come on, Malcolm." Stéphane grabbed his fiancé by the big, beefy arm. "I know he'll be very pleased to meet you."

"Oh dear," said Josephine again.

The evening was not unfolding in the way Archie and his great-aunts had hoped or expected. With Stéphane and Malcolm gone, Archie knocked back his flute of champagne—and he never knocked back a drink—and held his glass out for a refill when a waiter passed.

"It won't last," Josephine assured Archie as from a distance they watched Stéphane introducing Malcolm to his most esteemed (for which read "wealthiest") guests.

"But Stéphane is going to marry that man. He loves him."

"There are all sorts of reasons for getting married and not all of them have to do with love. Doesn't he remind you of Macadam?" Penny asked Josephine.

"Malcolm? Oh yes." Josephine laughed. "Yes, indeed."

"Who's Macadam?" Archie asked.

"We must have told you about him, dear. He was your great-grandfather's prized Highland bull. Terror of the Glens. Big muscles. Great hair . . ."

"Thick as mince," added Penny. "Which is I suppose how the poor thing ended up . . . I mean, all that guff about how hard it is to play a Resistance hero. I ask you."

"Quite," said Josephine. "He's very pleased with himself. *And self-praise is no recommendation.*" Penny chimed in with that last sentiment. As did Archie. It was one of their favourite sayings.

The sisters were trying to cheer Archie up but they hadn't raised a smile. "*Toujours gai,*" Penny reminded him, with a squeeze to his knee. "Plenty more frogs in the pond."

"You can't say that in Paris."

"I believe I just did."

It wasn't often that Archie's great-aunts couldn't coax a smile from him but their efforts that evening were in vain. Archie's disappointment went deep. It wasn't only that Stéphane, who had occupied a place in his heart for so very long, had finally chosen another. It was the kind of man he had chosen. So . . . er, basic (wasn't that what the modern kids said), with his muscles and his hair and his big white teeth that he'd probably bought in Turkey. He hadn't taken his method acting so far that he'd let his teeth get stained, Archie bitterly observed.

On several occasions over the years, Stéphane had openly admired Archie's style—the impeccable forties suits, his insistence on old-school elegance in style and manners—but here was the truth of it. Despite any number of old adages that maintained that looks didn't matter, they really did. They really, really did. Stéphane had never looked at Archie like that—the way he looked at Malcolm now. Stéphane had fallen in love with a handsome meat-head.

Archie's wrist still throbbed from Malcolm's furious handshake, as if to remind him that he would never be able to bench press his own body weight. Or even the body weight of a small dachshund, without feeling a warning tweak in his badly-healed ulna. He wished he hadn't come. Why hadn't Stéphane told him about Malcolm before, so that Archie could have made his excuses and avoided this awful moment altogether?

"Aunties, you know what, now that we've seen Stéphane, why don't we just go back to the hotel? He's very busy. You've both had a long day and I'm sure you'd be happy with a nightcap and early to bed, wouldn't you? I shouldn't have dragged you here. Shall we skedaddle?"

Josephine seemed quite happy with the idea but, to Archie's surprise, Penny shook her head.

"No, Archie, no," she said. "If meeting Stéphane's fiancé has made you feel like leaving, then we absolutely must stay. At least for a little while longer. Otherwise, it will be perfectly obvious what's going on."

Rats. Auntie Penny had rumbled him.

"This is just like that birthday party in Hyde Park in 1993 when you wanted to take your cricket stumps home because a little girl had bowled you out," she added.

"That girl cheated," Archie insisted.

"That might well have been the case, but you did yourself no favours by storming off the pitch in a fit of pique. And that's exactly what it will look like you're doing if you insist on leaving this party now."

"I'm very happy to go. You can use me as an excuse," said Josephine.

"Absolutely not," said Penny. "Archie Williamson, don't you dare let that knucklehead get the better of you. We're staying for at least another half hour and we're going to look like we're really enjoying ourselves. Fake it 'til we make it. Come on, laugh!"

She faked a guffaw and tried to get Archie join in. He didn't.

"If we're staying, I need some more champagne," said Josephine.

Archie pulled himself up, straightened his shoulders and, muttering "*toujours* bloody *gai*," he set off to find a wine waiter.

LATER, WHILE ARCHIE wistfully watched Stéphane's progress around the room and Josephine was in conversation with Natalie about the canapés, Penny surveyed the reception with a practised eye. She imagined it must be reaching peak capacity by now. Chatter filled the room, bouncing off the walls and glass cabinets so that it was hard to pick out any one conversation from the many dozens in different languages that were going on around her. Penny scanned the other guests, using the skill that her husband Connor had so admired, to pick out the embedded security from the genuine punters. It wasn't hard. While the punters greedily sank the free champagne and twittered and preened, the security team were staying sober and alert. Not so alert that they gave Penny a second glance, however. Why would they? She was no threat. A woman her age was used to being disregarded. Had been for many years.

Hold on, she reminded herself. *That's what you thought in Peter Jones.*

That bloody crystal elephant, which Penny had to pretend she adored for dear Archie's sake, was an ugly reminder that she must not make too many assumptions. "Never forget." She had to employ the same care as she had when she was just starting out, back in the 1940s.

"Check the room again."

The three chaps in almost identical black suits, standing by the buffet table, were definitely security. They weren't drinking. One of them kept putting a forefinger to his ear. Badly-fitted earpiece? "Must keep an eye on the whereabouts of those three at all times," Penny decided. But now was the moment, while everyone was so excited and distracted and before Stéphane brought the hubbub to a halt by getting up on stage to make a speech.

While Archie was making small-talk with another guest and Josephine was off spending another penny, Penny got up. No one watched as she crossed the room with determination in her small blue eyes. She was just a little old lady, drifting through the crowd of the young, the beautiful, and the rich, as though she were already a ghost. She was invisible and that was how she wanted it.

Slowly she made her way to the table where lots seven to thirteen were on display. Lot thirteen was an eighteen-carat gold ring mounted with an eight-carat emerald surrounded by three-carats' worth of diamonds in a peerless ballerina setting.

Penny stopped in front of the toughened glass case and murmured, "We meet again."

Thirty-Two

• • • • •

Antibes, 1966

"Penny? Penny Williamson? Is that you?"

Penny spun round, alarmed at the sound of her name, and looked about the hotel lobby for this person who thought he knew her. She could see only a very tanned middle-aged man with no hair, wearing a pair of overly tight white trousers.

He opened his arms as he walked towards her.

"Gilbert?"

"Penny! It is you. I knew it. You have not changed at all."

Penny wished she could say the same. She was still trying to reconcile the man standing in front of her with her childhood friend and long-ago lover. While he had no hair left on his head, Gilbert Declerc was sporting an extravagant moustache that put her in mind of the fox fur tippet she'd recently inherited from one of her godmothers. Full of moths, the horrible thing was. That bequest had cost Penny half her cashmere.

"But what are you doing here?" Gilbert asked.

"I'm on honeymoon," Penny said, wishing that Connor could be on time for once.

"Well, this is a happy coincidence! I'm on honeymoon too. Isn't this wonderful," Gilbert said, leaning in close so that she was almost over-whelmed by his cologne. "Two old lovers meeting like this. Imagine how embarrassing it would have been were I newly married and you still the spinster."

"Quite," said Penny, tightly.

"But where is he, this lucky man, who has captured the heart of England's most beautiful rose?"

Where was he indeed? Even before Gilbert turned up, Penny was starting to worry as she always did whenever Connor went to "see a man about a horse." It was worse since the hotel was buzzing with news about a violent gang that was targeting foreign tourists heading to their hotel knowing they would be laden with cash to pay for their accommodation. The Grand Hôtel des Anges would not take cheques or Connor's new-fangled credit card. Everyone wanted to see that card but nobody would accept it.

"Ah! Here is my wife."

Gilbert motioned towards a young woman who was standing just inside the hotel doors, scanning the lobby myopically through big red Lolita-style sunglasses. She was carrying an enormous number of bags. Behind her came one of the doormen, pushing a trolley piled high with more shopping. As Penny watched, the young woman skidded on the polished marble floor of the lobby, which was death to anyone in smooth-soled shoes, and dropped half her haul. Before Gilbert could get to his wife and offer his support, another man was already by her side, crouching down on the floor next to her, helping to gather up her scattered packages.

Connor.

"Of course," thought Penny. Where there was a mini-skirt . . . She shook her head as her incorrigible husband gazed at the young woman with his best "smiling" Irish eyes.

Gilbert looked distinctly uneasy as he raced to rescue his newly-minted spouse. Penny was right behind him.

Gilbert pulled his wife to her feet and crouched down to finish picking up the mess. He locked eyes with Connor, who was still twinkling. Penny gave Connor a little shove with the toe of her sandal, a signal that he should stand up now, before Gilbert suspected him of looking up his wife's dress.

Penny made the introductions. "This is my husband, Connor O'Connell. Connor, this is Gilbert Declerc. We knew each other as children." The phrase "as children" put him firmly in the past and, in Penny's mind at least, erased that awful, embarrassing week in 1947. Definitely best forgotten.

"I'm Veronique," said Gilbert's wife, gently offering Penny her right hand, which was as delicate as the rest of her doll-like self. Her insubstantial hand and wrist were weighted down by the jewels heaped upon them: three impressively thick diamond eternity bracelets and a ring with an octagon-cut sapphire. Penny had to try hard not to stare at it. It dwarfed the sapphire she was wearing on her own left hand. She knew Connor would have noticed it too.

The two couples stood in the lobby for a little longer, making small talk. though Penny could not wait to get away. She could feel Gilbert's eyes upon her, appraising her, deciding whether the chassis had aged as well as the bonnet. He was appraising Connor too, though she was less worried about that. For some reason Connor was the kind of man men liked.

Then, to Penny's horror . . .

"You must have dinner with us tonight," said Connor.

"But they're on honeymoon," said Penny quickly. "I'm sure they want to be *à deux*."

"We're on our honeymoon too," Connor reminded her. "They've got the rest of their lives to be *à deux*. As have we, my darling. It isn't every night you bump into one of your childhood friends. You must have a lot to catch up on."

Penny inwardly winced but meeting eyes with Connor she knew she shouldn't continue to protest. Let Gilbert make the decision for all of them. She had a feeling that decisions weren't the lovely Veronique's department.

"That would be very nice," said Gilbert.

"Good choice, my man." Connor clapped Gilbert on the shoulder. "I'll have the concierge reserve a table for four in the restaurant tonight. Have you tried the *sole meunière* here, Veronique? It's by far the best I've ever tasted."

CONNOR O'CONNELL HAD all the patter. A one-time jockey from County Kildare, he'd ridden horses for the great and the good: Saudi princes, European royalty, even the Queen. His reputation in racing circles was of a man who made winners. He could have ridden a donkey to victory in The Gold Cup at Cheltenham. At least, that was the way he told it.

When the news broke that Connor was going to marry Penny Williamson, there were expressions of open-mouthed surprise up and down the United Kingdom and the Republic of Ireland. It was widely believed that at almost forty-five, Penny Williamson remained unmarried because she "was not that way inclined." Meanwhile, Connor was a notorious bachelor. No woman could tie him down. Then along came Penny and Connor was smitten.

They were married at the Chelsea Register Office and held their reception in the garden at the Chelsea Arts Club. They were neither of them artists, but several of the members frequented the poker games Connor held in his tumble-down South Kensington house and thus he'd become an honorary member. They were toasted from "lunchtime till Christmas" as Connor described it. A couple of quite notable painters staged a sort of duel, scribbling portraits of the bride and groom. The wedding photographs were taken by a society snapper who'd come straight from photographing The Beatles.

"My beautiful wife," Connor began his speech. He looked at Penny with such softness in his eyes then that those guests in attendance who had been running a book on how long the marriage would last—"Six months tops"—began to revise their estimates upwards. Love really was a mysterious thing.

"Why him?" Josephine had asked, quite reasonably, the evening before the wedding. "Why now?" Josephine had been married since 1950, when she finally accepted Gerald Naiswell's proposal, but Penny had always insisted that she did not need a man in her life. Josephine didn't know about Frank because then she would have to know about everything else. At least, that was how Penny saw it. Instead Penny said she was happy to earn her own way and live according to her own rules. She'd never had any desire to have children, saying that the children she'd cared for in her role as a social worker had scratched that itch for good. Especially after what happened with Jinx. After everything she had done for her that girl had broken Penny's heart. She didn't have to be a parent to understand King Lear's complaint, "How sharper than a serpent's tooth it is, to have a thankless child."

"Connor and I understand each other," said Penny.

It seemed a good enough answer. And seeing Connor's smile as he looked at Penny's face, anyone might have believed it.

WITH AN HOUR to go before dinner at the hotel, Penny found herself in front of the mirror, wondering what to wear.

"Pink or blue," she asked her husband.

"You'll look great in either one," he assured her without looking up.

Penny didn't expect that kind of attention from her husband. She chose the blue. When Connor went into the safe to get some cash for the evening, he brought out her jewellery box at the same time, knowing she would want to accessorise. She might not be able to compete with the young Mrs. Declerc when it came to the dewy sheen of youth, but she could give her a run for her money when it came to her rocks.

Connor nodded in approval as Penny took off the sapphire and instead slid a diamond solitaire onto her ring finger, to nestle perfectly against the thick gold wedding band she'd bought for herself. He fastened a thick diamond rivière around her neck and pulled up the last inch of her zip, taking care not to touch her skin as he did so.

"Perfect."

Connor offered Penny his arm as they walked into the hotel bar. She shot him a smile which he returned with something approaching appreciation. Yes, they made a good team.

WHILE GETTING TO know Veronique, Penny kept one ear on the men's conversation. Gilbert was telling Connor that though he'd trained as a lawyer, he was in property these days. He'd recently bought a faded old hotel in Juan-les-Pins and intended to turn it into the chicest pension on the Riviera. There was a great deal of money to be made in hospitality.

Veronique grew more beautiful as the evening progressed and the champagne turned her peachy cheeks pinker. Penny found she liked the younger woman despite herself. It was easy to see why Gilbert had fallen in love with her. But why had she reciprocated?

"He was friends with my father," Veronique explained. "I thought perhaps he was too old for me but he is, how you say, young inside."

Penny had not asked Veronique how old she was but she estimated that she was not more than twenty-two. Her manner was occasionally younger.

"Gilbert makes me very happy. How did you meet your husband, Penny?"

Whenever Penny answered this question, she did not describe the very first time she met Connor, in the back room of a bookies in Willesden with Frank, but instead described what was actually the second time, when they found themselves at the same party in Chelsea, a month after Penny broke it off with Frank, and Connor sought her out.

"I've been thinking about you," he said. "Wondering what you've been up to."

"Keeping busy," Penny told him.

"Perhaps you and I ought to get out of here and go to supper some place."

Penny told Veronique the official version of the story. "We went to a tiny restaurant in Soho, all lit by candles. We ate steak and drank the most marvellous wine. Connor knows a lot about wine. And by the end of the evening, I had agreed to go with him to Deauville. We drove there in his sports car, taking the crossing from Dover to Calais. It was the craziest thing I ever agreed to do—go to France for the weekend with a man I'd only just met—but I suppose I knew at once that I could trust him. We had the most wonderful time, eating seafood, drinking champagne, and walking on the beach. And now here we are, happily married."

Veronique thought the story was wonderful. So romantic, so daring to take a chance on love like that. Veronique was so swept up by the thrill of it all that Penny was almost swept up too. She could very nearly picture herself, walking on the sand with her handsome Irish beau, letting him feed her oysters before retiring to their separate rooms (of course), and thinking about him all night, falling desperately in love.

The reality of that weekend was altogether different. There were oysters, but there were no separate rooms, because that weekend in the Deauville was the first Penny and Connor spent as a "married couple."

"Mr. and Mrs. Dillon Corry" was how they signed the hotel register. For various reasons it was best not to use their real names, though they wouldn't be coming back. Not until everyone had forgotten their faces.

Penny changed the subject back to this "real" honeymoon.

"This is our last stop," she said. "We've been on a European tour of sorts. We started out in Amsterdam, then took the train to Vienna, then onwards to Rome . . ."

"Oh, I've always wanted to go to Rome," said Veronique. "I've heard it's such a beautiful city."

"It is," agreed Penny. "One could spend a lifetime exploring Rome. It's a shame that we had just a day."

The next night, the two honeymooning couples dined together again. Different dresses for the ladies, different jewellery. Penny wore gold earrings and a matching ring by Andrew Grima. His brutal, almost architectural style was shockingly, thrillingly new. Veronique wore a pair of classical diamond chandelier earrings that lent a halo effect to her face which, Penny thought a little wistfully, hardly needed the help.

"Gilbert has very good taste in jewellery," Connor told Veronique approvingly. "Though I've the feeling I could make a ring out of a sweetie wrapper and you would make it look like it was worth a fortune."

It was true, thought Penny. Some women had the ability to make a chip of glass look like a million dollars while there were others—including several of the women in the restaurant that night—who could make a million-dollar diamond look cheap. Veronique Declerc was one of the former.

By the time dessert was served, a third night as a foursome had been proposed.

"Do we have to?" Penny asked when she and Connor got back to their room.

"Gilbert has some interesting deals going on," Connor said. "And they're going back to Paris the next morning. Who knows when you might see your old friend again?"

The truth was, Penny didn't mind spending time with Veronique. She was young but she wasn't uninteresting. She asked intelligent questions and listened attentively to the answers. Penny wanted to hug the girl when she admitted that she had not been able to get the kind of education she would have liked but was determined things would be different for any daughter she might bring into the world.

"Did you never want to have children, Penny?" she asked.

Penny's mind flickered briefly to her last meeting with Jinx.

"You're lecturing me about dishonesty, Penny? You taught me everything I know . . ."

"I don't think I'd have made a very good mother," Penny told Veronique.

FOR THE THIRD night, Penny pulled out a choker by Bulgari. Or should she say by someone who was very good at faking Bulgari. She wasn't sure it was entirely flattering but it was fashionable. She'd had her hair done at the hotel's salon. Really, all this dressing up was tiring. It gave her some sympathy for Sophia Loren, whom she'd once met at a party at Elstree Studios. The Italian screen goddess had been quite charming. A woman's woman, Penny decided, the sort who was so comfortable in her own skin that she was happy to be surrounded by other women, not feeling the need to compete. Sophia had had some serious jewellery. Penny remembered the impressive weight of the diamond necklace that disappeared in an infamous robbery a few nights after the party. Sophia had gone on television to appeal for her jewellery's return.

"Fat chance," Frank had muttered as he and Penny watched the appeal from a hotel bed.

Connor fastened the choker around Penny's neck.

"I like your hair like that," he said. "You could blend in anywhere with that do. Frank was right about that. You're a chameleon."

"Let's not talk about Frank," said Penny.

VERONIQUE AND GILBERT were waiting in the bar. Veronique wore a shimmering silver lamé mini-dress and matching pointed shoes. From her ears dangled a pair of emerald drops. And on her left hand . . . on her left hand . . .

An emerald as big as a Fox's Glacier Mint, surrounded by a glittering sunray skirt of smaller baguette-cut diamonds. A "ballerina mount," as it was called. The setting was different but surely there weren't many emeralds that big in that particular cut. In a lifetime of being interested in jewellery, Penny had only seen one other.

"It belonged to Gilbert's paternal great-grandmother," Veronique said, when she noticed Penny staring. "Isn't it just *magnifique*?"

In an instant, Penny knew the truth about the Declerc family's surprise inheritance. And at the same time she also knew with horrifying clarity that, on a lazy afternoon in the summer of 1939, it was she who had unwittingly signed Leah and Lily Samuel's death warrant.

Thirty-Three

• • • • •

Paris, July 1939

It was a Thursday. Josephine and August had given Penny a handful of centimes to look after August's little sister Lily so they could spend the afternoon holding hands and talking about untranslatable things in the Tuileries without interruption. Lily was much more excited at the prospect of the hours ahead than Penny was.

"We're going to have such a good time," she said with determination. "I've made a shop. Come and look."

Lily took Penny by the hand and pulled her into the bedroom where she had arrayed all her toys in a queue to visit a boutique run by her favourite doll.

Penny was minded to suggest, "Why don't you play shops while I read," but Lily's enthusiasm made her heart squeeze, reminding her as it did of the disappointment she herself had so often felt as a child upon hearing that the person she had earmarked as a playmate—usually Josephine—had better things to do.

"I'd be delighted to play shops with you," Penny told her little friend. She was rewarded with a beaming smile.

"You are by far my favourite," Lily said then, which was gratifying. "Do you think your sister will marry my brother?"

"Would you like that?" Penny asked.

Lily shrugged. "I suppose then you and I shall be sort of sisters too," she said. "I'd like that. *Alors*, I think to begin with I should be the shopkeeper and you can be my customer. I haven't got a bell but you can make the noise when you come through the door."

Penny stepped back out onto the landing and re-entered in the character of "Madame De La Plume De Ma Tante."

Lily too stepped into her role, showing Madame De La Plume the latest fashions.

"This would suit you beautifully," she said, as she invited Penny to feel the quality of one of Madame Samuel's old housecoats.

"Oh my!" said Penny, getting into the spirit of the game by trying the housecoat on. "This is fabulous but it's so very expensive. I can't afford it. Could I pay you in instalments?"

"Certainly not," said Lily. "No credit here."

While Lily rearranged her store, Penny looked out of the window into the courtyard.

"Shall we ask Gilbert to play with us too?" Penny asked, seeing him down there on the bench. He was probably reading Baudelaire.

"Yes!" Lily was enthusiastic. "He can be the policeman, who comes to arrest you for stealing the dress."

Penny whistled to catch his attention. It was a loud, unladylike whistle that would have got her a telling off at home, but Gilbert was impressed.

The trio played shops for another hour, until even Lily was bored. When Gilbert suggested a game of hide and seek, Lily clapped her hands together.

"That is the best idea!"

She wanted to hide first.

"You two must wait in the bathroom until you have counted to a hundred," she said. "Then you can both come and look for me."

Penny and Gilbert sat side by side on the edge of the bath, the edges of their hands just touching.

"Are you counting? Or am I?" Penny asked.

"You."

Penny tailed off after she got to twenty. They could hear Lily shrieking and giggling to herself as she looked for a hiding place elsewhere in the apartment. It sounded as though she would need longer than a hundred.

"Want to see something you shouldn't?" Penny asked.

"Are you going to take your dress off?" Gilbert asked.

"What? I am not. It's this."

Penny rolled back the bathmat and found the loose floorboard. As she tried to prise it up, the board kept escaping her grasp. Had August used something to get it open? She couldn't remember. Either way, she couldn't persuade the floorboard to give way.

"Underneath here is the Samuel family safe," Penny whispered.

"How do you know?" Gilbert asked.

"August showed me and Josephine the other day. There's half the jewels of Austria in there. Diamonds, sapphires, emeralds. The lot. You've never seen anything like it."

"I don't believe you."

"You don't have to," said Penny. "Help me get this board up and you'll see for yourself."

"No," said Gilbert firmly. "No. You shouldn't have told me. And August shouldn't have shown you. Put the mat back and never mention it to anyone again. It's the Samuel family's private property."

"You're such a goody-goody," said Penny.

"It's about trust," Gilbert said. "August is my friend."

Then Lily called out. "I'm ready!"

Gilbert and Penny carefully replaced the bathmat and went in search of their little charge, pretending for a good five minutes that they couldn't see her feet in their red velvet slippers poking out from beneath the curtains in the sitting room.

NEARLY THIRTY YEARS later, the memory of that afternoon made Penny's head swim. Lily was so sweet and so trusting. She'd thrown her arms around Gilbert's waist when he walked into the apartment and he had seemed enchanted by her in return. He'd made such an effort to play the policeman with sufficient gravitas and Lily had been thrilled. Penny and Gilbert were, Lily said, so much more fun than Josephine and August, who wanted to do nothing but kiss. And how excited Lily had been to play hide and seek even though she was so very bad at hiding.

While Connor and Gilbert discussed the wine list and Veronique chattered about a shopping trip to Cannes, Penny couldn't bat away the memory of Lily's tiny feet poking out from beneath the curtains. She imagined the young girl hiding for real when the French policemen came to take her away at the behest of the Nazis. Had Madame Samuel tried to keep her little chatterbox quiet when they hammered on the door? Had she pretended they were playing a game or had she let her daughter know that, this time, they were hiding in deadly, deadly earnest?

How could anyone ever want to hurt such a beautiful, innocent child? What did it take to make someone think that handing over a young girl to the Nazis was the right thing to do? Penny knew what it took. There were psychopaths out there. There were people too who had believed everything Hitler said. There were as well a great many cowards. Penny understood that most of the people who had collaborated with the Nazis had done so only to save their own skins. And then there were the people who perhaps thought they might benefit from their neighbours' distress.

How long had the Declercs waited before they let themselves into the Samuel family's flat and lifted the floorboards in the bathroom?

Thirty-Four

• • • • •

Antibes, 1966

Penny did not confront Gilbert about the ring, though many years later she might wish she had. But if she'd asked him to tell her the truth as they sat opposite one another at the dining table that night, what difference would it have made to hear it? Instead, she told Connor and the Declercs that she was suddenly feeling unwell. It must have been the fish she'd eaten for lunch. Gilbert suggested they ask the hotel to call a doctor. And if it was the fish, he would help her sue the restaurant. He evinced genuine concern. Penny assured him, "I'm sure I'll be fine." When she left the table, Connor stayed. It was Gilbert's turn to pay.

The following day, Penny stayed hidden in her hotel room until she was sure the Declercs had left to catch their flight. She didn't want to bump into them. When she thought they must be gone, she went down to the bar to read that day's newspapers. The leading story in that morning's edition of the Paris *Herald Tribune* was about the criminal gang targeting tourists up and down the Côte. Naturally, the local police had decided the gang wasn't French but more likely Italian, coming over the border to make their attacks before disappearing into the mountains where they divided their bounty with their mafioso friends.

Italy had its own crime wave. A smaller story on page three described how a high-end jewellery store in Rome had been hit by a daring thief who simply walked out with a fistful of diamonds. She was described as a woman in her thirties, five feet two, slim, blonde hair, her accent indefinable but possibly American. The store owner said, "She was very delicate," which was why he could hardly believe that she had managed to walk away with diamonds worth many, many hundreds of thousands of dollars. It wasn't worth trying to calculate the total in lire. There weren't enough noughts in the world.

"Jinx."

It had to be. The description certainly fit. Penny shook her head, half in admiration, half in exasperation at her former protégée. No wonder the jewellers in Rome were being frustratingly careful when Penny passed through a few days later.

The newspaper article went on, "The theft in Rome bore many similarities to recent thefts in Amsterdam, Monaco, and Vienna, leading police to believe that a serial jewel thief may be at work. In each case, a woman worked alone." She'd told the store owner in Amsterdam she was from Kentucky. She'd told the store owner in Monaco she was from California. The target of the Vienna theft, however, was convinced that the jewel thief who'd targeted his shop was French.

Penny re-read the scant information about the perpetrator of Viennese hit.

". . . definitely French, not at all beautiful, and middle-aged," the jeweller there thought.

"Perhaps there's more than one thief at work," the reporter concluded.

Not at all beautiful? And what counted as middle-aged, Penny mused as she folded the paper shut. Was that how she appeared to people now? She supposed she must be middle-aged. She was in her forties. If she lived only as long as her own mother, who had died the previous year, then she was well past the middle already. It was a sobering thought that had Penny summoning the waiter to bring her a whiskey and soda with her coffee. As she sipped it, she consoled herself that she had at least passed as French.

But the saga of the well-dressed female jewel thief (or thieves) was far from the biggest news at the hotel that morning.

Another tourist couple had been attacked by the modern highwaymen on their way to the airport. Despite trying to give the impression that she was busy reading by quickly snatching up her paper again, Penny found herself cornered by an American woman she'd seen around the hotel all week. The woman's diamond earrings—so big they looked fake, though they definitely weren't—jiggled along with her dowager duchess jowls as she relayed the story of the robbery with the demeanour of a chicken still clucking wildly hours after a fox has passed the hen house.

"It's no coincidence, is it? That this keeps happening to people who've stayed in this hotel? The taxi drivers must be in on it. Or somebody who works here."

"I'm sure it's random," said Penny. "This isn't the only hotel on the Côte D'Azur."

"But Des Anges is the best. They must be scoping us out. Well, I am very glad we have our own driver. We have given him instructions that when we leave to fly home tomorrow morning, he is not to stop anywhere between here and the airport. Not even if someone is lying bleeding in the middle of the road. They do that, you know, fake an accident so you stop to help. Next thing you know." She mimed pulling a knife across her throat and shuddered.

"Gosh," said Penny.

"I don't know how you can be so calm about it," the American woman said.

AT LUNCH IN the hotel restaurant, the latest highway robbery was on everybody's lips. As the story passed from table to table, it gathered detail. Someone had worked out that the victims must have been "that nice French couple. The handsome man with the much younger wife." They'd been ambushed within a mile of the hotel gates. The robbers had engineered a crash. The couple's car was a write off. Of course they had to get out before it exploded. There'd been a struggle. The robbers were armed with knives. And guns! Don't forget the guns! By the time the police got to the scene, the young wife had all but bled to death. She was rushed to hospital. She was not expected to survive.

While the restaurant echoed with barely muted gasps of horror from the guests, the waiting staff continued their serene progress about the room, as if deaf to anything but direct instructions. A young man appeared at Penny and Connor's table to take their drinks order.

"Champagne to toast my clever bride," said Connor.

Connor had been out all morning. He'd already had a drink. Penny could tell by the colour in his cheeks.

"Did you hear about the robbery on the road into town?" Penny asked. Connor nodded.

"I heard someone had to be taken to hospital."

Connor shrugged. "I didn't know about that."

"Where have you been all morning?"

"Here, there, everywhere. Went to see a man about a horse."

Penny snorted. Connor wouldn't be drawn but instead started telling her how the hotel concierge had suggested they take a trip from Cannes out to the Île Sainte-Marguerite. "I'll hire a boat. We'll take a picnic."

"The weather's supposed to be bad tomorrow," Penny observed. "It might be dangerous."

"I never had you down for a scaredy-cat."

The champagne arrived. Once the waiter stepped away, Connor reached into the inside pocket of his linen jacket and pulled out a bright white hand-kerchief, bundled into a ball. He tossed it into Penny's lap. She opened it with an odd feeling of trepidation. Wrapped in the soft cotton was a ring.

"Happy three-week anniversary," Connor said.

He tilted his champagne glass towards Penny in a toast while she stared at the ring in her lap as though Connor had presented her with a dead spider.

A moment later, the American woman burst into the dining room, ex-claiming as she did so, "She's dead!"

LATER THAT AFTERNOON, Penny walked out through the hotel gates, ig-noring various hotel staff who asked if they could call her a taxi. She walked down into the town, hoping that if she went far enough, the ghosts would give up their pursuit.

Lily Samuel and her family were dead because of Penny. Now Vero-nique too?

The American woman was right. There was someone at the hotel who had connections with the criminal gangs that were menacing holidaymak-ers on the road between Antibes and Juan-les-Pins. But it wasn't a member of the hotel staff. That someone was Penny's own husband.

That ring. That bloody ring. Why had she even mentioned it to him? It must have sealed Veronique's fate. As she marched along, her eyes cloudy with tears, Penny cursed her bastard spouse. He'd broken his promise. They'd had a deal. From the day they got together, they'd had an understanding. They stole from stores and from companies, not from individuals. Nobody ever got hurt.

At the first church she came to, Penny stopped and went inside. Might this be the moment to make her first confession? Where to start?

By the time Penny got back to the hotel, the ring was gone and Connor's body was almost cold.

Thirty-Five

. . . . .

Paris, 2022

There's a degree of simple genetic luck involved in living to a grand old age but there's also a question of having sufficient motivation to push on through the years when your bones ache and your eyes have dimmed and the soundtrack to your day-to-day life is the whine of a faulty hearing aid. Of course someone who loves their life and all the people in it wants to hang around for as long as they possibly can. But there are other reasons for clinging on too: pig-headedness, unfinished business, the prospect of glorious revenge.

Thinking about Lily again made Penny feel unsteady as she walked across the room. Gathering herself, she put the young girl from her mind in order to focus on the plan at hand. She could think about Lily afterwards, when she was using the proceeds from that blasted ring to build a new girls' school in the DRC in Lily's honour. If she was ever going to steal the ring back, she had to do it now.

Penny had chosen her moment, now she had to choose the right assistant. There were three assistants at the table where the emerald ring was being displayed: two men and a woman. Having studied them carefully, Penny picked the woman as her mark. It wasn't always the case that the woman was the best assistant to go to when there was a choice; over the years Penny had found that men were usually less observant of what was going on right under their noses—at least that had been the case when she was younger and could still be bothered to flirt up a storm—but in this situation, the woman was obviously distracted by Malcolm, who was evidently well-known from French TV. Her eyes were following him around the room. Every time he looked in her general direction, still chewing his stupid straw, she would give a slight pout and flick out the ends of her long blonde hair.

Good luck, sweetheart, Penny thought.

It took the assistant a moment or two to notice that Penny was even standing in front of her. Snapping to attention, she bestowed upon Penny a smile that Penny had come to know well over the past couple of decades. She'd first started to see it when she hit her seventies. It was a smile that suggested the assistant was expecting a question regarding the whereabouts of the nearest loo. Penny was neither incontinent nor incompetent but of course she played up to it. If this vain dimwit wanted a sweet little old lady, then that was what she would get.

"Oh, hello dear," said Penny. "Don't mind me. I just wanted to get a closer look at the rings."

"Of course."

"They're very beautiful. Is that a sapphire?" Penny pointed out lot number eleven.

"It is." The assistant trotted out the statistics in a bored sort of way. The weight of the stone. The provenance—it was one of the items belonging to the famous actress whose fabulous collection was anchoring the sale. The guide price. Her eyes kept drifting back towards Malcolm as she spoke.

"I don't suppose it would be possible for me to try it on?" Penny said in perfectly composed but such appallingly-accented French that it hurt her own ears.

"Hmmm?" said the assistant.

"Try it on? I'd like to try on the sapphire, please. If I may?"

The assistant glanced at her more senior colleague but he was busy helping another guest.

"I don't see why not," the assistant said after a moment's hesitation. She fetched out a velvet-lined tray from beneath the table and reached into the cabinet for the ring with white-gloved hands. She gave the stone a quick rub with her thumb before she lay the ring on the tray.

Penny picked it up and slipped it onto her right ring finger. She gave it an experimental twiddle. It spun around her finger freely. There would be no need for butter and ice to get this ring off again as had happened one disastrous afternoon in Asprey many years ago. First rule of sleight of hand, make sure you have slight-enough hands.

"Well, it is very lovely," Penny said. "But I'm not sure it looks quite right on this old finger."

"It's like a beautiful blossom on a wizened old tree," said the auction assistant. She probably meant to be charming but it just made Penny feel less bad for what she was about to do. Patronising young fool.

Penny handed the sapphire back. She then asked to try on a yellow diamond solitaire.

"Not my colour."

The ruby.

"Oh dear. Really not me."

The emerald?

"I'll need to ask my superior," the assistant said. The emerald was in a locked box within the case, as befitted its significance and value. The assistant's colleague duly appeared with the key. He looked at Penny quizzically but, seeing that she had already asked to try on three other rings, seemed convinced it might be worth accommodating Penny's request. Everyone at the reception that evening was a specially invited guest and they wouldn't have been invited if there weren't a chance they might make a credible bid in the auction later that week . . .

"Wizened old tree," Penny muttered under her breath as she slid the emerald onto her finger and turned her hand this way and that.

The assistant recounted the story of the ring's origins. The stone was Colombian but the cut suggested the emerald itself had first been set as jewellery in Russia. The identity of its original owner was unknown.

"How did it come to be in Paris?" Penny asked.

"Since the late nineteenth century, it has belonged to an important wine family in Bordeaux. It was passed down through the generations, ending up with its current owners at the end of the Second World War . . ."

It was the story Madame Declerc must have told her new daughter-in-law all those years ago. Penny nodded along, adding the occasional "how interesting."

"It is the finest piece in the Declerc collection."

"I'm sure it is."

Still wearing the ring, Penny sneezed. Over the years, she had perfected the art of the small, elegant sneeze, which nonetheless gave her an excuse to delve straight into her handbag for a handkerchief. And no one would find it odd that a little old lady would take a while to find her handkerchief in a capacious, old-fashioned handbag full of goodness only knew what. To add a little authenticity, Penny took out some of the rubbish she kept in her bag for exactly such an occasion and placed it on the display table, almost entirely covering the black velvet tray which still held the last ring Penny had tried on—the ugly ruby.

The assistant smiled tightly but nonetheless she still smiled, which was a good sign. And, of course, she was distracted by the mess Penny was making on the table. While Penny went back to rummaging in her bag, the assistant was transfixed by the half-finished packet of cough sweets, the battered glasses case and the well-thumbed copy of *Fifty Shades of Grey* that Penny had given her to look at. Penny knew that the assistant would be thinking of the ruby that lay concealed beneath those salacious pages.

Assured that no eyes were really upon her for the moment, Penny slipped the emerald ring off, letting it fall to the bottom of the bag. Then she fished the fake ring out of the bag's key pocket, sliding it into place as she did so. When it didn't quite work first time, Penny faked a fumble and said, "Goodness me! The ring fell off! I almost lost it. Now wouldn't that have been a disaster?" When she pulled her hand out of her bag, she was holding the fake between thumb and forefinger. She passed it to the assistant who took it from her with unseemly haste.

"And I still haven't found my handkerchief," Penny said.

The assistant passed her a tissue from a box beneath the table. Thank goodness she hadn't thought of that before.

After blowing her nose theatrically, Penny repacked her fluffy cough sweets, her glasses case, and the book while the assistant sprayed cleaner onto the ring Penny had given her and polished it up for the next punter.

"Thank you for letting me try all those rings on, dear," said Penny. "When you get to my age, there really isn't much to look forward to. No excitements."

The assistant said, "*Avec plaisir*," with a tight smile but her attention was already on a much more likely customer. Dragomir Georgiev pointed at the emerald ring and grunted. The assistant translated that to mean that the model draped around his shoulders would like to try the ring on. Except he didn't mean that. He wanted to try the ring on himself. He jammed the fake onto his little finger, where it looked reassuringly ridiculous. Penny would be very happy indeed if that man in particular paid a small fortune for the replica ring she'd had made by her dodgy jeweller in Hatton Garden back in 1967. Penny knew exactly how Georgiev had made his money. Though he didn't seem to remember her, they had old friends in common. He sold arms. Yes, of course he sold arms: to the good guys, to the bad guys, to anyone who wanted them.

"It suits you," she told him and he looked at her quizzically. "I really hope you end up with it."

THE WHOLE THING had gone like a dream. Though she had not lifted anything of particular value in a great many years, the past few weeks of intense practice had paid off and all of Penny's old skills and talent had come back to her.

Now all there was left to do was to get out of there, get back to the hotel and find a secure hiding place for the ring until they left for London, where Penny would have it broken up and sold. It wouldn't be worth as much broken down as it was in one piece but it would still be worth enough to fund all manner of exciting things that would make a real difference to people who deserved a little luck.

The world was a ridiculous place, where a stone such as the one she now had in her handbag could cause people to lose their minds, to hand over hundreds of thousands of euros, to steal and to kill. Yes, of course, she was in the process of stealing the damn thing herself but what she was doing was different. She had a higher purpose. The ring would be taken apart, some useful idiot would buy the stones and she would use the money raised to fund the Foundation and build schools, build clinics, help families stay together . . . The emerald was just a rock—a beautiful rock but a rock nonetheless—thrown up by geological quirks of a planet that was entirely indifferent to the perfection of its colour and the astonishment of its size.

Penny was determined that this piece of lucky dust would never again be the cause of someone's death. It was going to change lives for the better.

She paused by Archie to tell him, "I'm going back to the hotel."

"On your own? You can't, Auntie Penny. What if something happens to you?"

"I am nearly a hundred years old, Archie. Every day I long for something to happen to me."

"Auntie Penny," Archie said in a scolding tone. "Be careful what you wish for. Give me a moment to gather up Auntie Josephine and we'll come with you. There's not much point in hanging around here. Not now," he added ruefully. On the other side of the room, Malcolm laughed out loud as if on cue.

"I don't think I have ever seen anyone open their mouth that wide," Penny observed. "One could get lost in there."

"Tell me about it," said Archie. "Wait here. I'll fetch Auntie Josephine and we'll blow this joint. Perhaps we could stop and have a bite to eat at Willi's Wine Bar."

"On the Rue des Petits Champs? Oh yes. I do like Willi's."

"Me too," said Archie.

Archie left Penny standing close to the door, while he went to find her sister. This exit was taking rather longer than Penny had hoped but when she glanced back in the direction of the table where the ring had been on display, nothing yet seemed amiss. The assistant had obviously been fooled by the replica Penny left behind and had put it into the cabinet in the original's place.

All the same, Penny thought it wise to make another plan. What would she do if someone wanted to check her handbag on the way out? That hadn't happened on the way in but there seemed to be more security guards on the door now. Would their having nothing much to do for the moment mean they were more or less keen to do a thorough search? On the pretence of getting another tissue out of her bag, Penny transferred the ring from her bag to the palm of her hand and thence to her mouth. They wouldn't look in there. She lodged the ring between her gum and her cheek. Once upon a time she'd have swallowed it to make absolutely sure it wouldn't be found until she wanted it to be—with practice, she'd got very good at swallowing gems without so much as a sip of water—but that was when her digestive system was somewhat more reliable.

Where was Archie and why was he taking so long?

Ah, she could see him now, leading Josephine through the crowd towards her. Was he carrying a half-finished plate of canapés?

"I just need to find someone who can put these in a box," he told Penny. "For Auntie Josephine."

"I thought we were going to Willi's."

"They might have shut the kitchen by the time we get there," said Josephine. "Waste not, want not."

"You're moving your mouth a little strangely," Archie observed to Penny.

"Dentures," she said, before he could start worrying about a stroke.

"Well, we'll get them looked at as soon as we're back in London."

Archie went in search of a member of catering staff. While he was gone, another waiter carrying a tray full of champagne glasses tried to get by. Josephine helped herself to another glass of fizz.

"You can never have too much champagne," she said, taking one for Penny too. Josephine was well on her way to being hammered.

Penny discretely spat the ring back out into her handkerchief and held it balled in her fist.

"We're supposed to be leaving."

"What's the hurry?"

Penny huffed. She must be the only master criminal in the world in danger of being foiled by her sister's devotion to the doctrine of "waste not, want not." She should have just walked out the moment she had the ring in her possession. She could have got the staff at The Maritime to call Archie and tell him she was safely back at the hotel. Now she was stuck. This was why it was always better to work alone.

"I don't think Archie is having a very good time," Penny said. "He's only staying here for us and we only came here for him."

And now Penny could see that there was some kind of commotion around the table where up until ten minutes ago a priceless emerald had been on display. If they didn't go in the next thirty seconds . . .

"Penny Williamson!"

Penny froze, not wanting to turn and find out who had identified her; as if there was still a chance she could blend into the crowd and slip away as she had once been trained to do.

"It is you!"

"You're not dead," said Penny, recognising at once the pretty brown eyes in the leathery old face.

"And neither are you," Veronique Declerc observed.

Thirty-Six

. . . . .

"Well, isn't this the most wonderful surprise," said Veronique. "To meet again after all these years. When Stéphane told me that his friends, two British veterans, would be at the party this evening, I had no idea that one of them would be you."

Archie had rejoined the sisters now and looked with interest between his great-aunt Penny and the tiny French woman in the wheelchair in the hope that someone would fill him in on the connection.

"I'm Veronique Declerc." She offered Archie her tiny hand which, Penny noted, sported only a very plain wedding ring. No glittering solitaire. No watch. No sparkling bracelets. "And Penny is your grandmother?"

"My great-aunt . . ."

"How lovely. Your great-aunt and I met many years ago in the South of France. I've never forgotten it. We were both on honeymoon."

"Oh, with Uncle Connor!" Archie exclaimed. Then, "Sorry, Auntie Penny. You probably don't want to be reminded."

Veronique tilted her head, curious to know why.

"Your uncle Connor and my husband, Gilbert, got along very well. Gilbert hoped they might even be able to do business together but . . . but you didn't get in touch," she admonished Penny.

"Connor died the day you left the hotel," Penny said matter-of-factly. "Heart attack."

"What? But he was so fit. So young."

He wasn't that young, thought Penny. It wasn't until after Connor died that she got a proper look at his real passport. To think he'd had the cheek to refer to her as his "old bird."

"But you should have told us, Penny."

"I didn't know how to find you," said Penny. She didn't add, "Neither did I think there would be any point trying. Given you were supposed to have died in a robbery on the road to Nice airport." Penny had never looked for the news reports, not even all these years later when you could find anything on the internet. Convinced that she had catalysed Veronique's death, she could not bear to see the murder confirmed and risk seeing a photograph of the young woman innocent and happy.

"Well, this is terrible news. We had all been having such a lovely time," Veronique explained to Archie. "Your auntie Penny and my husband, Gilbert, knew each other as children. Which must mean he knew you too?" Veronique turned to Josephine.

"Yes," she said.

"You're Josephine? He talked of you often."

Penny noticed the past tense.

"Gilbert died last year. Just before our fifty-fifth wedding anniversary. What a lucky woman I am to have spent so many years with such a wonderful man."

"And now you're selling the family jewels," said Penny.

"Yes," said Veronique brightly. "Just the last few things now. What use does an old lady like me have for diamonds and pearls? Sadly, we didn't have any children to pass them on to. But the money? Oh, there's plenty I could do with that. Gilbert and I have been supporting a couple of girls' schools in Bangladesh since the 1970s. Whatever Stéphane and his team manage to raise for my old baubles will go towards building another."

"What a noble idea," said Archie.

Stéphane, who had come over to greet this very important client, agreed.

"Everyone at Brice-Petitjean is honoured you've chosen to let us help you achieve your ambitions, Madame Declerc."

"Isn't it a good idea, Auntie Penny? A school. You should talk to Veronique about your trust."

"It is a very good idea," said Penny. "How generous of you and Gilbert to think of such a thing."

"You know, for all these years, I've remembered that conversation you and I had over dinner in the Hôtel des Anges, Penny, about how important it is for women to be educated. How the education of girls is the very basis of a happy society, improving the lot of every generation that follows. You inspired me that night. That was the ethos behind our first school. I'm lucky that Gilbert agreed with the idea."

"Well, yes," Penny snapped. "I'm sure it must have salved his conscience somewhat."

An expression of confusion flickered across Veronique's face. "His conscience?"

"I'm sure you know what I mean."

Veronique tilted her head. She turned to Stéphane. "Stéphane, my dear, I wonder if I might try on my emerald ring one last time. That ring was very special to me. I always thought it brought me luck. You know, I actually lost it on my honeymoon. Gilbert had only just given it to me, as a wedding present, but it was too big for my hand and it must have slipped off. I thought it would be lost forever. It might have fallen off anywhere—in the hotel, in a shop, on the beach. The last time I remember seeing it was when we had that final dinner together, Penny, when you were taken ill. The following morning, I couldn't find it anywhere but three days after we got back to Paris, the newspapers reported that a priest in Antibes had found a priceless emerald in the offertory box at his church. It wasn't quite priceless, of course, but poor Gilbert had to make quite the offering in order to get it back. After that, I called it my lucky ring, though Gilbert always said that it brought us nowhere near as much luck as it should have done for the price."

"What a story," said Archie.

"I've often wondered who took the ring to the church. Such a kind thing to do. Though Gilbert said a truly honest person would have taken the ring straight to the police. He maintains it was stolen from our hotel room and the thief got cold feet when they realised it would be too difficult to sell on. There was a criminal gang operating on the Côte at that time. Several people from our hotel were robbed. But you, Penny. You lost the most precious thing. Poor Connor. He was so full of life. I am so sorry."

"It was a long time ago now," said Penny.

"But the loss of true love never gets any less painful, I think." Veronique reached out to Penny. "Come with me to see my lucky ring."

The ring that Connor must have taken straight from her hand without her noticing, Penny realised now. He could do that. It was his party piece. He'd hold your hands while looking deep into your eyes and the next thing you knew, he'd be showing you your own wedding ring in the palm of his hand and you would have no idea how he'd done it.

"Actually, I have to spend a penny."

"Spend a penny! I do love that phrase. Gilbert used to say it. He told me he learned it from you sisters."

Penny was already on her way to the door, moving surprisingly fast.

"Auntie Penny!" Archie called after her. "The powder room is over here."

Penny did not stop. She was fuelled by fury; fury that Gilbert Declerc might yet manage to turn his crime into a cause for beatification. God, how sick he must have felt to have to pay for the ring he and his mother had stolen from the Samuels when it reappeared at the church. Penny had never been able to work out for sure how it ended up in that offertory box. The last time Penny saw that ring, it was on the floor in the hotel room where she'd flung it in disgust as she and Connor argued. The only explanation was that the chambermaid who found Connor dead in bed a couple of hours later must have taken the emerald then thought better of it when the police arrived to investigate Connor's death.

And so it had ended up back with the Declercs, who were obviously *not* the newly-married couple car-jacked on the way to the airport. That damn American woman and her gossip. If Penny hadn't thought that Connor had arranged a hit on the Declercs, she would not have had to walk away from him that day. If she hadn't left him alone, he might have survived the heart attack that killed him. Though she'd never quite believed it was a heart attack . . . He was as fit as one of his horses.

As well as fury, Penny was also moved by fear now. Surely when Veronique saw the ring in the cabinet, she would know at once that it wasn't the same ring she had given to Brice-Petitjean for the sale. The fake was good but not that good. If Veronique didn't realise it, then Stéphane surely would. It was time for a fast exit.

With the real ring back between her teeth, Penny made for the door onto the street. She was about to walk through when she became aware of some sort of kerfuffle. The security guards scattered as three people in masks pushed their way in. In her dash for the exit, Penny collided with the first masked man's chest.

"Get back inside," he said in French. "You aren't going anywhere."

In her surprise, Penny swallowed the emerald in one big gulp.

Thirty-Seven

• • • • •

With the ring halfway down her oesophagus and threatening to come back up, Penny allowed herself to be marched back into the auction house. What choice did she have? The young man had a gun, as did his two companions. It was an unwelcome eventuality that she had not planned for.

There was a surreal moment as the four of them—three gunmen and one nonagenarian in danger of choking on a priceless emerald—entered the grand salon together. The party guests continued to drink champagne and chatter. No one was watching what was happening at the door. The young man's angry shout went unheard over the gossip and the valiant playing of the string quartet to which no one had been listening all evening.

"Right," the gunman said. "Let's do this."

With his hand on Penny's shoulder, he fired a single shot into the air to attract the party's attention. It brought down half of an expensive 1960s Murano glass light fitting, which was thankfully hanging over a large table and not over anyone's head. Even then, it was a second or two before anyone seemed to realise that the light fitting had been brought down deliberately.

"Ladies and gentlemen," Penny's captor announced over the hubbub. "May I have your attention, please. This is a siege and you are being taken hostage. Please sit down on the floor with your hands on your heads and nobody will be hurt."

"Oh dear," said Penny, as she thumped her chest to help the ring go down. It had been a long time since she'd swallowed anything so unyielding and she could hardly believe she'd ever done it. "Sit on the floor? I'm afraid I'm not sure I can manage that."

Around the room, most people remained standing in confusion. What had the masked man said? they asked one another. Was this some sort of performance art specially put on for the party? Since the pandemic, masks had become so much a part of daily life that they no longer registered as sinister in quite the same way as they used to. It took another shot into the ceiling to really draw everyone's attention.

"Floor. Now. Please," the chief gunman commanded. "Hands on your heads."

Slowly realising that this wasn't a joke or the beginning of a witty art piece, the elegantly dressed guests started to lower themselves slowly to the parquet and arrange themselves cross-legged, like school children. Anyone who tried to slip away—and there were a couple—was swiftly blocked by the masked man's accomplices, who had taken up a position by the main door. The auction house's official security team were nowhere to be seen, having made their escape while the gunmen were pushing their way in. The security guards obviously had it clear in their minds which was the more valuable: their jobs or their lives. If any of the punters had brought their own security, they too were suddenly elsewhere.

"What's going on?" came the murmur from every corner. "Who are these people?" The guests outnumbered the gunmen by a factor of a hundred but they allowed themselves to be subdued by the sight of the weapons, as well they might.

It wasn't long before only three people apart from the gunmen remained standing. Penny wasn't even trying to sit down. Archie stood alongside Josephine—who, like Penny, could not get down onto the floor on a whim—and Veronique, in her wheelchair. The young man who had been pushing Veronique's chair was already on the floor. Archie still had Josephine's treasured leftovers in his hand.

"Get down," one of the two junior hostage-takers demanded. "That means all of you."

"Would you mind?" Archie handed the plate of leftovers to Veronique, who cradled them in her lap. He then did his best to help Josephine to the floor but it was hopeless.

"I should never have given up yoga," Josephine attempted a joke.

"You can't expect these ladies to get down on the floor," Archie told the chief gunman. "My great-aunts are ninety-seven and ninety-nine years old."

"I don't care. Sit down," said the chief gunman.

"I definitely can't," said Penny. "I'll never get back up."

"Sit down."

"They can't sit on the floor. And I won't sit down either," said Archie. "Unless you allow me to get these ladies some chairs first."

The chief gunman levelled the barrel of his gun at Archie.

"What?"

"Archie," said Josephine. "I think we'll just have to do as the young man asks."

But it wasn't happening. The entire room held its breath as Archie and Josephine performed a funny little dance that got her absolutely no closer to sitting cross-legged.

"Is this going to take long?" Penny asked the gunman.

"We'll be here as long as we have to be."

"Then we probably will need chairs."

"What? Get them some chairs then," the gunman barked at Archie. "But don't try anything funny or I'll blow this lady's head off."

He put the gun to Penny's temple.

"Gosh," said Penny. She gave Archie a little nod.

"One of the gilt ones," she instructed. "The other ones are too low for my back."

"Thank you," said Archie to the gunman. He went to fetch two gilt chairs, apologising to his fellow hostages as he stepped over their legs.

"Excuse me. Sorry. Excuse me."

"Archie," Stéphane hissed at him from knee-height. "What are you doing? Be careful."

"My great-aunts cannot sit on the floor," said Archie, sounding a good deal braver than he felt in that moment. "I'm doing what I have to do."

"Put the chairs on the stage," the gunman instructed—motioning to the platform from which Stéphane had planned to give a charming speech at about this time. "Come on. Quickly."

"Quickly really isn't in my repertoire anymore," Penny warned him. "And who are you again, dear? If we're being kept hostage, I should really like to know why we've all been so unlucky."

"Shut up," was the only response she got.

"Manners cost nothing," Penny muttered.

The gunman glared at her. Penny mimed pulling a zip across her mouth.

WHAT IS GOING ON? Penny asked herself. Was this a robbery gone wrong or something else?

Penny decided that if the masked men—though perhaps the smallest of the three was a woman—had been there simply to rob the auction house, they would have swiped the booty they were after and used their guns to clear a quick escape path, like the robbers who'd recently targeted the Chanel store on the Rue Cambon. They would have hoped not to have to involve any bystanders at all. They certainly wouldn't have struck during a party, knowing there would be hundreds of people in attendance and security all over the place. So this was something different. Everything suggested an ideological motivation. Ideology was far more dangerous than greed. They weren't taking jewels. They were taking hostages.

The gilt chairs were on the stage now. Archie settled Josephine in place then stepped down again to fetch Penny. The other hostages watched wide-eyed as Archie helped his great-aunt up the steps oh so carefully, as if they had all the time in the world.

The chief gunman barked his disapproval.

"Come on!"

"We're moving as fast as we can," said Penny, though the truth was, she could probably have moved a little faster. A lot faster. She wanted time to get the measure of the situation from a standing position. "Honestly, some people . . ."

As Archie helped Penny to her chair, he offered her some comforting thoughts.

"I don't know what's going on here, Auntie, but you're not to worry. I'm sure this place is full of security cameras and the police must be fully aware of what's happening and already be on their way. They're probably outside right now, planning to rush in and end this nonsense at any moment."

Archie was right that the auction house was full of security cameras, but as Penny looked for them—she thought she knew where all of them were—she wasn't at all sure they were working. The ease with which the gunmen had entered the building perhaps even suggested an inside job, with the auction house's security system disabled. She would have expected there to be a cacophony of alarms by now otherwise.

"Now get on the floor," the chief gunman motioned for Archie to sit.

Flipping up the tails of his jacket so they didn't get creased, Archie sat on the stage between his great-aunts' feet, just as he'd done when he was small. Before he put his hands on his head, he gave them both the "thumbs up." Then, correctly seated at last, he tapped out in Morse on his crown.

"Et well bi uk."

He never could get the vowels right.

Up until that moment, Penny had remained quite sanguine, as her decades-old training allowed, but the sight of Archie's bald patch—just like his father's and his grandfather's before that—as he mis-tapped his Morse was in danger of bringing a lump to her throat.

If only she'd just said, "Of course we should go" when he suggested they leave the party after Stéphane had introduced them to that lump of a fiancé. If only. But she'd had to get that cursed ring. Was the damn thing about to do its worst again?

With everyone seated, the hall was uncannily calm. The chattering was utterly silenced. The string quartet that had played so enthusiastically and determinedly over the chit-chat sat on the floor next to their chairs, with their instruments in their laps, and hands on their heads. Thus posed, the lead violinist was unable to stop her violin from slipping onto the parquet, where it landed with a strange clatter and twang. The chief gunman switched his attention to her, like a hawk spotting a mouse in long grass. But his gaze did not rest on her for long. He went back to sweeping the room in search of the real reason for this surreal interruption to one of the biggest social engagements of the year.

While his colleagues kept the hostages covered with their guns, the chief gunman set up a tripod. Then he took out his phone and took a panoramic shot of the room on video, before he settled the phone on the stand and began to talk directly into its camera lens.

"Good evening, Facebook. I'm not going to tell you my real name, but you may call me Angel, since I am here to bring retribution."

A frisson went around the room. Retribution for what?

"I am a citizen of a state which has long since turned its back on democracy; where our esteemed leaders are nothing but robber barons. I am a fatherless child and a childless father. My family has been torn apart by quarrels that mean nothing to us, perpetrated on land that should have been used to feed our children, not to further enrich those who knew their loved ones would never have to stand on the front line.

"My apologies to you all," he said to the auction house guests. "With the exception of you," the masked man pointed his gun now at Dragomir Georgiev. "You know exactly who we are and why we're here. To the rest of you, it is with great regret that I tell you this evening that because of this man and his associates back in my home country, some of you may die."

There was an understandable murmur of distress.

The gunman addressed Georgiev directly. "Uncomfortable, isn't it, to be on the wrong end of one of these? I believe this particular gun is one you supplied to the militia that stormed my village a couple of years ago."

Georgiev looked hot and wretched in his Loro Piana dinner suit.

"Come up here, my old friend."

Prodded in the back by another gunman, Georgiev got to his feet and reluctantly joined Archie and the sisters on the stage. "Tell these good people how you came to be among them? Tell them how you made your many, many millions? Don't want to? I can understand why. Well, if you don't want to talk, I'll carry on."

As Georgiev was forced to sit down on the stage next to the sisters, Angel looked into the camera of his phone again. "In exchange for the life of this man, and the rest of the innocent bystanders now trapped in this room, we require the release of the following political prisoners."

He read out a list of names. At the end of the list, he told his audience,

"We expect a response to our demands within half an hour and if that response doesn't come, we will kill our first hostage. Every fifteen minutes after that, we'll kill another one."

"No!" someone shouted. "I have children."

"So did I. Once upon a time." Angel levelled his gun at the shouter. The shouter looked down at the floor.

Angel turned back to his phone camera. "Now, we start the countdown to justice." He glanced up at the clock on the auction house wall, as did everybody else.

"*Kiip culm*," Archie tapped on his head in bad Morse.

AS IT WAS, Penny did feel quite calm again. Having heard Angel's speech, she felt certain that he did not want this situation to end badly any more than his audience did. She remembered a long-ago lecture delivered by Frank during F Section training, about what to look for in recruiting partisans to a resistance cell. How to tell who would be a reliable colleague and who a dangerous hothead. She had a feeling that Angel was not the latter. Which wasn't to say that they weren't still in a difficult position. She wished she could send Archie a signal that reassured him, just as he was trying to reassure her. But he wouldn't be able to see her tapping on her knee. Josephine could though. Penny tapped out "TG" for "*toujours gai.*" Josephine risked a little smile in her direction.

"Observe." Penny heard Frank in her head.

There were instances when one needed to move quickly, on instinct, and instances when it was better to take the time to make a plan. Penny thought this was a situation for watching and waiting.

But while Penny was doing just that, down on the auction house floor, someone else decided to take action. Malcolm, Stéphane's fiancé, suddenly scrambled to his feet and made a run for the door. He did not get far before he tripped over Dragomir Georgiev's scantily-dressed girlfriend's endless pins. As Malcolm was righting himself, the smallest of the gunmen was upon him. Malcolm flailed his arms and legs in what might have been taekwondo but looked like a total mess from where Penny was sitting. It was distracting but ineffectual. When the smallest gunman discharged a bullet into the ceiling, Malcolm dropped to the floor as though he'd been hit. He hadn't.

Malcolm got to his knees and put his hands together in prayer. "I can't die!" he cried. "I can't. I'm nothing to do with this." He pointed at Georgiev. "I don't even know who that man is. I'm just an actor. I come at everything in life from a place of truth and love."

When Malcolm stood up again, Angel pointed his gun right at Malcolm's head, causing the actor to pull one of the Brice-Petitjean assistants to her feet to use as a human shield. She squeaked in indignation.

"If you let me go," Malcolm continued. "I can spread your message—whatever it is—in the outside world. I have fans, followers, millions of them. Just look at my Facebook page. I can be your mouthpiece. I'm playing a Resistance fighter in my latest film so I understand your struggle. Let me leave the building now and I will have a professional camera crew back here within the hour. I swear it. You can tell the whole world what your problem is then. My face will give you an international platform. You must know who I am?"

"I'm afraid I don't," Angel said, voice heavy with contempt. "Bring him up here."

The young auction house assistant wriggled free of Malcolm's unaffectionate embrace and the smaller gunman marched the actor up to the stage.

"You might have won yourself a new role," Angel told him. "As first man to die."

Malcolm fell to his knees. "Nooo! I still have so much to give the world," he wailed.

"The clock is ticking," Angel addressed his phone. "Thirty minutes, or we begin to take reparations for Georgiev's crimes. An eye for an eye. Starting with him . . ."

Malcolm sank onto his belly and beat his fists against the floor like a child having a tantrum. He railed against the gods and cried out for his mother. It was the most affecting performance he'd given in his twenty-year acting career. If only he were acting.

Penny wondered whether there was method in it. Was Malcolm distracting their captors before going for some kind of capoeira kick? Angel watched open-mouthed, as did everyone else. No daring martial arts move was forthcoming.

"Get up," Angel told Malcolm. "I don't want to have to shoot you in the back."

"Noooo!" Malcolm rolled around like an upended beetle. "I can't die. I'm at the height of my powers."

"Ahem," Archie cleared his throat to catch Angel's attention.

"What now?"

"Perhaps I could take Malcolm's place?"

"No!" cried the sisters and a good half of the room.

"No," said Angel. "No. Not you. I will spare this . . . this invertebrate." Angel prodded Malcolm with his toe. "But I want his replacement to send a proper message about strength and bravery. So, worm, you can join the rest of our audience again, but only if you're willing to swap your place with this little old lady."

Angel swung his phone around and pointed the lens and his gun at Penny.

Malcolm could not get off the stage fast enough.

"Oh dear," said Penny. "What a pickle."

Thirty-Eight

• • • • •

1943

When Penny and Josephine spoke at history festivals up and down the UK, members of the audience would sometimes ask how they had lived through the war so unafraid. That was without even knowing what Penny's war had really entailed. She would tell them in response, "I simply never for one moment thought that I was going to die."

That wasn't entirely true. There had been one moment when Penny very much *did* think she was going to die.

PARACHUTE TRAINING SPLIT the F Section recruits into two groups. Those who were excited about jumping from a plane and those who were quietly terrified. Penny was quietly terrified.

There were so many people one had to trust when it came to leaping from a plane. In the first place, you had to trust that the parachute had been properly made. Next you had to trust that the rigger who packed that parachute had not been having a bad day. You had to trust that the pilot of the plane that took you up would reach the right altitude over the right landing place. You had to trust that the person who had chosen the landing place knew what they were doing and wasn't a double agent, waiting to hand you over to the Gestapo the moment you touched down. You had to trust that God would provide the right jumping conditions: a clear moonlit night with no crosswind. You had to trust that the parachute trainer had told you the right way to exit the hold. You had to trust that the dispatcher would pick the perfect moment to shout "Go." Then you had to trust that your parachute would actually open.

Penny had never even been in a plane before her commando training with the SOE. Ahead of the first flight she ever took, from the south of England up to Arisaig, she stood trembling and silent as she waited for her turn to board. Though she understood something of the mechanics of flying, having read about it in one of her father's library books, it was hard to believe that the physics would apply to this plane, the one she was about to go up in. It looked so heavy and that was before the candidates and all their kit were loaded on board. Penny desperately wanted to ask one of her fellow trainees to reassure her that planes just like this one made safe flights all the time, but that would only be construed as weakness, and weakness was not something for which she wanted to be known.

Jerome was sitting opposite her in the hold.

"Happy?" he asked her. "You're looking awfully green."

"It's the uniform," Penny snapped back. "Khaki really isn't my colour."

The laughter of the others, which told Penny she'd won the point, gave her enough of a boost to make it through take-off. Even Jerome had to smile.

All the same, she could not quite shake the thought that they might run out of oxygen as the plane climbed into the sky. And the landing was terrifying. She was convinced that the pilot would never be able bring the plane to a stop. Evidently, the landing was not as smooth as it might have been and she wasn't the only one looking a little unwell as they filed off.

A month later, her paramilitary course complete, Penny was sent to Tatton Park near Manchester in preparation for her first parachute jump. Initial training took place in a hangar, from a tall tower built specially for the purpose, on which they could learn both how to exit a plane and land correctly. What nobody had told Penny was that jumping from that tower was, in many ways, harder than jumping from an actual plane. Once you were off the edge of the platform, it was a helluva rush to the ground. Penny would have volunteered for another round of having her head dunked in ice water in an instant if it meant she could avoid that leap.

And all the time Jerome seemed to be watching, waiting for her to make a mistake he could point out to the other candidates with glee.

"Get on with it, Bo Peep," he shouted from the ground, as Penny perched above him on the edge of the platform's trapdoor, the "Joe hole" as Jerome and his fellow Americans called it. Joe hole was slang for an outdoor toilet.

Jerome's goading made Penny angry enough to do it, to face that drop—much too short—and the sickening sensation of being jerked to a standstill in mid-air.

After that, the trainees were taken outdoors to the airstrip and loaded into an enormous wicker basket that was lifted into the air by a barrage balloon. The trainers remained on the ground, bellowing their instructions up into the sky through a megaphone. The basket was supposed to simulate the hold of a plane. When your number was called, you shuffled to the basket's Joe hole, dropped your legs through and waited for go. When it was Penny's turn, her trainer shouted, "Remember what your mother always said and keep your knees and feet together!"

Penny tipped him a sarcastic salute.

It seemed like an age between that "go" and the opening of Penny's chute but she executed a textbook landing and made sure she was safely out of sight before covering her face with her hands to stave off a small panic attack.

Less than a week later, as the veteran of three real parachute jumps, Penny was ready for the all-important night jump. She got on board the Halifax that would take them up and took her seat without even pausing in her conversation with the next agent in training. She even found a moment to reapply her lipstick.

When the time came for her to jump, she took her place at the Joe hole and looked down at the darkened countryside flying by beneath them. Where once she had been too nervous to look out of a plane window, now she happily searched out landmarks as they whizzed by below. She was relieved that she had managed to get through that particular fear.

Earlier that day, the trainees had been talking about another female agent, who'd exited the plane clumsily and caught her head on the edge of the hatch on her way out. They called it "ringing the bell," misjudging your exit from the plane like that. The agent (whom Penny would come to know of years later as Violette Szabo) was lucky that the damage she sustained was superficial. She still went on to undertake her mission. Now for some reason, she popped into Penny's head just as she moved forward to take her own jump.

Penny had already made three perfect jumps from a bomber. Each one she'd enjoyed more than the last. Now she made her fourth jump, and this time she was the clapper . . .

For a second Penny thought she had been shot in the side of the head. As her parachute unfurled like a beautiful chrysanthemum above her head, she gazed up at the billowing silk, lit by the moon, in a daze. When the parachute was fully filled, it jerked her briefly upwards, then she continued a more stately fall. She was unconscious by the time she hit the earth.

It wasn't such a bad thing, landing in a faint. Penny did not resist the ground as she made contact. Instead, she crumpled gracefully and probably hurt herself far less badly than she might have done had she been awake and panicking.

The drop zone team were there the moment she touched down, quickly getting her free of the parachute and rolling her onto her back, checking she was breathing and assessing her for damage.

"Get the stretcher," she heard someone say.

"What happened?" someone else asked.

"She rang the fucking bell," said Jerome.

"Fuck, what a mess."

Penny thought she recognised that voice. Was it Frank? Opening her eyes, she strained to reach a hand towards his face.

"Frank," she said. "I love you, Frank. Do you love me?"

"Frank?" mused Jerome.

"She's concussed," the parachute trainer said.

A WEEK IN sick bay later, Penny was declared fit for her own first mission in France.

She was going in with two other agents. The disappointment she'd felt when she discovered that Jerome was one of them seemed to be mutual. Dropping into France with them was an agent going by the alias of Remi. He'd grown up in Normandy. Penny was glad, hoping that his genuine Frenchness might offset Jerome's tendency to swear loudly in American English whenever something didn't go his way.

The night before the drop, they had something of a Last Supper at the country house—not for nothing was the SOE nicknamed "Stately 'Omes of England"—where they were taken through final preparations for the mission.

Jerome held his hand out towards Penny as they filed into the dining room. "Hostilities suspended 'til all this is over?"

Penny nodded.

"I'm glad to be going in with you," he said then. "I know you and I haven't always seen eye to eye, Bo Peep, but I do trust you. I think you know what you're doing."

"I hope *you* do," she replied.

That evening, Penny saw a different side to Jerome. They'd all changed over the past few weeks. Aged wasn't quite the word for it. Matured, perhaps. In Jerome's case, gone was the preening braggard who seemed to devote all his energy to tormenting her. She could see in this new version of Jerome—quiet and contemplative—what the F Section recruitment team must have seen in him: a good soldier, thoughtful and serious, someone who was devoted to the cause.

At the end of dinner, she and Jerome toasted each other.

"I'll make sure you get back in one piece," Jerome said.

"I'll make sure *you* get back in one piece," Penny echoed.

A FANY OFFICER was assigned to keep Penny company during her last evening in England. She had Penny write letters to her loved ones that would be sent at regular intervals while she was overseas and another set to be sent in the event of her demise. She'd already had to write a will but she wrote to her mother, *Please take some money out of my post office account to buy Mrs. Glover a new handbag and Sheppy a bone. George can have the rest, though not to spend on sweets.*

She wrote to Josephine.

Dear Josie-Jo, If you get this, then I've had it. I have left this mortal coil. I'm sorry we didn't get a chance to say goodbye. Bloody war.

Josie-Jo, you have been the very best of sisters. Even when you went through that phase of pinching me whenever Ma and Pa weren't looking. I will miss you. If it's possible to miss someone from the other side. Look after our parents and our little brother too. I'm sure I'll see you somewhere at some point; perhaps even in heaven if you're good! In the meantime, keep sticking it to Adolf and ensure you remain toujours gai.

She handed the letter over then asked for it back, to add a PS.

PS. I really do love you.

Everything about Penny's deployment had been thought of, down to the very last detail. She was given a set of clothes, old clothes, sourced in France, that she would wear instead of her FANY uniform. She wasn't even allowed to wear her own underwear, lest she find herself being searched by a Gestapo officer who recognised English knickers.

Every possible thing by which she might be identified as British had to be left behind. Her most treasured family photograph, which she had thought looked neutral enough, was confiscated straight away.

"The house you're posing in front of is very obviously not in France."

Even her Yardley lipstick had to go. She was given a new one—a French brand—and was delighted to discover it suited her far better than the one she had to give up.

As the hour of take-off approached, the FANY officer, who said Penny should feel free to call her Betty, despite her superior rank, seemed much more upset about the looming departure than Penny was.

"I will be coming back," Penny assured her. "It's not my time to die."

All the same, at the airfield, Penny was offered the legendary tin, containing sleeping tablets, amphetamines, and a single capsule of cyanide— the "L" pill. "L" for "lethal."

Vera Atkins—whom Penny had first met at those meetings in Baker Street where everyone remained anonymous—turned up to see her off.

She briefly held Penny's hands.

"I wish I could be coming with you," she said. It didn't feel like a platitude. "How are you, Agent Bruna?"

"I'm excited," said Penny.

"Not too excited, I hope. Keep your head." Vera tugged the zip on Penny's camouflage flight suit—the "striptease" suit that had to be buried on landing—fully closed, and gave her a last affectionate pat on the shoulder.

During the practice sessions, there was always a bit of banter, but on this flight the hold of the Halifax was silent. Penny kept her eyes closed, until her brain decided that now would be a good time to rerun the film of her last jump, of ringing the bell. Instead of watching that movie on the back of her eyelids, she looked up and examined her fellow agents in the gloom. She had never seen Jerome so still or so serious before. She studied his profile and wondered what he was thinking about. Who had he left behind? A sweetheart? A wife? A child? She had no idea. Would they ever share their true stories with one another? Their real names? Would they have a drink and a laugh, when the Nazis were defeated and they were on their way back home? Would they ever come back home?

"*Toujours gai*," Penny muttered to herself, as for just a moment her mind wandered to the unthinkable notion that she might never see her sister or brother again.

When the pilot announced that they would soon be over the drop zone, Jerome caught her eye and chanced a small thumbs-up. They performed the last pre-jump checks on their equipment: straps were tightened, buckles tested, prayers were muttered. Down below, the Resistance cell they would be joining had marked out the drop zone with just enough torchlight to guide them in without attracting the wrong sort of attention. The order of jumping had already been decided. Remi first, then Penny, then Jerome.

"Action station number one," said the dispatcher.

Remi advanced to the Joe hole and balanced there in the ready position, waiting for the green light.

"Go."

Remi exited into the ether as if he were just jumping into a pool.

"Action station number two."

Penny shuffled forward next. She looked down but could focus on nothing. Her head swam. She looked to the dispatcher. He was checking to be sure Remi was well clear of the plane. Satisfied that he was, the dispatcher gave the command.

"Go."

Penny didn't go.

"GO!" the dispatcher shouted, in case she hadn't got the signal over the noise of the propellers.

But Penny couldn't do it.

"No," she suddenly turned round, fell to her hands and knees and scrabbled away from the hatch. "No, I can't."

"Bo Peep," Jerome said. "What the hell? Come on."

"I can't. I can't. I can't."

Her heart hammered. She pressed herself against the wall of the fuselage, as far from the hatch as she could get.

"We've got seconds," Jerome told her. "Come on. You're next. We need you. I need you. You're our radio girl."

But Penny had missed her chance and now the timing was all messed up. The pilot took the Halifax back around to line up with the drop zone again. Every extra moment they were in the sky was an extra moment for the Germans to spot them and bring them down.

"I can't, I can't, I can't." Penny muttered the words over and over, with her hands over her ears.

"If you say you can't, of course you fucking won't be able to. Someone push her out there," Jerome exploded.

"No. She'll screw up," was the dispatcher's opinion.

"Bo Peep." Jerome took her hands and looked deep into her eyes. "Come on. You're the maddest bitch I ever met. You're not scared of anything. You can do this."

But something had snapped inside her and she couldn't stop the tears.

"I can't do it. I can't. I'm sorry. I just can't."

There was no time to argue.

"No one's going to make you," said Jerome.

The plane was back over the landing zone.

"Action station number three," said the dispatcher.

"I've gotta go," Jerome told her. "See you soon."

"Go."

Jerome jumped. Once Jerome's parachute was safely opened, the dispatcher closed the hatch after him. In silence, he helped Penny out of her parachute harness, as the pilot turned the Halifax back towards the Channel and home.

● ● ●

IF THE GROUND crew were disappointed or angry to see that Penny had not been successfully deployed over France, they didn't show it. They were consummate professionals, leaving the uncomfortable debriefing to the shadowy powers that be. The day after her unexpected return to base, Penny was called in to see a senior officer she had not previously met. He listened patiently to Penny's version of events.

"I couldn't stop thinking about ringing the bell. I just had this feeling I would do it again and be dead before I landed."

The officer nodded. "I understand."

"But I'm not afraid of being there, on the ground. I know I could still do everything expected of me if there were just some other way of getting me to France. It's only the jump. You've sent some of the other agents in on Lysanders, haven't you? Or by boat via the south. I could go in like that. I wouldn't be scared once I was there, I swear it. You know I've been an exemplary student. It was only about the jump."

The officer made notes and promised Penny that everything would be taken into account when her former trainers met to decide where Penny would end up next.

Thirty-Nine

· · · · ·

Where Penny ended up next was back in Scotland, on a period of gardening leave in the "cooler" at Inverlair, just long enough for everything she had been told about her abortive mission and her colleagues at F Section to become irrelevant.

Once she had sat out her gardening leave—all the while pretending in her letters to her mother and to Josephine that she was still doing secretarial work at the commando school—Penny was allowed to spend a weekend at home. It was the first time she'd been back to the house in almost two years. It seemed quite different from the last time she'd seen it. Smaller. Shabbier. There was no gardener anymore—all the village men between the ages of eighteen and forty-five were away at the war.

George had grown gangly and his voice was deep. He was full of stories about the brave men parachuting in behind enemy lines to support partisans all over Europe. The temptation to correct his wild fantasies about those agents was hard. He didn't even know that women were being trained for the same work. Would he have believed it? Penny longed to tell him but she had promised that she would never share what happened on the night she was supposed to parachute into France, or during the months before at the big country houses where she had trained in Morse, unarmed combat, and burglary. Even George, her own little brother, who was a patriot to his bones, might inadvertently let something slip that would endanger the people with whom she had trained.

In truth, Penny was too ashamed to want to tell anyone what a waste of time and resources her training had been. Night after night she relived the moment she failed to jump: Jerome's disbelief and the desperation in his voice as he tried to persuade her to join him. The long flight back across the Channel with only the dispatcher for company in the hold. The quiet confusion in the eyes of the ground crew as she stepped off the plane at the base she had left only hours before with a hero's send-off. She promised herself that if she was given another chance, she would not let them down again. But she was not given another chance. Her days as an F Section agent were over. No one would ever carve her name with pride. It was a humiliation from which she thought she would never recover.

Though when it was first suggested that she go back to the FANY rank and file Penny had smarted at the idea, she did know that she still wanted to be part of the war effort. She could still be useful, especially with her telegraphy training. Reporting back to FANY HQ, she was invited to apply for a posting overseas. Not in France or any of the occupied nations, of course, but the location of the job she applied for was still top secret.

At the beginning of February 1944, she joined a group of FANYs in Liverpool for a mystery voyage. Though they were, for the most part, older than she, they somehow seemed much younger. Their chatter didn't interest Penny at all. None of them knew where they were going, though they were definitely going somewhere warm. They'd been handed new uniforms—tropical uniforms—when they mustered at the dock.

They sailed in a convoy of troop ships, protected by a small fleet of Royal Navy destroyers to ward off attackers. There was a moment when a rumour went around the ship that the convoy was being tailed by a wolf pack of U-boats. When the FANYs gathered on deck for a lifeboat drill, the atmosphere was solemn. One of the FANY officers had known a Wren who'd gone down with the *Empress of Canada* in March 1943. The stories that had come out of that sinking were in every FANY's mind as they leaned against the rail on the top deck and looked out over the implacable sea.

The U-boats were deterred and Penny's ship made it safely to her destination, with no calamity bigger than the tuck shop having run out of her favourite kind of chocolate en route.

Penny was to be stationed in Algiers. She fell in love with the North African city the moment they docked there. As she felt the warm breeze on her face, she knew she had come a very long way from home in more ways than one. It was as though she had lived three lifetimes in the last three years.

From time to time—well, every day really—she wondered about her F Section colleagues. Who had been parachuted in as her replacement in Jerome and Remi's cell? What was Frank doing? Did he think of her? Did he even know that she'd been sent to North Africa? He must do. Every now and then she recited "Invictus" to herself, as if that could bring him back, feeling sure that their story could not end here.

In fact, it ended in a hotel in Germany, more than twenty years later.

IT WAS 1965 and Penny and Frank were preparing to steal a diamond "as big as The Ritz."

As they lay in bed smoking, having gone over the plan for the day ahead, Penny asked the question that she'd swallowed down for twenty years.

"What really happened in '43, Frank? Who was it who made the call not to send me back into the field?"

In the pale light of dawn, Frank was unguarded. He ran his fingers along her bare arm as he told her, "It was me."

"What?"

"It was me."

"Frank? No." Penny propped herself up on her elbow and stared down at him.

"Don't look at me like that, Penny. The others wanted to send you back in—God knows we needed all the trained agents we could get—but I told them you weren't ready, that ringing the bell had changed you."

"Why? Why would you do that?"

Frank took a long pull on his cigarette and blew the smoke back out in a plume that looked like a ghost leaving his body.

"I did it because I loved you."

It was the first time he had had ever mentioned loving her.

"Because you *loved* me?"

"Love you."

"But I wanted to serve my country. To serve France."

"Come on, Penny. It was suicide mission."

"I was prepared for that."

"No you weren't. You were lucky to get out of it. The cell you were supposed to join was already compromised. Do you know what happened to Jerome and Remi? They were rounded up two days after they landed. Do you know how they died? They died like dogs. You would have died the same way. And for what?"

"It was my choice to take that risk."

"You were nineteen years old. You didn't know what you were doing."

"I was old enough to fuck."

"Don't say it like that."

Penny got out of bed and began to gather the clothes she had thrown aside with such abandon the night before.

"What are you doing?"

"I'm leaving," she said.

"Penny . . . Come on. I'm just telling you the truth. I'm sorry you didn't get the chance to be a hero but what does it matter now?"

"It matters because I've spent the last twenty years thinking I wasn't good enough. Do you have any idea how the shame of not jumping that day has eaten away at me? Of course you don't."

"Plenty of people refused to jump. People much bigger and uglier than you were."

"But they were sent into France by other means. They weren't left to feel like failures. Like *cowards*."

"Anyone who ever met you knew you weren't a coward. If anything, you were too fucking brave."

"Stop. I can't even look at you. You betrayed me."

"I didn't betray you. I gave you the chance to have a life. The war wasted so many lives. I didn't want it to have yours as well. You're kidding yourself if you think your dying too would have made the slightest bit of difference."

"You don't know that. You don't know what I might have been able to do. Who I might have been able to save."

Frank's expression was downcast. He gave a small nod and admitted, "That's true."

"But you didn't trust in me enough to let me go."

"You were a child," Frank said again, more forcefully this time. "And I'd had enough of sending children off to war. You were high on hope and patriotic fervour and ready to lay down your life for what? Yes, the Nazis had to be defeated but what's really changed since then? All that blood and terror didn't buy us peace and love. So long as there's money to be made, there will always be war. Old men talking, young men dying. Always."

Holding her blouse to her breast, Penny seemed for a moment to be in agreement with him, but then she shook her head and carried on dressing.

"You robbed me of the chance to do the right thing."

"But you lived and you came back to me and ever since you've been doing the right thing, helping people in your own way."

"Don't patronise me. I never want to see you again."

"Penny, stop. How does this change what we've had for the past fifteen years?"

"What *have* we had for the past fifteen years, Frank? You've had a wife and a family, and adventures and sex with me whenever you could find the time. I've had . . ." Penny shrugged. "Whatever it is, I don't need it anymore. I don't need you."

"You're overreacting. Let's talk about this later. After we've done the job."

"I'm not doing the job. Not today. You can do it yourself. I'm flying home."

"Penny, don't do this."

She stood at the door, eyes burning with fury.

"I wanted to keep you out of trouble," Frank said. "I *saved* you."

"Saved me for what?"

TRUE TO HER word, Penny refused to speak to Frank again, though he tried his best to persuade her to forgive him. He even asked Jinx to act as go-between.

Jinx thought the sun shone out of Frank's arse. Had done ever since she first met him, when Penny's "family money" story unravelled and she'd had to bring Jinx in on the act. Jinx was an excellent apprentice for a jewel thief. With her sweet face, she could have walked out of the Tower of London carrying the Koh-i-Noor.

"If you don't want to work with Frank, I will," Jinx announced.

After that, the two women didn't talk either. But it was Jinx who broke the news about Frank's death to Penny in the summer of 1966. He died the same week Connor did—shot in the chest by an East End gangster in a deal gone horribly wrong. By coincidence, Jinx was in the South of France when she got the call. She tracked Penny down via Josephine and came to the hotel. When Josephine arrived shortly afterwards, of course she thought Penny's desperate tears were for Connor. She could not be consoled.

Josephine had to care for Penny for weeks after they got back to England. She was surprised at the depth of Penny's grief. She'd not sensed such a depth of love when Penny and Connor took their vows.

Josephine did not know that Penny really *had* lost the love of her life, and all she had left of him was a metal matchbox engraved with a verse from "Invictus." Jinx passed it on, after one of Frank's colleagues gave it to her at the funeral Penny could not attend.

Nothing but a matchbox. However years later Penny realised that, on that morning in Germany, Frank had also unwittingly handed her back her courage. Knowing that her commanding officers at F Section thought she could have gone back into the field, were it not for Frank's sentimental veto, Penny knew she could face anything. So when Angel levelled the barrel of his gun at Penny in that auction house, she felt an old calm descend. He had picked on the wrong old lady.

Forty

· · · · ·

Paris, 2022

Perhaps it was the cocktails and the sneaky tot of rum, but by the end of dinner, Davina Mackenzie seemed to have mellowed.

"Arlene," she said. "I am really very grateful to you for being here to help me tonight. I'm sure you had better things to do."

"Not at all," Arlene lied. "I'm glad I was here to take over from Hazel."

"Yes, well. I will have to call the agency and tell them next time they should send someone sturdier. Someone like you."

Arlene wasn't sure that was entirely a compliment but she decided to accept it as one. In any case, it was a beautiful evening to be gently wheeling two World War Two veterans through the streets of Paris. The four women paused on a bridge to watch the Eiffel Tower glittering on the hour. Sister Eugenia asked a passer-by to take a photograph for the convent's online newsletter.

"I do hope the Williamson sisters have been having as much fun this evening as we are. I find it hard to believe that anyone could have had a better time than we four," she said, as she scrolled through the shots the passer-by had taken and deleted the ones in which her eyes were half-closed. "I look half-cut," she complained.

"Well, you are, dear," said Sister Margaret Ann kindly.

When they arrived at Le Grande Bretagne, the hotel where Davina and Sister Eugenia were staying, Arlene went to the front desk to fetch the keys to their rooms. This hotel was not like The Maritime, where liveried staff attended to your desires before you even knew you had them. The receptionist at Le Grande Bretagne was glued to the huge television that hung on the wall opposite his desk. It was showing a news channel. When he didn't seem to notice Arlene standing there in front of him, her eyes were drawn upwards, wondering what was so compelling. She had little French apart from menu items and swear words and thus the words that the presenter spoke in rapid fire, which also scrolled along the bottom of the screen, didn't make much sense to her. The pictures however . . .

"Is that the auction house? Brice-Petitjean?" she asked the receptionist.

The receptionist nodded. He said something in French.

"I'm sorry. I don't understand. *Je ne peux pas parler Français.* Has something happened?"

The receptionist typed a word into his phone and showed Arlene the translation.

"There's a *siege*?"

IT WAS ALMOST ten o'clock. Archie and the sisters would have been back at The Maritime hours ago, surely? Archie had texted Arlene at around quarter to eight, telling her that he didn't think they would be staying out long after all. The party wasn't as exciting as he'd hoped. "Post-mortem later," he'd promised.

The television screen focussed on the face of a young man, who was evidently reading out a list of demands which he'd broadcast via Facebook Live.

Arlene called Archie as she watched, wanting reassurance that he and the sisters were nowhere near the situation unfolding on the news. Archie didn't pick up the call.

That didn't necessarily mean he was in trouble. Perhaps he had gone to bed. Or was in the hotel bar in conversation with someone interesting. She knew that Archie would very rarely pick up the phone if he was in company. He had the most impeccable manners.

Sister Eugenia and Sister Margaret Ann were alongside Arlene now. Sister Margaret Ann translated the words on the screen for the older nun.

"They're demanding the release of political prisoners in exchange for the life of an . . . an arms dealer, I think. If they haven't had a response from their government within the next half hour, they're going to start to shoot hostages. Beginning with . . ."

The young man shifted focus from his own face to the hostages. The first to fill the screen was a man dressed in a very strange outfit indeed. As he realised his predicament, the man rolled on the floor as though he'd already been shot.

"Who is that?" the women wondered.

Then all of a sudden Archie faced the camera.

"He volunteered to die in that other man's place," Sister Margaret Ann explained. "But the gunman has refused his offer and said the first man can only swap with . . . oh my goodness me!"

"Penny!" Arlene shrieked, as her employer's face smiled out from the television. "They're going to kill Penny! Aaaaaghhhh! Aaaaaghhh! Aaaaaaaggghhh!"

"CALM DOWN," DAVINA Mackenzie instructed.

When Arlene didn't immediately calm down, Davina blew her whistle. The familiar noise cut straight through Arlene's panic, stopping her wailing mid-flow.

Davina sharply tugged on Arlene's sleeve to pull the younger woman down to the level of her wheelchair.

"What?"

"You must calm down," said Davina.

"How can I?" Arlene asked.

"You have to. There is absolutely no point in losing your head. It isn't going to help anybody."

"But I don't know what to do. What can we do? Penny and Josephine are being held hostage. And Archie! Oh my god, Archie. What's happening over there? Why aren't the police storming in?"

"Because they understand the possible dangers. First rule of everything," said Davina. "Assess before you act. We do not yet know if armed intervention is necessary."

"We? What are you talking about? That man has a gun."

"Ah. But does he intend to use it?"

"He just said he did."

"No point waving one around if you don't. Arlene, when I was in the plotting room in Liverpool, marking down radar signals from my brother's destroyer, which was being tailed by a U-boat wolf pack across the Atlantic, do you think I lost my head like you are now?"

"I don't imagine so."

"Exactly. And I made sure than none of my team lost their heads either. Stand up straight, woman. Big girl pants on."

"Do they say that in the navy?"

"I believe I learned that phrase from you."

"But how can I pull my pants up when Penny is in danger of being shot?"

"Whether you decide to pull your pants up or not, I need you to stop being so distracting. This situation requires concentration."

"But what can we do?"

Davinia got out her whistle again and blew the signal Arlene recognised as the "shut up and sit down." It wasn't an official naval signal, but it was effective. Arlene slumped into a plastic chair.

Sister Eugenia was also watching the screen closely. She nodded to herself, then mimed her need for a notepad and pen to the hotel receptionist. He handed one over.

As Sister Eugenia started jotting things down in what looked like shorthand to Arlene, she explained to the others, "Earlier today, when we were at the ceremony, I noticed that Penny and Josephine seemed to be doing a lot of fidgeting. I mean, more so than you would expect even if someone had Parkinson's. I realised it wasn't random. They were making dits and dahs."

"Making whats?" said Davina, adjusting her hearing aid.

"Dits and dahs. Morse, Davina. Morse. They were talking to one another in Morse code."

"They do that!" Arlene confirmed.

"Well, this morning they were talking about me. They called me . . ." She took a deep breath and blushed. "They referred to me as the *Prinz Eugen*."

Davina understood the insult at once. "How dare they?"

"Oh, I'm sure they didn't mean any harm. Eugen does sound a bit like Eugenia, after all. But what I'm trying to say is, I bet Penny and Josephine will be signalling to each other in Morse right now. If only that silly young man would stop talking and show the sisters again, we might be able to pick up something useful."

The camera panned around and landed on the two old ladies on the stage. Sister Eugenia focussed on Josephine.

"There we go," said Sister Eugenia. "Joséphine just tapped out, 'guns— three?' I'm sure of it. She's asking Penny how many gunmen there are in the room."

"See. She's assessing the situation. Once a Wren, always a Wren," said Davina proudly.

"Penny tapped back 'three. Kitchen.' Hmm. I wonder . . . I think perhaps she's looking for exit routes."

"Arlene, move my chair closer to the television," Davina commanded. "Sister Margaret Ann, have that young man on the desk summon a policeman to the hotel at once. We need to pass this information on. It could be valuable."

"I don't know if they'll send someone here . . ."

Davina held up a finger to silence the young nun. "As the granddaughter of an admiral, I am not used to being ignored. And as a former third officer, I am taking charge."

"Ahem," Sister Eugenia coughed. "I was also a third officer by the time I left the Wrens, you know."

"Oh." Davina looked crestfallen. "Then . . ."

"But I'm sure you would have eventually outranked me had the war continued a moment longer," Sister Eugenia added kindly. "I'm happy to be under your command, former Third Officer Mackenzie."

"Good. Sister Margaret Ann, please translate the following for this chap . . ."

The receptionist did call the police but could not seem to make the operator at the end of the line understand the situation. Possibly because, as Sister Margaret Ann did not translate word for word, he said, "There's a mad old English lady in my reception shouting about the hostages at the auction house. Possibly needs locking up."

"If the mountain will not come to Mackenzie . . ." said Davina, when she heard the disappointing news that no police officer would be dispatched to Le Grande Bretagne that night. "Arlene, Sister Margaret Ann, to your places, please. We're going to the auction house."

Forty-One

. . . . .

Davina and Sister Eugenia were right. Between them the Williamson sisters *were* trying to assess the situation. Two ancient veterans versus three youthful gunmen. The odds were not on their side. But when youthful exuberance was weighed against experience perhaps the odds shifted somewhat. The gunmen had been more than a little exuberant since they arrived, firing shots off into the ceiling with abandon, wasting bullets. How many were left?

Penny tapped out, "No killer," with regard to the smallest of the three, who seemed jumpy—they flinched every time they fired their gun. Not that that wasn't dangerous in itself.

Regarding number two, "Big but slow."

Josephine tapped back, "Others? Guns? Three?"

"Three total," Penny was pretty sure of that.

It was time to form a plan. The gunmen had obviously scoped out the venue before tonight but this was a big room for the three of them to hold and Penny knew from her own research that there were angles they hadn't considered. They seemed to have overlooked the door through which the waiting staff had been bringing canapés all evening. Unless they had someone stationed on the other side. That was a possibility. But if they didn't, Penny tried to recall the old floor plan.

Angel was pacing up and down the stage as he talked into his phone. He was so focussed on getting his message across, he wasn't paying any attention to the people behind him.

"You trip him," Penny told Josephine. "I get gun."

It was a basic but solid strategy. Angel definitely wouldn't be expecting it. However he never seemed to get quite close enough to be in danger of Josephine's little feet, which only just reached the floor as she sat on her gilt chair.

"Can't reach," Josephine tapped as the gunman evaded her size four feet again.

Penny couldn't reach either. Her legs were even shorter than her sister's. She needed another strategy.

"In ten minutes' time," Angel was saying, "the bloodshed begins."

Begins with me, thought Penny.

Archie craned his neck to see her, then tapped out a Morse message on his head.

"Dan't warry. Wan't lit huppin."

Penny wasn't about to let it happen either.

As the clock ticked down, another idea began to form. Perhaps she could use the fact that she was first in line to her advantage. Angel would want to milk the drama of the moment for his viewers, whoever they were. She would get him to stoop down in front of her on the pretence of letting her send a last message to the world —it wasn't too much to ask to be able to say a final goodbye before he killed her, was it? Once he was within range, she would strike. She would use her lucky matchbox, hidden in her fist, to smash him in the side of the face. He'd never see it coming and it could work. The odds, according to Fairbairn, were two to one that The Matchbox Attack knocked your opponent out. She just had to be fast and hit him in the right spot. She could be fast one more time if she had to.

Angel had paused mid-stage to deliver another message to the government that had yet to make a response. ". . . your immoral trade has robbed children of their families and their futures. This is your chance to make amends or see more bloodshed in your name. This woman's had a long life," he said, gesturing towards Penny. "But I am ready to end it to make you take notice."

"Cheers," Penny said, through gritted teeth.

The sad thing was, Penny was sympathetic to Angel's cause. Who wouldn't be? Who wouldn't object to a small cadre of people making a fortune by beggaring their nation or sponsoring distant wars? Frank was right. As long as there was money to be made, there would always be conflict. It was easy to feel as if it didn't matter, when it wasn't happening on your doorstep and you watched it from far away. It was easy to turn a blind eye when the dirty money washed up in your auction house, or your art gallery. It was clever of Angel to have chosen this place to make his point.

In Angel, Penny almost thought she saw a kindred spirit, wanting to right injustice and restore the balance. Except that he was not prepared to do it quietly. Penny had tried to change the world one precious gem at a time, redistributing wealth in her own way. Angel was . . . Well, Jinx would have said that Angel was being honest. He was prepared to die for change. That must be a risk. Where were the police? When they turned up, they'd surely turn up prepared for a gun fight, ready to fire before they were fired upon. It struck Penny that if she could disarm Angel before they arrived, she might save his life too.

Forty-Two

• • • • •

When Former Third Officer Davina Mackenzie issued the call to action, Arlene and Sister Margaret Ann jumped. They would go to the auction house. But there were no taxis to be seen on the street outside Le Grande Bretagne. Neither did Arlene's Uber app offer any hope of a minicab before midnight. There was nothing to be done except push the two older ladies to the nearest taxi rank, with Sister Eugenia doing her best to follow the siege for any more Morse messages on Arlene's iPhone.

Despite his doubts to their sanity, the hotel receptionist was persuaded to join the four women (a crisp fifty euro note helped), working in a sort of relay with Arlene and Sister Margaret Ann, as they navigated the narrow streets with all the deeply frustrating bollards that may have prevented people from parking on the pavement but also made it hellishly hard for wheelchair users to use the pavements too.

Arlene, Sister Margaret Ann, and Eric, as the receptionist was called, did their very best but by the time they reached the Pont de La Concorde, all three of them were about ready to collapse. They needed a lift but the ranks were empty and every taxi that passed was already occupied. The one taxi driver that did have his light on swiftly turned it off again when he realised what a complicated pick-up stopping might involve. That's when Davina had Arlene push her halfway across a crossing to face down a double-decker bus that had been converted to a moving restaurant.

"They'll mow us down," Arlene suggested.

"They would not dare!" said Davina, holding one arm aloft as she blew hard on her bosun's whistle.

It worked. The bus stopped. Davina sent Sister Margaret Ann on board to explain the emergency.

"Might save some lives," the young nun finished her speech.

The driver was reluctant to change her route but the hen party from Dublin, who had rented the bus for the evening, insisted on bringing the veterans and their wheelchairs on board.

Once safely on the coach, Davina blew her whistle to focus everyone's attention. "We are on a very important mission," she told the hens, with Sister Margaret Ann and Eric translating. "And we need you all to be absolutely silent until we reach our destination. Third Officer Sister Eugenia is taking down vital comms."

Sister Eugenia waved Arlene's iPhone in the air.

Fascinated by their new commanding officer and her second, the hens obliged.

And so the curious party headed onwards to Brice-Petitjean, with Sister Eugenia watching for Morse signals whenever Penny and Josephine were on screen and Sister Margaret Ann taking down notes, while Arlene and Davina looked on anxiously and Eric gratefully accepted a glass of Crémant from their hosts.

The hens behaved in exemplary fashion, refraining from singing or shouting. Even holding off on their drinks, in case Davina needed them to form some sort of scratch commando unit when they reached their destination. It wasn't long before they were ready to follow the centenarian into any battle.

The police were already outside the auction house and of course the coach was not allowed to even turn into the street where the action was unfolding. Remaining on board, Davina commanded that Arlene, Eric, and Sister Margaret Ann bring a police officer onto the coach to hear their suit. Two officers took up the challenge. They were young-looking. Low-ranking.

"I don't think you understand," Davina said in loud English. "We need to speak to your superiors. We have vital information relating to the siege in the auction house."

Sister Margaret Ann translated apologetically.

"The older ladies are speaking in Morse," Davina said. "Giving the movements of the captors in the room and transmitting details of their blind spots. And they're outlining a plan. You would do well to take it into consideration when forming a plan of your own. I assume you are forming a plan."

The police officers remained unconvinced.

"Give them the details, Honorary Cadet Margaret Ann."

Sister Margaret Ann translated Sister Eugenia's notes. "Josephine was supposed to trip the main gunman over but she couldn't reach. Neither could Penny. Short legs. Now Penny is going to try to get him to crouch down next to her and knock him out with a matchbox . . . Sister Eugenia, that can't be right. A matchbox?"

"My Morse is rusty," said Sister Eugenia. "But that is exactly what Penny Williamson coded."

"And it can be done!" Arlene interrupted. "You can use an old-fashioned metal matchbox as a deadly weapon. Archie showed me how you do it in some old book he had and I know Penny has one of those matchboxes!"

"What else?" asked Davina.

"Once Penny has taken the main man down with the matchbox, Josephine is to kick the gun to Archie—that's their nephew. He should cover gunman two. Gunman three is not a big threat. No ammo left after firing at the ceiling."

The more senior of the two fairly junior police officers sat down beside Sister Eugenia. "And what are they saying now?"

"Penny is telling Josephine what to do if it goes wrong. If she dies."

"Which is?"

"She is saying . . ." Sister Eugenia watched Penny tap out a long sequence. She started to speak but then hesitated. "I think she's just saying she's not going to die. Not tonight."

"Such bravery," said Davina Mackenzie, thumping her fist against her heart. "It's hard to believe that Penny Williamson wasn't a Wren. Now, if one of you officers could get me a floor-plan of the auction house, I could mark out the current enemy position in the field so that you can send your team in the most efficient fashion."

"I think we'd better take these ladies down to the control centre," said the junior officer. "Let them watch the CCTV feed."

The hen party cheered them on their way.

Forty-Three

. . . . .

Inside the auction house, the captives had no idea that the police were mustering outside, along with two elderly veterans and a hen party. They were all watching the clock, as ten minutes passed, fifteen minutes, twenty . . . Were they witnessing the last ten minutes of a poor old lady's life?

Not if Penny could help it.

She had her plan now. Slowly, so as not to draw attention, Penny opened her handbag and reached inside it for her metal matchbox. She'd had it close to hand, day in, day out, for almost sixty years; ever since the day that Jinx brought it to the house in South Kensington, saying, "Frank would have wanted you to have this, not me. He loved you, Penny. You were the love of his life."

Penny had hoped never to have to use it for anything more serious than lighting a cigarette but here she was. In a different context, she thought she would have liked Angel, but he had threatened her life and the lives of everyone in the room. And if she died, who would be next? Anyone who threatened the health or happiness of Archie or Josephine would have to come through her on their way into hell.

Just as on that long-ago day when Alfred the army man grabbed her by the thigh, any fear Penny might have felt had been replaced by a low electric fizz of excitement. If this was to be her last action, it was going to be one worthy of the F Section agent she should have been, would have been, were it not for Frank's foolish attempt to keep her out of trouble. The young girl who'd broken her date's nose in the theatre back in 1942 was still within her, and that girl remembered exactly how to knock a man out with a metal matchbox turning her fist into steel.

Angel would not know what hit him.

Penny rehearsed the matchbox knockout in her mind as she rifled through her bag. Mental rehearsal was key. Calm, slow breathing. Focus. Deadly accuracy. She needed to get just one good strike to Angel's jawbone while parrying away his gun with her other hand. She could do it.

But the matchbox was not in Penny's bag that night. It was in her great-nephew's breast pocket.

"HELL'S TEETH." PENNY cursed under her breath. How could she have forgotten she'd given the matchbox to Archie just that afternoon? Her best weapon, gone. What could she use instead? Cough sweets? That bloody copy of *Fifty Shades of Grey*? Perhaps if she read him a particularly shocking passage . . . What about a pen? She had no pen either. Her Swiss army knife was back in South Kensington. "You won't get that through security," Archie had warned her, as they packed for the journey. She'd let him persuade her not to try. Now here she was with absolutely nothing left to work with.

"Pen?" Penny tapped to her sister.

"No," Josephine tapped right back.

"Hair pin?"

"No!"

"Cheese knife?"

"No!"

ARCHIE WAS OBLIVIOUS to the sisters' frantic messaging behind him. In front of him, Stéphane's face shone out from the sea of frightened faces. Archie chanced a little smile in his direction. Oh, Stéphane. Was this really how it was going to end?

Archie had never been very good at sitting on the floor and after nearly half an hour on the hard parquet, he was starting to lose sensation in his buttocks. He knew it was nearly half an hour because, like everyone else, he had been watching the clock on the wall, wondering if Angel's thirty minutes was a real deadline. Was anybody out there going to give in to his demands or at least suggest they might with a bit of negotiation? Did they even know he was making those demands? Of course they must. Angel was beaming his phone footage straight to Facebook. The world would be watching the countdown, possibly with popcorn at hand. Wasn't that how it worked these days?

"Twenty-nine minutes are up," Angel addressed his phone and the audience beyond. "And it seems to me that you don't think I'm serious. And so we come to the final minute," he said. "Sixty seconds until this elderly woman meets her maker."

"I don't think he'll have me," Penny said.

"Sixty seconds, starting now . . . fifty, forty-five, thirty, fifteen . . . Bye-bye, Grandma."

"No! No! I won't have it!" Suddenly Archie was on his feet. And then he was flat on his back.

But the distraction of Archie's unexpected fall was all the opportunity Penny needed to jump up and punch Angel in the kidney, with or without a weapon. She knew how to make a good fist. While Angel stared down at Archie, Penny made her move. But she didn't get as far as punching anyone. Instead as she leapt up, she gasped in surprise as a pain like the point of a compass in the middle of her chest made her slump back in her chair. She clutched at her chest. Angel lowered his gun.

Josephine tapped, "SOS."

Penny didn't tap back but kept her hands pressed to her heart. She closed her eyes and muttered, "Dear God, at least save Archie."

This was one fight she was not going to win.

Forty-Four

• • • • •

As he came back to consciousness on the hard wooden floor, for a second or two Archie had no idea where he was. When he did remember, he gasped in distress. He was under siege by some maniac in the glamorous hall at Brice-Petitjean. And then he remembered how he had come to be on his back. In the moment when he could have saved his great-aunt and become a hero, Archie had managed only to faint.

Was Penny dead?

"No!" he wailed. "Please, no!"

"No one's dead yet," said Angel, looming over him. "Though you just bumped yourself up to second in line. Any more heroes out there want to have a go?" he asked the room.

Oh, it was really too much. All his life all Archie had ever wanted was to be a hero, like the men and women who had served alongside his great-aunts in the war. Instead, he was on his back on the floor and that lunatic Angel was still waving his gun around. Penny and Josephine and Stéphane and all the other unfortunate hostages were still in danger. How had he got his attempt to defend Penny so horribly wrong?

Tears started to form in Archie's eyes. He was useless to anyone now. He was pathetic. Pathetic. A long line of brave and magnificent ancestors stretched out behind him—war heroes, adventurers, pioneers all. Archie was the end of the line. Just as the terrifying dinosaurs had eventually evolved into chickens, in Archie the magnificent Williamsons had reached their nadir. No one would write books about Archie the Ignoble.

It was all so unfair. What's more, he had brought this awful situation upon himself and his great-aunts. If he hadn't been so keen to see Stéphane, if he could have played it cool, he would not have brought them here. Penny and Josephine could be back at The Maritime hotel now, sipping brandy and telling him stories about the times they'd spent in Paris as children, with their godparents Godfrey and Claudine. Instead, they were likely going to die in this room, and for what? Though Angel had expounded at length, Archie still didn't really know what the siege was about. His French wasn't good enough. What were they dying for? Likes on Facebook? Angel was carrying on again now, giving the people who might accede to his demands another five minutes in the light of the recent kerfuffle.

"Because I am a reasonable man," he said in English this time.

Reasonable? Someone needed to take his block off. There must be someone in the room who could do it. Where was Malcolm with his "capoeira" moves now?

"Don't think, Archie, just act. Take the battle into the enemy's camp."

Archie could hear Auntie Penny in his head, explaining how she'd saved them from that mugger in New York. The man had waved a knife in her face as he demanded her handbag.

"Not bloody likely," she'd said, jabbing the tip of her umbrella under his chin. She might as well have been kicking away an amorous Cockapoo for all the fear she showed.

And going further back, he remembered her writing on his plaster cast.

"There are no rules. Only kill or be killed."

"You can get that tattooed on your arm when you're eighteen," she'd said when she finished printing it in her very best handwriting.

"Why not suggest he gets 'love' and 'hate' tattooed on his fists while he's at it," said Josephine at the time. "Come here, Archie. Let me give you a cuddle."

The sisters had given Archie so much. Without them, Archie knew his life would have been so much less interesting, so much less thrilling. They might have driven him crazy on occasion with their constant need for "excitements," but he would not have changed a thing about all the wonderful times they'd spent together. He was *not* going to say his goodbyes from the parquet.

Closing his eyes, Archie did an inventory of his body. No part of him had really been hurt in the faint except his pride. His wrist ached but then it always did. He was bruised but not broken. Wasn't that the "Invictus" line? No. *Bloody, but unbowed.* That was it. That was the line written on the matchbox in his pocket.

From his place on the floor, Archie did his best to work out exactly what was going on around him. Above him, Angel paced back and forth. He was right at the edge of the stage. All it would take was for someone to catch hold of his legs and pull him over, take the gun—he'd be bound to drop it in the fall—change the story. Finish him off with a punch to the jaw.

Take the battle into his camp. Act, Archie. Act. Kill or be killed.

Archie knew he could not just stand up and grab the man—well, not like he'd tried to do last time—but there was another way.

Archie took a deep breath. One, two, three . . .

WATCHING THE CCTV footage in slow motion later, martial arts experts all over the world would hail Archie as a true master of the forgotten art of Defendu. Angel was too busy with his demands to notice Archie carefully shifting into position, laying out his right arm at ninety degrees to give himself leverage, turning his head to the left, tightening his stomach muscles, getting ready for the flip, raising his legs from the waist, and then shooting them over his shoulder.

When he executed the move, Archie moved so quickly from being prone to being on his feet that it seemed like a magic trick. He grabbed Angel around the knees, toppling him from the podium. Angel dropped his weapon and his phone just as Archie had expected him to, but he was still dangerous. Angel scrambled to get back up, eyes blazing hate. He pulled back his fist.

Luckily, Archie had another trick in his pocket . . .

He had always wanted to try The Matchbox Defence, the move that W.E. Fairbairn warned could end in death. "Never practise this manoeuvre at full pressure," the books said. "And certainly never practise it upon yourself."

Kill or be killed.

With his hand around the matchbox, Archie smashed his fist into Angel's cheek just as Angel's fist made contact with the side of Archie's face.

The matchbox gave Archie the advantage. He punched harder, stronger and in exactly the right place. It was a knockout blow. Angel crumbled.

Falling arse-first upon Angel in a move straight out of WWE, Archie moved fast to secure him, while he was still dizzy from the punch.

"I think we've had enough of this siege," said Archie, tucking the matchbox back into his pocket.

ARCHIE'S BRAVERY GAVE others in the room confidence to move. The two other gunmen were taken down in an instant, without a shot being fired, just as the police finally, finally stormed in, using the unattended kitchen door.

Archie cried for someone else to take hold of Angel while he rushed to be with his great-aunts. Penny was still slumped in her chair, clutching the centre of her chest. Josephine was white with the excitement of it all.

"Hold on," Archie instructed them both. "The paramedics are coming. *Toujours alive*, please, Aunties. *Toujours . . .*"

Josephine pushed herself up from her seat to go to her little sister. Her brave and crazy little sister.

"My Perfect Penny," she cooed at her.

"Josie-Jo," said Penny. "If this is the end, you know what to do."

Josephine nodded.

"This is not the end," said Archie firmly.

He was right.

The denouement of the siege might have been utterly bloodless, but in the confusion that followed the arrival of the police, Dragomir Georgiev had grabbed the gun that skittered across the floor when Archie brought Angel down. Now Georgiev took aim at his accuser, his eyes narrowed with pure hatred as he pulled the trigger. And missed.

Missed his intended target, at least. Angel felt the shot fly right past him.

Josephine flew backwards, lifted from her tiny feet by the force of the bullet as it hit her in the chest.

Forty-Five

• • • • •

1940

"Well, you've got yourself into a right mess, Josie-Jo Williamson," was the first thing Connie Shearer said when they were finally alone.

Josephine had known Connie Shearer for almost her whole life. They were born the same year, if in entirely different circumstances. Connie was the daughter of the cook at Grey Towers, home of Josephine's paternal grandparents. When Christopher Williamson took his family to their ancestral home for high days and holidays, his daughters always rushed straight down to the enormous kitchen, to forage for biscuits and ask if little Connie could come out to play.

Between the ages of five and twelve, Josephine and Connie were on almost the exact same trajectory, but at fourteen, both girls donned new uniforms—Josephine for her smart new boarding school, St. Mary's, and Connie for a kitchen maid's role, following in her mother's and her grandmother's footsteps. After that, the girls were no longer encouraged to fraternize. Josephine was upstairs. Connie most definitely downstairs. In public, they were polite and distant but in secret, they still sought each other out and when Josephine arrived at the house in the January of 1940, Connie greeted her with a wink that said, "Hello, old pal." At night, when the household was in bed, Connie crept into the room where Josephine had been billeted. It wasn't Josephine's usual room. She'd been banished to the servants' floor this time. Her predicament was too obvious to risk her being seen about the formal rooms by her grandparents' social peers.

"Come on. Tell me everything," Connie said. "Who's the father? And is he going to marry you?"

"I don't think that's going to happen," said Josephine. She filled Connie in on the details.

Connie grimaced. "I'll bet your dad isn't happy."

"He doesn't know."

Christopher Williamson had left for Salisbury with his regiment before Cecily caught a glimpse of her daughter's belly straining her thin muslin nightdress and finally put two and two together. There followed three nights of long, anguished conversations about what should be done. They got as far as agreeing that Josephine should continue her pregnancy in Scotland, so as not to create gossip in the village. Neither should her father be told. Beyond that, Josephine still didn't know what was supposed to happen when the baby eventually came.

"I expect your ma will pretend it's hers," Connie suggested. "Pass it off as your little brother or sister. Happens all the time."

Josephine didn't know whether she liked that idea or not.

The days ahead were miserable. Josephine's paternal grandfather, who had once been so proud of her—"Always top of her form"—would not speak to her at all. He looked acutely distressed if they accidentally passed on the stairs. Her grandmother spoke only to express her disapproval.

"I don't know what your parents were thinking, letting you go to Paris in the first place. And to stay with that drunken godfather of yours and his floozy of a wife. You were always going to get into trouble."

It was easier to keep out of both her grandparents' way.

Josephine had her meals in the kitchen. The staff—apart from Connie—were polite but reserved. When Josephine needed fresh air, she would shuffle around the family graveyard—the high walls held back the worst of the icy wind that swept down from the mountains—reading the names on the pets' headstones. The highlight of her day was the moment the lights went out and Connie would creep into her room to talk.

Josephine knew that Connie was the only person in that house who didn't judge her. She was also the only person in the house who gave Josephine any hint of what was to come as her pregnancy reached its final furlong. Though Doctor Muir visited every few days to make sure Josephine's pregnancy was progressing as expected, he made it clear by his demeanour that he was not there to answer questions.

"I'm scared," Josephine admitted to Connie, as the moment drew nearer.

"You mustn't be. My sister's been popping out one a year since she was our age. She has a bit of a lay down then she gets straight back to work, with the new baby hanging off her tit."

Josephine winced.

"Oh lord. Sorry, Josie. I'm just trying to say it'll be alright. If my sister can do it—and she makes a fuss about anything—then you can do it too. You'll be alright."

Connie folded Josephine into a hug, made slightly awkward by the expanse of Josephine's belly.

"Will you stay with me when it happens?" Josephine asked.

"If I'm allowed," said Connie. They both knew that was unlikely.

"DO YOU WANT to have children, Connie?" Josephine asked on another night.

Connie shook her head quickly. "No thanks. I've seen enough, looking after my nieces and nephews. Besides . . ."

"Besides what?"

"I don't think I could do what I had to to, you know . . ." She waved at Josephine's bump.

"It just sort of happens naturally when you're in love," said Josephine. It was rare that she was more experienced in something than her friend. "You'll meet the boy of your dreams and you'll find that you want to."

Connie shook her head again. "I don't think I'll ever find the boy of my dreams, Josie-Jo."

"Oh you will . . ."

"Not me. I want a different kind of life. A different kind of sweetheart. Someone . . . Not a man."

Josephine's mouth dropped open.

"Don't tell anyone," said Connie.

Josephine mimed buttoning her lip.

"Anyway the minute I'm eighteen, I'm going to London, where nobody knows me."

"What will you do there?"

"I'm not going into service, that's for sure. I'm going to do my bit for the war effort. I saw a Red Cross advert in the post office window. They need ambulance drivers. I can do that. I've been driving the estate van since half the gardeners went off to war."

"Aren't you afraid of being bombed?"

"I'm more afraid of never getting out of here. I don't want to have the life my parents did, spending their days cleaning up after their betters. I'm sorry, Josephine," she added quickly. "I know you are my better." She doffed an imaginary cap.

"Stop it."

"It's not for me, being someone's servant or someone's wife. I want to choose my own destiny. I want to do what I want and love who I want and never have to answer to anybody else ever again."

"That sounds lovely," said Josephine, suddenly feeling the weight of her own destiny very heavily indeed.

"You could run away with me and bring the baby. Really, we could run away together. Set up home in London. What do you say?"

The two girls held hands and locked gazes. Over the years, they had made a great many plans to run away, mostly to avoid getting into trouble with their parents over some childish escapade. Once, when they were both nine years old, they'd packed their favourite toys and stole food from the kitchen and made it almost as far as the train station before Penny—furious at being left out—had sounded the alarm and Josephine's grandmother called the station manager to warn him that two runaways were heading in his direction. Now however, there was a seriousness in Connie's suggestion this time that made tears prick Josephine's eyes. They were almost grown women. No conductor would stop them boarding the train for wherever they wanted to go. They knew how to look after themselves. Well, Connie definitely did . . . Josephine had a little bit of money saved up.

"We could do it."

"I can't," Josephine said. "I can't."

Connie stroked her cheek. "Well, I'll go first and you can come and find me later."

● ● ●

FOR THE LAST month of Josephine's pregnancy, the weather had been terrible—the sun barely seemed to bother getting up, reflecting the mood inside the house. But the day before her baby's birth, the sun finally broke through the gloom and it felt as though the whole world was ready to begin anew.

Though Connie had done her best to tell Josephine what to expect, her second-hand knowledge of labour was sketchy. Connie hadn't explained to Josephine that her waters would break, so when she woke up on a damp bed Josephine assumed she must have wet herself. She started hauling the sheets off, thinking she could get them changed before anyone noticed the mess, but a cramp had her bending double and she sat down with the job half finished. She was in so much pain. It couldn't possibly be right. She had never felt such waves of agony. Was she dying?

It was the middle of the night. The house was quiet. She wanted to call for help but even in this moment of fear and distress, she didn't want to risk waking her grandmother. If she got her out of bed for nothing—just to tell her she'd soiled the sheets—she would be furious. But the pain was making it hard to think straight. What were her choices? Make her grandparents angry—angrier, than they were already—or die?

Instinctively, she got down on all fours on the floor next to the bed and tried to find a comfortable position. When the pain came, she screwed up her face and held her cries inside. But she couldn't do that forever. She crawled to the bedroom door and called out into the corridor, her voice thin and wavering.

"Can somebody help me? Please? Connie?"

Connie, whose bedroom was two empty rooms away, was awake, reading, and heard her call.

"I think it's coming."

"I know what to do," Connie said, as much to comfort herself as Josephine. "I've seen my sister do it enough times."

The truth was that neither of the girls really had any idea how the last stages of labour should unfold. Connie's bravado was misplaced. She'd always stayed at the head end of the bed when her sister was in labour.

Racked by another contraction, Josephine bit down on a pillow to soften the urge to scream. Connie rubbed her back and whispered encouragement and occasionally asked if she shouldn't wake her mother, to which the answer was always an emphatic "No. Please, no. Not yet. I just want you."

With every contraction, Connie shyly checked Josephine's progress, then exhaled deeply to stop herself from fainting at the sight.

"I'm breaking in half. Is this what's supposed to happen?" Josephine managed to pant.

"Yes, yes," Connie assured her. "You just keep pushing."

"I don't know how. I'm too tired."

"Hold my hand and really, really squeeze. Then imagine doing the same with your, your you-know, at the same time."

"Make it stop, Connie."

"I can't. Nobody can. You just have to keep on pushing."

It was too late now.

Kneeling on the floor between Josephine's legs, Connie caught the baby as he suddenly slid out and onto her lap. She was speechless.

"Give the baby to me," Josephine had to tell her. "Give it here."

Connie handed the baby over and then lay down on the floor in a swoon.

The baby was a boy. Josephine held him in her arms, umbilical cord still attached. His eyes were screwed tight shut as if in indignation at being hauled out into this cold, strange place. What kind of world had Josephine delivered him into?

When he did finally open them, his eyes were small, dark, and shiny, and already ancient though he was just a few minutes old. They seemed to search hers out.

"I'm here," she said. "Mummy's here."

The baby didn't cry. He was as quiet and still as she and Connie had been, as if he understood that they were not to make a fuss at such an ungodly hour. Josephine didn't know what she was supposed to do now she had him. When he mewed, she put her finger in his mouth. He sucked on it fiercely.

Sitting up again, Connie just gazed at the pair of them, her expression like one of the kings in Rubens' *Adoration of the Magi*. Josephine would never forget it, how Connie had looked at her baby that night. Pure love.

"I'll get some scissors," Connie said eventually, backing out of the room. "For the cord. You stay there."

"Don't be long!" Josephine begged.

But when Josephine next looked up at the creak of the door, it wasn't Connie who had come back. It was her grandmother, with Connie's mother, the cook, alongside her.

Her grandmother was angry. "Why didn't you wake us?"

"I didn't want to . . ."

Grandma Williamson was already barking instructions to Connie's mother.

"Send the boy to fetch the doctor then bring some hot water up here. We need to get you cleaned up," she said to Josephine. "Give me the baby."

"Not yet. I can't. I don't want to let him go."

But she did let him go.

Josephine heard her baby crying for the first time as he was bathed in another room.

DR. MUIR ARRIVED SHORTLY afterwards. He'd already attended another birth that morning, down in the village. The butcher's daughter had delivered her first son.

"Beautiful child. The family is delighted," he told Mrs. Williamson. But Dr. Muir examined Josephine without a word—not of reassurance or congratulation—announcing his verdict, "She'll be fine," to her grandmother instead.

"And my baby?" Josephine asked. "Have you examined him?"

The doctor and her grandmother shared a look.

"I'll leave you to it, Mrs. Williamson," Doctor Muir said.

Mrs. Williamson followed him out into the corridor.

Josephine strained to hear the hushed conversation between her grandmother and the doctor outside her bedroom, but the walls of her grandparents' house were built for Scottish winters and she could not make out the words though the tone of the exchange seemed heated. The conversation continued out onto the driveway. Josephine thought she heard the sound of her baby crying out there too, which couldn't be right. Eventually, Dr. Muir left. She heard the wheels of his car spinning on the gravel outside, as though he couldn't wait to get away.

Though she begged and cried, Josephine was not allowed to see her son again. She was not even allowed out of her room while a housemaid—not Connie—changed the bed sheets and brought a clean white nightdress to replace the one smeared with blood.

The house fell silent. When her grandmother came back to the bedroom around an hour after the doctor's visit, her face was stone-hard.

"What's going on?" Josephine asked her.

"The baby is dead."

"But I heard him crying outside not fifteen minutes ago."

"You're imagining it. The doctor pronounced him dead when he got here. He thought it would be better if I told you. The baby was too small," her grandmother said.

That made no sense either. The baby was at least as big as George had been when he was born. Bigger even.

"Is it my fault? Did I do something wrong?" Josephine asked.

Her grandmother made no move to suggest that Josephine hadn't. She didn't answer the question. Instead she said, "The doctor says you are to stay in bed and get some sleep."

"I want to see my baby."

"You can't," her grandmother all but shouted. "He's dead and it's for the best. What's done is done, Josephine. Just be glad it's over."

DOCTOR MUIR HAD left something behind to help her sleep. Josephine didn't want to sleep but her grandmother must have slipped the powder into her milk anyway. When she woke up again, it was a whole day later. She was told that her baby had already been buried.

She hardly dared ask where. And later, when she did dare ask, she would wish she hadn't.

Connie too, was gone.

"She had altogether too much to say for herself," said Josephine's grandmother. "London can have her. Now you'd better write a letter to that boyfriend of yours, telling him what he put you through. I'll get the cook to post it when she's next in town."

A week later, Josephine was on her way home, breasts bound tight to stop the milk, under strict instructions to "forget she ever had a baby and move on with her life."

When she picked her daughter up from the station, Cecily Williamson did not mention the reason for Josephine having been away. The baby— whom Josephine had named Ralph in her heart—was never spoken of again.

MEMORY IS A strange thing. In her old age there were days when Josephine could hardly remember what she'd had for breakfast, but she would never forget the first time August Samuel took her hand in the summer of 1939, or their first kiss, or their baby's small brown eyes shining in the early morning light on the one day he spent on this earth. Neither would she ever forget Connie's goofy smile at the sight of the child she had delivered. In fact, it seemed the further the events retreated into the past, the stronger those memories became. Was it because as time moved ever faster they were coming closer from the opposite direction? Were they coming for her now? Her old lover? Her old friend? Her child?

On the floor of the auction house, Josephine struggled to open her eyes and when she did, she saw nothing but white light. Yes. This must surely be the end. She was surprised not to feel in the least bit afraid. On the contrary, she was happy. It felt like the right time to say goodbye at last.

Forty-Six

. . . . .

Paris, 2022

"Stand back, please. Stand back. Give the lady some air."

It wasn't a heavenly glow that lit the back of Josephine's eyeballs. It was a torch.

"There's a reaction," said the paramedic.

"I'm not dead," Josephine said out loud. "Though I feel as though I ought to be."

"You probably should be," the paramedic agreed. With infinite care, she helped Josephine into a more comfortable position. "Someone must be looking out for you."

Though the media would later report that Josephine had been saved from a bullet by her *Légion d'honneur* medal, the glitzy medallion wasn't quite that strong. In fact she had been rescued from death by another secret layer of protection. Beneath the medal, in the breast pocket of her favourite navy-blue jacket, was that piece of lucky shrapnel that she had carried on her person for more than eighty years. That tiny piece of bomb casing built to kill in a German munitions factory had saved her. The paramedics marvelled at the small square of dull metal with its perfect bullet-head-shaped dent.

While the gunmen and Dragomir Georgiev were bundled into separate police vans and whisked away from the scene, Josephine was loaded into an ambulance to be taken straight to the hospital where she could be more thoroughly checked.

In the ambulance alongside her was Penny, who had been wired up to all sorts of machines. First thought when dealing with chest pain was always "heart attack" and goodness knows the siege should have been enough to bring on one of those in someone fifty years younger. Penny was pale, which was consistent with a cardiac event, but she was also loudly insisting, "I feel absolutely fine now. I don't know what was going on in there but I really do not need to go to hospital. Please send me back to the hotel."

Though she chatted with the nice paramedic all the way and that was a good sign, there was no way Penny was going to be allowed to leave without a proper check-up. Likewise Veronique, who couldn't stop shaking from the shock of it all. She was in the ambulance behind, together with Archie, who had a bump on the back of his head the size of a chicken's egg from his faint. He also thought he'd done something to his wrist again when he pulled that Defendu backflip.

Stéphane had been the first to Archie's side once the police had neutralised all the weapons in the auction room.

"My darling boy!" he called him, wrapping him in his arms.

Malcolm tried to get in on the act, suddenly looking much smaller than he had before.

"Oh, go away," said Stéphane. "You would have let me die in there. You'd have let all of us die. You let an old lady take your place in the firing line. A ninety-seven-year-old lady. Where's the heroism in that. Thank God, Archie saved us all."

"It was PTSD from rehearsals for the film," Malcolm pleaded. "Faced with a gun, I was reliving René Tremblay's last moments before the firing squad."

"Oh, take your bloody method acting and shove it up your arse," was Stéphane's retort. "You're not brave enough to say that Resistance hero's name."

Archie tried not to look triumphant as Malcolm slunk away.

"I can't believe I fainted," Archie said. "I feel like such a wimp. I was so frightened."

"You didn't faint from fear," Stéphane reassured him. "You fainted because you'd been sitting cross-legged with your hands on your head for half an hour. You didn't have any blood in your legs. No wonder they buckled beneath you. And after that, you absolutely redeemed yourself. Bloody hell, Archie. Where did you learn those moves?"

AT THE HOSPITAL, Penny's doctors were surprised to discover that according to an ECG her heart was in perfect working order, beating as strongly and evenly as that of someone decades younger. But the chest pain Penny had experienced had been strong enough to bend her in two. Had they missed something? Stress? Indigestion? A broken rib? Elderly bones might break at the slightest provocation.

"I absolutely don't need a scan," Penny said crossly when one was suggested. "Please concentrate your efforts on my sister."

Josephine had already been examined. She was bruised and in shock but the prognosis was good.

"You have a least another decade in you," the chief medic said kindly. However she would not be going back to the hotel that night.

"And neither will you," the medic told Penny. "Unless we can be sure you're entirely fit. And that means finding out what gave you that chest pain."

Arlene, who had come to the hospital to act as Penny's advocate (not that she wanted one) agreed.

"You're ninety-seven," she reminded her.

"So I should probably know my own mind," Penny retorted.

Penny was sure she was as fit as she might expect to be. She had also remembered by now exactly what must have caused that pin sharp jab that had knocked her off her feet. The sharp edges of a ballerina mount.

"I refuse to have any sort of scan," she said firmly. "Though I would appreciate it very much if somebody could find me some sort of laxative. Fast-acting, if you please."

Forty-Seven

• • • • •

The following morning, the sisters and Archie were reunited in Josephine's hospital room.

"Well," said Archie. "I think we had enough excitements to last a lifetime last night, don't you?"

The sisters agreed. For the moment. There was, however, still work to be done. As soon as Josephine and Penny's doctor gave the green light, Police Inspector Emile Allard and his junior, Detective Nathalie Urban, arrived to take the sisters and Archie's statements regarding the previous evening's events at Brice-Petitjean. Penny claimed that her recollection of events in the run-up to the arrival of Angel and his accomplices was a little murky. "I just had a little potter around the room and looked at some of the jewels," she said. "I'd asked Archie to take me back to the hotel. At my age, one doesn't like to stay up too late."

The detectives were understanding and didn't press Penny for too much detail. They had the hostage-takers and Georgiev in custody, after all.

"We hope not to have to bother you again," said Detective Urban.

But there were other visitors to come. A little later, Arlene brought the remaining contingent of elderly British veterans to the hospital, so that Davina and Sister Eugenia could explain their part in the way the evening had unfolded.

"Sister Eugenia was telegraphy. I was command and control," Davina explained. "Eugenia gave the police a minute-by-minute feed of your Morse conversation and I plotted coordinates on a map."

"Well, I never," said Josephine.

"Did I say anything rude?" asked Penny.

Sister Eugenia looked up to the ceiling. "Let's just say, I wasn't translating verbatim."

Then Stéphane arrived, with armfuls of flowers, and charmed them all.

"If I had known I would be in the presence of so many beautiful women, I would have dressed up," he told them. He was of course, immaculate, in the way that only a French man can be.

He handed one of the bouquets to Archie. The look that passed between them made all the ladies sigh.

"Is Malcolm OK?" Archie asked in what was obviously meant to be a nonchalant fashion.

Stephane visibly bristled. "I believe he's in a meeting with the producers of his film, who think they might want a couple of casting changes before they go ahead with the shoot. The optics from the auction house weren't exactly edifying. But enough about that. I thought you would like to see the newspapers. There are some lovely photographs of us all."

"But I look awful," said Archie. One of the papers had a photograph lifted from CCTV footage, which showed Archie all but lifting the gunman off his feet with the power of an old metal matchbox.

"You look like a hero," Stéphane assured him.

The auction house siege had made all the papers—French and international—but it had been knocked off the top spot in Paris that morning by another piece of local news, which perhaps explained why it had taken so long for the police to form their initial response to events at Brice-Petitjean. While the siege was underway, half the city's police force was already in the sixteenth, responding to an emergency that required the evacuation of three whole apartment blocks.

A young couple—"Totally Bobo," as Stéphane described them—had made a shocking discovery while renovating their recently-purchased apartment.

"It's a Resistance arms cache. Guns, bullets, grenades. You name it. All under their bathroom floor. Just imagine. It's been hidden there for nearly eighty years. It could have gone up at any moment. The police estimated there was enough live ordnance beneath those floorboards to have blown up the entire building and half the street in each direction. I imagine it's put their renovation plans back a couple of months."

Penny pored over the photographs. The exact address of the apartment block in question had not been given but the building looked familiar. The pictures of the police cars and army bomb disposal team outside were supplemented by a photograph of the same building "believed to be taken in the 1930s." Was that Madame Declerc scowling from the door that led from the street to the courtyard where Penny and Josephine once played?

Penny snatched up another paper, looking for another angle on the story. More pictures. None of the stories said exactly where in the building the apartment was but the fact that the Resistance arms cache wasn't the only thing hidden beneath the floor in the bathroom gave another clue. The police had also found a safe, full of cash, letters, and a small velvet bag full of gems. Including a ring set with a green stone the size of a Fox's Glacier Mint. There was a photograph.

"Efforts will be made to reunite the jewellery with the descendants of its owner . . ."

While the conversation in the room returned to Archie's heroism—"I remember when he was learning Defendu," said Josephine. "Wrecked an Ercol standard lamp. His mother was not in the least bit happy"—Penny excused herself to the bathroom. She had a feeling that the Declercs' cursed "lucky" emerald was ready to make its return.

AS IT HAPPENED, the Declercs' emerald was not ready to come out, but having seen the photographs in the newspapers, Penny had another reason to feel slightly unwell. The apartment with the arms cache and the safe beneath the bathroom floor had to be the apartment that once belonged to the Samuels and then the Declercs. The safe had lain there untouched for years. It must have been in place in 1947, when Penny tried to prise the floorboard up again before she was interrupted by Madame Declerc's return. Gilbert and his mother had not found the Grand Duchess's ring or the hand grenades.

Had they looked? Penny remembered Gilbert's face when she told him about the secret stash of gems. His sense of integrity had shone through. He did not want to know a secret about his friend that his friend had not already thought to share.

"You shouldn't have told me." That was what he'd said to her. "It's about trust. August is my friend."

Had Penny got Gilbert all wrong? And his mother too?

For decades, she had hated Gilbert Declerc, for betraying the Samuel family and buying a new life for himself with their riches, only to discover that the "stolen emerald" was a peridot. Penny could see that even from the pictures. The colour was entirely different. All those years ago, young August must have embellished the stone's provenance for his audience. The ring August claimed had belonged to a Grand Duchess wasn't quite worthless but it would be worth just a fraction of the real thing—the emerald ring that Gilbert Declerc must really have inherited from the mysterious great-uncle from Bordeaux.

Penny emerged from the bathroom, looking as green as the ring which remained nestled somewhere inside her.

Sister Eugenia beckoned Penny to sit beside her and whispered in her ear. "You were a terribly long time in the bathroom, dear. I always carry Ex-Lax in my bag, if it might be of any help."

"I'm perfectly fine," Penny told her.

"But you told Josephine about a ring in Morse, didn't you? Said that you'd swallowed it. I left that out of my decoding."

"Have you told anyone since?"

"I decided to ask God for guidance first."

"And what did God say?"

"He said 'Mind your own business, Prinz Eugen.'"

STÉPHANE MADE HIS excuses. Once the police had finished extracting evidence from the auction house, he and his team would be making an inventory of the auction lots that had been on display.

"There's no reason to think that anything would have gone missing, but with all the chaos you never know."

He left the others watching a news show which featured the siege and then the story of the Resistance arms cache.

"It's unlikely that the sender of the letters found at the Rue du Mont Olympe is still alive," the police spokesperson said.

But Josephine knew exactly to whom those fragile old letters had once belonged.

"Archie, will you make a telephone call for me?" she asked.

Forty-Eight

• • • • •

The letters from the Rue du Mont Olympe were delivered to the hospital that afternoon and brought to Josephine's room on a tray decorated with a rose in a bud vase. It was a sweet touch, confirming that Josephine was already a firm favourite with the staff. Several news channels had asked for interviews—they were camping outside the hospital—but Josephine refused them all. This was not something she could do with an audience. Not even Penny was beside her as she opened the first of the envelopes and began to re-read her side of a correspondence that had once meant so much.

The letters were all in date order. Josephine hoped that was how they had been found. She hated the idea that a stranger had read through them all and carefully filed them before they were handed over, though she knew that must have happened. Who wouldn't at least have opened a couple of the envelopes and flicked through the yellowed pages inside, eager to be the first to read those words in eighty years?

THOUGH THESE WERE Josephine's own letters, she found herself surprised by the lightness of the earliest notes in the little pile: the ones she'd sent from school in the autumn of 1939. The margins were full of doodles—lots of little love hearts and unkind caricatures of the teachers at St. Mary's to illustrate Josephine's complaints about the same. It was surprising that Matron had let those slip by.

"Really, could any teacher be more appropriately named than Miss Bull?"

"The Jolly Girls made short work of the lacrosse team from The Laurels yesterday afternoon . . ."

"Penny has now been knitting the same sweater sleeve for six weeks in a row. Talk about knitting for victory . . ."

There was a little section in code at the bottom of each note. A very easy code that should hardly have passed the censorship of matron. It said, *"I love you. I am forever yours."*

The letters looked well read and they were all still in the envelopes they'd been sent in. They'd been treasured. That made Josephine happy. But then she came to the first letter she sent from Scotland. The one she had written under the supervision of her grandmother. The one telling August that she no longer wanted to be in correspondence. Her grandmother had practically dictated the words.

"Ours was a summer romance and I realise it would be foolish for both of us to continue to pretend it has a future."

The last line, *"Yours sincerely, Josephine,"* so very formal, was smudged with what looked like a tear. Had it been hers or August's? Josephine could weep anew both for the girl who sent that letter and for the young man who received it.

Yet here was the letter Connie had smuggled out for her a few days later. The one which told the truth.

"They made me write that horrible letter, August. I still love you. I will love you forever. I am having our child!"

And then the last from Scotland, which her grandmother said would be posted by the cook, Connie's mother.

Our baby was born on Thursday morning. He lived for just a couple of hours. The doctor said he was too small to survive. I am so sorry, my darling August. When I held him in my arms, I felt so full of love. When he opened his eyes, it felt as though you were looking out at me from his face. He wrapped his tiny fingers around mine and held on so tightly. He seemed so strong. I had no idea that he would be called away so soon.

I named him Ralph. You once said you liked that name, remember? It was the name of the hero in a book you were reading. I don't remember the title. My grandmother had the vicar come and perform a funeral on Saturday while I was dead to the world thanks to some kind of sleeping draught from Doctor Muir. He is buried in the family graveyard at Grey Towers.

I hope you can forgive me. I think about you every day. I love you. I am forever yours.

Reading that eighty-year-old letter, the pain of losing Ralph was just as fresh as it had been at the moment she heard of his all-too-early death. The sharp stab of it to her heart made Josephine wish she hadn't insisted on being alone to read the letters. She needed someone to hold her hand now. She needed Penny. She needed Archie. She needed them both.

While Josephine was waiting for her sister to pick up the telephone in her room at The Maritime, she put the last letter from the pile back in its envelope. Laying it upside down in her lap, she noticed for the first time that someone had scribbled something on the back of that envelope in pencil, in small cramped handwriting, that seemed familiar somehow. Just four words in English and a pair of initials.

"He is not dead. CS."

Forty-Nine

• • • • •

After a delicious lunch with Arlene, Davina, and Sister Eugenia, and an afternoon of television and radio interviews about the siege, Archie and Penny were relaxing in Penny's hotel room when Josephine called.

"We'll both go to the hospital," Archie said. He was eager to see these old letters, which he could imagine going into a book proposal. Having seen reportage of the siege on the internet, an acquaintance of Archie who worked as an editor had left three voicemails, eager to get a contract in place before another publisher swept in with a better offer.

In the taxi to see Josephine, Archie fielded emails. There was another one from Maddie Scott-Learmonth, with more information about her father. She'd attached a photograph this time. While Penny looked out of the taxi window at the Parisians going about their day-to-day, Archie surreptitiously compared Penny's profile with that of Maddie's father as a young man. There was definitely some similarity. That upturned nose. The interesting ears.

As if sensing Archie's gaze upon her, Penny turned towards him.

"Are you alright, dear?" she asked.

Archie had been wondering when to break the news to the sisters that perhaps there was a hidden branch to the Williamson family tree. Was now the moment? He nonchalantly informed Penny, "You know I sent off for a DNA test a short while ago . . ."

"What inspired that particular madness?" Penny asked.

"I wanted to find out who my grandfather was."

"But you know who he was. He was our little brother George. Oh, I do wish he was still around to have seen you be the hero last night. He would have been very proud."

"Thank you, Auntie Penny. But I meant my other grandfather. There seems to be a question around my mother's parentage."

"Oh dear. That is unfortunate."

"So I sent off for a DNA test and got back a notification telling me I've got a cousin in Canada. I thought that would solve the mystery of Mum's roots but in fact it's made things rather murkier. You see, there doesn't seem to be a connection on my mother's side at all. Instead this cousin says her father was adopted from Scotland in 1940. She says his mother was Connie Shearer. I've seen her grave at Grey Towers, haven't I? Connie Shearer's? She worked there, didn't she? She died in the Blitz."

"Yes. Driving an ambulance," Penny remembered. "Poor girl."

"But she was the cook's daughter, at Grey Towers?"

"Yes, we used to play with her when we were children, whenever we were in Scotland for the holidays. She much preferred Josephine. They were closer in age. Connie used to pinch me black and blue. They both did. Though I suppose I did give them plenty of reason with all my tale-telling."

"So she was at Grey Towers but why would anyone related to her be related to me? I mean, if she was the daughter of the cook and I'm definitely descended from the family. Unless perhaps . . ."

Penny frowned. "Archie, what are you trying to say?"

"ARCHIE THINKS OUR grandfather had an illegitimate child with Connie Shearer," was the first thing Penny said when they got to Josephine's room. "He's found some sort of cousin on DNA dot wotsit. Can you imagine, Josie-Jo? Have you ever heard such a thing?"

While Archie explained his theory and Penny continued to scoff at the very idea of it, Josephine held out the last envelope from 1940. Her hand was shaking in a way that they had never seen.

"Archie, I think that child might have been mine."

IT MADE SENSE now—the note on the back of the letter. "*He is not dead.*" CS. Connie's initials. And the postcard Connie sent when she got to London, telling Josephine, "*I need to see you. There are things I have to tell you that I can't put down in writing.*"

This was what Connie had wanted to tell Josephine. She wanted to tell her that Ralph hadn't died on that long-ago morning. Josephine hadn't imagined the cry she heard from the courtyard. Ralph must have been taken away from the house on the day of his birth, presented to the registrar by the GP as Connie Shearer's child—Connie's reputation, as a housemaid, being considered less valuable—then adopted by a respectable local couple who were about to move to Nova Scotia.

"They told me they'd buried him in the pets' garden," Josephine told her astonished sister and great-nephew. "Next to Zephyr."

Zephyr was their grandfather's favourite dog. The German shepherd that had bitten all the Williamson children at least twice.

Seeing the horror on Archie's face, Josephine rushed to comfort him. "They loved their pets more than most humans so it's not the demotion you think."

Penny had to agree.

"But to tell you that." For once Archie was of a more modern view. "I can't believe it. It's horrific."

"It was a different time. And I'd rather concentrate on the fact that I think at last I know the truth thanks to you, our dear family historian. But is he? Is he?"

Josephine couldn't finish the sentence.

"Alive now? Yes, Auntie Josephine. Yes, he is."

Fifty

• • • • •

"Is there a term for feeling as though one might explode from happiness?"
Josephine asked her sister. "Because that is how I'm feeling right now."

"The Germans must have a word for it," said Penny. "We'll have to ask
Archie to google it when he comes back."

Archie was outside the hospital, making calls to his gallery in London,
leaving the sisters alone with each other for the first time in quite a while.

"My son has been alive all these years," Josephine said in a tone of wonder.

"Bloody amazing, isn't it?" said Penny.

"That's an understatement." Josephine sniffed back a tear. "You know,
the funny thing is, I think I always knew. They told me he was dead and
that was the story I told myself, but deep down there was always a part of
me that never quite believed it. You remember when we went to Paris in '47
and Gilbert told us about August?"

Penny nodded. "How could I forget?"

"I could feel it . . . I could feel that he was gone the moment I heard the
words. But it was *never* like that for my baby. No matter how many years
passed, I could still feel his presence. Though logic told me I was being
ridiculous—why would our grandmother have lied about his dying—I
looked out for him everywhere. I would see a little boy in a playground,
with August's thick brown hair, and my heart would leap out of my chest.
I was so certain I would see him. Every year on his birthday, I felt him
so strongly, Penny. So strongly. I would find a place to be alone and sing
'Happy Birthday' as loudly as I could so that he could hear me wherever he

might be. And then I would push my love out across the universe so that it would get to him and wrap around him and let him know that I never stopped thinking about him or loving him for a single second. My head said he was gone but my heart—never! And now he's back and I can tell him in real life."

She pressed her fingers to her eyes to stop the tears from rushing in again. It was a hopeless exercise. Even Penny's nose was pink with the effort of keeping her own tears back.

"He's still alive."

When Josephine opened her eyes again, she picked up the printout Archie had asked the hospital receptionist to make of the photograph his new cousin had sent him. The moment Josephine saw that picture, she knew that this was her child. There was no doubting it.

"Look at this face," she said to Penny, for the twentieth time. "How could he not be mine?"

He had the Williamson nose. He had August's eyes. He had the same widow's peak as dear Archie.

"He's got all our family's best bits," Penny agreed.

"He's perfect," said Josephine. "He's my boy."

Josephine would be talking to her son later that evening, as soon as Madeleine Scott-Learmonth got to his house and helped him make a Zoom call on her laptop.

"What am I going to say?" Josephine asked her sister. "So many years of sadness. I can't believe they're coming to an end at last. Do you think he'll forgive me?"

"What is there to forgive, Josie-Jo? You were lied to."

Josephine's hands trembled as she lifted the photograph to her face and kissed it.

"My son. My darling son." She held the photograph towards Penny and chuckled. "Your nephew."

Penny pressed the heels of her hands to her eyes. "Stop it. You're making me cry." When she dared to look at her new nephew's face again, Penny said, "There's something of George about him too," remembering the little brother they both still missed so much. "Thank goodness Archie put aside his horror of spitting to do that DNA test."

"Thank goodness."

Josephine pressed the picture to her chest. The thought of how lucky she'd been that Archie was such a genealogy nut was dizzying.

"Can I be here when you take the call from Canada?" Penny asked.

"I want you right beside me." Josephine reached for Penny's hand. "Ralph needs to know what sort of family he's getting into, warts and all."

"I promise not to be a bad influence."

"Only he's not called Ralph now, is he? He's Edgar. That's going to take some getting used to."

"Edgar is a good solid name," said Penny.

"Yes," Josephine agreed. "It is. Edgar. My boy."

"My nephew." Penny tried out the word for size.

"My son," said Josephine. Then once more with emphasis. "My *son*."

Fifty-One

· · · · ·

"We have a lot to talk about, you and I," said Penny, a little later. "I can't believe you didn't tell me you had a baby. I might have helped you. Why didn't you trust me enough to say?"

"I think I thought you might have guessed, but when you didn't ever ask . . ."

"You could have told me. If not then, at least at some point in the last eighty years. I've never kept anything from you. Not a *thing*."

Josephine snorted.

"I haven't!" Penny insisted.

"Then tell me, what exactly did you mean when you tapped out in Morse last night that you'd swallowed a ring?"

"Did I say that? I must have got my code wrong."

"You said it." Josephine cocked her head. "Well? Has it worked its way back out into the world yet? That's why you asked the nurse for laxatives, yes? So what ring? And where did you find it?"

"Oh, it was a mistake."

"Penny, I think this is the moment for truth."

It came out in a rush. "I thought the ring that Veronique Declerc had for sale in the auction was the ring that August showed us all those years ago. The one he said belonged to the Russian Duchess. I thought it because I told Gilbert about the safe hidden beneath the Samuel family's bathroom floor and I was certain he told his mother after Leah and Lily were taken away. How else to explain the Declercs' sudden change in fortune? So I decided to steal it back. I asked to try it on and swapped it for a toy ring I had that looked a bit like it."

Penny shrugged as though what she was saying was quite reasonable. Quite commonplace.

"Goodness knows what I thought I would do with it," she concluded.

"Same as you did with all the others?" Josephine suggested.

"I don't know what you're talking about."

"Penny. Please. I know all about it. I know how you've been funding the Foundation. I know how you funded all your charity work before that. 'Clever investments.' You know Gerald once said to me that perhaps we should entrust you with our life savings, given the returns you seemed to get no matter how choppy the markets."

"I've just been very lucky."

"You have been lucky. Lucky not to end up in jail. Jinx told me everything. She came to see me just before you got married."

"She came to see you?"

"You always wanted her to consider our family her own. Gerald and I were very fond of Jinx. She was worried about you. What circles you moved in, Penny. What men you chose to love. Twenty years in an affair with a crooked cop then you got yourself mixed up with a gangster."

Penny didn't deny it.

"When you called to tell me Connor had died in the south of France, I have to admit, I felt relieved. I thought that with the life insurance payout upon Connor's death, you might finally decide to go straight. Like you wanted Jinx to do."

"If you thought what I was doing was so bad, why didn't you confront me then?"

"What difference would it have made? You haven't listened to me since you were old enough to talk. And there were years when I hated you, when it seemed like you were so happy and carefree while I had a hole in my heart where August should have been that would never, ever heal."

"But you had Gerald."

"I was Gerald's beard. He wasn't interested in women and I wasn't interested in anyone but August. We were the perfect match. I saved him from the possibility of gossip and arrest for being gay. He saved me from sex. I'm not saying I didn't grow to love him. Love comes in all shapes and sizes. He was one of the best people I ever knew. As are you. My funny, brave, crazy little sister. But blimey . . . What a way to live.

"What are you going to do about the Foundation, Penny? Time is running out and we owe it to Archie to have everything squared away before we go."

"I keep meaning to tell him the truth."

"You can never tell Archie the truth. Because then he would have to know the truth about so many things, including how the QE2 dowager's diamond came to end up in his pocket on his birthday trip to New York. You know he'd be appalled to know how you made him your unwitting partner in crime."

"You're right," said Penny. "Archie was never going to follow me into the family business. He's such a decent man. So open-hearted and trusting."

"Like his granddad—our little brother. Let Archie think of you as a hero, Penny. You should tell him about F Section."

"How do you know about that? No one knows about that."

"You're not the only one who signed the Official Secrets Act," said Josephine.

"And what does that mean?"

"I could tell you but then I'd have to kill you." Josephine smiled. "A diplomat's wife hears a lot of things at parties."

"MI6?"

Josephine's lips twitched into a smile.

"I might have bloody known," said Penny.

"No comment," said Josephine.

"You always went one better."

"Better than an F Section agent? I don't think so. You got the family balls."

"I failed in the one mission I had."

"But you've been trying to set it right ever since. All those lives you've made better with the O'Connell Foundation. Which is ironic too. You know Jinx also told me that after you got married, Connor planned to kill you for the insurance money."

"How did she know all this?"

"He was hoping she would help but she was too loyal for that. Did you kill him first?"

"No," said Penny. "No, I did not. You have to believe that."

"I do."

"Josephine, are you very ashamed of me for everything I've done?"

"No. I'd be ashamed of you if you'd kept all the proceeds of your crimes to yourself but you haven't. Everything you've ever done came from a good place. Are you ashamed of me?"

"Why would I be?"

"I had a baby out of wedlock."

"That's nothing to be ashamed of. It's our grandparents who should be ashamed. And Ma."

"She thought my baby died too. I believe that."

"But he's still alive."

"And he's eighty! It's absolutely obscene to have a child that old. But I can't wait to meet him."

"Me too. Another nephew. After that, I think I might be ready to die."

"Not yet. We both have to make sure Archie is settled. I think Stéphane may have woken up to what a catch he is by now." They knew Stephane had been texting Archie constantly while he was supposed to be doing the inventory at the auction house.

"Oh, I'm not dying before that happens," said Penny. "How did we get so lucky? Having Archie in our lives? Josephine," Penny asked then. "What am I going to do with this bloody ring of Veronique's if it ever makes a reappearance? I can't tell Archie. It's too hot to sell on."

"Take it to a church," said Josephine. "And put it into the poor box. I'm sure it will find its way home."

ARCHIE HAD FINISHED his phone calls. He came into Josephine's room backwards, pushing the door open with his bottom. He was carrying three ice cream cones from a nearby artisan gelateria.

"Strawberry for you, Auntie Josephine. Mint choc chip for you, Auntie Penny. And vanilla for me."

Archie always had vanilla. It was a little quirk of his that always made Penny's old heart hurt when she was reminded of it. He didn't need anything fancy to be happy; just plain ice cream, a weak martini (very weak in Penny's opinion), an afternoon spent watching *In Which We Serve* for the hundredth time. He could never have been a master criminal. He was good and kind and honest and that was perfectly alright.

The mint chocolate ice cream seemed to have an enlivening effect on Penny's digestive system and before she left the hospital, she was able to assure Josephine, "It's out."

On the way back to the hotel, Penny told Archie she wanted to light a candle. She chose the church in the square at the top of the Rue du Mont Olympe. It was the church where Madame Declerc had tried to teach Madame Samuel how to pass as a good Catholic woman, in a Paris where to be anything else might be a death sentence. She thought of Madame Declerc differently now, remembering her not as the termagant concierge who had chased the girls with a broom or the newly rich heiress playing at aristocracy but as a brave woman who knew what it was like to lose a loved one to war, who had seen a fellow woman and mother in need of support and help, and who had risked her own life to protect that fellow woman as best she could.

Gilbert too, she remembered differently now. Penny wished she could hold his hands one more time and look into his gentle brown eyes and tell him she was sorry for having ever let herself believe that he might have betrayed August Samuel, his best friend and fellow Resistant. She was sure now that he would never have willingly sent little Lily to her death. How could she not have seen the way his decency shone through when he berated her for having revealed the existence of the Samuels' safe all those years ago? Veronique's revelation that she and Gilbert had used their fortune to endow schools for girls who might not otherwise have access to formal education should have come as no surprise.

She had been such a bad judge of character. Thinking the worst of pure souls like Gilbert while missing the truth beneath her nose when it came to real bastards like Connor O'Connell.

Jinx—her one-time mentee and soul sister—always had a better instinct for good and bad. They'd argued about it. Penny thought Jinx disliked Connor because she was jealous. She remembered now that she thought she had glimpsed her—Jinx—on the day that Connor died. She was coming out of a church in Antibes. She was wearing sunglasses that covered half her face and a scarf over her hair but Penny would have recognised her anywhere. Her mouth, her walk. It must have been Jinx who had taken the emerald ring from Penny's hotel room, then left it in the church's offertory box. Perhaps she had taken Connor's life at the same time.

"Kill or be killed."

Unlike Archie, Jinx *did* have that W.E. Fairbairn quote tattooed in black ink on the inside of her right forearm.

Stepping into the darkness of the Parisian church, Penny watched an old man—though he was almost certainly younger than she—dip his fingers into the holy water and make the sign of the cross. She followed suit, though she couldn't be sure she was doing it the right way. She'd been raised firmly C. of E. She took a turn around the church. There was no one to take confession, but that was probably a good thing. She didn't have all day. Then she put the ring into the black metal money box where you were supposed to deposit a euro in exchange for a candle. Given the magnitude of her donation, Penny decided that she might reasonably help herself to five candles.

One for Lily, one for Leah, one for August, one for Gilbert. And one for Madame Declerc.

Remembering the Jewish benediction, she'd once heard Leah Samuel say, Penny whispered over the flames, "May their memory be a blessing."

Fifty-Two

• • • • •

At last it was time to go home. When Josephine was discharged from hospital, it was to a guard of honour comprised of the nursing staff who had overseen her recovery. Archie made sure she wore her battered *Légion d'honneur* medallion for the occasion. Her lucky shrapnel, which was infinitely more precious, she had tucked inside her purse awaiting that moment when she could hand it over to her newly-found granddaughter. Archie and Maddie had been talking several times a day to finesse the details of Maddie's first trip to the United Kingdom, which would naturally take in a visit to Grey Towers. Josephine's son Ralph, who was now called Edgar, was recovering from a hip replacement but would be visiting in due course. Josephine and Edgar had spoken via Zoom—a moment for tears all round.

At The Maritime, Archie gave the sisters their instructions for the journey home.

"We are booked on the 11:13 train back to London, which means we will need to be at the Gare du Nord by half past nine local time to go through passport control and security. I have ordered a taxi for half past eight. The journey should not take an hour but I am allowing time for traffic and toilet breaks."

"Very sensible," said Arlene.

"Though please let's do our best to ensure there are no toilet breaks. Even your bladder should last sixty minutes, Auntie Pee-Pee."

THE FOLLOWING MORNING, there was the usual kerfuffle at the breakfast buffet, when Penny and Josephine were overwhelmed by the sheer number

of ways they could have their eggs. They both plumped for scrambled. Archie was convinced the hesitation might make them late for their taxi, but
Arlene had the sisters in the lobby for 8:25.

"I think that's 8:30 naval time," she said proudly.

The manager of The Maritime came down in person to see them off.

"This must be what it's like to be a celebrity," Josephine commented, as
they posed for a photograph for The Maritime's Instagram account.

"Famous or notorious?" Arlene joked.

All the same, they were surprised when, upon arrival at the Eurostar
terminal, the Williamson team was met by another farewell party.

"Good to see you again," Archie said to Inspector Emile Allard and Officer Nathalie Urban, who had taken their statements on the morning after
the siege. "Have you come to make sure we leave the country, before we
attract any more trouble?"

Archie's joke did not raise a smile.

Officer Urban gave an order via her radio. Archie didn't catch what she
said but Penny, with fresh batteries in her hearing aid, caught every word.

"Nous avons apprehende le suspect . . ."

There was no point trying to run. Penny's running days were long since
over. All she could do was play dumb. Or demented. Yes, whatever they
were about to accuse her of, she had almost certainly forgotten.

Inspector Allard addressed the party in perfect English. "I'm afraid
we're here to take Madame Penny Williamson back to the station for questioning, in relation to an incident at Blanchet, the luxury jewellery store,
on the Place Vendôme."

SO MUCH HAD happened since they'd arrived in Paris, that Archie had
completely forgotten losing his younger great-aunt outside The Ritz only
to find her trying on diamonds in Blanchet. He'd certainly forgotten all
about that moment at the Gare du Nord, when Penny was targeted by a
young female beggar as they disembarked the train.

The young woman had tried the old "ring trick," offering Penny a cheap
piece of costume jewellery that she claimed was a real diamond ring, for a
bargain price.

"Fifty euros," was what she'd asked for.

"Oh dear, I don't have that much on me in cash," Penny said.

But Penny had clung on to the woman's hand, swapping the ring for a single euro coin that would feel the right weight and keep the young woman from knowing what was going on until Penny was well out of the way.

Penny had taken the ring for fun but it wasn't quite the cracker-quality crap Penny had been expecting. Rather she could see how someone less cynical might have been taken in and believed it was the real deal. It was good. Good enough to use in a little rehearsal for the performance she had planned for the reception at Brice-Petitjean. At Blanchet on the Place Vendôme, she swapped the beggar's surprisingly convincing fake for a three-carat diamond ring.

"There must be some mistake," Archie told Inspector Allard. "My great aunt is ninety-seven years old. She's been awarded the *Légion d'honneur*."

"So have half the world's dictators," said Inspector Allard. "Madame Williamson?"

"Archie," said Penny. "I'm sure this can all be sorted out. Please don't worry. I will go along quietly, but may I just spend a penny first?" she asked Officer Urban to whom she was cuffed. Penny hoped she'd be able to choke down another ring in the time it took to fake a widdle.

STÉPHANE ARRANGED FOR a lawyer, Christophe Chastain, to meet Penny at the police station while Archie, Josephine, and Arlene waited anxiously at Stéphane's flat. Penny assured Chastain that she didn't have a clue what Inspector Allard was on about.

"I may have a little light dementia," she said.

In the interview room, the charges were laid out.

The assistant at Blanchet remembered that the English woman came into the shop just after lunchtime. The woman was old—definitely—but seemed sprightly for her age. She'd asked to see several rings and a parure. She'd been wearing a knitted beret. The assistant thought that was a witty nod to their being in France. It was quite distinctive. When the assistant heard about the siege at Brice-Petitjean the following night, she was fascinated by the story. And there on the television was the old lady she remembered from the day the diamond ring went missing. She was convinced now that the harmless-looking biddy had swiped a solitaire worth fifty thousand euros, exchanging it for a worthless chip of glass.

"Well, how ridiculous," said Christopher Chastain. "My client is ninety-seven years old and she has never before been accused of dishonesty. She has devoted her life to the service of others, first as an officer in Britain's First Aid Nursing Yeomanry. The Fa-*nay*." Penny had never before heard it pronounced quite so beautifully. "And later at the helm of the Connor O'Connell Foundation, providing healthcare, housing, and education for some of the most disadvantaged children in the world. She is a decorated veteran and a chevalier of the *Légion d'honneur*."

That medal had been taken off her at the front desk, along with all her other personal items.

"How can you look at this woman, this humble, honest, elderly woman, and believe she could be a jewel thief? Where is your evidence? I very much hope you are able to explain why you're wasting Madame Williamson's precious time. All the more precious, for her being in her tenth decade." He was really laying it on.

Inspector Allard was unmoved. "There is CCTV footage," he said.

On the screen of Allard's computer, the Blanchet showroom flickered in grainy black and white. There at the desk was the young assistant Penny remembered. She was tap-tapping away on a laptop, while the heavy who manned the door watched the goings-on outside. There was always something going on in the Place Vendôme. Tourists taking selfies in front of Napoleon's vast triumphal column, business people heading for meetings, little old ladies dashing in and out of luxury hotels in desperate need of a wee.

After a few moments during which nothing much happened, the heavy swung the boutique door open to admit a customer. A small woman, obviously elderly, wearing a beret at a very jaunty angle. She kept her beret on as she approached the desk and sat down with her handbag on her knees. After a brief exchange, the assistant moved from cabinet to cabinet, assembling a collection of items on a velvet-lined pad.

Penny tried not to smile as she watched the collection on the velvet pad growing. Five items, seven, ten . . . an insurance nightmare. Much too hard to keep track.

On screen the assistant swept a hand across the jewels she'd arrayed. Though there was no soundtrack to the footage, Penny could hear the sales patter inside her head. "Our finest . . . exclusive to Blanchet . . . one of a kind . . ." Meanwhile, the client was picking items up and trying them on, until suddenly she sneezed and delved into her handbag for a tissue.

"That's the moment when the priceless solitaire was exchanged for a fake," explained Inspector Allard. "Just like that incident in Boodles in London, when that woman swapped a bag of pebbles for five million euros' worth of diamonds."

"That was a seriously amazing steal," Officer Urban said.

"So there you have it," said Allard when the film was finished. "What do you have to say?" He draped one arm across the back of his chair. Easiest case he'd ever had to solve.

Penny put her hand on her lawyer's arm and beckoned him closer so she might whisper in his ear.

"Well," Chastain said. "That's a very clever old lady you've captured on film there. And perhaps she was indeed English. But as anyone with half a brain can see, she's obviously not my client."

"What?"

"Play the last minute again. Look closer."

Allard looked more closely. He stared at the film. He stared at Penny. He stared at the film. He had to play the footage twice more until he too could be convinced that the woman who actually looked up at the CCTV camera and winked as she left the store was not the same old dear now sitting in front of him.

"But you do own a knitted beret," Allard persisted.

"As does that old lady," said Penny. "They're very fashionable." The detectives, the lawyer, and Penny all watched the footage one more time. "But that isn't me."

"It really isn't," Chastain confirmed. "I can see how mistakes might have been made," he said as he shuffled his papers into a neat pile ready to be put away. "But I don't think there's any justification whatsoever in questioning Madame Williamson for a moment longer. Except to hear your apology."

It did not take long to secure Penny's release after that. As they left the police building, Penny was very satisfied to hear Allard tearing into his junior.

"You made me look a fool in there. How could you have made such a mistake?"

"Old ladies all look the same to me."

"Did you just say that? Did you just actually say that? Old ladies all look the same? How were you raised? Did you never have a grandmother? How could you be so disrespectful? And now we have another suspect to track down in a world full of identical old ladies. According to you . . ."

"I could tell at once that it wasn't you," said Chastain.

"Thank you, yes," said Penny. "While I do have a knitted beret, I would not be caught dead in shoes like that. *Mouton* dressed as *agneau*."

Chastain helped Penny into the back seat of his chauffeured car. Who said crime didn't pay? He must have had some extremely successful clients.

"I wonder if they'll catch their daring thief," Chastain mused when he was buckled in beside her. "It can't be every day the police encounter find themselves looking for such an . . ." He was about to say "ancient," Penny knew. "Such an *experienced* criminal."

"The cost-of-living crisis is forcing everyone to work for longer these days," Penny said.

"But what a woman," Chastain nodded in admiration. "Right under the assistant's nose."

"She used quite a basic technique actually." Penny couldn't resist pointing that out because Penny knew exactly who the elderly woman in the CCTV footage was. She wasn't about to tell anyone—not even her lawyer. There was still a little honour to be found amongst thieves—but the thief in question was her erstwhile apprentice. Good old Jinx. How nice to know she wasn't yet dead. Wily little thing.

"I wonder," Penny asked then. "Do you think you might take me via a pharmacy on the way to meet the others? I need to take some laxatives again."

Epilogue

• • • • •

Three months later

Archie Williamson no longer subscribed to the view that nothing bad could happen at Peter Jones because he now knew that absolutely was not true. As he entered the store on his way to his lunchtime rendezvous, he scanned the ground floor china department for items that might accidentally end up in an old lady's handbag, like a new parent scanning a room for plug sockets and sharp corners. Peter Jones was a veritable den of temptation. Fortunately Arlene had promised to bring the sisters straight to the Top Floor Restaurant, via the lift, to minimise the risk of the wrong kind of excitements.

Already waiting in the café was Archie's newly discovered second cousin Maddie Scott-Learmonth of Halifax, Nova Scotia, who had spent the morning in Green Park admiring the floral tributes to the late Queen. Maddie had been in London for a week now—staying with her grandmother Josephine and great-aunt Penny in South Kensington—and in that time she and Archie had become firm friends. The following weekend they would be going up to Scotland together, to Grey Towers, to see the land of their ancestors and to pay their respects to Connie Shearer, whose scribbled note on the back of Josephine's last letter to August had been so important in finally bringing Edgar and Josephine together again. They'd been discussing the possibility of arranging for her to have a new, bigger headstone, to better commemorate the heroine she truly was.

Maddie couldn't get enough of hearing about the moment when Archie saw the faded pencil scribble on the back of his great-aunt's letter to August Samuel and solved the mystery of their complicated family connection. Naturally, that led to a wider discussion of the trip to Paris and the various excitements and near-death experiences it had involved.

"Yes, the moment we thought Josephine had been shot was heart-stopping," said Archie. "But I don't think I ever felt closer to death than at that time when the gendarmes turned up to arrest Penny at the Eurostar terminal. Can you imagine? Jewel theft? At her age? I was mortified. The worst of it was, I wouldn't have put it past her, not after what happened here back in April with that awful elephant ornament."

"She's such a card," Maddie agreed. "I wish I had grown up around Auntie Penny. What excitements you must have had over the years."

"You don't know the half of it. Perhaps you ought to learn some Defendu if you're thinking of sticking around . . ."

WHEN ARLENE AND the sisters finally arrived, they were half an hour late.

"What took you so long?" Archie asked. "You were supposed to be here at one o'clock, naval time."

"My fault," said Arlene. "Josephine persuaded me that we needed to stop on the ground floor to choose my birthday present."

Arlene showed them an elegant silver-topped cocktail shaker.

"Not entirely an altruistic purchase," Josephine admitted. "Now perhaps she'll make better martinis."

"I'm desperate to learn how to make a good *soixante-quinze*," said Maddie.

"For that you need the *Prinz Eugen*. I mean, Sister Eugenia," said Josephine. "She and Davina Mackenzie will be at our house tomorrow afternoon, dear. Dan Snow is going to be recording a special podcast about the excitements in Paris. Hopefully, I'll be able to get a word in."

"I'll make sure you do," said Arlene.

Arlene was not going to be working for the sisters for very much longer, having decided to go part-time while attending an access course so she might do a fashion degree. It was Davina Mackenzie who'd helped her to fill out the online application forms. She had forgiven Arlene for the Jamaica lie and almost apologised for having pushed Arlene to make it. "I know I'm a tough old bird," she'd admitted. "But I also know what it feels like not to be able to follow your heart. As the granddaughter of an admiral, I have always felt the weight of other people's expectations. Arlene, you must follow your heart and go to fashion school. Apart from anything else, they might encourage you to experiment with less . . . less strident colours."

Archie had news for the sisters too. He showed them a photograph that Stéphane had attached to an email sent that morning. The rescheduled "important early twentieth-century jewellery sale" had taken place at Brice-Petitjean the previous evening, with Veronique Declerc's emerald ring fetching a record price. There had been a lot of interest in the sale, generated by the fact that when Stéphane and his team did their post-siege inventory, they'd discovered that the valuable emerald had been swapped for a fake. The recovery of the real ring a few days later had made all the papers.

"They've still got no idea how the original turned up in the poor box at that church though," said Archie. "But all's well that ends well. It went for twice the price expected and that means two new schools."

Penny agreed that was the very best outcome.

With everyone settled, Archie took the ladies' orders for sandwiches, scones, and various pieces of cake.

"Do they serve alcohol here in Peter Jones?" Penny asked then. "I forget."

"I think they might," Archie said. "What is it you fancy, Auntie Penny?"

"I think we deserve a small glass of fizz, don't you?"

"Well, if we can't get that here, we'll go to Colbert afterwards. But what are we celebrating?"

"There's always something to celebrate," said Josephine.

"Got to be *toujours gai*, right?" said Maddie. She was learning fast.

"*Toujours gai*," the others agreed.

While Archie looked out for a Peter Jones partner who might be able to help them procure something sparkling, Penny rifled through her handbag for a tissue. The news about the sale of the emerald ring had made her just a little tearful, especially to be hearing it as she sat opposite Maddie, who looked so much like her paternal great-grandmother, Madame Leah Samuel.

Around that table in Peter Jones, the past reached into the present and Penny saw a future she would not be a part of for long, but for which she was still very happy, knowing that Archie and his new-found cousin Maddie had so many excitements still ahead of them. She felt her breath catch in her throat at the thought.

Penny found no tissues in her handbag that afternoon, but from next to a fluff-covered roll of cough sweets, another small crystal elephant gaily waved his twinkling trunk.

Acknowledgments

· · · · ·

The Top Floor Restaurant,
Peter Jones

LONDON, JANUARY 2023

Dear Reader,

Thank you for taking a chance on my book. I hope you've had as much fun reading it as I've had writing it.

I owe a debt of gratitude to a great many people for this adventure. First and foremost, my friends Patricia Davies and Jean Argles, two real-life World War Two veterans (and sisters), whose exciting and occasionally hair-raising stories about their time in the women's services never fail to inspire me. Likewise, the marvellous Christian Lamb, for sharing her wartime experiences in the Wrens. Then there's my dear friend Simon Robinson, agent to all the best nonagenarians, who first introduced me to the concept of "excitements" on one of our life-saving lockdown telephone calls. Thank you, Simon, for so generously sharing your encyclopedic knowledge of the thirties and forties with me and for always being ready with an impression from *Brief Encounter*.

Thank you to my old pal Dr. David Jordan for letting me geek out about World War Two and for introducing me to the work of the legend that was W.E. Fairbairn. I can't think of anyone in whose company I would rather await the controlled explosion of a World War Two bomb.

The first people to read an early version of this book were Alexandra Potter and Victoria Routledge, two of my very favourite women and wonderful writers to boot. Thank you both for your gentle but oh-so-useful feedback and for your unwavering support through the dark days between that first flash of inspiration and this final draft. Tea and cake at Peter Jones is on me!

Thank you to the wonderful gang at United Agents. Jim Gill, Amy Mitchell, and Amber Garvey, I'm so grateful to you for your encouragement and support and for getting my fledgling story in front of all the right people. Talking of the right people: Maria Runge, Marie Misandeau, Rachel Kahan, Susanne Von Leeuwen, Paola Confalonieri, and Giulia De Biase— thank you all for taking a chance on Penny and Josephine.

Thank you to my fabulous editor Sam Eades, the most excellent Sanah Ahmed, and the rest of the team at Orion for championing *The Excitements* all the way. You've made me feel so very welcome at your venerable publishing house. I'll make sherry lovers of you all yet . . .

Thank you copy-editor Laura Gerrard for putting my punctuation where it should be and for catching my mistakes. Hachette rights director, Rebecca Folland, thank you for finding a home for this book in the US.

Special thanks are due to my goddaughter Josephine Hazel and her siblings Penelope and George for lending my heroines and their little brother their perfect names.

Thank you to my family—especially Lukas and Harrison—for being the best cheerleaders a writer could have. And no, I'm still not doing TikTok.

I'd also like to take this opportunity to remember the late Johnny Johnson, a real Dambuster, whose whispered advice to me at the unveiling of his portrait by Dan Llywelyn Hall in May 2018 nudged me to change the direction of my writing, setting me off on this new and exciting path.

Finally, thank you to my beloved Mark, without whose confidence in me, I wouldn't have made it to the end. I promise that one day soon, I won't bring my laptop on holiday.

CJ Wray